and Shar...
of ...

"Space opera isn't just ripsnortin' adventure, though Lee and Miller give us plenty of that. The thing about space opera is that it's more than nifty science, the clash of customs, the evolution of ideas, interesting planets, cool tech, and new pioneers, it's also and above all about character . . . and one cares about the characters, about their further adventures, and their families' adventures, and even about the villains. The Liaden Universe stories are very good space opera."
—Sherwood Smith,
author of *Journey to Otherwise*

"The authors have a rare gift for creating vivid characters that you care deeply about, and weaving complex, fascinating stories that are worthy of their creations. From the very first page you will find yourself drawn in, compelled to keep reading until you reach the end, and then wishing immediately for more stories from these gifted authors."
—Patricia Bray, author of *Devlin's Luck*

"No other authors can compare to their skill at bringing characters to full and robust life, half convincing me that there is a time portal to the future hidden up in Maine, through which Sharon and Steve have been watching and recording the lives of the Liadens for years."
—Jennifer Dunne, author of *Raven's Heart*

continued . . .

local custom

sharon lee and steve miller

ACE BOOKS, NEW YORK

LOCAL CUSTOM

An Ace Book / published by arrangement with
Meisha Merlin Publishing, Inc.

PRINTING HISTORY
In Meisha Merlin Publishing, Inc. hardcover and trade paperback
editions of *Pilots Choice* / February 2001
Ace mass-market edition / February 2002

Visit our website at
www.penguinputnam.com
Check out the ACE Science Fiction & Fantasy newsletter!

ISBN: 0-441-00911-5

ACE®
Ace Books are published by The Berkley Publishing Group,
a division of Penguin Putnam Inc.,
375 Hudson Street, New York, New York 10014.
ACE and the "A" design
are trademarks belonging to Penguin Putnam Inc.

PRINTED IN THE UNITED STATES OF AMERICA

10 9 8 7 6 5 4 3 2 1

Introduction to Local Custom

by Anne McCaffrey

Now and again one reads a book and, when finished, sighs that it has ended and the magic of it is closed between the covers. One can often think, "Gee, I wish I'd written that." Or "Gee, if I could write like that." And "Golly, what a great idea and it worked out."

That's called "Balance"—the cost of buying the book has been balanced by the enjoyment you had reading it. And rereading it.

I discovered the Liaden series by Sharon Lee and Steve Miller in the late '80s, 1980s that is to keep our centuries straight. My first one was *Agent Of Change* and, since it was published by Del Rey, I nagged at Shelly Shapiro to get the second, *Conflict Of Honors*, which had just been published and got the third, *Carpe Diem* in galleys. I nagged again at Shelly for surely such a viable series would have *more*. One can get quite Twistian about *good* novels, and exciting characters, like Miri, Val Con, Shan, Priscilla, Gordon, even a parapsychic Tree. One can get quite upset that 'someone' is out after them with malice aforethought and erasure as the exercise. And no Balance involved for the victims.

I even wrote to Sharon and Steve to ask when the next Liaden book was coming out. By now, we're in the late '90s. I have worn out my copies of the first three: they have accompanied me as my "comfort books" to two hospital stays, three holidays and those odd glitch-ful days when I *have* to be somewhere else for a little while to attain "balance" within me. ("Balance," you see, is a very Liaden thing.)

Then Sharon became much more visible as SFWA Executive Secretary—a position I held back in 1968–1970 so I know a lot about that job! And I could plague her directly to find to my joy that there is a website for Liaden, there was a new book *Plan B* about to be published from Meisha Merlin and that there were several shorter works already in booklet form.

However, being as how I was such a staunch fan, I got *Plan B* in manuscript and didn't stop reading once I'd started. But then, as the last page joins the tumbled pile of sheets, it was over (please read in a pathetic tone). I reread some of the good bits. When the published version arrived, I called a Liaden day, sat down on my bed, and reread it. Then, of course, to be sure I had the saga all correct in my head, I reread all three and the two novellas.

Consequently, when Sharon asked me would I comment on *Local Custom*, d'you honestly think I'd say "no"? Of course not.

I read until my hands froze. As soon as I answered my email the next morning, I read the last of it. Wow! This is a really good love story about Er Thom yos'Galan and Anne Davis, the parents of Shan yos'Galan, and it ends with a very interesting resolution of "balance": a fine Liaden tradition.

And there's a second one on its way (oh, have patience, my beating heart), concerning the parents of Val Con yos'Phelium. All part of the rich pageant of the original trilogy and filling in and explaining how Shan and Val Con came to be.

One of the never-failing joys of re-re-rereading this series is the crisp language, the well-turned phrases, the very exciting action, not to mention the confrontation of two vastly different cultures that, on the macroscopic canvas, are antagonistic, yet find, between themselves, the balance needed to endure, love, overwhelm, and survive! Not an easy balance to achieve but Korval's motto, *I Dare*, is well taken.

Reading the above, you might say I like the series. I won't go all hyper on you, dear reader, because there's more than enough hype about some books. But I *like* these. They have become my "comfort books" and sit on a shelf above my bed where they are easy to reach. Sometimes I just look at the cover, relive some of the scenes I now know almost by heart and eye. And I feel better. Re-rereading a book is proof of its lure, its basic worth, all the clever reader hooks and bits and pieces of "custom," like Liaden Balance, that are memorable.

Local Custom does fill in some of the beginnings so well expressed in the original trilogy, introducing you to Er Thom and Anne Davis, and the power of the Delm in Liaden society. Sharon and Steve say there is another planned: *Scout's Progress*: the two combining into the second omnibus *Pilots Choice.*

Can I last until they're published? Or shall I just reread the seven already on my comfort shelf?

•

Anne McCaffrey
Dragonhold-Underhill
June 2000

CHAPTER ONE

Each person shall provide his clan of origin with a child of his blood, who will be raised by the clan and belong to the clan, despite whatever may later occur to place the parent beyond the clan's authority. And this shall be Law for every person of every clan.

—From the Charter of the Council of Clans
Made in the Sixth Year After Planetfall,
City of Solcintra, Liad

"No?" his mother echoed, light blue eyes opening wide.

Er Thom yos'Galan bowed hastily: Subordinate Person to Head of Line, seeking to recoup his error.

"Mother," he began, with all propriety, "I ask grace . . ."

She cut him off with a wave of her hand. "Let us return to 'no.' It has the charm of brevity."

Er Thom took a careful breath, keeping his face smooth, his breath even, his demeanor attentive. Everything that was proper in a son who had always been dutiful.

After a moment, his mother sighed, walked carefully past him and sat wearily in her special chair. She frowned up at him, eyes intent.

"Is it your desire, my son, to deny the clan your genes?"

"No," said Er Thom again, and bit his lip.

"Good. Good." Petrella, Thodelm yos'Galan, drummed her fingers lightly against the chair's wooden arm, and continued to gaze at him with that look of puzzled intensity.

"Yet," she said, "you have consistently refused every possible contract-alliance the head of your line has brought to your attention for the past three years. Permit me to wonder why."

Er Thom bowed slightly, granting permission to wonder, belatedly recognizing it as a response less conciliatory than it might be, given the gravity of circumstances. He glanced at his mother from beneath his lashes as he straightened, wondering if he would now receive tuition on manners.

But Petrella was entirely concentrated upon this other thing and allowed the small irony to pass uncriticized.

"You are," she said, "captain of your own vessel, master trader, pilot—a well-established melant'i. You are of good lineage, your manner is for the greater part, pleasing, you have reached your majority and capably taken up the governing of the various businesses which passed to you upon your thirty-fifth name day. It is time and past time for you to provide the clan with your child."

"Yes," murmured Er Thom, because there was nothing else to say. She told him no more than the Law: Every person must provide the clan with a child to become his heir and to eventually take his place within the clan.

His mother sighed again, concern in her eyes. "It is not so great a thing, my child," she offered with unlooked-for gentleness. "We have all done so."

When he remained speechless, she leaned forward, hand extended. "My son, I do not wish to burden you. Necessity exists, but necessity need not be oppressive. Is there one your heart has placed above others? Only tell me her name and her clan, negotiations will be initiated . . ." Slowly she sank back into the chair, hand falling to her knee. "Er Thom?"

"Mother," he murmured miserably, eyes swimming as he bowed. "I ask grace . . ."

Grace, after all, had not been forthcoming. He had scarcely expected it, with him tongue-tangled and kittenish as a halfling. His mother had no time to waste upon baseless sentiment, not with her illness so hard upon her. She had granted grace to one child already—and those genes lost to Clan Korval forever by reason of her leniency.

So there was to be no grace given Petrella's second child and the hope of Line yos'Galan. Er Thom wondered at himself, that he had dared even ask it.

Wondering still, he turned down the short hallway that led to his rooms and lay his hand against the lockplate. Late afternoon sun bathed the room beyond in thick yellow light, washing over the clutter of invoices and lading slips on his work table, the islands of computer screen, comm board and keypad. The message waiting light was a steady blue glow over the screen.

Er Thom sighed. That would be the file on his wife-to-be, transferred to him from his mother's station. Duty dictated that he open it at once and familiarize himself with the contents, that he might give formal acquiescence to his thodelm at Prime meal this evening.

He went quietly across the hand-loomed imported rug, thoughts carefully on the minutiae he would need to attend to, so he might stay on Liad for the duration of his marriage, as custom, if not Law, demanded. Another master trader would have to be found for *Dutiful Passage*, though Kayzin Ne'Zame, his first mate, would do very well as captain. The upcoming trip would require re-routing and certain of their regular customers notified personally . . . He pushed the window wide, letting the mild afternoon breeze into the room.

Behind him, papers rustled like a startled rookery. Er Thom leaned out the window, hands gripping the sill, eyes slightly narrowed as he looked across the valley at the towering Tree.

Jelaza Kazone was the name of the Tree—Jela's Fulfillment—and it marked the site of Korval's clanhouse, where Er Thom had spent his childhood, constant companion and willing shadow of his cousin and foster-brother, Daav yos'Phelium.

Er Thom's eyes teared and the Tree broke into a hundred glittering shards of brown and green against a sky gone milky bright. The desire to speak to Daav, to bury his face in his

brother's shoulder and cry out against the unfairness of the
Law, was nearly overmastering.

Compelling as it was, the desire was hardly fitting of one
who kept adult melant'i. Er Thom tightened his grip on the
sill, feeling the metal track score his palms, and closed his
eyes. He would *not* go to Daav with this, he told himself
sternly. After all, the younger man was facing much the same
necessity as Er Thom—and Daav lacked even a parent's guid-
ance, his own mother having died untimely some five Standard Years before.

Eventually the compulsion passed, leaving him dry-
mouthed and with sternness at least awakened, if not full
sense of duty.

Grimly, he pushed away from the window, marched across
the room and touched the message-waiting stud.

The screen flickered and the lady's likeness appeared, his
mother being no fool, to waste time fielding dry fact when fair
face might easily carry the day.

And she was, Er Thom thought with detached coolness,
very fair. Syntebra el'Kemin, Clan Nexon, was blessed with
classic beauty: Slim brows arched over wide opal-blue eyes
fringed with lashes long enough to sweep the luscious curve
of her cheekbones. Her skin was smooth and flawlessly
golden; her nose petite; her mouth red as clemetia buds. She
looked at him coyly from the screen, dark hair pulled back
and up, seductively displaying tiny, perfect ears.

Er Thom swallowed against a sudden cold surge of sick-
ness and glanced away, toward the window and the Tree, towering into twilight.

"It is—not possible," he whispered and ground his teeth,
forcing his eyes back.

Beautiful, serene and utterly Liaden—even as he was utterly Liaden—Syntebra el'Kemin beckoned from the depths
of the screen.

That the rest of her person would be as guilesome as her
face, he knew. *Knew.* He should in all honor seek out his
mother and kneel at her feet in gratitude. Nothing in the Law
said that the lady must be comely. Indeed, Korval's own law
required merely that a contract-spouse be a pilot, and of vig-
orous Line—all else as the wind might bring it.

Lower lip caught tight between his teeth, Er Thom stared into the lovely face of his proposed wife, trying to imagine the weight of her hair in his hands, the taste of her small, rosy-gold breasts.

"No!"

The chair clattered back and he was moving, pilot-fast, through the adjoining kitchenette to his bedroom. Fingers shaking, he snatched open his jewel-box, spilling rubies, pearls and other dress-gems carelessly aside. His heart clenched for the instant he thought it gone—and then he found it, stuffed into a far corner, half-hidden by a platinum cloak pin.

A scrap of red silk no longer than his hand, that was all. That, and a length of tarnished, gold-colored ribbon, elaborately knotted into a fraying flower, through which the red silk had been lovingly threaded.

"It is not possible," he whispered again, and lay his cheek against the tarnished flower, blinking back tears that might stain the silk. He swallowed.

"I will not wed."

Fine words, the part of him that was master trader and a'thodelm and heir to the delm jeered. *And what of duty to the clan, not to mention the Law and, easing of one's mother's pain?*

If there is one your heart has set above all others . . . his mother pleaded from memory and Er Thom's fingers clenched convulsively on the scrap of silk. She would never—he dared not—It was against everything: Code, custom, clan—duty.

He took a deep breath, trying to calm his racing thoughts. The clan required this thing of him, the clan's dutiful child, in balance for all the clan had thus far given him. It was just. The other—was some strange undutiful madness that should after so many years have passed off. That it remained in this unexpectedly virulent form told a tale of Er Thom yos'Galan's sad lack of discipline. He would put the madness aside once and forever, now. He would burn the silk and the tawdry ribbon, then he would read the file on Syntebra el'Kemin, bathe and dress himself for Prime meal. He would tell his parent—

Tears overflowed and he bowed his head, fingers tenderly bracketing the red and gold token.

Tell his parent what? That for three years, steadfast in his refusal of all prospective spouses he had likewise taken no lover nor even shared a night of bed-pleasure? That new faces and old alike failed to stir him? That his body seemed to exist at some distance from where he himself lived and went about the work that the clan required of him? That food tasted of cobwebs and wine of vinegar and duty alone forced him to eat sufficient to fuel his cold, distant body?

Tell his mother that, Er Thom thought wretchedly, and she would have him to the Healers, quick as a blink.

And the Healers would make him forget all that stood in the way of duty.

He considered forgetfulness—such a little bit of time, really, to be erased from memory, and so very—long—ago.

The thought sickened him, nearly as much as the face of the woman his mother proposed to make his wife.

He blinked his eyes and straightened, slipping the rag of silk and the frazzled ribbon into his sleeve-pocket. Carefully, he put his jewelry back into the box and lowered the heavy carved lid.

In the office, he saved Syntebra el'Kemin's data to his pending file, and left a message for his mother, expressing regret that he would not be with her for Prime.

Then he quit the room, shrugging into the worn leather jacket that proclaimed him a pilot.

The papers on his worktable rustled irritably in the breeze from the open window and across the valley the first stars of evening glittered just above the Tree.

CHAPTER TWO

The giving of nubiath'a, the parting-gift, by either partner signals the end of an affair of pleasure. The person of impeccable melant'i will offer and accept nubiath'a with gentleness and grace, thereafter referring to the affair by neither word nor deed.

—Excerpted from the Liaden Code of Proper Conduct

"I surmise that the lady is a two-headed ogre— and ill-tempered, besides?" Daav yos'Phelium splashed misravot into a crystal cup and handed it aside.

"Another face entirely," Er Thom murmured, accepting the cup and swirling the contents in counterfeit calm, while his pulses pounded, frenzied. "The lady is—very—beautiful."

"Hah." Daav poured himself a cup of the pale blue wine and assayed a sip, black eyes quizzing Er Thom over the crystal rim.

"Your mother, my aunt, exerts herself on your behalf. When shall I have the felicity of wishing you happy?"

"I have not—that is—" Er Thom stammered to a halt and raised his cup to taste the wine.

In general, he was not as fond of misravot as was his brother, finding the burnt cinnamon taste of the wine cloyed rather than refreshed. But this evening he had a second sip, dawdling over it, while his mind skipped in uncharacteristic confusion from this thought to that.

He sighed when at last he lowered the cup, and raised his head to meet his brother's clever eyes.

"Daav?"

"Yes, denubia. How may I serve you?"

Er Thom touched his tongue to his lips, tasting cinnamon. "I—am in need. Of a ship."

One dark eyebrow arched. "Is it ill-natured to recall," Daav wondered, "that you are captain of a rather—substantial—ship?"

"A quicker ship—smaller," Er Thom said swiftly, suddenly unable to control his agitation. He spun away and paced toward the game table, where he stood looking down at the counterchance board, dice and counters all laid to hand. Had things been otherwise, he and Daav might even now be sitting over the board, sharpening their wits and their daring, one against the other.

"There is a matter," he said, feeling his brother's eyes burning into his back. He turned, his face open and plain for this, the dearest of his kin, to read. He cleared his throat. "A matter I must resolve. Before I wed."

"I see," Daav said dryly, brows drawn. "A matter which requires your presence urgently off-world, eh? Do I learn from this that you will finally assay that which has darkened your heart these past several relumma?"

Er Thom froze, staring speechless at his brother, though he should, he told himself, barely wonder. Daav was delm, charged with the welfare of all within Clan Korval. Before duty had called him home, he had also been a Scout, with sensibilities fine-tuned by rigorous training. How could he not have noticed his brother's distress? It spoke volumes of his melant'i that he had not taxed Er Thom with the matter before now.

"Have you spoken to your thodelm of this?" Daav asked quietly.

Er Thom gave a flick of his fingers, signaling negative. "I—would prefer—not to have the Healers."

"And so you come on the eve of being affianced to demand the Delm's Own Ship, that you may go off-planet and reach resolution." He grinned, for such would appeal to his sense of mischief, where it only chilled Er Thom with horror, that necessity required him to fly in the face of propriety.

"You will swear," Daav said, in a surprising shift from the Low Tongue in which they most commonly conversed to the High Tongue, in the mode of Delm to Clanmember.

Er Thom bowed low: Willing Obedience to the Delm. "Korval."

"You will swear that, should you fail of resolution by the end of this relumma, you shall return to Liad and place yourself in the care of the Healers."

The current relumma was nearly half-done. Still, Er Thom assured himself around a surge of coldness, the thing ought take no longer. He bowed once more, acquiescence to the Delm's Word.

"Korval, I do swear."

"So." Daav reached into the pocket of his house-robe and brought out a silver key-ring clasped with an enameled dragon. "Quick passage, denubia. May the luck guide you to your heart's desire."

Er Thom took the ring, fingers closing tightly around it as his eyes filled with tears. He bowed gratitude and affection.

"My thanks—" he began, but Daav waved a casual hand, back in the Low Tongue.

"Yes, yes—I know. Consider that you have said everything proper. Go carefully, eh? Send word. And for the gods' love leave me something to tell your mother."

"**Good-night,** Shannie." Anne Davis bent and kissed her son's warm cheek. "Sleep tight."

He smiled sleepily, light blue eyes nearly closed. "'night, Ma," he muttered, nestling into the pillow. His breathing evened out almost at once and Anne experienced the vivid inner conviction that her child was truly asleep.

Still, she hung over the truckle-bed, watching him. She extended a hand to brush the silky white hair back from his forehead, used one careful finger to trace the winging eyebrows—his father's look there, she thought tenderly, though the rest of Shan's look seemed taken undiluted from herself, poor laddie. But there, she had never hankered after a pretty child. Only after her own.

She smiled softly and breathed a whisper-kiss against his hair, unnecessarily fussed over the quilt and finally left the tiny bedroom, pulling the door partly shut behind her.

In the great room, she settled at her desk, long, clever fingers dancing over the computer keyboard, calling up the student work queue. She stifled a sigh: Thirty final papers to be graded. An exam to be written and also graded. And then a whole semester of freedom.

More or less.

Shaking her head, she called up the first paper and took the light-pen firmly in hand.

She waded through eight with the utter concentration that so amused her friends and enraged her colleagues, coming back to reality only because a cramped muscle in her shoulder finally shouted protest loudly enough to penetrate the work-blur.

"Umm. Break-time, Annie Davis," she told herself, pulling her six-foot frame into a high, luxurious stretch. Middling-tall for a Terran, still her outstretched fingers brushed the room's ceiling. *Bureaucratic penny-pinchers,* she thought, as she always did. *How much would it have cost to raise the ceiling two inches?*

It was a puzzle without an answer and having asked it, she forgot it and padded into the kitchen for a glass of juice.

Shan was still asleep, she knew. She sipped her juice and leaned a hip against the counter top, closing her eyes to let her mind roam.

She had met him on Proziski, where she had been studying base-level language shift on a departmental grant. Port Master Brellick Gare himself, a friend of Richard's, had invited her to the gala open house, sugaring the bait with the intelligence that there would be "real, live Liadens" at the party.

Brellick knew her passion for Liaden lit—Liadens themselves were fabulously rare at the levels in which Terran professors commonly moved. Anne had taken the bait—and met her Liaden.

She had seen him first from across the room—a solemn,

slender young man made fragile by Brellick Gare's bulk. The introduction had been typically Gare.

"Anne, this is Er Thom yos'Galan. Er Thom, be nice to Anne, OK? She's not used to parties." Brellick grinned into her frown. "I'd show you around myself, girl-o, but I'm host. You stick close to this one, though, he's got more manners than a load of orangutans." And with that he lumbered off, leaving Anne to glare daggers into his back before glancing in acute embarrassment toward her unfortunate partner.

Violet eyes awash with amusement looked up into hers from beneath winging golden brows. "What do you suppose," he asked in accented Terran, "an orangutan is?"

"Knowing Brellick, it's something horrible," Anne returned with feeling. "I apologize for my friend, Mr. yos'-Galan. There's not the slightest need for you to—*babysit* me."

"At least allow me to find you a glass of wine," he said in his soft, sweet voice, slipping a slim golden hand under her elbow and effortlessly steering her into the depths of the crowd. "Your name is Anne? But there must be something more than that, eh? Anne what?"

So she had told him her surname, and her profession and what she hoped to discover on Proziski. She also let him find her not one but several glasses of wine, and go in with her to dinner and, later, out onto the dance floor. And by the time the party began to thin it had seemed not at all unnatural for Er Thom yos'Galan to see her home.

He accepted her invitation to come inside for a cup of coffee and an hour later gently accepted an invitation to spend the night in her bed.

She bent to kiss him then, and found him unexpectedly awkward. So she kissed him again, patiently, then teasingly, until he lost his awkwardness all at once and answered her with a passion that left them both shivering and breathless.

They hadn't gotten to the bed, not the first time. The rickety couch had been sturdy enough to bear them and Er Thom surprised again—an experienced and considerate lover, with hands, gods, with hands that knew every touch her body yearned for, and gave it, unstinting.

Time and again, he came back to her lips, as if to hone his skill. When at last she wrapped her legs around him and pulled him into her, he bent again and put his mouth over hers, using his tongue to echo each thrust until her climax triggered his and their lips were torn apart, freeing cries of wonder.

"Oh, dear." Anne set the juice glass aside, moving sharply away from the counter and wrapping her arms around herself in a tight hug. "Oh, dear."

He was gone, of course. She had known he would go when the trade mission had completed its task, even as she would go when her study time had elapsed.

But it had been glorious while it had lasted—a grand and golden three-month adventure in a life dedicated to a calm round of teaching and study and research.

Shan was the living reminder of that grand adventure—of her own will and desire. She had never told Er Thom her intention to bear his child, though it seemed she told him everything else about herself. Shan was hers.

She sighed and turned, half-blind, to put the glass properly in the rack to be washed. Then she went into the great room and shut the computer down, shaking her head over the double work to be done tomorrow.

Crossing the room, she made certain the door was locked. Then she turned off the light and slipped into the bedroom, to spend the rest of the night staring at the invisible ceiling, listening to her son breathe.

Er Thom had not come to Prime.

Oh, he had sent word, as a dutiful child should, and begged her pardon most charmingly. But that he should absent himself from Prime meal on the day when he was to have agreed at last to wed could not fail to infuriate.

And Petrella was furious.

Furious, she had consigned the meal composed of her son's favorite dishes to the various devils of fifteen assorted hells, and supped on a spicy bowl of *gelth,* thin toast and strong red wine, after which she had stumped off to her office on the arm of Mr. pak'Ora, the butler, and composed a sizzling letter to her heir.

She was in the process of refining this document when the comm-line buzzed.

"Well?" she snapped, belatedly slapping the toggle that engaged the view-screen.

"Well, indeed." Her nephew, Daav yos'Phelium, inclined his head gravely. "How kind of you to ask. I hope I find you the same, Aunt Petrella?"

She glared at him. "I suppose you've finally stirred yourself to call and allow me to know your cha'leket my son has dined with you and that you are now both well into your cups and about to initiate a third round of counterchance?"

Daav lifted an eyebrow. "How delightful that would be! Alas, that I disturb your peace for an entirely different matter."

"So." She eyed him consideringly. "And what might that matter be?"

Daav shook his dark hair out of his eyes, the barbaric silver twist swinging in his right ear.

"I call to allow you to know that my cha'leket your son has gone off-world in the quest of resolving urgent business."

"Urgent business!" She nearly spat the words. "There is a contract-marriage dancing on the knife's edge and he goes off-planet?" She caught a hard breath against the starting of pain in her chest and finished somewhat more calmly. "I suppose you know nothing about the alliance about to be transacted with Clan Nexon?"

"On the contrary," Daav said gently, "I am entirely aware of the circumstance. Perhaps I have failed of making myself plain: The delm has allowed Er Thom yos'Galan the remainder of the relumma to resolve a matter he presents as urgent."

"What is urgent," Petrella told him, "is that he wed and provide the clan with his heir. This is a matter of Line, my Delm, and well you know it!"

"Well I know it," he agreed blandly. "Well I also know that any clan wishing to ally itself with Korval may easily accommodate half-a-relumma's delay. However, I suggest you begin inquiry among our cousins and affiliates, in order to identify others who may be available to wed the lady and cement the alliance with Clan Nexon."

"For that matter," Petrella said spitefully, "it happens that the delm is yet without issue."

Daav inclined his head. "I shall be honored to review the

lady's file. But ask among the cousins, do." He smiled, sudden and charming. "Come, Aunt Petrella, every trader knows the value of a secondary plan!"

"And why should I have a secondary when the prime plan is all-important? You are meddling in matters of Line, my Delm, as I have already stated. Chapter six, paragraph twenty-seven of the Code clearly outlines—"

Daav held up a hand. "If you wish to quote chapter and page to me, Aunt, recall that I have the longest memory in the clan."

She grinned. "Could that be a threat, nephew?"

"Now, Aunt Petrella, would I threaten you?"

"Yes," she said with a certain grim relish, "you would."

"Hah." His eyes gleamed with appreciation, then he inclined his head. "In that wise, aunt, and all else being in balance—ask among the cousins—feel free to contact Mr. dea'Gauss, should the enterprise put you out of pocket. In the meanwhile, the delm is confident of the return of Er Thom yos'Galan by relumma's end. As you should be."

Petrella said nothing, though she wisely refrained from snorting.

Daav smiled. "Good-night, Aunt Petrella. Rest well."

"Good-night, child," she returned and cut the connection.

CHAPTER THREE

"Of course you are my friend—my most dear, my beloved . . ."
Shan el'Thrasin leaned close and cupped her face in his two
hands, as if they were kin, or lifemates.

"I will love you always," he whispered, and saw the fear
fade from her beautiful eyes. Achingly tender, he bent and
kissed her.

"I will never forget . . ." she sighed, nestling her face into
his shoulder.

"Nor will I," he promised, holding her close as he slipped
the knife clear. No whisper of blade against sheath must warn
her, he told himself sternly. No quiver of his own pain must
reach her; she was his love, though she had killed his partner.
He would rather die than cause her an instant's distress.

The knife was very sharp. She stirred a little as it slid be-
tween her ribs, and sighed, very softly, when it found her
heart.

—From "The Trickster Across the Galaxy: A Retrospect"

"Jerzy, you're a doll," Anne said gratefully.

Her friend grinned from the depths of the comm-screen
and shook his head. "Wrongo. *He's* the doll. I love this kid.
Name the price; I gotta have him."

Anne laughed. "Not for sale. But I'll let you watch him
tonight. Purely as a favor to you, understand." She sobered.

"How about letting me do a favor in return? We're getting a little top-heavy, here."

"What're you, Liaden? Take some advice and skip that meeting. Go home, eat something sexy, glass of wine, play yourself a lullaby and go to sleep. Tomorrow's your study day, right? Jerzy will deliver kid latish in the a.m. If I don't decide to steal him, instead."

"Jerzy—"

"Enough, already! Seeya tomorrow." The screen went blank.

Anne sighed, closed the line at her end and sat looking at the screen long after the glow had faded into dead gray.

There had to be a better way, she thought, not for the first time. Certainly, there were worse ways than the path she was pursuing—the Central University creche leapt forcibly to mind, with its sign-in sheets and its sign-out sheets and its tidy rows of tidy cribs and its tidy, meek babies all dressed in tidy, identical rompers. Horrible, antiseptic, unloving place—just like the other one had been.

She was doing all right, she assured herself, given the help of friends like Jerzy. But she hated to impose on her friends, good-natured as they were. Even more she hated the hours she was of necessity away from her son, so many hours a day, so many days a week. She was growing to resent her work, the demands of departmental meetings, class preparations. Her research was beginning to slack off—fatal in the publish-or-perish university system. Her allotted study days more and more often became "Shan days" while she tried to cram the work that needed to be done into late nights and early mornings, using her home terminal to the maximum, piling up user fees she could have easily avoided by using her assigned terminal at the Research Center.

Abruptly, she stood and began to gather her things together. Her own mother had been a pilot, gone six months of every local year, leaving her son and daughter in the care of various relatives and, one year, at the New Dublin Home for Children.

Anne shuddered, scattering a careful stack of data cards. That had been the worst year. She and Richard had been sequestered in separate dorms, allowed one comm call between them every ten days. They had found ways to sneak away after lights-out, to hold hands and talk family talk. But sneaking away was against the rules, punishable, when they were inevitably caught, by hard labor, by imposed silence, by ostracism. The year had seemed forever, with their mother's ship long overdue, and Anne certain it was lost . . .

She looked down at her clenched fists, puzzled. It had all been so long ago. Her mother had died three years ago, peacefully in her bed. Richard was a pilot in his own right, and his last letter had been full of someone named Rosie, whose parents he was soon to meet. And Anne was a professor of comparative linguistics, with several scholarly publications to her name, teaching a Liaden Lit seminar that was filled to capacity every session.

Anne shook her head and wearily bent to pick up the scattered cards. Jerzy was right; she was tired. She needed a good meal, a full night's sleep. She'd been pushing things a little too hard lately. She needed to remember to relax, that was all. Then, everything would be fine.

Wearily, Er Thom climbed the curving marble staircase that led to the Administrative Center for University's Northern Campus. It was slightly warmer in the building than it had been outside, but still cool to one used to Liad's planetary springtime. He left his leather pilot's jacket sealed as he approached the round marble counter displaying the Terran graphic for "Information."

A Terran woman of indeterminate years came to the counter as he approached. She had a plenitude of dark hair, worn carelessly loose, as if fresh-tousled from bed, and her shirt was cut low across an ample bosom. She leaned her elbows on the pinkish marble and grinned at him.

"Hi, there. What can I do for you?" she asked, casually, and with emphasis on "you."

He bowed as between equals—a flattery—and offered a slight smile of his own.

"I am looking for a friend," he said, taking extreme care with the mode-less and rough Terran words. "Her name is Anne Davis. Her field is comparative linguistics. I regret that

I do not know the name of the department in which she serves."

"Well, you're on the right campus, anyhow," the woman said cheerfully. "You got her ident number, retinal pattern, anything like that?"

"I regret," Er Thom repeated.

She shook her head so the tousled dark curls danced. "I'll see if it flies, friend, but it's not much to go on with the size of the faculty we've got . . ." She moved away, muttering things much like her counterparts in the East and West offices had muttered. A few meters down-counter she stopped and began to ply the keypad set there, frowning at the screen suspended level with her eyes. "Let's see . . . Davis, Davis, Anne . . ." She turned her head, calling out to him over her shoulder. "Is that 'Anne' with an 'e' or not?"

He stared at her, unable to force his weary mind to analyze and make sense of the question. "I—beg your pardon."

"Your friend," the clerk said, patiently. "Does she spell her name with an 'e' or without an 'e'?"

An 'e' was the fifth letter of the Terran alphabet. Surely, he thought, half-panicked, surely he had at some time seen Anne's written name? He closed his eyes, saw the old-fashioned ink pen held firmly in long, graceful fingers, sweeping a signature onto the mauve pages of an ambassadorial guest book.

"A—" he spelled out of memory for the clerk's benefit. "n, n, e. D, a, v, i, s."

"Hokay." She turned back to her board as Er Thom opened his eyes, feeling oddly shaken.

The clerk muttered to herself—he paid her no mind. Terran naming systems, he thought distractedly, Terran alphabet, and, gods help him, a Terran woman, bold and brilliant—*alien*. But a woman still, with Terran blood in her and genes so far outside the Book of Clans that—

"OK!"

Er Thom shook himself out of his reverie as the clerk's cry of jubilation penetrated, and stepped forward.

"Yes?"

She looked up at him, lashes fluttering, and he saw that she was not so young as he had thought. Cosmetics had been used to simulate the dewy blush of first youth across her cheek and her eyes were artfully painted, with silver sequins sprinkled across her lashes. Er Thom schooled his face to calm politeness. Local custom, he reminded himself sternly. As a trader he dealt with local custom in many guises on many worlds. So on this world faces were painted. Merely custom, and nothing to distress one.

"Don't know if this is your friend or not," the woman was saying, "but she's the only Davis in Comparative Ling. Wait a sec, here's the card." She frowned at it before handing it over. "Lives in Quad S-two-seven-squared. You know where that is?"

"No," he said, clutching the card tightly.

The woman stood, leaning over the counter to point. Her breasts flattened against the marble, and swelled toward the margin of the low-cut blouse. Er Thom turned to look along the line of her finger.

"Go back out the way you came," she told him, "turn right, walk about four hundred yards. You'll see a sign for the surrey. Go down the stairs and hit the summonplate. When the surrey comes, you sit down and code in *this* right here, see?" She ran her finger under a string of letters and numbers on the card he held.

"Yes, I see."

"OK. Then you lean back and enjoy the ride. The surrey stops, you get out and go upstairs. You'll be in a big open space—Quad S. Best thing to do then is either ask one of the residents to help you find the address or go to the Quad infobooth, punch up your friend's code—that's right under the name, there—and tell her to come get you. Clear?"

"Thank you," said Er Thom, bowing thanks and remembering to give a smile. Terrans set great store by smiles, where a Liaden person would merely have kept his face neutral and allowed the bow to convey all that was necessary.

"That's OK," said the woman, flashing her silvered lashes. "If your friend's not home, or if it turns out it's *not* your friend, come on back and I'll see if I can help you some more."

There was an unmistakable note of invitation there. Hastily, Er Thom reviewed his actions, trying to determine if he had inadvertently signaled a wish for her intimate companionship. As far as he could determine, he had indicated no such thing, unless the smile was to blame. Bland-faced, he bowed once more: Gratitude for service well-given, nothing else.

"Thank you," he said, keeping his voice carefully neutral. He turned on his heel and walked away.

Behind him, the Information clerk watched him wistfully, twining her fingers in her hair.

The surrey ride was longer than he had expected from the clerk's explanation. Er Thom sat rigid in the slippery plastic chair, clutching the thin plastic card and occasionally looking down at it.

"Anne Davis," the Terran letters read. "ID: 7596277483ZQ." He committed the ID to memory, then the Quad code, department number and assignment berth. It did not take long; he had a good head for cargo stats, manifest numbers and piloting equations. After checking himself three times, he put the card in his belt-pocket with infinite care and tried to relax in the too-large, Terran-sized seat, hands tightly folded on his knee.

It had been a weary long trip from Liad to University— three Jumps, which he had taken, recklessly, one after the other, pushing the reactions and the stamina of a master pilot to their limits. And at the end of that reckless journey, this endless day of searching, campus to campus, through a bureaucracy that spanned an entire planet—

To this place. Very soon now he would see Anne—speak to her. He would—for the last time in his life—break with the Code and put his melant'i at peril.

He would speak to one to whom he had given nubiath'a. The heart recoiled, no matter that necessity existed. Necessity *did* exist—his own, and shame to him, that he use his necessity to disturb the peace of one who was not of his clan.

A tone sounded in the little cab, and a yellow light flashed on the board. "Approaching Quad S. Prepare to disembark," a man's pleasant voice instructed him.

Er Thom slid forward on the seat as the surrey slowed. He

was on his feet the instant the door slid open and had run halfway up the automated stairs by the time it closed behind him.

The local sun was setting, bathing the tall buildings that enclosed the quad in pale orange light. Er Thom stopped and looked about him, spinning slowly on one heel, suddenly and acutely aware of his empty hands. It was improper of him to go giftless to an evening call; he had not thought.

There must be shops, he thought. *Mustn't there?*

A group of four tall persons was crossing the Quad a few yards to his right. He stretched his legs to catch them, fishing in his belt for the plastic card.

His dilemma produced a slight altercation among three of his potential aides. It seemed that there were several ways to arrive at the dwelling indicated; the question addressed was which of several was the "best" way. Er Thom stood to one side, having rescued his card from one gesticulating well-wisher, and tried to cultivate patience. He heard a low laugh and turned to look at the fourth member of the party, a short-ish Terran male—though still a head taller than Er Thom—with merry dark eyes and a disreputable round face.

"Listen to that bunch and you'll get lost for sure," he said, dismissing his companions with a flutter of his fingers. "I live a couple halls down from your friend's place. I don't guarantee it's the *best* way, but if you follow me, I can get you there."

"Thank you," said Er Thom, with relief. "And—I regret the inconvenience—if there would be a shop selling wine?"

"Oh, sure," said his guide, turning left. "There's the Block Deli, right where we get the lift. Step this way, and keep an eye out for falling philosophers."

CHAPTER FOUR

Relations between Liad and Terra have never been cordial, though there have been periods of lesser and greater strain. Liad prefers to thrash Terra roundly in the field of galactic trade—a terrain it shaped—while Terra gives birth to this and that Terran-supremacist faction, whose mischief seems always to stop just short of actual warfare.

—From "The Struggle for Fair Trade," doctoral dissertation of Indrew Jorman, published by Archive Press, University

The surrey's *ding* woke her; she got a grip on her briefcase and went up the autostairs in a fog.

On the Quad, the sharp night breeze roused her and she stopped to stretch cramped leg and back muscles, staring up into a sky thick with stars. It was a very different night sky than Proziski's, with its gaggle of moons. She and Er Thom had counted those moons one night, lying naked next to each other on the roof of the unfinished Mercantile Building, the end of a bolt of trade-silk serving as coverlet and mattress. She liked to think Shan had come from that night.

She shook her head at the laden sky and took one last deep breath before turning toward the block that held her apartment.

She walked past the darkened deli and rode the lift to the seventh floor, trying to remember if she had eaten the last roll that morning for breakfast. She recalled a cup of coffee, gulped between feeding Shan and getting him ready for his trip to Jerzy's place. She remembered having to go back for her notes for the afternoon's lecture.

She didn't remember eating breakfast at all, and she had been too busy with a promising research line to break off for lunch . . .

Anne sighed. *You need a keeper,* she told herself severely. The lift door cycled and she stepped out into the hallway.

A slim figure turned from before her door and began to walk toward her, keeping scrupulously to the center of the hall, where the lights were brightest. Anne hesitated, cataloging bright hair, slender stature, leather jacket—

"Er Thom." She barely heard her own whisper, hardly knew that she had increased her stride, until she was almost running toward him.

He met her halfway, extending a slim golden hand on which his amethyst master trader's ring blazed. She caught his fingers in hers and stood looking down at him, wide mouth curved in a smile no dimmer than the one he had treasured, all this time.

"Er Thom," she said in her rich, lilting voice. "I'm so very happy to see you, my friend."

Happy. What a small word, to describe the dazzling, dizzying joy that threatened to engulf him. He hung onto her hand, though it would have been more proper to bow. "I am—happy—to see you, also," he managed, smiling up into her eyes. "They keep you working late . . ."

She laughed. "A departmental meeting—it dragged on and on! I can't imagine what they found to talk about." She sobered. "Have you been waiting long?"

"Not very long." Hours. He had despaired a dozen times; walked away and returned two dozen . . . three . . . He showed her the bag he held. "Are you hungry? I have food, wine."

"My thoughtful friend. *Starved.* Come in." She tugged on his hand, turning him back toward the anonymous door that marked her dwelling place. "How long are you stopping, Er Thom?"

He hesitated and she looked at him closely.

"More than just today? Don't tell me that stupid meeting has kept me away for half your visit!"

"No." He smiled up at her. "I do not know how long I am staying, you see. It depends upon—circumstances."

"Oh," she said wisely, "*circumstances.*" She let go his hand and lay her palm against the door's lockplate. With a grand, meaningless flourish, she bowed him across the threshold.

Just within and to one side, he stopped to watch her cross the room, past the shrouded half-chora to the wall-desk, where she lay her briefcase down with a sigh. It struck him that she moved less gracefully than he recalled, and nearly gasped at the sharpness of his concern.

"Anne?" He was at her elbow in a flicker, searching her face. "Are you well?"

She smiled. "Just tired, my dear—that absurd meeting." She reached out, touching his cheek lightly with the tips of her fingers. "Er Thom, it's so good to see you."

He allowed the caress. Kin and lifemates alone touched thus: face-to-face, hand-to-face. He had never told her so; he did not tell her now. He turned his face into her palm and felt the icy misery in his chest begin to thaw.

"It is good to see you, also," he murmured, hearing the pounding of his heart, wanting—wanting . . . He shifted slightly away and held up the bag. "You are tired. I will pour you wine—is that proper?—and you will sit and rest. All right? Then I will bring you some of this to eat." He pointed to a dark alcove to the right. "That is the kitchen?"

She laughed, shaking her head. "That's the kitchen. But, my friend, it can't be proper to put a guest to work."

"It is no trouble," he told her earnestly. "Please, I wish to."

"All right," she said, astonished and bewildered at the way her eyes filled with tears. "Thank you. You're very kind."

"Rest," he murmured and disappeared into the kitchen corner. The light came on, adding to the dim illumination of the living area. Anne sighed. There were signs of neglect everywhere: dust, scattered books and papers, discarded pens. Under the easy chair a fugitive rubber block crouched, defiant.

She turned her back on it deliberately, pulled off her jacket and curled into a corner of the couch, long legs under her, head resting on the back cushions. She heard small sounds from the kitchen as Er Thom opened and closed cabinets. The air filtering unit thrummed into sluggish life . . .

"Anne?"

She gasped, head jerking up. Er Thom bit his lip, violet eyes flashing down to the glass he held and back to her face.

"I am inconvenient," he said solemnly, inclining his head. "Perhaps I may come again to see you. When you are less tired. Tell me."

"No." Her changeable face registered guilt, even panic. "Er Thom, I'm sorry to be a bad host. I'd like you to stay. Please. You're not *inconvenient* —never that, my dear. And if you leave now and your circumstances mesh, then you might not be able to come again. You could be gone again tomorrow."

He set the glass aside, caught the hand she half-extended and allowed himself to be drawn down to sit beside her.

"Anne . . ." Fascinated, he watched his fingers rise to her cheek, stroke lightly and ever-so-slowly down the square jaw line to the firm chin.

"All will be well," he said, soothing her with his voice as if she were a child instead of a woman grown. "I will be here tomorrow, Anne. Certainly tomorrow. And you—my friend, you are exhausted. It would be wrong—improper—to insist you entertain me in such a case. I will go and come back again. Tomorrow, if you like. Only tell me."

Her eyes closed and she bent her head, half-hiding her face from him. He held onto her hand and she did not withdraw it, though her free hand stole upward, fingers wrapping around the pendant at the base of her throat.

Er Thom's eyes widened. She wore the parting-gift, even now; touched it as if it were capable of giving comfort. And he, he here by her, *touching* her, speaking on terms that would lead any to assume them lovers, if not bound more closely still.

The magnitude of his error staggered; the cause that had brought him here suddenly showing the face of self-deception. He should never have given Anne nubiath'a.

He should never have sought her out again . . .

"Er Thom?" She was looking at him, dark brown eyes large in a face he thought paler than it might be.

"Yes, my friend?" he murmured and smiled for her. What-ever errors were found in this time and place were solely his own, he told himself sternly. Anne, at least, had behaved with utmost propriety.

"I—I know that I'm not very entertaining right now," she said with a tentativeness wholly unAnne-like, "but—unless you have somewhere else you need—would rather be—I'd *like* you to stay."

"There is no other place I wish to be," he said—and that was truth, gods pity him, though he could think of a dozen places he might otherwise be needed, not forgetting his mother's drawing room and the bridge of the trade ship orbiting Liad.

He picked up the wineglass and placed it in her hand as he rose. "Drink your wine, my friend. I will be back in a moment with food."

It was some time later, after the odd sweet-spicy food was eaten and the wine, but for the little remaining in their glasses, was drunk, before she thought to ask him.

"But, Er Thom, what are you doing on University? Another trade mission? There isn't anything to trade for here, is there?"

"To trade for? No . . ." He took a sip of the sticky yellow wine, then, with sudden decision, finished the glass.

"I am not here to trade," he told her, watching as if from a distance as his traitor body slid closer to her on the sofa and his hand lifted to fondle her hair. "What I am doing is seeing you."

She laughed softly as she set aside her glass. "Of course you are," she murmured, gently mocking.

She did not believe him! Panic galvanized him. She *must* believe, or all he had meant to accomplish by this mad break-ing with custom was gone for naught. The Healers would take him, and reft him of distress, and it would be forgot, un-known, lost in a swirl of blurry dreaming . . .

His fingers tightened in her hair, pulling her down as he tipped his face up to hers, hungrily, despairingly.

She came willingly, as she ever had, her mouth firm and sweet on his, calling forth the desire, the need, that had been touched by no other, before or since. The need that burned away names, clans and duty, leaving only she . . . and he.

• • •

Later yet, and she asleep. Er Thom shifted onto an elbow, letting the light from the living area fall past his shoulder and onto her.

A Liaden would not count her beautiful. He believed that even among Terrans she was considered but moderately attractive. Certainly her face was too full for Liaden taste, her nose too long, her mouth too wide, her skin merely brown, not golden. And while chestnut was a very pretty color for hair, Anne wore hers with an eye to ease of care.

The rest of her was as strange to the standard of beauty he acknowledged: Her breasts, brown as her face and rosy brown at the very tips, were round and high, larger than his hand could encompass. She was saved from being top-heavy by the width of her hips, flaring unexpectedly from a narrow waist, and she moved with a pilot's smooth grace. Her hands were long-fingered and strong—musician's hands—and her voice was quite lovely.

He thought of the face of the latest proposed to him: Properly Liaden, well-mannered and golden. A person who understood duty, who would do as she was bid by her delm. And who would very properly rebuke Er Thom yos'Galan, should he but reach out a finger to trace the line of her cheek, or lay his lips against hers.

But I do not want her! he thought, plaintive, childish, undutiful—strange. As strange as lying here in this present, in a too-large bed, his arms about a woman not of his kind, who expected him to sleep next to her the night full through; to be there when she awoke . . .

Carefully, he slid down until his eyes were on a level with her closed eyes. For a long while, he stared into her unbeautiful, alien face, watching—guarding—her sleep. Finally, he moved his head to kiss her just-parted lips and said at last the thing he had come to tell her, the thing which must not be forgotten.

"I love you, Anne Davis."

His voice was soft and not quite steady, and he stumbled over the Terran words, but it hardly mattered. She was asleep and did not hear him.

CHAPTER FIVE

Melant'i - *A Liaden word denoting the status of a person within a given situation. For instance, one person may fulfill several roles: Parent, spouse, child, mechanic, thodelm. The shifting winds of circumstance, or 'necessity,' dictate from which role the person will act this time. They will certainly always act honorably, as defined within a voluminous and painfully detailed code of behavior, referred to simply as 'The Code.'*

To a Liaden, melant'i is more precious than rubies, a cumulative, ever-changing indicator of his place in the universal pecking order. A person of high honor, for instance, is referred to as "a person of melant'i," whereas a scoundrel—or a Terran—may be dismissed with "he has no melant'i."

Melant'i may be the single philosophical concept from which all troubles, large and small, between Liad and Terra spring.

—From *A Terran's Guide to Liad*

Late in the morning, loved and showered and feeling positively decadent, Anne stood in front of the tiny built-in vanity. A few brush-strokes put her shower-dampened hair into order, and she smiled into her own eyes as her reflected fingers found and picked up her pendant.

"Anne?"

She turned, transferring her smile to him. An elfin prince, so Brellick had described him, enticing Anne to meet a real, live Liaden. And elfin he was: Slim and tawny and quick; hair glittering gold, purple eyes huge in a beardless pointed face; voice soft and seductively accented.

The eyes right now were very serious, moving from her hand to her face.

"Anne?" he said again.

"Yes, my dear. What can I do for you?"

"Please," he said slowly, gliding closer to her. "Do not wear that."

"Don't wear—" She blinked at him, looked down at the fine golden chain and pendant seed-pearls, artfully blended with gold-and-enamel leaves to look like a cluster of fantasy grapes.

This is a misunderstanding, she told herself carefully; *a problem with the words chosen.* Er Thom's command of Terran tended to be literal and uneasy of idiom—much like her careful, scholar's Liaden. It made for some interesting conversational tangles, now and then. But they had always been able to untangle themselves, eventually. She looked back into his eyes.

"You gave this to me," she said, holding it out so he might see it better. "Don't you remember, Er Thom? You gave it to me the day *Dutiful Passage*—"

"I remember," he said sharply, cutting her off without a glance at the pearls. He lay a hand lightly on her wrist.

"Anne? Please. It was—it was given to say good-bye. I would rather—may I?—give you another gift."

She laughed a little and lay her hand briefly over his.

"But you won't be here long, will you? And when you leave again, you'll have to give me another gift, for another good-bye . . ." She laughed more fully. "My dear, I'll look like a jewelry store."

The serious look in his eyes seemed to intensify and he swayed closer, so his hip grazed her thigh.

"No," he began, a little breathlessly. "I—there is a thing you must hear, Anne, and never forget—"

The doorbell chimed. Anne glanced up, mouth curving in a curious smile, and raised her fingers to touch his cheek.

"That's Jerzy," she said, laying the pendant back in its carved ivory box. She moved past him toward the living room. "Er Thom, there's someone I want you to meet."

He stood still for a moment, running through a pilot's calming exercise. Then, he went after her.

The man who was coming in from the hallway was not large as Terrans go; he was, in fact, a bit under standard height for that race, and a bit under standard weight, too. He had rough black hair chopped off at the point of his jaw and a pale face made memorable by the thick line of a single brow above a pair of iron-gray eyes. He was carrying a cloth sack over one shoulder and a child on the opposite hip. Both he and the child were wearing jackets; the child also wore a cap.

"Jerzy delivers kid latish in the a.m., as promised. Notice the nobility of spirit which would not allow me to steal him, though I was tempted, ma'am. Sore tempted."

"You're a saint, Jerzy," Anne said gravely, though Er Thom heard the ripple of laughter through her words.

"I'm a lunatic," the young man corrected, bending to set the child on his sturdy legs. He knelt and pulled off the cap, revealing a head of silky, frost-colored hair, and unsealed the little jacket, much hampered by small, busy hands.

"Knock it off, Scooter. This is hard enough without you helping," he muttered and the child gave a peal of laughter.

"Help Scooter!" he cried.

Jerzy snorted. "Regular comedian. OK, let's get the arms out . . ."

"I can do that, you know," Anne said mildly, but Jerzy had finished his task and stood up, sliding the bag off his shoulder and stuffing the small garments inside.

"And have you think I don't know how to take care of him? I want him back, you know. Say, next week, same time?"

"Jerzy—"

But whatever Anne had meant to say to her friend was interrupted by a shriek of child-laughter as young Scooter flung himself hurly-burly down-room, hands flapping at the level of his ears. Er Thom saw the inexpert feet snag on the carpet and swooped forward, catching the little body as it lost control and swinging him up to straddle a hip.

The child laughed again and grabbed a handful of Er Thom's hair.

"Good catch!" Jerzy cried, clapping his palms together with enthusiasm. "You see this man move?" he asked of no one in particular and then snapped his fingers, coming forward. "You're a pilot, right?"

"Yes," Er Thom admitted, gently working the captured lock of hair loose of the child's fingers.

The young man stopped, head tipped to one side. Then he stuck out one of his big hands in the way that Terrans did when they wanted to initiate the behavior known as "shaking hands." Inwardly, Er Thom sighed. Local custom.

He was saved from this particular bout with custom by the perpetrator himself, who lowered his hand, looking self-conscious. "Never mind. Won't do to drop Scooter, will it? I'm Jerzy Entaglia. Theater Arts. Chairman of Theater Arts, which gives you an idea of the shape the department's in."

An introduction. Very good. Er Thom inclined his head, taking care that the child on his hip did not capture another handful of hair. "Er Thom yos'Galan, Clan Korval."

Jerzy Entaglia froze, an arrested expression on his forgettable face. "yos'Galan?" he said, voice edging upward in an exaggerated question-mark.

Er Thom lifted his eyebrows. "Indeed."

"Well," said Jerzy, backing up so rapidly Er Thom thought he might take a tumble. "That's great! The two of you probably have a lot to talk about—get to know each other, that kind of stuff. Anne—seeya later. Gotta run. 'Bye, Scooter—Mr. yos'Galan—" He was gone, letting himself out the door a moment before Anne's hand fell on his shoulder.

"Bye, bye, bye!" the child sang, beating his heels against Er Thom's flank. He wriggled, imperatively. "Shan go."

"Very well." He bent and placed the child gently on his feet, offering an arm for support.

The boy looked up to smile, showing slanting frosty eyebrows to match the white hair, and eyes of so light a blue they seemed silver, huge in the small brown face. "Shank you," he said with a certain dignity and turned to go about his business.

He was restrained by a motherly hand, which caught him by a shoulder and brought him back to face Er Thom.

"This is someone very important," she said, but it was not clear if she was talking to the boy or to himself. She looked up, her eyes bright, face lit with such a depth of pride that he felt his own heart lift with it.

"Er Thom," she said, voice thrilling with joy, "this is Shan yos'Galan."

"yos'Galan?" He stared at her; looked down at the child, who gazed back at him out of alert silver eyes.

"yos'Galan?" he repeated, unable to believe that she would—without contract, without the Delm's Word, without—He took a breath, ran the pilot's calming sequence; looked back at Anne, the joy in her face beginning to show an edge of unease.

"This is—our—child?" he asked, trying to keep his voice steady, his face politely distant. Perhaps he had misunderstood. Local custom, after all—and who would so blatantly disregard proper behavior, melant'i, *honor* . . .

Relief showed in her eyes, and she nearly smiled. "Yes. Our child. Do you remember the night—that horrible formal dance and it was so hot, and the air conditioning was broken? Remember, we snuck out and went to the roof—"

The roof of the yet-unfinished Mercantile Building. He had landed the light-flyer there, spread the silk for them to sit on as they drank pilfered wine and snacked on delicacies filched from a hors d'ouevre tray . . .

"Fourteen moons," he whispered, remembering, then the outrage struck, for there was no misunderstanding here at all, and no local custom to excuse. "You named this child *yos'-Galan*?" he demanded, and meant for her to hear his anger.

She dropped back half-a-step, eyes going wide, and her hands caught the boy's shoulders and pulled him close against her. She took a deep breath and let it sigh out.

"Of course I named him yos'Galan," she said, very quietly. "It is the custom, on my homeworld, to give a child his father's surname. I meant no—insult—to you, Er Thom. If I have insulted you, only tell me how, and I will mend it."

"It is improper to have named this child yos'Galan. How could you have thought it was anything else? There was no contract—"

Anne bowed her head, raised a hand to smooth the boy's

bright hair. "I see." She looked up. "It's an easy matter to change a name. There's no reason why he shouldn't be Shan Davis. I'll make the application to—"

"No!" His vehemence surprised them both, and this time it was Er Thom who went back a step. "Anne—" He cut himself off, took a moment to concentrate, then tried again, schooling his voice to calmness. "Why did you not—you sent no word? You thought I had no reason to know that there was born a yos'Galan?"

She moved her hands; he was uncertain of the meaning, the purpose, of the gesture. The child stayed pressed against her legs, quiet as stone.

"I wanted a child," she said, slowly. "I had decided to have a child—entirely my own choice, made before I met you. And then, I did meet you, who became my friend and who I—" Again, that shapeless gesture. "I thought, 'why shouldn't I have the child of my friend, instead of the child of someone I don't know, who only happened to donate his seed to the clinic?' " She moved her head in a sharp shake.

"Er Thom, you were leaving! We had been so happy and— is it wrong, that I wanted something to remind me of joy and the friend who had shared it? I never thought I'd see you again—the universe is wide, my brother says. So many things can happen . . . It was only for my joy, my—comfort. Should I have pin-beamed a message to Liad? How many yos'Galans are there? I didn't think—I didn't think you'd *care*, Er Thom—or only enough to be happy you'd given me so—so fine a gift . . ." She bent her head, but not before he'd seen the tears spill over and shine down her cheeks.

Pity filled him, and remorse. He reached out. "Anne . . ."

She shook her head, refusing to look at him, and Shan gave a sudden gasp, which quickly became a wail as he turned to bury his face against her legs. She bent and picked him up, making soothing sounds and stroking his hair.

Er Thom came another step forward, close enough to touch her wet cheek, to lay his hand on the child's thin shoulder.

"Peace, my son," he murmured in Liaden while his mind was busy, trying to adjust to these new facts, to a trade that became entirely altered. He thought of the proposed contract-marriage that must somehow be put off until he had done duty

by this child—*his* child—a half-bred child, gods—whatever
would he say to his mother?

"No!" Anne jerked back, holding the sobbing child tightly
against her. Her face was ashen, her eyes shadowed with some
dire terror.

"Anne?"

"Er Thom, he is *my* son! He is a Terran citizen, registered
on University. *My* son, of whom your clan was never told—
for whom your clan doesn't care!"

Harsh words, almost enough to strike him to anger again.
But there, Terrans knew nothing of clans.

"The clan knows," he said softly, telling her only the truth,
"because I know; cares because I care. We are all children of
the clan; ears, eyes and heart of the clan."

The fear in her eyes grew, he saw her arms tighten about
Shan, who put out renewed cries.

Whirling, Anne carried him into the bedroom.

She stayed in the bedroom a long time, soothing Shan and
convincing him to lie down in his little pull-out bed. She sat
by him until he fell asleep, the tears dried to sticky tracks on
his cheeks.

When she knew he was sleeping deeply, she rose and
pulled the tangled blankets straight on her own bed. She
strained her ears for a sound—any sound—from the next
room. The apartment was filled with silence.

Go away! she thought fiercely and almost at once: *Don't
go!* She shook her head. He would go, of course; it was the
nature of things. They would resolve this misunderstanding;
she would change her son's surname and he would be easy
again. They would be friends. But sooner or later Er Thom
would go, back to his round of worlds and trade-routes. She
would take up again the rhythm of her hectic life . . .

There was no sound from the living room. Had he gone already? If he was still here, why hadn't he come to find her?

She glanced at the pull-out, stepped over to make sure the
bed-bars were secure, then she took a deep breath and went
into the living room.

He was sitting on the edge of the sofa, hands folded on his

lap, bright head bent. At her approach he stood and came forward, eyes on her face.

"Anne? I ask pardon. It was not my intent to—to cause you pain. My temper is—not good. And it was a shock, I did not see . . . Of course you would not know that there are not so many yos'Galans; that a message sent to me by name, to Liad or to *Dutiful Passage,* would reach me. I am at fault. It had not occurred to me to leave you my beamcode . . ." *And who leaves such,* he asked himself, *for one who has taken nubiath'a?*

She tried a small smile; it felt odd on her face. "Maybe this time you can leave me the code, then. I'll contact you, if something—important—happens. All right?"

"No." He took her lifeless fingers in his, tried to massage warmth into them. "Anne, it cannot continue so—"

She snatched her hand away. "Because he's named yos'-Galan? I'll change that—I've said I would! You have no right—Er Thom—" She raised her hand to her throat, fingers seeking the comfort that no longer hung there; she felt tears rising.

"Er Thom, don't you have somewhere else you need to be? You came here for a purpose, didn't you? Business?" Her voice was sharp and he nearly flinched. Instead, he reached up and took her face between his hands.

"I came to see you," he said, speaking very slowly, as clearly and as plainly as he knew how, so there could be no possible misunderstanding. "I came with no other purpose than to speak with you." Tears spilled over, soaking his fingertips, startling them both.

"Anne? Anne, no, only listen—"

She pulled away, dashing at her eyes.

"Er Thom, please go away."

He froze, staring at her. Would she send him away with all that lay, unresolved, between them? It was her right, certainly. He was none of her kin, to demand she open her door to him. But the child was named yos'Galan.

Anne wiped at her face, shook her head, mouth wobbling.

"Please, Er Thom. You're—my dear, we're still friends. But I don't think I *can* listen now. I'm—I need to be by myself for a little while . . ."

Reprieve. He licked his lips.

"I may come again? When?"

The tears wouldn't stop. They seemed to come from a hole in her chest that went on and on, forever. "When? I don't—this evening. After dinner." What was she saying? "Er Thom . . ."

"Yes." He moved, spinning away from her, plucking his jacket from the back of the easy chair and letting himself out the door.

For perhaps an entire minute, Anne stared at the place where he had been. Then the full force of her grief caught her and she bent double, sobbing.

CHAPTER SIX

Any slight—no matter how small—requires balancing, lest the value of one's melant'i be lessened.

Balance is an important, and intricate, part of Liaden culture, with the severity of rebuttal figured individually by each debt-partner, in accordance with his or her own melant'i. For instance, one Liaden might balance an insult by demanding you surrender your dessert to him at a society dinner, whereas another individual might calculate balance of that same insult to require a death.

Balance-death is, admittedly, rare. But it is best always to speak softly, bow low and never give a Liaden cause to think he has been slighted.

—From *A Terran's Guide to Liad*

It was a crisp, bright day of the kind that doubt- less delighted the resident population. Er Thom shivered violently as he hit Quad S and belatedly dragged on his jacket, sealing the front and jerking the collar up.

Jamming his hands into the fur-lined pockets, he strode off, heedless both of his direction and the stares of those he passed, and only paused in his headlong flight when he found water barring his path.

He stopped and blinked over the glittering expanse before him, trying to steady his disordered thoughts.

The child's name was yos'Galan.

He shivered again, though he had walked far enough and hard enough for the exercise to warm him.

His melant'i was imperiled—though that hardly concerned him, so much had he already worked toward its ruination—and the melant'i of Clan Korval, as well. A yos'Galan born and the clan unaware? Korval was High House and known to be eccentric—society wags spoke of "the Dragon's directive" and "Korval madness"—but even so strong and varied a melant'i could scarcely hope to come away from such a debacle untainted.

Er Thom closed his eyes against the lake's liquid luster. Why? Why had she done this thing? What had he done that demanded such an answer from her? So stringent a balancing argued an insult of such magnitude he *must* have been aware of his transgression—and he recalled nothing.

Abruptly he laughed. Whatever the cause, only see the beauty of the balance! A yos'Galan, born and raised as Terran, growing to adulthood, building what melant'i he might, clan and line alike all in ignorance . . . If Er Thom yos'Galan had been a stronger man, one who knew enough of duty to embrace forgetfulness without once more seeking out the cause of his heart-illness . . . It was, in truth, an artwork of balance.

But what coin of his had purchased it? If Anne had felt herself slighted, if he had belittled her or failed someway of giving her full honor—

"Hold." He opened his eyes, staring sightlessly across the lake.

"Anne is *Terran,*" he told himself, as revelation began to dawn.

There were some who argued that Terrans possessed neither melant'i nor honor. It was a view largely popular with those who had never been beyond Liad or Liad's Outworlds. Traders and Scouts tended to espouse a less popular philosophy, based on actual observation.

He himself had traded with persons unLiaden. As with Liadens, there were those who were honorable and those who were, regrettably, otherwise. Local custom often dictated a system strange to Liaden thought, though, once grasped, it

was seen to be honor, and consistent with what one knew to
be right conduct.

Daav went further, arguing that melant'i existed independent of a person's consciousness, and might be deduced from
careful observation. It was then the burden of a person of conscious melant'i to give all proper respect to the unawakened
consciousness and guard its sleeping potential.

Er Thom had thought his brother's view extreme. Until he
had met Anne Davis.

He knew Anne to be a person of honor. He had observed
her melant'i first-hand and at length and he would place it, in
its very different strengths, equal to his own. She was not one
to start a debt-war from spite, nor to take extreme balance as
bolster for an unsteady sense of self.

Is it possible, he asked himself, slowly, *that Anne named
the boy so to* honor *me?*

The lake dazzled his eyes as the paving stones seemed to
move under his feet. He grappled with the notion, trying to accommodate the alien shape, and he grit his teeth against a desire to cry out that no one might reasonably think such a thing.

Facts: Anne was an honorable person. There had been
nothing requiring balance between them. The child's name
was yos'Galan. Therefore, Anne had meant honor—or at the
least no harm—to him by her actions.

He drew a deep breath of chill air, almost giddy with relief,
that there was no balancing here that he must answer; that he
need not bring harm to her whom he wished only to cherish
and protect.

There remained only to decide what must properly be done
about the child.

It was mid afternoon. Shan had eaten a hearty dinner, resisted
any suggestion of sleep and fell easy prey to *Mix-n-Match*.

Anne shook her head. She'd had to upgrade the set three
times already; Shan learned the simple patterns effortlessly, it
seemed. He needed a tutor—more time than she could give
him, to help him learn at his own rate, to be sure that he received balanced instruction, that he didn't grow bored . . .

"A tutor," she jeered to herself, not for the first time. "Sure,

Annie Davis, an' where will ye be getting the means for that madness?"

It was a measure of her uneasiness that she sought comfort in the dialect of her childhood. She shook her head again and went over to the desk, resolutely switching on the terminal. "Get some work done," she told herself firmly.

But her mind would not stay on her work and after half-an-hour's fruitless searching through tangential lines, she canceled the rest of her time and went over to the omnichora.

She pulled the dust cover off and folded it carefully onto the easy chair, sat on the bench, flipped stops, set timings, tone, balance, and began, very softly, to play.

Er Thom was not coming back. Intellectually, she knew that this was so: The abruptness of his departure this morning told its own tale. It was no use trying to decide if this were a good thing or a bad one. She had been trying to resolve that precise point all morning and had failed utterly.

Her hands skittered on the keys, sowing discord. Irritably, Anne raised her hand and re-adjusted the timing, but she did not take up her playing. Instead, she sat and stared down at the worn plastic keys, fighting the terror that threatened to overwhelm her.

It cannot continue so, he insisted in memory and Anne bit her lip in the present. Er Thom was an honorable man. He had his melant'i—his status—to consider. Anne had, all unwitting, threatened that melant'i—and Er Thom did not think a mere change of Shan's surname would retire the threat.

Liaden literature was her passion. She had read the stories of Shan el'Thrasin compulsively, addictively, searching back along esoteric research lines for the oldest versions, sending for recordings of the famous Liaden prena'ma—the tellers of tales. She knew what happened to those foolish enough to threaten a Liaden's melant'i.

They were plunged into honor-feud, to their impoverishment, often enough. Sometimes, to their death.

It didn't matter that she loved Er Thom yos'Galan, or what his feelings might otherwise be for her. She had put his status at risk. The threat she posed must be nullified, her audacity answered, and his melant'i absolutely reestablished, no matter what hurt he must give her in the process.

He might even be sorry to hurt her, and grieve truly for her misfortune, as Shan el'Thrasin had grieved truly for his beloved Lyada ro'Menlin, who had killed his partner. She had paid fully and Shan had extracted the price, as honor demanded, and then mourned her the rest of his life . . .

She gasped and came off the bench in a rush to go across the room and sweep her son up in a hug.

"Ma no!" yelled that young gentleman, twisting in her embrace.

"Ma, yes!" she insisted and kissed him and rumpled his hair and cuddled him close, feeling his warmth and hearing the beat of his heart. "Ma loves you," she said, fiercely, for all that she whispered. Shan grabbed her hair.

"Ma?"

"Yes," she said and walked with him to the kitchen, back through the living room to the bedroom. "We'll go—someplace. To Richard." She stopped in the middle of the living room and took a deep breath, feeling beautifully, miraculously reprieved. She kissed Shan again and bent down to let him go.

"We'll go to Richard—home to New Dublin. We'll leave tonight . . ." Tonight? What about her classes, her contract? It would be academic suicide—and Er Thom would find her at her brother's house on New Dublin, she thought dejectedly. He would have to find her. Honor required it. Her shoulders sank and she felt the tears rise again.

"Oh, gods . . ."

The door chime sounded.

She spun, some primal instinct urging her to snatch up her son and run.

Shan was sitting on the floor amidst his rubber blocks, patiently trying to balance a rectangle atop a cube. And there was no place, really, to run.

The chime sounded again.

Slowly, she walked across the room and opened the door.

He bowed in spite of the parcels he held, and smiled when he looked up at her.

"Good evening," he said softly, as if this morning had never happened and he had never looked at her with fury in his eyes. "It is after dinner?"

Speechless, she looked down at him, torn between shutting

the door in his face and hugging him as fiercely as she had hugged Shan.

"Anne?"

She started, and managed a wooden smile. "It's after Shan's dinner, anyway," she said, stepping back to let him in. "But he's being stubborn about going to bed."

Er Thom glanced over to the boy, absorbed in his blocks. "I see." He looked up at her. "I have brought a gift for our son. May I give it?"

She looked at him doubtfully. Surely he wouldn't harm a child. No matter what he might feel he owed her, surely his own son was safe? She swallowed. "All right . . ."

"Thank you." He offered the smaller of the two parcels. "I have also brought wine." He paused, violet eyes speculative. "Will you drink with me, Anne?"

She caught her breath against sudden, painful relief. It was going to be all right, she thought, dizzily. To drink with someone was a sign of goodwill. It would be dishonorable to ask a feud-partner to drink with one. And Er Thom was an honorable man.

The smile she gave him this time was real. "Of course I'll drink with you, Er Thom." She took the package. "I'll pour tonight. And provide dinner. Are you hungry?"

He smiled. "I will eat if you will eat."

"A bargain." Her laughed sounded giddy in her own ears, but Er Thom did not seem to notice. He was walking toward Shan.

The boy had succeeded in building a bridge of a rectangle across two cubes. Gracefully, Er Thom went to one knee, facing the child across the bridge, and laying down the large parcel.

"Good evening Shan-son," he said in soft Liaden. Anne swallowed around the lump of dread in her throat, clutched the wine bottle and said nothing.

"Jiblish," Shan said, glancing up from his task with a smile. "Hi!"

"I've brought you a gift," Er Thom pursued, still in Liaden. "I hope that it will please you."

To Shan's intense interest, he removed the wrapping from the package and held out a stuffed animal. It was a friendly sort of animal, Anne thought, with large round ears and rounder blue eyes and a good-natured smile on its pointy face. Shan gave it thoughtful consideration, uttered a crow of laughter and fell upon its neck.

Er Thom echoed the laugh softly and reached out to touch the small brown face. Shan pulled his new friend closer and caught the man's finger in his free hand, crowing again.

Anne quietly turned and went into the kitchen for glasses and for food.

She busied herself in the kitchen rather longer than was necessary; cutting the cheese to nibble-size, and the fruit, too. She stood for a ridiculous amount of time, trying to decide which crackers to offer.

Throughout it all relief warred with lingering fear. It went against everything she knew to distrust Er Thom. He was her friend, the father of her son. This morning had been a regrettable misunderstanding—a conflict of custom—and she ought to thank all possible gods, that Er Thom had been able to forgive her assault on his melant'i. She would need to be very careful not to threaten him again. Even fondness for a lover could not be expected to stay a Liaden's hand twice . . .

When she finally returned to the living room, it was strangely quiet. Er Thom smiled up at her from his seat against the sofa. Shan was spread out across his lap, head on Er Thom's shoulder, one small hand gripping the stuffed animal's round ear. He was fast asleep.

"Oh, no!" Anne laughed, nearly upsetting the wine glasses on the tray. "My poor friend . . ." She sat the tray down and knelt on the floor next to them, holding out her arms. "I'll put him to bed."

The stuffed animal proved a stumbling block. Even in sleep her son's grip was trojan, but Er Thom patiently coaxed the sleeping fingers open, and offered the liberated toy to Anne. She took it and led the way as Er Thom carried Shan into the bedroom and lay him gently on the pull-out bed.

He waited quietly while she settled both friends comfortably and allowed her to proceed him back into the living room, pulling the door half-closed behind him.

CHAPTER SEVEN

The delm shall be face and voice of the clan, guarding the interests of the clan and treating with other delms in matters of wider interest. The delm is held to be responsible for the actions of all members of his clan and likewise holds ultimate authority over these members. The delm shall administer according to the internal laws of his clan, saving only that those laws do not circumvent the Laws agreed upon by all delms and set forth in this document.

—From the Charter of the Council of Clans

"Go to Liad?" Anne set her glass carefully aside. "I have no reason to go to Liad, Er Thom."

"Ah." He inclined his head, keeping his manner in all ways gentle. It had been ill-done to show her his anger; he had not missed the wariness in her face when he had asked entrance this evening. Nor did the continued tension in her shoulders and the unaccustomed care with which she addressed him escape notice. He met her eyes, as one did with a valued friend, and brushed the back of her hand with light fingertips.

"Our child must be Seen by the delm."

She took a slow, deep breath. "I believe," she said with that care which was so different from her usual way with him, "that the matter need not concern your delm. I said this morning that I will change Shan's surname to Davis, and I meant it. I have an early day tomorrow. I'll go to Central Admin and file the request through Terran Census. Three days, at the most, and—"

"No." He caught her hand in both of his, keeping his voice soft with an effort. "Anne, is Shan not the—the child of our bodies?"

She blinked, slipping her hand free. "Of course he is. I told you."

Irritation there, and rightly so. Who was Er Thom yos'-Galan to question the word of an equal adult? He bowed his head.

"Forgive me, friend. Most certainly you did tell me. It is thus that the delm's concern is engaged. You have said that the child of our pleasure is yos'Galan. It is the delm's honor to keep the tale of yos'Galans and ensure that the clan—" here he stumbled, sorting among a myriad of words of Terran possibility, all the wrong size or shape to describe the clan's obligations in this matter.

"I've said," Anne stepped into the space his hesitation had created, "that his name will be changed to Davis. In three days, Er Thom, there will be no new yos'Galans for your delm to count."

"You have said he is yos'Galan. Will you unsay it and forswear yourself?" It was not his place to rebuke her, nor any of his concern, should she choose to tarnish her melant'i. But his heart ached, for he had taught her to fear him, and now fear forced her to dishonor. "Anne?"

She sighed. "Er Thom, he's the same child, whether his name is Davis or yos'Galan!"

"Yes!" Joy flooded him, so that he caught her hands, laughing with sheer relief, for she did not after all turn her face from honor. "Precisely so! And thus the delm must certainly See him—soon, as you will understand. I shall pilot— you need not be concerned—and the ship is entirely able. To Liad is—"

"Hold it." Her face held an odd mix of emotion—a frown twisted curiously about a smile—and she shook her head, a pet gesture that did not always signal negative, but sometimes also wonder, or impatience, or sadness. She took one of her hands from his and raised it to his face, running her knuckles whisper-soft down his right cheek. Once more, wonderingly, it seemed to him, she shook her head.

"It's really important for your delm to see Shan now?"

Important? It was vital. To be outside the clan was to be outside of life.

"Yes," he told her.

"All right. Then let your delm come here."

"Hah." She was within her right to ask it, though there were few so secure in their melant'i as to bid Korval come to them. Er Thom inclined his head.

"It is, you see, that—until his own children are of an age— I am the delm's designated heir. Wisdom dictates that we both not be off-planet at the same time. Your grace would be the clan's delight, could you instead go to Korval."

"You're the delm's heir?" Anne was frowning slightly. "I didn't know that."

There was no reason for her to know; such information was not commonly shared with pleasure-loves. Yet Anne knew much else about him, he realized suddenly. It was possible that only Daav knew more.

"Forgive me. I am a'thodelm—heir to my mother, who is thodelm of yos'Galan. And I am nadelm—named to take the place of the delm, should—necessity—dictate." He paused, biting his lip, and then made her a gift: "The delm is Daav yos'Phelium, who is also my cha'leket—you would say, my foster-brother."

"And master trader, and master pilot," Anne murmured, naming the two facets of his melant'i she had cause to know well. "That's quite a hat-rack."

His brows twitched together. "Your pardon?"

"I'm sorry," she said, laughing lightly. "An old Terran joke had to do with the number of duties a single person was assigned to perform. Each of the duties was referred to as a 'hat,' and the traditional question was: 'What hat are you wearing today?' "

He stared at her. A joke? But—

"That is melant'i," he said, around a sense of wondering bafflement.

"More or less," Anne agreed with a shrug. "It's pretty old—a scholar's joke, you know." She changed the subject abruptly. "If your delm needs to see Shannie *now*, the solution is for you to go home so he can come to University. I certainly can't leave *now* —exam week is just beginning—and I don't have any other reason to go to Liad, Er Thom. Though I'm certain," she added, with a return of that unnatural caution, "that I would *want* to accommodate your delm."

"Of course you would." True enough. Who sane deliberately thwarted Korval? Er Thom reached for his wine, eyes sweeping down the column of her throat, to where her breasts pushed tight against the fabric of her shirt.

"When," he asked softly, dragging his eyes away with an effort and trying to ignore his hammering pulse. "When might you be able to leave University, were you interested in a visit to—to Liad?"

Anne shook her head, sharply, he thought, and seemed to shift her eyes from his face all a-sudden. "I—three weeks. About that, with getting in final grades, and—" She took a hard breath. "Er Thom."

"Yes." He slid nearer to her on the sofa, setting his leg against hers, and raised a hand to stroke one delightful breast through her shirt—deliberately teasing—and felt the quiver of her desire.

Lightly, he smoothed his fingertips across her nipple, feeling it harden as his own passion mounted, hard and demanding. He shifted closer, urgent fingers at the fastening of her shirt.

"Shan—" she began.

"Is asleep," he whispered, and brought his gaze up to her face. "Isn't he?"

Her eyes seem to lose focus—an instant only and he half-swooning with a desire that seemed only to build, and build, until he must—"Anne?"

"Asleep." She was back with him fully, fingers busy with his own clothing. "Er Thom, I need you. Quickly."

"Quickly," he agreed, and the passion built to a wave, hesitated in a pain that became ecstasy as it crashed, engulfing them entirely.

• • •

"**The** Right Honorable Lady Kareen yos'Phelium," Mr. pel'Kana announced with unnerving formality, and bowed low.

The lady's brother bit back a curse, spun his chair to face the door and swept his hand across the computer keypad, banishing the files he had been reviewing. The last move was sheer instinct: Kareen never hesitated to busy herself about any bit of business within the clan, a right she claimed as Eldest of Line. That Daav did not agree with this assessment of her melant'i barely slowed her and had never, so far as he knew, stopped her.

"Young brother." Kareen paused on the threshold long enough to incline her head—Elder to Younger—and allowed Mr. pel'Kana to seat her.

Inwardly, Daav sighed. True enough, Kareen could give him ten years, but it wearied one that she must always be playing that point. A variation, he thought, would add piquancy to a game of spite and dislike that had become all too predictable. Alas, that Kareen was not imaginative. He moved his hand, catching the servant's attention.

"Wine for Lady Kareen," he murmured.

This done, Mr. pel'Kana quit the room, with, Daav thought, marked relief. The Council of Clans rated Kareen expert in the field of proper action and called upon her often to unravel this or that sticky point of Code. It was to be regretted that she demanded expert's understanding of all she met.

Expert's understanding required that he rise and make his bow, honoring the eldest of Line yos'Phelium, and bidding her graceful welcome.

Daav thrust his legs out before him and crossed them at the ankle. Lacing his fingers over his belt buckle, he grinned at her in counterfeit good-humor.

"Good-day, Kareen. Whatever can you want from me now?"

She allowed the merest twitch of a brow to convey her displeasure at being addressed in the Low Tongue, and lifted her glass, pointedly tasting the wine.

Setting the glass aside, she met his eyes.

"I have lately been," she murmured, still in the mode of

Elder Sibling to Younger, "at the house of Luken bel'Tarda, in the cause of visiting my heir."

Kareen's heir was six-year-old Pat Rin, recently fostered into the house of bel'Tarda by the delm's command. An imperfect solution, as the delm had admitted to his cha'leket, and one that had enraged Kareen unseemly.

Daav inclined his head. "And how do you find our cousin Luken?"

"Shatterbrained to a fault," his sister replied with regrettable accuracy. "As I had said to you on another occasion, sirrah, Luken bel'Tarda is hardly fit guardian for one of the Line Direct. However," she said, interrupting herself, "that is a different bolt of cloth." She fixed him with a stern eye.

"Cousin bel'Tarda informs me that yos'Galan searches for one of the clan to enter into contract-alliance with Clan Nexon, in the person of its daughter Syntebra el'Kemin."

"yos'Galan has the delm's leave for this search," Daav said lazily, moving his hand in a gesture of disinterest. Kareen's mouth tightened.

"Then perhaps the delm is also aware that Thodelm yos'-Galan had intended Syntebra el'Kemin as contract-wife for the a'thodelm." It cut very near disrespect, phrased as it yet was in Elder-to-Younger. But Kareen was expert in mode, as well, and kept her tongue nimbly in place.

"The delm is aware of the thodelm's intentions in that regard, yes." He lifted an eyebrow. "Is there some point to this, Kareen?"

"A small one," she said, "but sharp enough to prick interest." She leaned forward slightly in her chair. "The a'thodelm is gone off-planet, not to return before the end of the relumma, fleeing, one must conclude, the proposed alliance. Think of the insult to Nexon, that one intended for the contract-room at Trealla Fantrol should be shunted off to make do with—forgive me!—the like of Luken bel'Tarda."

"Luken is an amiable fellow," Daav said calmly. "Though I give you score—thought is not his best endeavor. As for the insult to Nexon—the contract has not yet been written, much less signed. If the lady hoped for an a'thodelm and nets instead a country cousin, still her clan gains ties with Korval, to her honor. I note that she is young, and while Nexon is all very well, it is hardly High House."

"Which matters to Korval not at all," Kareen said, with a touch of acid. "I recall that your own father was—solidly—Low House."

"But a pilot to marvel at," Daav returned, very gently. "So our mother praised him."

Kareen, who was no pilot at all, took a deep breath, visibly seeking calm.

"This does not address," she said after a moment, "how best to deal with the scandal."

Daav straightened slowly in his chair. He met his sister's eyes sternly.

"There will be no scandal," he said, and the mode was Ranking Person to Lesser. "Understand me, Kareen."

"I do not—"

"If I hear one whisper," Daav interrupted, eyes boring into hers, "one syllable, of scandal regarding this, I shall know who to speak with. Do I make myself plain?"

It was to her credit that she did not lower her eyes, though the pulse-beat in her throat was rather rapid. "You make yourself plain," she said after a moment.

"Good," he said with exquisite gentleness. "Is there something else to which you desire to direct your delm's attention?"

She touched her tongue to her lips. "Thank you, I—believe there is not."

"Then I bid you good-day," he said, and inclined his head.

There was a fraction of hesitation before she rose and bowed an entirely unexceptional farewell.

"Good-day."

Mr. pel'Kana met her at the edge of the hallway and guided her away.

Daav waited until he no longer heard her footsteps, then he got up and went across the room to the wine rack. Kareen's glass, full, except for the single sip she had taken, he left on the elbow table by her chair. Mr. pel'Kana would come back presently and take it away.

He poured himself a glass of misravot and had a sip, walking to the window and looking out into the center garden.

Flowers and shrubs rioted against the backdrop of Jelaza Kazone's massive trunk, threaded with thin stone walkways. Daav closed his eyes against the familiar, beloved scene.

Alone of all the orders he had from his mother, who had been delm before him, the mandate to preserve Kareen's life stood, senseless. It was doubtless some failing of his own vision, that he could not see what use she was to the delm she continually worked to thwart. The best that could be said of her was that she was an assiduous guard of the clan's melant'i, but such vigilance paled beside a long history of despite. Daav sighed.

Perhaps, as he grew older and more accustomed to his duties, he would acquire the vaunted Delm's Vision and see what it was his mother had found worth preserving in Kareen.

In the meanwhile, her latest bit of spite was put to rest, at least. Now if only Er Thom would finish with his mysterious errand, return home and mold himself to duty!

Not such an arduous duty, Daav thought, who had lately reviewed Syntebra el'Kemin's file. True, the lady was very young, and her second class pilot's license nothing out-of-the-way. But she would by all accounts make an agreeable enough contract-wife, and like to quickly produce an infant pilot.

Once the new yos'Galan was born, and accepted, and named, then Syntebra el'Kemin was free to return to her clan, richer by the mating-fee and bonus, with her melant'i enhanced by having married one of Korval.

Er Thom would likewise be free, to seek out *Dutiful Passage* and pick up his rounds as Korval's master trader.

And Daav would have a new niece or nephew to wonder over and nurture and guide—and a contract-wife to find for himself.

CHAPTER EIGHT

Love is best given to kin and joy taken in duty well done.

—Vilander's Proverbs,
Seventh Edition

The sound of water, splashing and running, brought him from dream to drowse, where he recalled that he lay on Anne's spring-shot sofa, covered over with the blanket from her own bed.

She had left him sometime in the early morning, amid a comedy of untangling limbs and wayward clothing, murmuring that the child had stirred. The blanket she had brought a moment later, and spread carefully on the sofa before bending and kissing him, too quickly, too lightly, on the lips.

"Thank you," she whispered and flitted away.

And for what did she thank him? Er Thom wondered, as the drowse began to thin. For breaking her peace and teaching her fear? Or for being so lost to decency that he twice allowed passion to overrule right conduct and made fierce, almost savage, love to a woman who was neither pleasure-love, wife, nor lifemate?

He twisted in his uncomfortable nest and inhaled sharply, smelled Anne's scent mingled with the blanket's scratchy, synthetic odor, and felt a surge of longing.

It was to have been so simple. He had only planned to find

her, to tell her of his love—that had seemed important. Vital. That done, knowing his truth held by one who treasured it, he thought he might have faced the Healers with calm. And he would have come away from them a fit husband for Nexon's daughter, no impossible might-have-beens shadowing his heart.

Instead, he found a child who must someway be brought to the clan, a woman who seemed etched into his bones, so deep was his desire for her—and no easy solutions at all.

"Hi!" Warm, milk-sweet breath washed his face.

Er Thom opened his eyes, finding them on a level with a serious silver pair, thickly fringed with black lashes.

"Tra'sia volecta," he replied, in Low Liaden, as one did with children.

The winging white brows pulled together in a frown.

"Hi!" Shan repeated, at slightly louder volume.

Er Thom smiled. "Good morning," he said in Terran. "Did you sleep well?"

The child—*his* child—gave it consideration, head tipped to one side.

"OK," he conceded at last, and sighed. "Hungry."

"Ah." The water continued to flow, noisily, nearby: Anne was doubtless in the shower. Er Thom wriggled free of the clinging blanket and stood. "Then I shall find you something to eat," he said and held out a hand.

His son took it without hesitation and the two of them went together into the tiny kitchen.

He found instant soy-oats and made porridge, sprinkling it with raisins from a jar on the cluttered counter. The cold-box yielded milk and juice: Er Thom poured both and stood sipping the juice while he watched his son assay breakfast.

Shan was an accomplished trencherman, wielding his spoon with precision. There were a few, of course unavoidable, spills and splashes, and Er Thom stepped forward at one juncture to help the young gentleman roll up the sleeves of his pajamas, but for the most part breakfast was neatly under way by the time Anne strode into the kitchen.

"Oh, no!" She paused on the edge of the tiny space, laughter filling her face so that it was all he could do not to rush over and kiss her.

"Hi, Ma," her son said, insouciant, barely glancing up from his meal.

Anne grinned. "Hi, Shannie." She looked at Er Thom and shook her head, grin fading into something softer.

"My poor friend. We impose on you shamefully."

He cleared his throat, glancing away on the excuse of finishing his juice.

"Not at all," he murmured, putting the glass into the washer. "The child was hungry—and I was able to solve the matter for him." He met her eyes suddenly. "What should a father do?"

Her gaze slid away. "Yes, well. What a mother should do is grab a quick cup of coffee and then get this young con artist ready to go see his friend Marilla."

"Rilly!" Shan crowed, losing a spoonful of cereal to the table top. "Oops."

"Oops is right," Anne told him, pulling a paper napkin from the wall dispenser and mopping up the mess. "Finish up, OK? And try to get most of it in your mouth."

"Clumsy Scooter," the child commented matter-of-factly.

"Single-minded Scooter," Anne returned, maneuvering her large self through the small space with deft grace. "Leave eating and talking at the same time to the experts—like Jerzy."

Shan laughed and adjusted his grip on the spoon. "Yes, Ma."

Anne shook her head and pulled her mug out of the wall unit. The acrid smell of chicory-laden synthetic coffee substitute—'coffeetoot,' according to most Terrans—was nearly overpowering. Er Thom stifled a sigh. Anne loved real coffee. He could easily have brought her a tin—or a case of tins—had he any notion she was reduced to drinking synthetic.

"Done," Shan announced, laying his spoon down with a clatter.

"How about the rest of your milk?" His mother asked, sipping gingerly at her mug.

"There is no need," Er Thom said, quietly, "for you to—cheat yourself of a meal. I can easily tend our child today."

She looked down at him, brown eyes sharp, face tense with reawakened caution. Er Thom kept his own face turned up to hers and fought down the desire to stroke her cheek and smoothe the tension away.

"That's very kind of you, Er Thom," she said carefully, "but Rilly—Marilla—is expecting Shan today."

"Then I will take him to her," he replied, all gentleness and reason, "and you may eat before you go to teach your class."

"Er Thom—" She stopped, and, heart-struck, he read dread in her eyes.

"Anne." He did touch her—he *must*—a laying of his hand on her wrist, only that—and nearly gasped at the electrical jolt of desire. "Am I a thief, to steal our son away from you? I am able to care for him today, if you wish it, or to take him to your friend. In either case, we will both be here when you come home." He looked up into her face, saw trust warring with fear.

"Trust me," he whispered, feeling tears prick the back of his eyes. "Anne?"

She drew a deep, shaking breath and sighed it out sharply, laying her hand briefly on his shoulder.

"All right," she said, and gave him a wobbling smile. "Thank you, Er Thom."

"There is no thanks due," he told her, and shifted away to allow her access to the meager cupboards and crowded counter. "Eat your breakfast and I will wash our son's face."

"**Not** coming today?" Marilla looked grave. "He isn't sick, is he, sweetie? Pel said there's a *horrific* flu-thing going through the creche—half the kids down with it and a third of the staff." She sighed, theatrically. "Pel's working a double-shift. Naturally."

"Naturally." Anne grinned, Pel was always finding an excuse to work double-shifts. Marilla theorized—hopefully—a late-shift love-interest. Anne privately thought that Marilla's fits of drama probably grated on her quieter, less demonstrative daughter.

"Shan's in the pink of health," Anne said. "His father's visiting and the two of them are spending some time together."

There, she thought, *it sounds perfectly reasonable.*

Marilla fairly gawked. "His *father,*" she repeated, voice swooping toward the heights. "Shan's father is *visiting* you?"

Anne frowned slightly. "Is that against the law?"

"Don't be silly, darling. It's only that—of course he's fabulously wealthy."

As a matter of fact, Er Thom never seemed at a loss for cash, and his clothes were clearly handmade—tailored to fit his slim frame to perfection. But the jacket he wore most often was well-used, even battered, the leather like silk to the touch.

"Why should he be?" she asked, hearing the sharpness in her voice. "Fabulously wealthy?"

Marilla eyed her and gave an elaborate shrug. "Well, you know—everyone *assumes* Liadens must be rich. All those cantra. And the trade routes. And the clans, too, of course. Terribly old money—lots of investments. Not," she finished, glancing off screen, "that it's any of *my* business."

That much was true, Anne thought tartly, and was immediately sorry. *It's only Marilla,* she told herself, *doing her yenta routine.*

"Rilly, I've got to go. Class."

"All right, sweetheart. Call and let me know your plans." The screen went dark.

My plans? Anne thought, gathering together the pieces of Comp Ling One's final. *What plans?*

During her free period, she banged back into her office for an hour's respite, juggling a handful of mail, the remains of Liaden Lit's exam and a disposable plastic mug full of vending-machine soup.

Dumping the class work into the 'Out' basket near the door, she sat down at her desk, pried the top off the plastic mug and began to go through her mail.

Notice of departmental meeting—*another* one? she thought, sighing. Registrar's announcement of deadline for grades. Research Center shutdown for first week of semester break. Request for syllabi for next semester. A card from the makers of *Mix-n-Match,* offering to upgrade Shan's model to something called an *Edu-Board.* A—

Her fingers tingled at the touch—a gritty beige envelope, with 'Communications Center' stamped across it in red block letters that dwarfed her name, printed neatly in one corner.

A beam-letter. She smiled and snatched it up, eagerly breaking the seal. A beam-letter meant either a note from her brother Richard or a letter from Learned Doctor Jin Del yo' Kera, of the University of Liad, Solcintra.

The letter slid out of the envelope—one thin, crackling sheet. From Richard then, she decided, unfolding the page. Doctor yo'Kera's letters were long—page upon page of scholarly exploration, answers to questions Anne had posed, questions reasked, reexamined, paths of thought illuminated . . .

It took her a moment to understand that the letter was not from Richard, after all.

It took rather longer to assimilate the message that was put down, line after line, in precise, orderly Terran, by—by Linguistic Specialist Drusil tel'Bana, who signed herself 'colleague'.

Scholar tel'Bana begged grace from Professor Davis for the intrusion into her affairs and the ill news which necessity demanded accompany this unseemly breaking of her peace.

Learned Doctor yo'Kera, Scholar tel'Bana's own mentor and friend, was dead, the notes for his latest work in disarray. Scholar tel'Bana understood that work to be based largely, if not entirely, on Professor Davis' elegant line of research, augmented by certain correspondence.

"It is for this reason, knowing the wealth of your thought, the depth of your scholarship, that I beg you most earnestly to come to Liad and aid me in reconstructing these notes. The work was to have been Jin Del's life-piece, so he had told me, and he likened your own work to an unflickering flame, lighting him a path without shadows."

Then the signature, and the date, painstakingly rendered in the common calendar: Day 23, Standard year 1360.

Anne sat back, the words misting out of sense.

Doctor yo'Kera, dead? It seemed impossible that the death of someone she had never physically met, who had existed only as machine-transcribed words on grainy yellow paper should leave her with this feeling of staggering loss.

In the hallway, a bell jangled, signaling class-change in ten minutes. She had an exam to give.

Awkwardly, she folded Drusil tel'Bana's letter and put it

in her pocket. She gathered up Comp Ling Two's exam booklets, automatically consulting the checklist. Right.

The five-minute bell sounded and she left the office, taking care to lock the door behind her, leaving the vending-machine soup to congeal in its flimsy plastic mug.

———

CHAPTER NINE

The delm of any given clan, when acting for the clan, is commonly referred to by the clan's name: "Guayar has commanded thus and so . . ."

To make matters even more confusing, it is assumed all persons of melant'i will have a firm grounding in Liaden heraldry, thus opening up vast possibilities for double-entendre and other pleasantries. "A hutch of bunnies," will indicate, en masse, the members of Clan Ixin, whose clan-sign is a stylized rabbit against a rising moon. Korval, whose distinctive Tree-and-Dragon is perhaps the most well-known clan-sign among non-Liadens, is given the dubious distinction of dragonhood and a murmured, "The Dragon has lifted a wing," should be taken as a word to the wise.

—From *A Terran's Guide to Liad*

Shan accepted the surrey ride with the cheerful matter-of-factness that seemed his chiefest characteristic. He settled into the oversized seat next to Er Thom, pulled off his cap and announced, "Jerzy Quad C. C. Three. Seven. Five. Two. A. Four. Nine. C."

Fingers over the simple code-board, Er Thom flung a startled glance at the child, who continued, "Rilly Quad T. T. One. Eight. Seven. Eight. P. Three. Six. T."

"And home?" Er Thom murmured.

"Home Quad S," Shan said without hesitation. "S. Two. Four. Five. Seven. Z. One. Eight. S."

Correct to a digit. Er Thom inclined his head gravely. "Very good. But today we are going elsewhere. A moment, please." He tapped the appropriate code into the board and leaned back, pulling the single shock-strap across his lap and Shan's together and locking it into place.

The child snuggled against his side with a soft sigh and put a small brown hand on Er Thom's knee.

"Who?" he asked and Er Thom stiffened momentarily, wondering how best—

The child stirred under his arm, twisting about to look into his face with stern silver eyes. "Who are you?" he demanded. "Name."

Er Thom let out the breath he had been holding. "Mirada," he said, the Low Liaden word for "father." "My name is Er Thom yos'Galan, Clan Korval."

The white brows pulled together. *Mirada?* " he said, hesitantly.

"Mirada," Er Thom replied firmly, settling his arm closer around the small body and leaning back into the awkward seat.

The boy curled once more against his side. "Where we go?"

Er Thom closed his eyes, feeling his son's warm body burning into his side, thinking of Anne, and of love, and the demands of melant'i.

"To the spaceport."

Dragon's *Way* admitted them, hatch lifting silently. Beyond, the lights came up, the life-systems cycled to full, and the piloting board initiated primary self-check.

Shan hesitated on the edge of the piloting chamber, small hand tensing in Er Thom's larger one.

"Mirada?"

"Yes, my child?"

"Go home."

"Presently," Er Thom replied, taking half a step into the room.

"Go home *now*," the boy insisted, voice keying toward panic.

"Shan." Er Thom spun and went to his knees, one hand cupping a thin brown cheek. "Listen to me, denubia. We shall go home very soon, I promise. But you must first help me to do a thing, all right?"

"Do?" Doubtful silver eyes met his for an unnervingly long moment.

"All right," Shan said at last, adding, "sparkles."

He lifted a hand to touch Er Thom's cheek. "Soft." He grinned. "Jerzy prickles."

Er Thom bit his lip. Jerzy Entaglia would be bearded, Terran male that he was. But why should Er Thom yos'Galan's son be familiar with the feel of an outsider's face?

He sighed, and forced himself to think beyond the initial outrage. Jerzy Entaglia stood in some way the child's foster-father. The success of his efforts in that role was before Er Thom now: Alert, intelligent, good-natured and bold-hearted. What should Er Thom yos'Galan accord Jerzy Entaglia, save all honor, and thanks for a gift precious beyond price?

"Come," he said to his son, very gently. He rose and took the small hand again in his, leading the boy into the ship. This time, there was no resistance.

Shan sat on a stool by the autodoc, watching curiously as Er Thom rolled up his sleeve and sprayed antiseptic on his hand and arm.

"Cold!"

"Only for a moment," Er Thom murmured, tapping the command sequence into the autodoc's panel. He looked down at his son and slipped a hand under the chin to tip the small face up. "This may hurt you, a little. Can you be very brave?"

Shan gave it consideration. "I'll try."

"Good." Er Thom went down on one knee by the stool and put his arm around Shan's waist. The other hand he used to guide the child's fingers into the 'doc's sampling unit. "Your hand in here—yes. Hold still now, denubia . . ."

He leaned his cheek against the soft hair, raising his free hand to toy with a delicate earlobe, eyes on the readout. When

the needle hit the red line, he used his nails, quickly, deftly, to
pinch Shan's ear, eliciting a surprised yelp.

"Mirada!"

The unit chimed completion of the routine; the readout es-
timated three minutes for analysis and match. Er Thom came
up off the floor in a surge, sweeping Shan from the stool and
whirling him around.

"Well done, bold-heart!" he cried in exuberant Low Liaden
and heard his son squeal with laughter. He set him down on
his feet and offered a hand, remembering to speak Terran.
"Shall I show you a thing?"

"Yes!" his son said happily and took the offered hand for
the short walk back to the piloting chamber.

Bronze wings spread wide, the mighty dragon hovered protectively above the Tree, head up and alert, emerald-bright
eyes seeming to look directly into one's soul. Shan took a
sharp breath and hung slightly back.

"It is Korval's shield," Er Thom murmured, though of
course the child was too young to understand all that meant.
He ran his palm down the image. "A picture, you see?"

The boy stepped forward and Er Thom lifted him, bringing
him close enough to run his own hand down the smooth
enameled surface. He touched the dragon's nose.

"Name?"

"Ah." Er Thom smiled and cuddled the small body closer.
"Megelaar."

"Meg'lar," Shan mispronounced and touched the Tree.
"Pretty."

"Jelaza Kazone," his father told him softly. "You may
touch it in truth—soon. And when you are older, you may
climb in it, as your uncle and I did, when we were boys."

Shan yawned and Er Thom felt a stab of remorse. A long
and busy morning for a child, in truth!

"Would you like a nap?" he murmured, already starting
down the hall toward the sleeping quarters.

"Umm," his son replied, body relaxing even as he was carried along.

He was more asleep than awake by the time Er Thom laid

him down in the bed meant for the delm's use and covered him with a quilt smelling of sweetspice and mint.

" 'Night, Mirada," he muttered, hand fisting in the rich fabric.

"Sleep well, my child," Er Thom returned softly, and bent to kiss the stark brown cheek.

On consideration, and recalling his own boyhood, he opened the intercom and locked the door behind him before going back to the autodoc.

"yos'Galan, indeed," he murmured a few moments later, carrying the 'doc's gene-map with him into the piloting chamber.

He sat in the pilot's chair, eyes tracing the intricate pattern revealed in the printout. yos'Galan, indeed. He glanced at the board, fingered the gene-map and looked, with distaste, down at his shirt. He was not accustomed to sleeping in his clothing, and then rousting about, rumpled and unshowered, for half-a-day afterward.

The board beckoned. Duty was clear. Er Thom sighed sharply and lay the gene-map atop the prime piloting board.

He wanted a shower, clean clothes. What better time than now, with the child, for the moment, asleep?

A shower and clean clothes, he thought, removing his jacket and laying it across the chair's back. Duty could wait half-an-hour.

"Er Thom? . . . Shannie!"

Anne let her briefcase fall as she darted forward, flashing through the tiny apartment: Empty bedroom, dark bathroom, silent kitchen.

"Gone."

Pain hit in a hammer blow, driving the breath out of her in a keen that might have been his name.

Er Thom! Er Thom, you promised . . .

But what were promises, she thought dizzily, where there was melant'i to keep? Anne swallowed air, shook her head sharply.

Shan was well, of that she was absolutely certain. Er Thom would not harm a child. She *knew* it.

But he would take his child to Liad. *Must* take his child to Liad. He had asked her to go with him on that urgent mission—and she—she had thought there was an option of saying no.

"Annie Davis, it's a rare, foolish gei ye are," she muttered, and was suddenly moving.

Three of her long strides took her across the common room. She smacked the door open and burst into the hallway at a dead run, heading for the Quad, the surrey station.

And the spaceport.

She should never have trusted him, Anne thought fiercely. She should have never let him back into her life. She should have never let him back into her bed. Gods, it had all been an act, put on to lull her fears, so that she would leave Shan with him—she saw it now. And she—she so starved for love, so besotted with a beautiful face and caressing ways, incapable of thinking that Er Thom would do her harm, willing herself to believe he would—or could—stop being Liaden . . .

She flashed down the stairs and out into the Quad, running as if her life depended upon it and, gods, what if he had already gone? Taken her son and lifted, gone into hyperspace, Jumping for Liad—how would she ever find him again? What Liaden would take the part of a Terran barbarian against one who was master trader, a'thodelm, and heir to his delm?

There are not so—very many—yos'Galans, Er Thom murmured in memory, and Anne gasped, speeding toward the blue light that marked the surrey station.

She was halfway across the Quad when they emerged, the boy straddling the man's shoulders. The man was walking unhurried and smooth, as if the combined weight of the child and the duffel bag he also carried was just slightly less than nothing.

"T'lanta!" the child cried, and the man swung right.

"Dri'at!" the boy called out then and the man obediently went to the left.

Anne slammed to a halt, fist pressed tight against her mouth, watching them cross toward her.

Shan was exuberant, hanging on to the collar of Er Thom's

battered leather jacket, Er Thom's hands braceleting his ankles.

"I'lanta!" Shan called again, heels beating an abbreviated tattoo against the man's chest.

But Er Thom had seen her. He increased his pace, marching in a straight line, ignoring it entirely when Shan grabbed a handful of bright golden hair and commanded, "I'lanta, Mirada!"

"Anne?" The violet eyes were worried. He reached up and swung the child down, retaining a firm hold on a small hand. His other hand lifted and stopped a bare inch from her face, while she stood there like a stump and stared at the two of them, afraid to move. Afraid to breathe . . .

"You're weeping," Er Thom murmured, hand hesitating, dropping, disappearing into a jacket pocket. "My friend, what is wrong?"

She drew a shaky breath, her first in some time, or so it felt, and found the courage to move her hand from before her mouth.

"I came home," she said, hearing how her voice wobbled, "and you were gone."

"Ah." Distress showed, clearly, for a heartbeat. Then Er Thom was bowing, graceful and low. "I am distraught to have caused you pain," he murmured, in Terran, though the inflection was all High Liaden. "Forgive me, that my thoughtlessness has brought you tears."

He straightened and moved Shan forward, relinquishing his hand. "Go to your mother, denubia."

"Ma?" The light blue eyes were worried; she felt his uncertainty as if it were her own.

Anne sank to her knees and pulled him close in a savage hug, her cheek against his.

"Hi, Shannie," she managed, though her voice still quavered. "You have a nice day?"

"Nice," he agreed, arms tight around her neck. "Saw Meg'lar. Saw—*spaceport*." He wriggled, proud of himself. "Saw ship and store and—and—"

He wriggled again, imperatively. Anne loosened her grip, found herself looking up into Er Thom's face.

Very solemn, that face, and the violet eyes shadowed so

that she longed to reach out and touch him, to beg his pardon
for having doubted—

Enough of that, Annie Davis, she told herself sternly. *You
touch the man and lose your sense—only see how it happened
yestereve.*

"It was necessary that I have clothes," Er Thom said gently, fingers brushing the bag at his hip. "Also, I have arranged
that food be delivered to your dwelling—" His hand came up,
fingers soothing the air between them. "It was seen that food
was in shortage. I mean no offense, Anne."

"No, of course not," she whispered, and cleared her throat.
She took Shan's hand and rose, looking down into her friend's
beautiful, troubled face. "Er Thom—"

His fingers flickered again—indicating more information
forthcoming.

"It is also necessary that I engage a—a *room*. This has not
yet been done. If you desire to keep our son by you, I will
complete this task." He hesitated, slanting a glance at her face
from beneath thick golden lashes.

"I ask—may I visit you this evening? After supper?" He
inclined his head. "It will be entirely as you wish, Anne, and
nothing else. My word upon it."

"A room?" she repeated, looking at him in astonishment.
She took a breath. "Er Thom, how long are you staying here?"

He glanced aside, then back to her face.

"Three weeks, you had said, until you might come to
Liad."

"I said no such thing!" she protested, and felt Shan's hand
tense in hers. She took another breath, deep and calming. "Er
Thom, I am not going—" Then she remembered the letter in
her sleeve and the unknown scholar's plea.

"Anne?"

She bit her lip. "I—perhaps—I will—need to go to Liad,"
she said, suddenly aware that it was cool on the Quad and that
she had dashed out without snatching up a jacket. "A friend of
mine—a colleague—has died, very suddenly, and I am asked
to—" She shook her head sharply. "I haven't decided. The
news just came this morning."

"Ah." He inclined his head and murmured the formal

phrase of sorrow for a death outside one's own clan:
"Al'bresh venat'i."

"Thank you," Anne said and hesitated. "You can stay with
us, you know," she heard herself say. "I know that the couch
isn't what you're used to . . ." She let the words die out, even
as Er Thom's fingers flickered negative.

"I do not think that—would be wise," he said softly,
though the glance he spared her was anything but soft. "May
I visit you, Anne? This evening?"

"All right," she said, around a surprising tightening of her
heart. "For a little while. I have—examinations to grade."

"Thank you." He bowed to her, touched his fingertips to
Shan's cheek.

"This evening," he murmured and turned, boot heels click-
ing on the Quad-stones as he walked back toward the surrey
station.

"'Bye, Mirada!" Shan called, waving energetically.

Er Thom glanced back over his shoulder and raised a hand,
briefly.

"C'mon, Shannie," Anne murmured, looking at her son so
she wouldn't have to watch her lover out of sight, as she had
done once before. "Let's go home."

CHAPTER TEN

The most dangerous phrase in High Liaden is coab min-shak'a: "Necessity exists".

—From *A Terran's Guide to Liad*

". . . guide the delm's attention to the appended gene-profile for Shan yos'Galan, who has twenty-eight Standard Months.

"The mother of this child is Anne Davis, native of New Dublin, professor of comparative linguistics, Northern Campus, University Central, Terran Sector Paladin.

"One regrets that a profile for Professor Davis is not at this time available. Although professional necessities have denied her the opportunity to pursue her own license, she is descended of a line of pilots. Her elder brother, Richard, holds first-class-pending-master; her mother, Elizabeth Murphy, had held first-class, light transport to trade class AAA. The records of these pilots are likewise appended, for the delm's information.

"It is one's intention to bring the child with his mother before the delm's eyes on the second day of the next relumma, the earliest moment Professor Davis may be released from the necessities of her work. One implores the delm to See the child welcomed among Korval, to the present joy and future profit of the clan.

"One also begs the delm's goodwill for Professor Davis. She is a person of melant'i who is owed balance of Korval through the error of the clan's son Er Thom.

"In respect to the delm . . ."

"Er Thom yos'Galan."

"Twenty-eight Standard Months?" Daav stared at the screen, torn between disbelief and a woeful desire to laugh. "I should allow that a matter to resolve, indeed!"

On the desk beside the pin-beam unit, Relchin lifted his head and stared daggers of outraged comfort, which tipped the scale firmly to laughter. Daav chucked the big cat under the chin and hit the advance key, calling up the appended gene-map.

"Well, and the child's out of yos'Galan," he admitted to Relchin a moment or two later. "But what's it to do with me if a Terran lady sees a way to combine profit with pleasure? Especially where there's young Syntebra so eager to wed an a'thodelm and do the thing by contract and Code, with no untoward scandals." He skritched the cat absently behind the ears.

"Er Thom wants to buy the Terran lady off, that seems the gist of the thing, don't you think? And he wants the boy for the clan, though as Aunt Petrella and my sister will no doubt both inform us, Shan is *not* a yos'Galan name." He frowned at the gene-map once more.

"Child might well be the devil of a pilot. Er Thom's very good, you know, Relchin. One needs make a push to stay abreast of him—though it won't do to let him know that, of course. The clan is always eager to welcome pilots . . . The matter comes down to the lady's price, as I see it—and the lady's price must be high, indeed, else why did he simply not pay it out of his private account?"

The cat vouchsafed no answer and after a moment Daav called up the records of the lady's brother and mother.

"Adequate, certainly, but the lady herself is no pilot. Who can say but she's no more than a bumble-fingered pretty-face and the child takes all from her? Only see how it is with Kareen, eh, Relchin? Though it must be recalled that yos'Galan, at least, has always bred true."

He was quiet for a time then, absently stroking the cat and staring not at the screen but at a point just above it.

"No, it won't do," he announced at last, snapping out of the chair and striding to the bar. He poured himself some misravot and wandered out into the middle of the room, holding the glass and glaring down at the rug.

"Has Er Thom run mad?" he inquired, perhaps of the cat, which was busily washing its back. "Implore the delm to See a child unacknowledged by yos'Galan? Put the clan into uproar, set thodelm against delm, open vistas untold to Kareen's despite and all for the sake of an untried child and some person named *Anne*—"

He stopped, dropping into a stillness so absolute the cat paused in its ablutions to stare at him out of wide yellow eyes.

"Anne Davis." He sipped wine, pensively, head cocked to a side. "Anne Davis, now." He sighed lightly. "It really is too bad, the things Scout candidates are required to read. But is it the identical Anne Davis, I wonder? And *was* it Anne Davis at all? Certainly it was linguistics—and rather startling in its way. My pitiful memory . . ."

Talking thus to himself, he went back to the desk, set aside the wine and opened a search program. In response to the command query he typed in a rapid half-dozen keywords, struck "go" and leaned back in his chair.

"Now—" he began, looking significantly at the cat.

He got no further. The first chime signaling a match had barely ceased when the second, third, fourth, fifth sounded. There was a pause of less than a heartbeat before the sixth and final match was announced and by that time Daav was blinking in bemusement at the screen-full of information his first keyword had produced.

"Ah yes," he murmured, touching the "continue" key. "Exactly so."

Anne Davis' list of publications ran two full screens, including the compilation and cross-check of major Terran dialects Daav had half-recalled. He noted the work had been upgraded twice since; the version he had read had been her doctoral paper.

He also noted that the focus of her study had undergone a fascinating shift of direction, the seeds of which were certainly to be found in that earliest work. Yet the intellectual courage required to begin the painstaking sifting and matching of Liaden and base-Terran, not to forget the language of the enemy—Yxtrang—seeking commonality . . .

"A concept worthy of a Scout," Daav murmured, ordering the entire bibliography for his private library with a flash of quick golden fingers across the board. "Bold heart, Scholar. Máy the luck show you fair face."

The biography, accessed next, jibed very well with Er Thom's letter. Heidelberg Fellow Anne Davis, author of many scholarly papers (list appended) in the field of comparative linguistics, was indeed a native of New Dublin in the Terran Sector of Faerie. She possessed one sibling, Richard Davis, pilot; and was descended of Elizabeth Murphy, pilot, deceased, and Ian Davis, engineer, also deceased.

She was listed as the parent of one child, Shan yos'Galan, born Standard Year 1357.

"And a matter of very public record," Daav commented wryly. "One begins to comprehend Er Thom's feelings in the matter."

Eyes still on the bio, he reached out and spun the pin-beam screen around.

"A person of melant'i, forsooth," he murmured, frowning at the letter. "Is it possible he begs a *solving* for the lady? True enough, she will have no delm to solve for her, and if the child is to come to Korval . . ." He rescued his wine glass and leaned back in the chair, staring at the cloud-painted ceiling and sipping.

On the desk, the cat stirred, stretched and walked over the small gap to the man's lap, leisurely making itself comfortable.

"It may be alliance she wants," Daav murmured, toying with the cat's ear. "No bad thing, there, Relchin—and Professor Davis in pursuit of a notion likely to have found approval with Grandmother Cantra. There's University of Liad, after all, just over the valley wall—and all the lovely native speakers . . ."

The cat purred and moved its head so the man's fingers were tickling its chin.

"Simple for you to say so," Daav complained. "*You're* not

asked to solve for one outside the clan! Nor is the coming of this child to Korval at all regular. What *can* Er Thom have been about?"

But the big cat only purred harder and kneaded Daav's thigh with well-clawed front feet.

"Stop that, brute, or I'll need a medic." Daav sighed. "Perhaps I should travel to University, see the lady and—no." He finished his wine and reached out a long arm to set the glass aside.

"Best to read the letter precisely as written, Relchin, eh? In which manner we must graciously respond to our erring a'thodelm and solicit details upon the nature of Korval's debt to Professor Davis."

So saying, and to the cat's disapproval, he spun the chair around to the pin-beam unit and began to compose his reply.

Shan made a hearty dinner and went to bed without demur, a circumstance so unusual that Anne felt his forehead for signs of fever.

There was none, of course, which she had known in that secret pocket of her heart where she also knew if he slept or waked, was calm or distressed. The child was tired, that was all.

"Mirada wore you out, laddie, didn't he just?"

"Mirada?" Shan's lashes flickered and the slanting brows pulled together. "Mirada?"

"Later, Shannie," Anne soothed, brushing the white hair back from the broad, brown forehead. "Go to sleep now."

But she had no need to coax; her inner sense told her sleep had already laid its spell.

Out in the great room a few minutes later, she shook her head at the parcels that had been delivered from the local grocer. Gods only knew where the man thought she was going to put all the various goodies he'd ordered, which included two tins of fabulously expensive, real-bean coffee.

"Well, and perhaps some of it will be for himself," she murmured, turning her back on the pile and resolutely picking up the first examination booklet.

She was very nearly halfway through the lot when the doorbell sounded, startling her into a curse.

"Ah, there, Annie Davis," she chided herself as she crossed the room, "always losing yourself inside the work . . ."

"Good evening." Er Thom bowed low as she opened the door—the Bow of Honored Esteem, she thought, frowning slightly. Most usually, he greeted her with the Bow Between Equals. She wondered, uneasily, what the deviation meant.

"Good evening," she returned, with as much calm as she could muster. She stepped aside, motioning him in with a wave of her hand. "Come in, please."

He did, offering the wine he carried with another slight bow. "A gift for the House."

Anne took the bottle, uneasiness growing toward alarm. Er Thom usually brought wine on his visits—a Liaden custom, she understood, which demonstrated the goodwill of the visitor. But he had never before been so formal—so *alien*—in his manner to her.

Clutching the symbol of his goodwill, Anne attempted her own bow—Gratitude Toward the Guest. "Thank you. Will you take a glass with me?"

"It would be welcome," he returned, nothing but stiff formality, with all of her friend and her lover hid down in the depths of his eyes. He moved a graceful hand, showing her the cluttered worktable and piles of exam booklets. "I would not, however, wish to interrupt your work."

"Oh." She stared at the desk, then at the clock on the shelf above it. "My work will take me another few hours," she said, hesitantly. "A break now, for a few moments, to drink wine with—with my friend . . ." She let it drift off, biting her lip in an agony of uncertainty.

"Ah." Something moved across his face—a flicker, nothing more. But she knew that he was in some way relieved. Almost, she thought he smiled, though in truth he did nothing more than incline his head.

"I suggest a compromise," he said softly. "You to your worktable and I to stow the groceries. The wine may wait until—friends—are able."

"Stow the groceries?" She blinked at him and then at the

pile of boxes. "All that stuff won't fit in my kitchen, Er Thom. I'd hoped some was for you."

Surprisingly, he laughed—sweet, rare sound that it was— and she found herself smiling in response.

"A cargo-balancing exercise, no more." He reached out and slipped the bottle from her grasp. "I shall contrive. In the meanwhile, you to your examinations, eh?"

"I to my examinations," she agreed, still smiling like a fool, absurdly, astonishingly relieved. "Thank you, Er Thom."

"It is nothing," he murmured, moving off toward the pile.

He paused briefly to take off his jacket and drape it over the back of the easy chair before continuing on to the kitchen.

Ridiculously light of heart, Anne went back to her desk and opened the next blue book.

True to his word, Er Thom found room for every blessed thing in the boxes, then neatly folded the boxes and slid them into the thin space between the coldbox and the washer.

He used the few extra minutes Anne needed to finish grading her last paper to rustle up some of the freshly-foraged foodstuffs and carry the snack, with wine and glasses, into the great room.

"That looks wonderful!" Anne said, eyeing the tray of cheese and vegetables and sauce with real appreciation. She smiled at Er Thom and stretched high on her toes to work out the kinks, fingers brushing the ceiling, as always.

"Blasted low bridge," she muttered, as she always did. "How much could it cost to add an extra two inches of height?"

"Quite a bit, I should think," Er Thom replied seriously. "Two inches on such a scale of building very soon becomes miles." He moved his shoulders, studiously watching the wine he was pouring into the glasses, rather than the delightful spectacle of her stretching tall and taut above him. "And cantra."

Anne grinned. "I expect you're right, at that. But it's a nuisance to always be bumping my fingers on the ceiling tiles."

She sank down into a corner of the sofa and took the glass

he offered her. "Thank you, my dear, for all your labors on my behalf."

For a moment he froze, panicked that she might somehow know of the plea he had made on her behalf to Daav—Then he shook himself, for of course she only meant the task this evening, which was in truth nothing to one accustomed to balancing the holding pods of a starship.

"You are welcome," he said, since she seemed to wish hear him say it, and was rewarded by her smile.

Carefully, he sat on the opposite end of the sofa, striving to ignore the way his blood heated with her nearness, the shameful desires that clamored for ascendancy over honor and melant'i . . . He sipped wine, set the glass gently aside and steeled himself to look up into her face.

"I regret," he said, clearing his throat because his voice had gone unexpectedly hoarse. "I regret very much to have caused you pain, Anne. It was not understood that you would arrive home at an early hour. I erred and I wish you will forgive me."

She blinked. So *that* was the reason for his earlier stiffness. Almost, she reached out to touch his cheek. It was only the memory of the searing, unreasoning passion that the least touch of him awoke that kept her hand resting lightly on her knee.

"I forgive you freely," she said instead, smiling at him warmly. "It was—foolish of me to have panicked that way. You had given me your word and I should have—" Dangerous ground here: Fatal to say that she had *doubted* his word. "—I should have remembered that."

"Ah." He gave her a slight smile in return. "You are kind."

He hesitated then, putting off the moment when he must, in honor, ask what melant'i trembled to conceive. And it was not, he admitted to himself, wryly, as he would admit it to Daav, honor's argument that most compelled him. Rather, it was happy circumstance that honor in this instance bent neatly 'round his heart's desire.

He sipped his wine and had a nibble of cheese, all but trembling with desiring her. Sternly, he pushed the passion aside. He had sworn that it would be precisely as Anne wished it, with none of Er Thom yos'Galan's unruly passions to disarm her. There were proposals to be considered here; trade to be engaged upon. He took a deep breath.

"Anne?"

"Yes, love?" The intensity of her gaze betrayed a passion as unruly as his own and almost in that instant of meeting her eyes he was lost again.

Gritting his teeth, he shifted his gaze and swallowed against the flood tide of desire.

"I have a—proposal," he managed, hearing his voice shiver with breathlessness. "If you will hear me."

"All right," she said. Her voice seemed odd, as well, though when he turned to look at her, she had her face averted, watching the wine glass she had set upon the table. "What proposal, Er Thom?"

"I propose—" Gods, his thodelm would berate him and his delm also—perhaps. She was outside the Book of Clans— Terran, Terran, Terran to the core of her. She was bread to nourish him, water to slake him—desire to torment him until he could do nothing else but have her, though it flew in the face of clan and Code and—yes—of kin.

"I propose," he repeated, forcing himself to meet her eyes with a calmness he did not feel, "that we two be wed."

CHAPTER ELEVEN

If fate decrees you'll be lost at sea, you'll live through many a train wreck.

—Terran Proverb

"Wed?" Astonishment overrode exultation—barely. With the force of both emotions rocking her, she heard her own voice, stammering: "But—I'm not Liaden."

Er Thom smiled slightly, slender shoulders moving in a fluid not-shrug. "And neither am I Terran," he said, with a certain dryness. He half-extended a hand to her, thought better of it and reached instead for his wine glass.

"It would be proper," he murmured, with exquisite care, for who was he to instruct an equal adult in proper conduct? "Proper—and well-intended—for you and I to be bound by contract—wed—at the time our son is Seen by Korval."

Exultation died with an abruptness that was agony. No lover-like words from Er Thom, Anne thought with uncharacteristic bitterness—when had she had even an endearment from him? This was expedience, nothing more. Unthinkable that a man of Er Thom yos'Galan's melant'i come home to show his delm a doxy and a bastard when he might, with only a little expense, show instead a wife and legitimate heir. Anne blinked through a sudden glaze of tears and willed herself to believe that the pounding of her heart was caused by anger, not anguish.

"No, thank you," she said shortly, proud that her voice was sharp and even. She turned her head, refusing to look at him, and reached for her glass.

"Hah." His hand—slim golden fingers, one crowned by the carved amethyst ring of a master trader—his hand lay lightly on her wrist, restraining her, waking fire in her belly.

"I have given offense," he murmured, taking his hand away. "My intention was—far otherwise, Anne. Please. What must I do to bring us back into balance?"

"I'm not offended," she lied, and managed to meet his eyes squarely. "I just don't want to marry you."

Winged golden brows lifted, eloquent of disbelief. "Forgive me," he said gently. "One recalls the joy shared just recently—as well as that which we knew—before . . ."

"Did I say I didn't want to go to bed with you?" Anne snapped, all out of patience with him—and with herself. "Far too much of that, my lad! But lust is less of a reason for marrying than, than because it's—*proper*—and I'm damned if I'll marry for either!" She took a hard breath, barely able to see his face through the dazzle of tears—*angry* tears.

"It's your own notion to be taking Shannie to show your delm, not mine. For all of me he can stay uncounted 'til the end of his days! He's a Terran citizen, which is good enough for quite a number of folk, who manage to have good, long, productive lives and—"

"Anne." He was very close, one knee on the sofa cushion while his hands caught her shoulders, kneading the tight muscles. "*Anne.*"

She gasped, half-choked and lifted a hand to wipe at her eyes. Unaccustomed, she looked up into Er Thom's face, heart melting at the distress in his eyes even as passion flared and took fire at his nearness.

Achingly slow, he lifted a hand, ran light, trembling fingers down her damp cheek, over her lips, purple eyes wide and mesmerizing.

"I love you," he whispered, "Anne Davis."

"No." It was a battle to close her eyes, to deny her body the solace of him. Every thread of her ached to believe that whispered avowal, saving only one small bit of sanity that clamored it was nothing but expediency, still.

"No," she said again, eyes shuttered against him, trembling with need. "Er Thom, stop this. Please."

Instead, she felt warm breath stir the hairs at her temple an instant before his lips pressed there.

"I love you," he said again, wonderful, seductive voice shaking with passion. He stroked her hair back with tender fingers, kissed the edge of her ear. "Anne . . ."

"Er Thom." Her own voice was anything but steady. "Er Thom, you gave me your word . . ."

She could have sworn she felt the jolt go through him, the icy jag of sanity that broke the flaming fascination of desire for the instant he required to jerk back and away, coming to his feet in a blur of motion—and going entirely still, hands firmly behind his back.

"Oh, gods."

Anne shuddered, finding his abrupt absence less easement than added torment. *What is this?* she asked herself, for the dozenth time since yesterday. She had felt a rapport with Er Thom yos'Galan almost from the first. But this—*compulsion*—reminded her of the ancient stories of the Sidhe, the Faerie Lords of old Terra, and the enchantments they wove to ensnare mere mortals . . .

Except one sight of Er Thom's sweat-damp face and anguished eyes proved beyond human doubt that if this was enchantment, then he was netted as tightly as she.

She let out the breath she hadn't known she was holding and straightened against the cushions. "Er Thom . . ."

He bowed, effectively cutting her off. "Anne, only think," he said quickly, his accent more pronounced than she had ever heard it. "You say you will be traveling to Liad, that there is duty owed one who has died. What better than to travel with one who is your friend, to guest in the house of your son's kin for as long as you like? Everything shall be as you wish—" He bit his lip and glanced sharply away, then back.

"If you do not wish us to wed, why then, there is nothing more to be said. I—certainly I cannot know your necessities. However, you must know that my necessities require our son to show his face to the delm no later than the second day of

the next relumma—three Standard weeks, as you had said."
He moved his hands, showing her palms, fingers spread wide,
concealing nothing.

"I tell you all," he said, the pace of his words slowing
somewhat. "Anne. I do not wish to wound you, or to frighten
you, or to steal our son away from you. But he *must* be
brought to the delm. He is yos'Galan! Provision must be
made—and yourself! Will you stand alone and without allies,
having borne a child to Korval?"

Anne stared, breathless with hearing him out. "Is that—
dangerous?" she asked.

"Dangerous?" Er Thom repeated, blankly. He moved a
hand, a gesture of tossing aside. "Ah, bah! It is games of
melant'i. Nothing to alarm one who is prudent." He tipped his
head, bit his lip as if unsure how to continue.

"It is prudent to gather allies," he said at last and Anne
heard the exquisite care he took now, lest he offend her. "Korval is not negligible, you understand. And the child is yos'-
Galan. None can deny basis for alliance. The marriage
I—wished for—would have brought you immediately into a
case of—of—*intended alliance.* You would have been seen to
be under the Dragon's wing *now,* rather than waiting upon the
trip to Liad and the drawing up of—other—contracts." He
took a deep breath, and met her eyes, his own wide and guileless.

"It distresses me to see you in peril," he said, very softly,
"when I have the means and the—desire—to give you pro-
tection."

"I—see," she managed, around the hammering of her
heart. She shook her head in a futile effort to clear it and made
a grab for common sense. This was University Central, after
all: Haven of scholars and students and other servants of odd
knowledge and arcane thought.

"No one's likely to come after my head here," she told
him, meaning it for comfort and an ease to the distress he
showed her plainly, and added a phrase with a flavor of High
Liaden: "Thank you for your care, Er Thom."

He hesitated, then bowed acceptance of her decision, or so
she thought.

"In three Standard weeks," he said, straightening, "I shall

pilot our son and yourself to Solcintra. We shall all three go to the delm and Shan shall be Seen. After, I shall take you to Trealla Fantrol—the house of yos'Galan—where you may guest until your duty to your friend has been completed."

It made sense, even if it was phrased rather autocratically. It solved her transportation and living problems. It solved Er Thom's pressing need to have the newly-discovered yos'-Galan added to Clan Korval's internal census.

It did *not* solve her disinclination for having the order of her life disrupted for as long as two months while she tried to sort out a colleague's private working notes.

And it certainly did not solve the fact that she would be staying those two months on Liad—in *Solcintra*, called "The City of Jewels" for the standard of wealth enjoyed by its citizens. At—Trealla Fantrol—she might well be Er Thom yos'-Galan's honored guest and recipient of every grace the House could provide. But in Solcintra she would be a lone Terran in the company of Liadens, with their fierce competitiveness and Liad-centric ways—

. . . in a society where the phrase, "Rag-mannered as a Terran," enjoyed current—and frequent—usage.

"I had thought perhaps of—not—going to Liad," Anne began, slowly. "It might be just as useful for me to copy my old letters to Jin Del—Scholar yo'Kera—and send them to his colleague. That way she—"

The doorbell chimed—and again, insistent.

"At this hour?" Anne was already moving, unaware that Er Thom had moved with her until he caught her hand, pulling her a step back from the widening door.

"Er Thom—"

"Anne!" Jerzy all but fell into her arms. "You're here! You're *safe*! Gods, gods—the whole damn pantheon! Down at the Quad S Tavern when the news came over—terrified you'd stayed late to grade exams—too stupid to find a call box—" He sagged against her shoulder and let a theatrical sigh shudder through him before he lifted his head to grin at Er Thom.

"Evening, Mr. yos'Galan."

Er Thom inclined his head. "Good evening, Jerzy En-

taglia," he said gravely. "Is there a reason why Anne should—
not—be safe?"

Jerzy blinked, straightening away from Anne's support and
glancing from her to Er Thom. "You didn't hear?" he asked,
eyes going back to Anne. "The bulletin, right in the middle of
the—" He stared around the room, spied the dark screen.
"Guess not. Well, all that exercise for nothing."

"Heard *what*?" Anne demanded. "Jerzy, it's past mid-
night! If this is one of your—"

"My jokes? No joke." He grabbed her hand, ugly face entirely serious. "Comp Ling's gone. The whole back corner of
the Language Block blew sky-high, two hours ago."

Petrella yos'Galan eyed the child of her deceased twin with
a noticeable lack of warmth.

"Felicitations, is it?" she said ill-temperedly. "And to what
event does my delm desire me to attach felicity? The continued absence of my heir, perhaps? Or the visit from Delm
Nexon this morning, inquiring of that same heir's health? Or
shall I find joy in the empty nursery and the absence of a child
to continue the Line?"

Daav had a sip of red wine. "Well, certainly you may rejoice in any such that may move you," he said agreeably. "I
had only meant to bring tidings of my cha'leket's return on
the second day of the next relumma."

"Three days later than the delm's deadline," she said with
asperity. "As I am certain the delm recalls, having so—long—
a memory."

He grinned. "Well-thrown, Aunt Petrella! But as it happens, your heir begged the delm's grace and received the ex-
tension, as insisting on the previous time frame would have
considerably inconvenienced the guest."

"Ah, the felicity not only of the return of one's son, but
also the inestimable joy of a guest!" Petrella flung her hand
high in mock jubilation. "How fortunate for the House, indeed. Is one to know more of the guest, I wonder? For the universe, you understand, is a-bursting with potential guests."

"Why, so it is!" Daav said, much struck by this viewpoint.
"I had not considered it thus, but I believe you are correct,

ma'am! How piquant, to be sure: An entire universe, panting to guest with Korval!"

"Yes, very good," she returned. "Play the fool, do, and amuse yourself at an old woman's expense. I note that details regarding the guest have not come forth."

He moved his shoulders. "The guest is a scholar of some repute."

"More delight," his aunt said acidly. "A scholar, to our honor! As if there were any more rag-mannered, saving only a—"

"A Terran scholar," Daav interrupted gently. He assayed another sip of the excellent red. "You may wish to remodel the Ambassadorial Suite."

Petrella was staring. "A Terran scholar?"

"Indeed, yes," her nephew said, and amplified: "A scholar who also happens—a mere accident of birth, I assure you!—to be Terran."

Petrella had closed her eyes and allowed herself to slump back into her chair. Daav watched her closely, seeking a sign by which he might know if this sudden sagging were an artifact of her illness or a ploy to divert him.

Petrella opened her eyes. "Er Thom is bringing a Terran scholar to guest in this house," she said, absolutely toneless.

"Correct," replied Er Thom's foster-brother and, when she still glared at him: "He being so scholarly himself, you see."

She snorted. "A master trader may not be an idiot, I allow. However, I confess that this scholarly aspect of my son's nature has heretofore escaped my notice." She waved a hand, and Daav saw sincere weariness in the gesture. "But there—a cha'leket will know what none other may guess."

"Exactly so," Daav murmured and finished his wine. Setting the glass aside, he rose and made his bow—affection and honored esteem. "If there is any way in which I may be of service, Aunt, do call. And if you would prefer not to meddle with the Ambassadorial Suite, the scholar may just as easily stay at Jelaza—"

"yos'Galan's guest," the old lady interrupted austerely, "stays in yos'Galan's house."

"Certainly," her nephew said and crossed over to bend and kiss her ravaged cheek and lay a light hand on the sparse, scorched hair. "Don't tire yourself. I am entirely able to assist you."

She smiled her slight, mocking smile and reached up to touch his cheek. "You're a good boy," she said softly, then waved an irritable hand. "Go away. I've work to do."

"Yes, aunt," he said gently and crossed the room with his silent, quick steps, melting down the hallway as if he had no more substance than a shadow.

Petrella sighed and slumped deep in her chair, concentrating on the breath that rasped, painful and hot, through her ruined lungs.

After a time, when she was certain she would not shame herself, she rang the bell for the butler.

CHAPTER TWELVE

The thing to recall about Dragons is that it takes a special person to deal with them at all. If you lie to them they will steal from you. If you attack them without cause they will dismember you. If you run from them they will laugh at you.

It is thus best to deal calmly, openly and fairly with Dragons: Give them all they buy and no more or less, and they will do the same by you. Stand at their back and they will stand at yours. Always remember that a Dragon is first a Dragon and only then a friend, a partner, a lover.

Never assume that you have discovered a Dragon's weak point until it is dead and forgotten, for joy is fleeting and a Dragon's revenge is forever.

—From *The Liaden Book of Dragons*

Er Thom let himself into his stuffy rented quarters, took off his jacket and flung it over the arm of the doubtful sofa. Spacer that he was, he barely noticed the lack of windows, though the rattle of the ventilator grated on senses tuned to catch the barest whisper of life system malfunction.

Surefooted in the dimness, he went across the common room to the pantry and poured a glass of wine from one of the bottles appropriated from *Dragon's Way.*

Honest red wine and none of Daav's precious misravot! he

thought, smiling softly. Leaning against the too-high counter, he closed his eyes and sipped.

He had almost lost her.

The thought horrified—and horrified again, for it transpired that on days when Marilla watched Shan, she most usually brought him to Anne's office in the evening, as Rilly went to teach a night class. Dependent upon the child's mood, Anne did sometimes stay late, grading papers, meeting with students, doing "housecleaning." If Er Thom had not had the tending of his son this day . . .

"An accident," Jerzy Entaglia had said, sitting on Anne's sofa and drinking a cup of real coffee. "Just one of those stupid damn things. That's what Admin's saying, anyway." He sighed, looking abruptly exhausted.

"'Course they haven't sorted the rubble yet, or counted the bodies—or even called up the folks who have back-wing offices, just to make sure they're all tucked up, safe and warm." He shook his head. "Likely they'll find huge chunks of a fusion bomb in the wreckage, when they get around to cleaning it up."

"Is there—forgive me," Er Thom had murmured at that point, though it was hardly his place to do so. "Has there been thought of—of a balancing . . . ?"

Jerzy blinked at him.

"An honor-feud, he means," Anne told her friend and shook her head. "It's not too likely, Er Thom. The whole wing went, remember? Not just one person's office. And anyway, how could there be a feud against a language department? We're just a bunch of fuzzy humanities-types. If it were a hard-science department, where they might possibly have gotten onto something someone didn't want them to have—but Languages? You might as well blow up Theater Arts!"

"A notion over-full with glamour," Jerzy announced, with the air of one quoting a passage of Code.

Anne laughed.

"Yah, well, I'm outta here," Jerzy said, levering himself up. "'Night, Anne—Mr. yos'Galan. Lucky thing you were here to take Scooter today." He stuck his big hand out.

Er Thom rose and offered his own, patiently enduring the stranger's touch and the up-and-down motion. Then he rescued his hand and bowed honor for his son's foster-father. "Keep you well, Jerzy Entaglia."

"Thanks," the other man had said. "Same to you."

He'd left then, and Er Thom soon after, to come back to these ragged apartments that were still slightly more spacious than Anne's normal living quarters. He pictured her in Trealla Fantrol, where the guesting suites boasted wide windows and fragrant plants and well-made, graceful furniture.

He pictured her walking the lawns with him, visiting the maze, and Jelaza Kazone—thought of showing her the Tree . . .

She had said she did not wish to wed.

Er Thom opened his eyes, frowning at the clock hung lop-sided on the wall opposite.

She had said she did not wish to marry him, but that was not true. She burned for him as he for her and dreaded the day when they would part. He knew it. In his bones he knew it, ir-revocably, absolutely, beyond doubt or even question of *how* he knew it.

So, Anne had lied. He was a master trader, after all. He knew prevarication in all its postures, tones and faces. Never before had he had a lie from Anne.

Why now? he wondered, and then recalled that he had taught her to fear him. Very likely the lie was credited to his account—and accurate balance it was.

Still, if she wished to wed and denied him out of fear, the matter might yet be managed. All his skill was in showing folk who had never seen an item why they must yearn to pos-sess it. How much easier a trade, when the one he traded with already desired that which he had to offer—

"Wait."

He came sharply away from the counter and paced into the common room, reaching up to slap at the ill-placed light-switch.

He had offered contract-marriage, he thought agitatedly. It was everything that he *could* offer—though it was extremely irregular and would doubtless require him to fall on his face before his thodelm and cry mercy. Yet, contract-marriage to Anne—especially with the child already fact!—lay within the realm of what was very possible.

Only—contract-marriages very soon expired and the

spouses separated—and Anne dreading their eventual separation as much as he.

"How," Er Thom asked the empty room, "if she wishes a lifemating?"

That became a matter for the delm. Giddy as the prospect of spending all his days with Anne Davis might render Er Thom yos'Galan, yet the delm was the keeper of the clan's genes, guardian of the lines' purity, arbiter of alliances. Korval was not as populous as once it had been and the delm might very well have use for Er Thom's genes elsewhere. A lifemating would put him beyond the possibility of future contract-marriages, which left the burden of such alliances to Kareen, which was laughable—and to Daav.

Korval might very well—and with all good cause—deny its son Er Thom the solace of a lifemating.

Or he might be allowed the lifemating—later. After he had done his full duty for the clan—however many years it might take.

"And I hardly able to keep myself from her for one night!" He finished his wine, ruefully. Still, it was out of his hands and firmly in the keeping of the delm, who would decide for the good of the clan and could do nothing at all until Er Thom laid the entire matter before him.

Thinking thus, though in no way comforted, and, indeed, with an unaccustomed dismay for the ways and necessities of the clan, he went back to the pantry for another glass of wine, which he carried with him to the wall desk.

"I shall put the thing before Daav," he said to himself. "He may best advise me of the clan's requirements, and what the delm might decide." And Daav at least, Scout as he had been, would not turn his face in horror from one who professed abiding love for a Terran . . .

Seated on the too-wide chair, booted feet just short of the floor, Er Thom opened the remote unit he had brought with him from the ship and touched the "on" key.

The message-waiting light blinked in the top right corner, blue and insistent.

So, then. Besides his message to the delm he had also sent word to his first mate, though not—guilt twisted in his stomach—to his mother. *Ever more unruly,* he thought. *Brother, only see what becomes of the one of us who had always been dutiful.*

He touched the access key and a heartbeat later was staring at a brief note from his delm, requesting details of Korval's debt to Respected Scholar Anne Davis and the error which led to this balancing.

"Hah." Er Thom cleared the screen and had a sip of wine, wondering how best to comply with his delm's request. As he put the glass aside, he saw the message light still blinking and touched the access key once more.

"Darling, what mad coil have you tangled yourself in?" Almost, he could hear Daav's voice through the words on the screen—and smiled. "Worse, how am I to do a brother's duty and aid you in ruining yourself unless I Know All? Worse still, I have informed your mother my aunt of your return date and the concomitant arrival of a guest, from which interview I barely escaped with my life. Please believe me willing to die for you, but may I at least know for what cause?

"I look forward to making the acquaintance of my new nephew, and of his mother, a lady I have long admired from afar. In preparation for her visit I have ordered and am now reading her entire bibliography, so you see I don't mean to shame you. In the case that you had been unaware of the scope of the lady's work, I most highly commend *Who's Who in Terran Scholars* to you.

"In the meanwhile, brother, do not hesitate to call upon me for whatever service I might render. Keep safe. Smooth journey. And may the luck ride your shoulder until we meet again.

"All my love."

"Daav."

"I love you, too, denubia," Er Thom murmured, then grinned. *Who's Who in Terran Scholars*, was it? As it happened, he was aware of the nature of Anne's work, though it would do no harm to read her published papers. His knowledge came from listening to her speak of her theories, her observations, more—he freely admitted!—because the sound of her voice soothed him in some profound, indescribable way than because her theories compelled him.

Still, it was the joke between his cha'leket and himself— that it was Daav who was bookish. What, after all, was a

Scout, save a scholar placed in peril? Meantime, Master Trader yos'Galan, with his penchant for statistics and passion for new markets, could most often be found reading a manifest.

Smile fading, Er Thom leaned back, wondering anew how best to put a situation that grew daily more tangled into lines of orderly words, for either delm or cha'leket.

He required a plan of action, he thought, sipping his wine thoughtfully. Best perhaps to first soothe Anne's wariness of him, and bring her gently to see that she must of course travel to Liad. Duty to her dead friend was clear, as he was certain she knew. It was fear speaking, when she talked of staying on University and not venturing forth to Liad. And certainly, anyone must be distressed at first encountering Solcintra society, though a guest of Korval would naturally be given all honor due the House. Society was prudent, if not particularly intelligent.

So, then. Anne gentled into making the trip. Shan Seen by the delm and then, gods willing, by Thodelm yos'Galan. He expected his mother would need some gentling herself, but, presented with one already Seen by Korval, she could hardly be churlish enough to refuse to take the child to yos'Galan, mixed blood or pure.

As yos'Galan's guest, Anne could become accustomed to Liad—*and Liad to Anne,* he thought wryly—and fulfill her duty. In the meanwhile, Er Thom would take thought as to how best to present his desires to the delm—and would speak to his cha'leket of the matter, face-to-face, over a glass or two, with the warmth of brotherhood between them.

It would do, he decided. It was not precipitate, and it held some promise for success—if he was very careful and played each counter with all the craft and skill in him. He recalled that Daav was a counterchance player to behold, and smiled.

Well, and now that he thought of it, there was a service his brother could perform for him. Er Thom pulled the remote onto his lap. He would write a quick note and then to bed, for he was to rise early and go to mind Shan while Anne went to Central Administration and found what now was required of her, with her place of work destroyed.

CHAPTER THIRTEEN

There are several million Traders in the galaxy, but only 300 Master Traders registered with the Trade Commission on VanDyk. Until recently, all 300 were Liaden. This has been changing slowly, as Terrans become more successful in the trade arena and able to afford the costly and extensive certification tests.

Terran or Liaden, a Master Trader's work is exacting, requiring intimate knowledge of the regulations of a thousand ports of call, as well as a sure instinct for what will gain a profit at each. Master Traders often chart their ships' course as the trade develops, some running as long as five years between visits to the home port.

Less exalted Traders most usually ply an established route, which has most likely been researched and planned by a Master Trader.

The very best Master Traders are described as coolheaded, analytical, persuasive generalists who are filled with the passion to deal.

—From A Young Person's Book of Trade

Er Thom frowned at the remote's cramped screen and wondered just how much—and who—Jyl ven'Apon had paid for the privilege of being known as a Master of Trade.

"Lithium, by all gods," he muttered, reaching for the mug

of tea set to hand. "An enterprise as substantial as moon-beams, and she begs my hundred cantra buy-in cool as if she has a right! What can she be about? And to claim she enjoys yo'Laney's support—and Ivrex!" He paused, sipping the horrible Terran tea and considering that so-blithe claim of support.

Neither yo'Laney nor Ivrex was master-class, but two solid, substantial traders from solid, substantial clans. By all rights, they should have smelled the overripeness of the scheme even as Er Thom had.

Was ven'Apon's claim of support false, upon which face she was even more foolish than he had suspected? Or was her claim *true*, and she out to lighten as many pouches as possible before she was called to face the Guild Masters and her license—

"Mirada!" The demand was punctuated by a bump on his elbow that barely missed sending the mug's contents into orbit.

Carefully, he put the tea aside and turned his chair so he faced his petitioner.

"Shan-son," he said in grave Low Liaden. "How may I serve you?"

The boy looked at him doubtfully, gripping the red plastic keyboard-and-screen unit with both hands.

Er Thom smiled and reached out to stroke the snow-white hair. *Such an odd color,* he thought. *Doubtless it will darken, when he is older . . .*

"My son," he murmured in his careful Terran, "what may I do for you?"

The small face relaxed into a smile and Shan swung the toy onto Er Thom's knees.

"All done," he said with the air of one making himself perfectly clear.

"Ah." Er Thom glanced down at the thing. Dirty white plastic letters spelled out *Mix-n-Match,* against the bright red case. The screen was narrow, and the keys overlarge—to accommodate those too young to possesses fine manipulative skills, Er Thom thought. He touched a key at random.

"This module has been satisfactorily completed," a

woman's bright voice told him. "Please insert upgrade module number *five* to continue progression."

"All done," Shan amplified, leaning cozily against Er Thom's thigh and pointing at the blank screen. "Need new, Mirada."

"A moment, if you please," Er Thom replied, putting his left arm around the child's body in a loose hug and adjusting the tiny screen for less glare. "I would like to look at the old . . ."

In very short order he had located and accessed the toy's resident manual, from which he learned that *Mix-n-Match* aimed to teach pattern recognition, eye-hand coordination, improve memory and lay the foundation for understanding of cause and effect. Module four, which Shan had just completed, was rated for the use of children having from 36 to 40 months. Er Thom frowned.

A bit more searching uncovered the module's database, which revealed the fascinating information that Shan's scores were in the ninety-eighth achievement percentile of all those who had completed the module.

"Well done," Er Thom said, touching the power-off and putting the simple computer onto Anne's desk. He bent and gave Shan a hug, rubbing his cheek against the soft, odd-colored hair. "Ge'shada, Shan-son. You have done very well, indeed."

Shan wriggled in his embrace. "Gee-shad-a," he announced and laughed.

Er Thom echoed the sound, softly, and let the child go. "Where are the new modules, then, my bright one?"

He had forgotten himself—the question was asked in Low Liaden. But Shan barely hesitated an instant before catching Er Thom's hand and pulling on it.

"Come on, Mirada. Needs new."

"So I am told." He stood and allowed himself to be tugged across the room to where Anne's ancient and battered half-chora slept, plastic-shrouded, atop a table made of real wood.

"Here," Shan announced, dropping Er Thom's hand to bend down and paw fruitlessly at the table's single drawer. He sighed gustily and straightened, looking up at Er Thom out of guileless silver eyes. "Stuck."

"I see." He bent and pulled.

The drawer *was* a little sticky, but not to signify. Once opened, however, it proved to be—empty.

"All gone," Shan discovered, peering into the depths. He shook his head. "Oh, well."

Oh, well, indeed, Er Thom thought. *And the child already outpacing the modules . . .*

"Shall I show you how my computer works?" he asked, holding down a hand. Shan took it with his usual lack of hesitation and they went back to Anne's desk.

Er Thom sat in the big chair and lifted the child onto his lap. He filed Jyl ven'Apon's audacious letter away for the moment and pulled the remote closer, adjusting the screen height.

Bintell Products was the manufacturer of *Mix-n-Match,* according to the resident manual.

"It happens," Er Thom murmured to his son, fingers moving over the keys, "that Korval trades with subsidiaries of Bintell Products. We should be able to locate an entire set of modules with very little trouble."

It took a few minutes, with Shan sitting rapt astride his knees, eyes never moving from the screen and the data flickering across it.

"There." He froze the screen, highlighted his choices and called for fuller information.

"I think perhaps we will have this *Edu-Board* for you," he murmured, absently and in Low Liaden. "You find *Mix-n-Match* far too simple, eh? *Edu-Board* has complexity—self-programming, individually-structured learning—yes. I think you will like this extremely, denubia." He issued the order—to be delivered, alas, to Trealla Fantrol, as a special shipment to University would not arrive until several weeks after Shan was on Liad.

"So then." He shut down the goods list and called up his work screen. On his lap, Shan gave a sigh of utter satisfaction.

"Fast," he commented, hand moving toward the remote's keyboard.

Er Thom caught the small, questing fingers in his and squeezed them lightly. "This is mine," he said in firm Terran. "You may watch me do my work, if you like, or you may do something else."

"Watch," his son decided without hesitation, and snuggled his back into Er Thom's chest. "Say—*tell*—me your—work—Mirada."

"Ah." He touched keys, accessing the information for *Mandrake*, one of Korval's lesser trade ships. "We must consider how best to utilize Dil Ton sig'Erlan upon this route. He is young, you see, though not entirely untried. Indeed, he may have the ability to achieve master-rank. It is the duty of one already master to give him opportunity to expand himself and hone his talent—but not too quickly. We do not wish to ruin him with too much failure—or with too much success . . ."

He leaned back and Shan did also, so that his head was under Er Thom's chin. The man smiled and lay his arms about the child and closed his eyes, considering Dil Ton sig'Erlan.

There was not much scope for creativity on the Lytaxin run. It was a minor route at best, encompassing a total of seven Outworlds, existing by reason of Korval's ancient ties with Erob, Lytaxin's ascendant clan. Still, there ought to be some way to test sig'Erlan's mettle, to place him out of context and force him into unexpected—

"Hah!" Er Thom opened his eyes, having bethought himself of a certain very odd something that had reposed, undisturbed, these several years in a corner of Korval's third Solcintra warehouse. "I believe that will do nicely, yes." He leaned forward and added the item to *Mandrake*'s manifest.

"What you do?" Shan demanded, grabbing at the man's sleeve.

"I have given young sig'Erlan a gift," Er Thom replied, touching the 'send' key. "May he reap joy of it."

He smiled and stretched, eye snagging on the time-bar in the upper corner of the remote's screen.

"Are you hungry?" he asked Shan, and received an enthusiastic affirmative.

"Very well." He lifted the child to the floor and stood, offering a hand. "Let us then eat lunch."

The sky was of a blue just tinged with green and the air was laden with flower-scents.

Daav yos'Phelium sent the sleek groundcar through the

various twists and turns of Treal!a Fantrol's drive with expert negligence. As he pulled into the carport, he saw Er Thom's mother sitting on the East Patio, taking the sun, a bound book unopened on her lap. He sighed, pushing aside the old sorrow as he walked across the grass toward her.

"Good morning, Aunt Petrella!"

She looked up, making no move to rise from her chair. A bad day, then.

"Good enough, I suppose, for those who have nothing better to do than fidget about in fancy cars."

He grinned. "Ah, but I have much more to do than fidget about! You behold me, in fact, atremble with busy-ness. I have this day received a pin-beam from my brother Er Thom, bidding me purchase in his name a concert-quality omnichora and have it delivered to this house immediately. In my brother's name I have done this thing. It should arrive this afternoon."

She glared at him. "An omnichora?"

"An omnichora," he agreed, with appropriate gravity.

"Er Thom does not play the omnichora," that gentleman's mother announced darkly.

"Ah. Then perhaps it is for the guest," Daav speculated, eyes wide with wholly counterfeit innocence. "It is our duty, you know, Aunt, to arrange all for the comfort and well-being of the guest."

"A lesson in Code, I apprehend," Petrella said scathingly. "Uncounted thanks to the instructor."

Bland-faced, Daav bowed, graciously acknowledging the offered thanks. Petrella sniffed.

"Awake upon all suits, are you? One supposes you know the name of the respected scholar who is to be our guest, but wonders when you will judge it proper to share that information."

"From you, Aunt Petrella, I have no secrets," her nephew told her audaciously. "The scholar's name is Anne Davis."

"Anne Davis," she repeated, mouth tightening. "And Anne Davis is—naturally!—a scholar of the omnichora. Met perhaps at some delightful musical soiree engineered by those who must delight in—"

"I believe," Daav interrupted gently, "that Anne Davis is a

scholar of comparative linguistics, attached to the Languages Department based upon University. If you wish, I will forward copies of her publications to your screen—" he bowed, "in order that you may enjoy informed conversation with the guest."

"Yet another lesson in manners! I am quite overcome. In the meanwhile, what has a concert-quality omnichora to do with a scholar of language?"

"Perhaps," Daav offered, ever more gently, "it is an avocation."

Petrella hesitated, considering him out of narrowed eyes. Daav was notoriously—even foolishly—sweet-tempered. Yet that tone of caressing gentleness was clear warning to those who knew him well: Daav hovered on the edge of displeasure, in which state even his cha'leket was hard-put to deal with him sanely.

Accordingly, Petrella relented somewhat in her attack and inclined her head. "Perhaps it is, as you say, an avocation. Doubtless we shall learn more when the scholar is with us." She glanced up, moving both hands in the formal gesture of asking. "One cannot help but wonder why the scholar comes to us at all."

There was a small pause.

"My cha'leket allows me to know that Scholar Davis had been a friend of Scholar yo'Kera of Solcintra University. Scholar yo'Kera has recently died and duty of friendship calls Scholar Davis to Solcintra."

"I see." An entirely reasonable explanation, saving only that the mystery of Er Thom's acquaintanceship with Scholar Davis remained—deliberately, as Petrella strongly suspected—unresolved.

Still, another measuring glance at her nephew's face argued the best course was to leave the matter until she might have the entire tale, start to finish, from the lips of her heir.

Embracing thus the more prudent course, Petrella inclined her head. "My thanks. Is there anything else one should know beforehand of the guest, so all may be arranged for her comfort and well-being?"

Amusement gleamed in the depths of Daav's dark eyes. He bowed slightly.

"I believe not. Now, if you will excuse me, Aunt, I must away. Duty calls."

"Certainly. Give you good day."

"Give you good day, Aunt Petrella." He was gone, noiseless across the blue-green grass.

An omnichora, she thought, watching Daav's car down the drive. *To be delivered this afternoon, by all the gods. And if the guest is an expert in her avocation . . .*

Grumbling to herself, she rang for Mr. pak'Ora.

"An omnichora will be arriving this afternoon. See it situated."

"Situated, Thodelm?"

She drew herself up in the chair, ignoring the pain the effort cost her. "Yes, *situated.* The Bronze Room is said to have good acoustics—put it there. We'll have a music room."

The butler bowed. "Very good, Thodelm," he said, careful of her mood, and left her.

Alone, she fingered her book, but did not open it. Eventually she nodded off in the warm sun and slept so soundly she did not hear either the arrival of the omnichora or of the technician hastily summoned to tend to the Bronze Room's acoustics.

CHAPTER FOURTEEN

*The Guild Halls of so-called "Healers"—interactive empaths—
can be found in every Liaden city.*

*Healers are charged with tending ills such as depression,
addiction and other psychological difficulties and they are
undoubtedly skilled therapists, with a high rate of success to
their credit.*

*Healers are credited with the ability to wipe a memory
from all layers of a client's consciousness. They are said to be
able to directly—utilizing psychic ability—influence another's
behavior; however, this activity is specifically banned by
Guild regulations.*

—From "The Case Against Telepathy"

The music built of its own will, weaving a tapes-
tried wall of sound that shielded her from her weary thoughts.

Er Thom was giving Shan a bath, a project that had been
under way when she arrived home, and also appeared to include laundering Er Thom's shirt. After a brief glance into the
tiny bathroom and hurriedly exchanged hellos with father and
son, Anne had retreated to the great room and, as she so often
did in times of stress, to the omnichora.

The music changed direction and her fingers obediently
followed, her mind beyond thought and into some entirely
other place, where sound and texture and instinct were all.

Eyes closed, she *became* the music and stayed thus for time unmeasured, until her attention was pricked by a subtle inner-heard unsound: Her son was with her.

Reluctantly, she became apart from the music, lifted her fingers from the keyboard and opened her eyes.

Shan stood beside her in his pajamas, silver eyes wide in his thin brown face. "*Beautiful* sparkles," he breathed.

Anne smiled and reached down to lift him onto her lap. "Sparkles again, is it, my lad? Well, it's a pretty line of chat. All clean, I see. Did your da live, too?"

"Does he see them often?" That was Er Thom, solemn and soft-voiced as ever, though his dark blue shirt was soaked as thoroughly as his hair. He moved his hand in a measured gesture as she glanced over to him. "The—sparkles."

"Who can tell if he sees them now?" Anne replied, ruffling Shan's damp hair. "Ask him where the sparkles *are* and all you'll get is a stare and a point into blank air." She bent suddenly, enclosing the child in a hug. "Ma loves you, Shannie. Sparkles and all."

"Love you, Ma." This was followed by an enthusiastic kiss on her cheek and an imperative wriggle. "Shan go."

"Shan go to bed," his mother informed him, adjusting her grip expertly and standing with him cradled in her arms.

"Mirada!"

But if he was hoping for sympathy from that quarter, he got none.

"To bed, as your mother wishes," Er Thom said firmly. "We shall bid you good-night and you shall go to sleep."

Anne grinned at him. "A plan. Even a good plan. Let's see how it holds up to practical usage."

"By all means." He bowed, slightly and with amusement, before preceding her across the room and opening the door to the bedroom.

"Not *sleepy*!" Shan announced loudly and tried one more abortive twist for freedom.

"Shannie!" Anne stopped and frowned down into his face. "It's bedtime. Be a good boy."

For a moment, she thought he would insist: He stared mulishly into her face for two long heartbeats, then sighed and leaned his head against her shoulder.

"Bedtime," he allowed. "Good boy."

"Good boy," Anne repeated. She carried him into the bedroom and laid him down next to Mouse.

"Good-night, Shannie. Sleep tight." She kissed his cheek and fussed at the blanket before standing aside to let Er Thom by.

"Good-night, my son," he murmured in Terran, bending to kiss Shan gently on the lips. He straightened and added a phrase in Liaden: "Chiat'a bei kruzon"—dream sweetly.

"'Night, Ma. 'Night, Mirada."

"Sleep," Er Thom said, gesturing Anne to proceed him.

She did and he followed, closing the door half-way.

In the common room he smiled and bowed. "A plan proved by field conditions. Shall you have wine?"

"Wine would be wonderful," she said, abruptly aware of all her weariness again. She shook her head. "But I'll pour, Er Thom. You're soaked—"

"Not now," he interrupted softly, testing his sleeve between finger and thumb. "This fabric dries very quickly." He ran a quick hand through bright golden locks and made a wry face. "Hair, however—"

Anne laughed. "Adventures in bathing! You didn't need to take that on, my friend. I know Shan's a handful—"

"No more than Daav and I were at his age," Er Thom murmured, leading the way into the kitchenette. "Based on tales which have been told. Though the process by which one may get soup into one's ears seems to have escaped me over time—"

"It's a gift," Anne told him seriously, leaning a hip against the counter.

"As well it might be," he returned, back to her as he ferreted out glasses, corkscrew, and wine bottle.

Anne put her arms behind her, palms flat on the counter, watching his smooth, efficient movements. Her mind drifted somewhat, considering the slim golden body hidden now beneath the dark blue shirt and gray trousers. It was a delightful body: unexpectedly strong, enchantingly supple, entirely, warmly, deliciously male—Anne caught her breath against a throttling surge of desire.

Across the tiny kitchen, Er Thom dropped a glass.

It chimed on the edge of the counter, wine freed in a glistening ruby arc, and surrendered to gravity, heading toward the floor.

In that instant he was moving, hand sweeping down and under, snatching the glass from shattering destruction and bringing it smoothly to rest, upright on the wine-splashed counter.

"Forgive me," he said breathlessly, violet eyes wide and dazzled. "I am not ordinarily so clumsy."

"It could have—happened to anyone," Anne managed, breathless in her own right. "And you made a wonderful recover—I don't think the glass broke. Here—"

Glad of a reason to turn away from those brilliant, piercing eyes, she pulled paper towels out of the wall dispenser and went to the counter to mop up, avoiding his gaze.

"Just a bit of clean up and we're good as new. Though it is a shame about the wine."

"There is more wine," Er Thom replied, voice too near for her peace of mind. She straightened, found herself caught between counter and table and looked helplessly down into his face.

He raised his hands, showing her empty palms. "Anne—"

"Er Thom." She swallowed, mind stumbling. The man could *not* have heard her lustful thinking, she assured herself and in the next heartbeat heard her voice stammering:

"Er Thom, do *you* see sparkles?"

"Ah." He lowered his hands, slowly, keeping them in full view until they hung, open and unthreatening, at his sides. "I am no Healer," he said seriously. "However, you should know—Korval has given many Healers—and—and dramliz as well."

The dramliz, for lack of a saner way to bend the language, were wizards, infinitely more powerful than Healers. Dramliz talents embraced interactive empathy and took off from there: teleportation, translocation, telekinesis, pyrokinesis, telelocution—every item on the list of magical abilities attributed to any shaman, witch or wizard worth their salt during any epoch in history.

If you believed in such things.

And Shan, Anne thought, somewhat wildly, *sees sparkles.*

"I—see." She took a breath and managed a wobbling smile. "I suppose I should have inquired further into the— suitability of your genes."

It was a poor joke, and a dangerous one, but Er Thom's eyes gleamed with genuine amusement.

"So you should have. But done is done and no profit in weeping over spoiled wine." He stepped back, bowing gently. "Why not go into the other room and—be at ease? I will bring the wine in a moment."

"All right." She slipped past, assiduously avoiding even brushing his sleeve, and fled into the common room.

"Oh, it's just a mess," she was saying some minutes later in answer to his query. "Admin's being as bitchy as possible. You'd think—oh, never mind." She sighed.

"The best news is that everyone seems to be accounted for—but the cost in terms of people's work! Professor Dilling just stood in a corner during the whole meeting and shook, poor thing. I went over to see if there was something I could do, but he just kept saying, 'Thirty years of research, gone. Gone.'" She sighed again, moving her big hands in a gesture eloquent of frustration, and sagged back into the corner of the sofa.

"But surely," Er Thom murmured, from his own corner, "the computer files—"

"Paper," Anne corrected him, wearily. "Old Terran musical notation—some original sheet music. I'd helped him sort things a couple of times. His office was a rat's nest. Papers, old instruments—wood, metal—all blown to bits. Little, *tiny* bits, as Jerzy would have it." She reached for her wine.

"And your own work?" Er Thom wondered softly.

Anne laughed, though not with her usual ration of humor. "Oh, I'm one of the lucky ones. I lost the latest draft of a monograph I'd been working on—but I've got the draft before that saved down in the belly of Central Comp—some student work, files, study plans—that's the worst of it. The important stuff—the recordings, notes, my letters—is in the storage room I share with Jerzy—all the way over in Theater Arts. I doubt if it even got shook up."

"You are fortunate."

This time her laugh held true amusement. "Paranoid, more likely. I didn't care to have my work sitting about where just anyone could pick it up and read it. As a rule, when I'm working on something, I keep the notes with me—in my briefcase—and I have a locked, triple-coded account in Central Comp." She smiled, wryly. "Welcome to the world of cutthroat academics. Publish or perish, gentlefolk, please state your preference."

"'Who masters counterchance masters the world'," Er Thom quoted in Liaden. He tipped his head. "Central Administration—there are new duties required of you, in the face of this emergency?"

"Not a bit of it!" Anne assured him. "All that is required of us is that we continue precisely as we would have done, had the Languages Department not been—*redecorated*—in this rather extreme fashion. Exams are to be given *on schedule*—Central Admin has located and assigned—alternative—classroom space! Grades are to be filed *on time*—no excuses." She threw her hands up in a gesture of disgust.

"Some of these people lost *everything*! The exams they've already given are buried under a couple of tons of rubble, alongside of the exams still to be given! It was just sheer, dumb luck that I brought my lot home with me last night, or else I'd be trying to issue final grades on the basis of guess-and-golly!"

"Hah." Er Thom sipped his wine. "The explosion—do they know the cause?"

"An accident," Anne said, rubbing her neck wearily. "Which means they don't know. Not," she added, "that they'd tell a bunch of mere professors if they *did* know."

She sipped her wine, eyes closed. Er Thom sat quietly, watching her shuttered face, noting the lines of weariness, hating the demands of necessity.

Tomorrow will be soon enough to speak of the journey to Liad, he told himself. *She is exhausted—wrought.*

He took a sip of wine, wondering if he might properly offer to fetch her a Healer. It struck him as outrageous, that those to whom she owed service had not provided this benefit. To barely miss being blown up with the building where one's work was housed—Healers should have been present at the meeting at Central Administration today, available to any who had need. Had one of his crew been subjected to such stress—

"This is wonderful wine," Anne murmured, opening her eyes. "You never bought this at the Block Deli!"

He smiled. "Alas. It is from the private store of *Valcon Melad'a*—the ship of my brother, which he—lent—to me for this journey."

"Is he going to be a little annoyed with you for drinking up all his good red wine?" she wondered, eyes curiously alert, though the question was nearly idle.

"Daav does not care overmuch for the red," Er Thom told her, with a smile for his absent kin. He moved his shoulders. "We are brothers, after all. How shall it be except that I own nothing that is not his, nor he something that is not also mine?"

"I—see." Anne blinked and had another appreciative sip of wine. "Is he much older than you are?"

"Eh? Ah, no, he is the younger—" He moved his hand, fingers flicking in dismissal. "A matter of a few relumma—nothing to signify. You will see, when you have come to be our guest."

It was little enough, and truly he meant to say no more than that, but Anne's mouth tightened and she straightened against the flat cushions.

"I have decided," she said, not quite looking at his face, "that I won't be going to Liad. And neither will Shan."

Without doubt, here was the opening of the trade, which must be answered, at once and fully.

"Ah." Er Thom sipped, delicately, tasting not so much the wine as sorrow, that she forced this now, with her less than able and he with necessity to his arm—and a Master of Trade, besides.

"It is, of course, your decision to make," he murmured, giving her full view of his face, "for yourself. For Shan, it is a different matter, as we have discussed. The delm must Know him. Necessity exists."

It was gentler answer than he would have given any other— by many degrees—and still it seemed to him that her face paled.

"Will you steal my son from me, Er Thom?" Nearly harsh, her voice, and her eyes glittered with the beginnings of anger.

"I am not a thief," he replied evenly. "The child's name is yos'Galan. You, yourself, named him. If there is question of—*belonging*—the law is clear." He tasted wine, deliberately drawing out the time until he looked back to her.

Her face had indeed paled, eyes bright with tears, mouth grooved in a line of pain so profound that he broke with the trade and leaned forward against all sense, to take her hand in his.

"Anne, there is nothing here for the Council of Clans—there is nothing between we two that must make one of us thief! Shan is our child. What better than we who are both his parents take him before the delm, as is proper and right? And as for declining the journey entire—what of your friend, who has died and left you duty? Surely you cannot ignore that necessity, aside from this other—" He was raving, he thought, hearing himself. What possible right had he to speak to her so? To demand that she embrace duty and turn her face to honor? What—

She snatched her hand away from him, curling it protectively against her breast.

"Er Thom," she said, and her voice shook, though her eyes were steady on his, "I am not Liaden."

"I know," he told her, his own voice barely more than a whisper. "Anne. I know."

For a long moment they sat thus, her eyes pinned to his, neither able to move.

"You're in trouble," she said slowly, and there was absolute conviction in her voice. "Er Thom, why did you come here?"

"To see you—once more," he said, with the utter truthfulness one owes none save kin—or a lifemate. "To say—I love you."

"Only that?"

"Yes."

"You've done those things," Anne said, and the tears were wet on her face, though she never moved her eyes from his. "You can go home now. Forget—"

"The child," he interrupted, hand rising in a sign of negation. "I cannot. Necessity exists." He flung out both hands, imploring, the trade in shambles around him. "Anne, I *am* Liaden."

"Yes," she said softly, putting her hands into his. "I know." She closed her eyes, long fingers cool against his palms, and he watched her face and wished, urgently, for Daav to be here just now, to show them the safe path out of this desperate muddle that only became more confused with each attempt at repair . . .

"All right." Anne opened her eyes. He felt her withdraw her hands from his with an absurd sense of loss.

"All right," she said again, and inclined her head.

"At the end of the semester, Shan and I will come with you to Liad," she said, intonation formal—a recitation of the conditions of agreement. "Shan will be seen by your delm and we will be the guests of Clan Korval while I help Professor yo' Kera's colleague sort out his notes. When that—duty—is done, my son and I will come home. Agreed?"

He retained enough wit to know he could agree to no such thing. Who was he, to guess what the delm might require? And there was yet that other matter between he and Anne, which the delm must adjudicate . . .

She was watching him closely, eyes sharp, though showing weariness around the corners.

"I hear you," he murmured, matching her tone of formality. He bowed as fully as possible, seated as he was, and looked back up into her face. "Thank you, Anne."

She smiled, dimly, with her face still strained, and reached out toward him. Just shy of his cheek, her fingers hesitated—dropped.

"You're welcome," she said softly, and sighed, all her exhaustion and strain plain for him to see.

"I shall leave you now," he said gently, though he wanted nothing more than to take her in his arms and soothe her, to sit the night through, if need be, and watch that her sleep went undisturbed.

Fighting improper desires, he rose and made his bow.

"Sleep well," he said. "I shall come tomorrow, as I did today, and care for our child while you are away."

"All right." Anne made no move to rise, as if she did not trust herself to do so without stumble. She gave him the gift of another tired smile. "Thank you, Er Thom. Chiat'a bei kruzon."

He bowed, profoundly warmed. "Chiat'a bei kruzon, denubia," he replied and was so lost to propriety that the endearment passed his lips without awaking the least quiver of shame.

CHAPTER FIFTEEN

*The Universe adorns
a flawless jewel.
Solcintra.*

—From *Collected Poems*
Elabet pel'Ongin, Clan Diot

Reluctantly, Daav lifted his cheek from the comfort of her breast.

"Olwen?"

"Mmm?" she murmured sleepily, raising a hand to push his head down. "Stop *fidgeting.*"

"Yes, but I have to leave," he explained, shamelessly nuzzling into her softness.

"You have to leave *now*?" Olwen released him and actually opened her eyes.

"I have uses for you yet, my buck," she told him severely. "I was only just considering which to subject you to next."

He grinned. "You tempt me, never doubt it. But duty is a sterner mistress."

"A hint in my ear, forsooth! Next time you'll not find me so gentle."

"And I with a dozen new bruises to explain," Daav said mournfully. "Ah, well. Those who would seize joy must expect a tumble or two."

"Hah!" Her laugh was appreciative. Rising onto a elbow, she reached out to stroke the hair back from his face, laughter fading as she studied him.

"Old friend." She sighed, touched the silver twist hanging in his ear. "I recall how you earned that," she murmured, "our first time as teammates. I wish—"

"I know," he said quickly, catching her hand and bringing it to his lips. He kissed her fingertips lightly. "I would still be a Scout, Olwen, if the universe were ordered to my liking. Necessity exists."

"Necessity," she repeated and grimaced—an entirely Scout-like reaction. "Does it occur to you that necessity has killed more Liadens than ever the Yxtrang have?"

"No, are you certain?" He gave her over-wide eyes and a face bright with innocence, winning another laugh.

"I shall formulate a data box and attempt to corroborate my statement, Captain." The laughter faded yet again, and she ran light fingers down his cheek. "Take good care, Daav. Until again."

"Until again, Olwen," he returned gently and slid out of her bed and left her, silently damning necessity.

Two hours until the end of Jump, according to the trip scanner set in the wall.

And after that, Anne thought, *maybe three hours through heavy traffic to setdown in the port.*

Solcintra Port.

"Annie Davis," she told herself, ducking her head to pass through the low doorway connecting the 'fresher unit to the sleeping compartment, "this has not been one of your better ideas."

She did *not* want to go to Solcintra. Yet careful scrutiny of the events leading to her approaching that very place in this lavish, uncannily efficient space-yacht failed to show her how she might have arranged things otherwise.

The conviction that Er Thom was in some sort of trouble persisted. Pressed, he had admitted to "difficulties" at home— and then hastened to assure her that they were neither "of her making nor solving."

As if, Anne thought grumpily as she pulled on her shirt, *that had any bearing on the matter.*

In the next instant, she allowed that it had every bearing. She simply could not allow him to face his "difficulties" alone.

She paused in the act of sealing her shirt to look into her own eyes, reflected in the low-set mirror.

He came to find me.

That in itself was extraordinary, for surely a man of Er Thom yos'Galan's position might easily call upon powers far beyond those mustered by an untenured professor of linguistics, had he need of aid.

And yet he had come to find *her*—a Terran. Come, so he had it—and would not be pushed from that bald statement— for the sole purpose of saying that he loved her.

The sort of thing, Anne thought, threading her belt around her waist and doing up the buckle, *a man comes to say when he's looked eye to eye at his death.*

She sighed and sat on the edge of the too-short bed to pull on her boots, then stayed there, elbows on knees, staring down at the sumptuous carpet.

"Now, Annie Davis," she murmured, hearing Grandfather Murphy's voice echoing in memory's ear. "Tell the truth, and shame the devil."

And the truth was, she wryly admitted to herself, that she was head over ears in love with the man.

"And will not marry him for propriety's sake, willful, wicked gel that ye are!" the gaffer thundered from life-years and light-years away.

Anne grinned and in the back of her mind, the gaffer laughed. "Well, and who can blame ye? The man might stir himself to a bit of lovemaking, after all."

Though lovemaking was not precisely the problem—or not in the ordinary sense, Anne thought, shaking her head. It was as if the years of separation had multiplied their desire for each other until a touch, a shared glance, a word held the potential for conflagration.

The sheer power of the passion—the bone-deep, burning *need* for him was—frightening.

"So why not marry the man?" she asked herself. "You've

agreed to everything else he's wanted. Take a bit for yourself and never mind he only asked because it was *proper*."

Except that he had offered contract-marriage, an arrangement very like a standard Terran cohabitation agreement, with each party going its separate way at the conclusion of the time-limit.

And the thought of letting him go again made her blood cold and her mouth dry and her stomach cramp in agony.

Just how she was going to manage herself upon quitting Liad at the end of semester break had not yet become clear.

I'll think of something, she assured herself, standing and heading for the door to the companionway. *Everything will be all right.*

She paused briefly in the alcove to pay respect to Clan Korval's shield with its lifelike Tree-and-Dragon and to consider yet again the bold, almost arrogant, inscription: *Flaran Cha'-menthi.* I Dare.

Not a very conciliatory motto, Anne thought and grinned. The history of Cantra yos'Phelium and her young co-pilot, Tor An yos'Galan, who had used an experimental space drive to bring the people who were now Liadens away from their besieged planet to a fair new world was the stuff of many stories and plays. Pilot yos'Phelium was characterized as a crusty sort who brooked no questioning of her authority. *I Dare* was probably an entirely accurate summation of her philosophy.

Still grinning, she bowed respect to the device and its motto, then reached out to stroke the dragon's muzzle and look into its bright green eyes.

"Keep good watch," she told it, surprised at how earnest her voice sounded. She stroked the dragon once more, fingers lingering on the cool enamel surface, then continued on in search of Er Thom.

They entered the piloting chamber from opposite doors and Anne noted once more how well-suited he was to this ship. Each doorway that insisted she bend her head for entry framed Er Thom's slender figure like a benediction. The small chairs with their short backs that forced her to bundle her long legs into a ludicrous, adolescent tangle beneath the seat welcomed and enclosed Er Thom as if they had been made for him.

Which, Anne thought wryly, *they very possibly had.*

He bowed now, graceful and smooth, smiling as he straightened.

"Anne. Did you sleep well?"

"Very well," she said, returning his smile and feeling her doubts about the wisdom of this journey begin to slip away. "I missed you."

"Ah." He came closer, fingers stroking her arm, featherlight and enticing, beautiful face tipped up to hers. "The pilot must be vigilant."

"Of course," she murmured, half-tranced by his eyes. She took one careful step back and turned her head toward the board. "About ninety minutes to the end of Jump."

"And another two hours to Solcintra Port," he agreed. "We shall be at Jelaza Kazone by late afternoon." He tipped his head. "Are you troubled, Anne?"

"Nervous," she said and gave him a quick smile. "I don't know much about your cha'leket the delm except that he used to be a Scout and that the two of you were raised together. And your mother—"

Here she faltered. The little she had gleaned of Er Thom's mother seemed to indicate the old lady was a high stickler, with, perhaps, a gift for sarcasm. She strongly suspected that Thodelm yos'Galan was not going to find Terran Scholar Anne Davis, the rather irregular mother of her grandson, much to her liking.

"My mother." Er Thom slipped his hand gently under her elbow, as he had done on the occasion of their first meeting, so long ago, and guided her across the pilot's room and into the alcove that served as a kind of snack bar.

"My mother," he repeated, after he ordered them both a cup of tea from the menuboard and they were sitting across from each other at the pull-down table. "You must understand, she is—ill."

"Ill?" Anne blinked at him, teacup halfway to her lips. "Er

Thom, if your mother isn't well, it would be—discourteous—of me to insist—"

"You are my guest," he interrupted her softly. "All is as it should be, and no discourtesy attached to you at all, who merely accepted invitation freely offered." He paused to sip tea.

"Several years ago," he said slowly, "a—tragedy—befell the clan. When all was accounted, we had lost the delm—Daav's mother, twin of my mother—and the a'thodelm of yos'Galan, my elder brother, Sae Zar."

Anne lowered her cup, eyes wide on his face, but he was staring at some point just beyond his own cup, which was cradled in the net of his fingers.

"Such a blow to the Line Direct could not easily be withstood. Of course, Daav was called home immediately to take up the Ring—and there was myself to—absorb—a'thodelm's duty—but we were neither of us yet full adult and looked to the remaining elder of the Clan to guide us." He sighed.

"Which she was not at first able to do, so desperate was her illness. We feared—for relumma—that she would follow sister and son and leave us—a halfling delm, as Daav would have it, and an unschooled thodelm—alone to guide Korval."

"But she didn't die," Anne breathed, unable to take her eyes from his averted face.

"Indeed," he murmured, "she gained strength. To a point. A very specific point, alas, and that more by will than any skill the medics brought. Damage from the radiation had gone too far, taken too much. She is not well. In fact, she is dying. And all the medics and the autodocs can do is somewhat ease the pain of her determination to live." He lifted his cup and drank, eyes still cast aside.

"I'm so terribly sorry," Anne managed and his eyes flashed to hers, brilliantly violet.

"It is not of your blame," he said, softly.

"No," she agreed, "but I still grieve for your grief. Was it—was it an honor-feud?"

"There was nothing honorable in it!" he said sharply, then moved a hand, fingers tracing a formal sign in the air between them.

"Forgive me. It was lies and treachery and outworld conniving and the stupidity of it is the trap was not even set for us! She who told the first tale, the one who set the bait—she had only been awaiting a master trader. One would have done as well as any other. Only ill luck that it was Sae Zar yos'-Galan who walked into the place where she waited and lay down his coin for a drink."

"I'm sorry," Anne said again, damning the inadequacy of the phrase. "Were you and your brother very—close?"

"Close?" He tipped his head, frowning. "Ah, I see. Not so—close. Sae Zar was eleven—twelve—Standard Years my elder. He brought presents to Daav and me, and took us with him to Port a time or two . . . He was kind, but old, you know, and we but children." He paused.

"There was—vast difference in our estates, you must understand," he said and the impression she had was that he was choosing his words with the utmost care. "It became—necessary—for the delm to provide the clan with another child. The elder child of yos'Phelium had then ten Standard Years and it was the delm's wisdom that the new child should have another of—near age—with whom to grow and learn. Thus she commanded her sister my mother to also wed, and then took the child of that union in fostering."

"Which is how you and Daav came to be cha'lekets," Anne murmured, shaking her head over this *commanding to wed.* "Er Thom—"

A tone sounded in the piloting chamber—one clear, bright note.

Er Thom stood. "Forgive me. We are about to re-enter normal space, and I must be at the board." He hesitated, flashing her a look from beneath golden lashes. "Would you care to sit with me there?"

A signal honor, Anne knew, to be asked by a master pilot to accompany him at the board. And honor beyond counting, that one who was not even a pilot should be offered that place.

Heart full, she inclined her head.

"I would be honored, Er Thom. Thank you."

"The honor is my own," he returned, which she knew was rote, and thereby sheer nonsense. He bowed and left the alcove then, Anne hard on his heels.

•   •   •

Traffic was not so heavy as she had imagined—or Delm Korval's pleasure-yacht commanded a clear approach whenever it appeared.

Which, she allowed, upon consideration, might not be so fanciful a notion, after all.

She leaned forward in the acceleration chair that was built all wrong for her size, and watched his face as he worked the board, listening to his matter-of-fact exchange of information with Solcintra Tower. There was nothing hurried in the rapid dance of his fingers over the various keys, toggles and switches—no hurry and no hesitation. Only pure efficiency enveloped by a nearly transcendent concentration.

"You love this," she breathed, barely knowing that she spoke aloud. "Really love this."

Purple eyes flashed to her face. "This—yes. Every liftoff is a privilege. Every homecoming is—a joy."

She was about to answer—and then started, abruptly alert on an utterly different level.

"Shan's awake," she said, rising and moving away. "I'll go and make him presentable."

But Er Thom was fully back in the pilot's beautiful, unfathomable dance and gave no sign that he heard her.

CHAPTER SIXTEEN

Each one of a Line shall heed the voice of the thodelm, head of that Line, and give honor to the thodelm's word. Likewise, the thodelm shall heed the voice of the delm, head of the clan entire, and to the delm's word bow low.

Proper behavior is that thodelm decides for Line and delm decides for clan, cherishing between them the melant'i of all.

—Excerpted from the Liaden Code of Proper Conduct

Er Thom led the way down, Anne coming after, holding Shan's hand. At the edge of the ramp, they were met by a woman in mechanic's coveralls, the Tree-and-Dragon emblem stitched on her sleeve.

"Sir," she murmured, bowing low.

Er Thom barely inclined his head. "There is luggage in the smaller hold to be sent on immediately to Trealla Fantrol," he said in the mode, so Anne thought, of Employer to Employee. "The ship shall at once be inspected and made ready according to its standard bill of orders."

The mechanic bowed, indicating understanding of her orders. "Sir," she said again and stepped aside.

Without further ado, Er Thom moved on, Anne a step still behind him, slowed by the shortness of her son's stride, and her own desire to crane around like a tourist and stare at everything.

"Hi!" Shan announced as they passed the mechanic, which earned him a flash of startled gray eyes and a bow nearly as low as the one given his father.

"Young sir," the woman said swiftly. Her eyes lifted and barely touched Anne's face before she bowed yet again.

"Lady."

Anne blinked, cudgeling her brain for the proper response. Clearly, her melant'i in no way approached Er Thom's, whose clan employed the woman. Nor did she have any notion of the relative status of learned scholars to starship mechanics, though she was inclined to think that, on the basis of practical abilities, the mechanic stood several orders above a mere professor of linguistics.

She was saved the necessity of making any decision at all by the arrival of the rest of the woman's crew, to whom she turned with rapid-fire orders. Reprieved, Anne walked over to Er Thom, Shan in tow.

"I need a scorecard," she muttered in Terran, and saw the gleam of a smile in his eyes.

"A guest of the House outranks a hireling of the House," he said softly. "She expected no response. Indeed, it was forward of her to offer greeting, except she was forced to it by this young rogue." He reached down to ruffle Shan's hair.

Anne sighed. "Shannie," she said, without much hope, "don't talk to strangers." She met Er Thom's eyes, adding wryly: "Not that he's ever met a stranger."

He frowned briefly, brows pulling slightly together, then his face cleared. "'Happy the one who finds kin in every port.'"

"Close enough," she allowed. "Except if the other person counts differently there's Hobbs to pay."

"Who is Hobbs?" Er Thom wondered and Anne laughed, shaking her head.

"I'm sorry," she managed after a moment. "Hobbs isn't—anybody—really. A figure of speech, like his brother Hobson, who's generally seen offering a choice." She paused, suddenly taken. "Actually, you may know Mr. Hobson. His choice goes like this: Take my terms or take nothing."

"Hah!" The smile this time was nearer a grin. "We have met." He slid his hand under her elbow, guiding her away from the cold-pad and toward a low building some distance away painted with the Tree-and-Dragon.

"A car awaits us," he said, "and then we may to Daav. In any case, we should clear the field."

As was only prudent, Anne thought. The field was a-buzz with activity. Jitney traffic was heavy, racing between cold-pads and the distant bulk of the main garage. Added to the speedy jitneys were fuel trucks, repair rigs, forklifts and ground-tugs, some with ships in tow.

The Tree-and-Dragon sigil was displayed on every piece of equipment, on every jitney and on several of the ships they passed.

"All this belongs to—to your clan?" Anne asked around a mounting sense of dismay.

He glanced up at her. "This is Korval's primary yard in Solcintra," he murmured. "We maintain three others here, and in Chonselta, two."

It may have been the staggering information that Clan Korval owned no fewer than *six* spaceship maintenance and repair yards that caused the lapse in her usual vigilance. Or it may have been the realization that *rich,* the descriptor she had vaguely attached to Er Thom's financial status, so far under-stated the matter as to be actually misleading.

Six repair yards, she thought dazedly, allowing herself to be guided through the hurrying traffic. These were not the holdings of a mid-level mercantile clan with a couple near-mythological heroes and a tradeship or two to its credit. This was stupefyingly wealthy, not merely Old House, but High—

"Er Thom," she began, meaning to demand an exact ac-counting of Clan Korval's melant'i here and now, before she or her son set foot beyond the repair yard's gate. "Er Thom, just precisely where—"

"Sparkles!" Shan shouted, snatching his hand free.

She spun at once, grabbing for him, but he was gone, run-ning as fast as his short legs could carry him, counter-cutting traffic, ignoring the lumbering repair rig entirely.

"Shannie!" She was moving—was caught, snatched aside with sudden, brusque strength—and a slim figure in a leather jacket was past her, running so quickly he seemed to skim the ground.

In the path of the rig, Shan stooped, fingers scrabbling at the blast-sealed tarmac. At the machine's crown, Anne saw the driver frantically slapping at his control board, saw the rig slow—not enough, not nearly enough—

Her terror made the rescue more dramatic than reality, or so Er Thom assured her afterward.

Truth or overheated imagination, she saw the enormous treads bearing the metal mountain inexorably toward her son, tiny and oblivious to his danger.

And she saw Er Thom, swift and unhesitating, flash between Shan and the mountain, catch the boy in his arms and roll away in a shoulder-bruising somersault.

The machine obscured her sight of them for a heart-searing minute, cleared her line of sight and ground, at last, to a halt.

Er Thom was standing, Shan held tightly in his arms, a new white scar showing on the shoulder of his battered brown jacket.

"Is he—?" The driver was shaking, braced against the side of his machine. He lifted eyes half-wild with horror in a face the color of yellow mud. "The child, Lady! By the gods, where is the child?"

"Here." Er Thom walked forward, Shan unnaturally still in his arms, silver eyes stretched wide.

"Compose yourself," Er Thom told the driver, coolly. "No hurt has been taken."

The man closed his eyes and leaned weakly back into the side of the machine. Anne saw his throat work, swallowing anguish.

"Thank gods," he rasped, and abruptly stiffened. Standing away from his support, he made a deep bow that was somewhat marred by his continued trembling.

"Your Lordship."

"Yes," Er Thom said, in Employer to Employee, which did not, Anne thought, finally getting her legs to move, lend itself to warmth. "You are Dus Tin sig'Eva, are you not?"

"Yes, sir," the man said, standing stiffly upright.

Anne made it to Er Thom's side and held out her arms. Shan smiled at her, somewhat unsteadily.

"Hi, Ma," he whispered. Er Thom never turned his head.

"You will call for assistance," he was telling Dus Tin sig'Eva, still in the cool tones of Employer to Employee. "When assistance arrives, you will accept the role of passenger back to your station, where you will report this incident to your supervisor. If you feel need of a Healer, that service will be provided you. In any case, you will be given the rest of this shift and all of your next shift off, with pay. It may be advisable for you to retrain on this piece of equipment."

The man bowed. "Your Lordship," he said, with, Anne thought, staggered relief. Straightening, he turned and swarmed up the ladder into the driver's compartment, to radio for assistance.

At last, Er Thom turned his head.

"And now you, my swift one—" he began in Low Liaden.

Shan shifted sharply in his arms. "Sparkles, Mirada!"

Er Thom looked grim. "Sparkles, is it?" he said in ominous Terran.

He swung the child to his feet, keeping a firm grip on one small hand. Anne grabbed the other and held tight. "Show me these sparkles."

Obediently, Shan marched forward, mother and father in tow. Just two steps from the rear of the repair rig, he stopped and bent his head to point with his nose, since neither parent would relinquish a hand.

"There!"

Embedded in the tarmac was a faceted blue gem, sparkling in the brilliant Liaden sunlight.

"Hah. And are these your usual sparkles or something a bit different, I wonder?"

Shan blinked, expression doleful. "Sparkles," he repeated, and tried to yank his hand away from Er Thom. "Shan *go*," he demanded, stamping a foot.

"Shannie!" Anne said warningly, but Er Thom let the small hand free.

"Sparkles!" Shan cried, pointing down at the glittering gem. "More sparkles!" His finger stabbed at a point just over Er Thom's bright head. "Ma sparkles! Jerzy sparkles! Rilly! Everywhere sparkles, but not to touch! This sparkle to touch! Touch this, touch more?"

"Ah." Er Thom went to one knee on the tarmac and looked

very earnestly into Shan's face. "Here," he said softly, and to Anne's amazement, pulled off his master trader's ring, the amethyst blazing gloriously purple. "Touch this sparkle, denubia."

Shan's fist closed greedily around the big gem. Enthralled, Anne knelt on his other side, letting his hand free, but keeping a firm grip on his shoulder.

"Can you now touch these other sparkles?" Er Thom asked.

There was a long, charged moment as Shan scanned the blank air above Er Thom's head, and extended a cautious, hungry hand.

"Nothing," he said, body losing all its unnatural tenseness at once. His eyes filled with tears, but he only shook his head. "Can't touch Mirada."

"Perhaps when you are older," Er Thom said gently, slipping the ring back onto his finger. "In the meanwhile, you see that there are—different sorts—of sparkles, eh? Those you can touch and those you can only see. Can you remember that?"

"Yes," Shan told him, utterly certain.

"Good. Then you must also remember never to run away from your mother again. It was ill-done and caused her pain. This is not how we use our kin, who deserve all of our love and all of our kindness. I am not pleased."

Shan swallowed hard, eyes filling again. "I'm sorry, Mirada."

"As is proper, for the fault is yours," Er Thom told him. "But you owe your mother some ease, do you not?"

Woefully, he turned to Anne. "I'm sorry, Ma."

"I'm sorry, too, Shannie," she said. "It was bad to run away like that, wasn't it?"

He nodded, then the tears escaped in a rush and he flung himself into her arms, burying his face against her neck. "I'm sorry, *sorry*!" he hiccuped, sobbing with such extravagance that Er Thom began to look alarmed.

Anne smiled at him and held up a finger.

"All right," she said, gently rubbing Shan's back, working loose the tight muscles. "I guess that's sorry enough. But you need to do something else for me."

"What?" Shan asked, raising his sodden face.

"Promise you won't run away again."

"I promise," he said and then sighed, tears gone as suddenly as they had appeared. "I won't run away."

"Good," Anne said and set him back so she could stand, remembering to keep a tight grip on his hand. She glanced over at Er Thom, who had also risen.

"Why does he cry like that?" he asked, trouble still showing in his eyes.

Anne grinned. "You can write a note and thank Jerzy. Shan had gotten cranky one day and started to whimper over something and Jerzy told him that if he wanted to be really convincing, he had to *project*—and proceeded to demonstrate. By the time I came in, the two of them were sitting on the floor in the middle of Jerzy's apartment, holding each other and sobbing their hearts out." She shook her head, suddenly serious.

"Are you OK?" she asked, extending a tentative hand and touching his shoulder. "That was quite a tumble."

"I am fine," he assured her solemnly.

"Your jacket's gotten scarred," she said, fingering the leather briefly before prudence took her hand away.

He glanced negligently at the scrape, shoulders moving. "If that is the worst of the matter then we may make our bow to the luck." He reached down and took Shan's hand.

"In the meanwhile, our car awaits," he said, and led them around the stalled repair rig and away.

CHAPTER SEVENTEEN

The number of High Houses is precisely fifty. And then there is Korval.

—From the Annual Census of Clans

The landcar was low and sleek and surprisingly roomy. Anne leaned back in a passenger's seat adjusted to accommodate her height, Shan dozing on her lap, and watched Solcintra Port flash by.

She gave an inward sigh of regret for the quickness of the tour as Er Thom guided the car through Port Gate One and into the city proper.

He glanced over at her, violet eyes serious. "Forgive me my necessity," he murmured, "and allow me to show you the Port another day—soon."

She blinked, then inclined her head. "Thank you, Er Thom. I'd like that."

"I, also," he answered and fell silent once more, driving the car with the same effortless efficiency he had demonstrated at the yacht's control board.

Anne settled against the back of her seat and watched him, content to let Solcintra City slip by with only a few cursory glances. Another day, and she would see it all, immerse herself—safely anchored by Er Thom's melant'i and knowledge—in all the wonder the City of Jewels could muster.

The car slid effortlessly around a flowered corner, under an ancient archway of shaped stone, negotiated a sweeping curve in a smooth uptake of speed and they were suddenly out of the city and moving through a landscape of plush lawns and wide gardens.

"Soon now," Er Thom said so softly she might have thought he was speaking to himself, except the words were in Terran.

The car accelerated once more, lawns and gardens flickering by—and changing. The houses became larger, set further back from the road, some hidden entirely, marked only by gates and driveways.

Er Thom sent the car right at an abrupt branching of ways. They climbed a sudden hill and a valley stretched before them. At the near end, Anne saw a cluster of trees, glimpsed roof top and chimneys through the leaves.

On the far side of the valley were more trees and, soaring high into the green-tinged, cloudless sky, a—Tree.

"What on—?" She sat forward in the seat, earning a sleepy grumble from Shan. "It *can't* be a tree!"

"And yet it is a tree," Er Thom said, as the car descended the hill to the valley floor. "Jelaza Kazone, Korval's Tree, which is at the house of my brother, also called Jelaza Kazone."

Jelaza Kazone, the professorial corner of her mind supplied helpfully, meant "Jela's Peace" or "Jela's Fulfillment". She stared at the impossible tallness of it, and licked lips suddenly gone dry.

"Who is Jela?" she murmured, barely knowing that she asked the question aloud, so absorbed she was by the Tree itself.

"Cantra yos'Phelium's partner, all honor to him, who died before the Exodus."

Anne managed to move her eyes from the Tree—from *Jelaza Kazone*—to Er Thom's profile. "But—'Jela's Fulfillment'? And he never made it to Liad?"

"Ah. But it had been Jela's Tree, you know, and he had made her swear to keep it safe."

"Oh." She eased back slowly, and several minutes passed in silence, until she said: "So the delm is the Dragon who

guards the Tree—the *actual* Tree. Your shield isn't an—alle-
gory?"

"Ale—?" He frowned, puzzlement plain. "Your pardon.
It—the delm's instruction, when we were children, was that
each of us holds the burden of Cantra's promise, and—should
there be but one of Korval alive, the life of that one was only
to keep the Tree."

Anne sighed, slowly, and shook her head. "It's *the* Tree—
Jela's original?"

"Yes," Er Thom murmured, slowing the car as they approached a cluster of low bushes.

"That makes it, what? Nine hundred years old?"

"Somewhat—older, perhaps," he said, flicking a glance at
her as he turned into one of those long, mysterious driveways.
"We arrive."

Jelaza Kazone, the house, was two stories high, overhung
with a sloping roof. A porch girded the second story; chairs
and loungers could be seen here and there.

It was, Anne thought in relief, a cozy sort of house, with
nothing of the mansion about it, never mind that it was big
enough to hold seventy apartments the size of her own on
University. Perhaps the benign presence of Jelaza Kazone, the
Tree, helped make it feel so comfortable.

For the Tree, pinnacle now lost to her sight, grew out of the
center of the house.

Questioned, Er Thom told her that the house had been built
piece-by-piece as the clan grew, until it now surrounded the
Tree on all sides.

"My rooms are—*were*—on the second story, facing the
inner court, where the Tree is." The car glided to a soundless
stop and Er Thom made several quick adjustments, before
turning in his seat to look at her.

"The delm will—very soon—See our child and the clan
will rejoice," he said earnestly, taking her hand in his and
looking up into her eyes. "Anne. If there is—a thing in your
heart—you—are welcomed—to lay it before Korval for—for
solving." The pressure of his fingers on hers was hard, nearly
painful, and she had the impression he was striving to impart
information of paramount importance.

"It is known—forgive me!—that you have none to speak

on your behalf. We would not—wish to be—backward—in
service to—to the guest." He drew a deep breath and released
her hands, looking doubtfully into her eyes.

"I mean no insult, Anne."

"No, of course not," she said gently, while her mind raced.
Traditionally, delms solved—spoke for—those of their own
clan. For Delm Korval to be willing to speak for someone outside his clan—and a Terran besides!—was something rather
extraordinary. Anne inclined her head deeply.

"I am—disarmed—by Korval's graciousness," she said
carefully. "You do me great honor. I will not hesitate to bring
any worthy matter to the delm's attention."

Er Thom's face relaxed into a smile.

"That is good, then," he said, and glanced down at Shan.
"Now, we must wake this sleepy one and take him within."

Master Daav, the stately individual who answered the door-
summons informed Er Thom with precision, was in the Inner
Court. If the Lord and Lady and Young Sir would follow,
please?

They did, down a well-lit, wood-paneled hallway, footsteps muffled on bright, thick carpet, past closed doors with
ancient china knobs set in the centers. Even Shan seemed
awed, and kept close to Anne's side, his fingers clutching at
hers.

Rounding a corner, they went down a slightly narrower
hall that ended in a glass door. Their guide opened the door
with a flourish and bowed them into the Inner Court.

Anne went three steps into the garden and stopped, blinking at the profusion of flowers and shrubs, the riot of bird
song and the flutter of jewel-colored insects.

Er Thom continued across the silky grass, glancing this
way and that among the unruly flowers.

"Well met, brother!" a cheery voice called from no particular direction.

Er Thom stopped, head tipped to one side. "Daav?"

"Who else? Had you a good trip?"

"Smooth and easy." Er Thom approached the monumental
Tree, and lay his palm flat against the silvery trunk as he

peered upward into the branches. "It is difficult to converse when I cannot see you."

"Easily solved. Climb yourself up."

"Might you not climb yourself down?" Er Thom inquired. "There are others present and matters that require your attention."

"Ah. You see how it is, brother: My manners have atrophied utterly in your absence."

"*Will* you climb down?" Er Thom demanded, a curious mix of laughter and frustration in his voice. Anne drifted closer, Shan silent and alert at her side.

"I will, indeed," said the Tree cheerfully. "Have a care, denubia, and stand away. It would not do for me to fall on you."

There was remarkably little movement among the silent broad leaves. When the lithe dark man dropped from the branches, it was as if he were part of a conjuror's trick: *Now you see him . . .*

"So then." He grinned at Er Thom and opened his arms, heedless of the twig caught in his hair and the smear of green across one wide, white sleeve.

Without hesitation, Er Thom went forward and the two embraced, cheek to cheek.

"Welcome home, darling," the dark-haired man said, his words in Low Liaden carrying clearly to Anne. "You were missed."

The embrace ended and Er Thom stepped back, though his cha'leket kept a light hand on his shoulder, thumb rubbing the new scar on the leather jacket.

"Perilous journey, pilot?"

"A tumble at the Port," Er Thom returned calmly. "Nothing to signify."

"Hah. But there are others present and matters that require my attention—or so recent rumor sings me! Lead on, brother; I am entirely at your disposal."

"Then you must come this way and make your bow to the guest," Er Thom told him, leading him the way across the grass to Anne.

He extended a hand on which the master trader's ring blazed and laid it lightly on her sleeve. "Anne," he murmured, switching to his accented, careful Terran, "here is my brother, Daav yos'Phelium, Delm Korval."

She smiled at the dark-haired man and bowed acknowledgement of the introduction. "I am happy to meet you, Daav yos'Phelium."

"Korval," Er Thom continued. "This is Anne Davis, Professor of Linguistics."

From beneath a pair of well-marked brows, bright dark eyes met hers, disconcertingly direct before he made his own bow.

"Professor Davis, I am delighted to meet you at last." His Terran bore a lighter accent than Er Thom's; his voice was deeper, almost grainy. He was a fraction taller, wiry rather than slim, with a face more foxy than elfin. A curiously twisted silver loop swung from his right earlobe and his dark brown hair fell, unrelieved by a single curl, an inch below his shoulders.

"And this . . ." Er Thom bent, touching Shan on the cheek with light fingertips. "Korval, I Show you Shan yos'Galan."

"So." Daav yos'Phelium moved, dropping lightly to his knees before the wide-eyed child. He held out a hand on which a wide band glittered, lush with enamel-work. "Goodday to you, Shan yos'Galan."

Shan tipped his head, considering the man before him for a long moment.

"Hi," he said at last, his usual greeting, and brought his free hand up to meet the one the man still patiently offered.

Wiry golden fingers closed around the small hand and Daav smiled. "Did you have a good trip, Nephew?"

"OK," Shan told him, moving forward a half-step, his eyes on his uncle's face. Reluctantly, Anne relinquished her hold on his hand and he took another small step, so he was standing with his toes nearly touching the man's knees.

"Do you see sparkles?" he asked, abruptly.

"Alas," Daav answered, "I do not. Do *you* see sparkles?"

"Yes, but not the kind to touch. Mirada on hand has sparkles to touch." He bit his lip, looking earnestly into the man's face.

"You *happen* sparkles," he said plaintively. "Can't *see* sparkles?"

The well-marked brows pulled together. "Happen sparkles?" he murmured.

"He means 'make,'" Anne explained. "You *make* sparkles."

"Ah, do I? I had no notion. Have you brought me a nascent wizard, denubia?" This last was apparently to Er Thom.

"Perhaps," that gentleman replied. "Perhaps a Healer. Or perhaps only one who has the gift of knowing when another is happy."

"Not too bad a gift, eh?" He smiled at Shan and then sent his brilliant black gaze to Anne's face.

"If Korval Sees this child, he is of the clan," he said, voice and eyes intently serious. "You understand this?"

Anne nodded. "Er Thom explained that it was—vital—for the delm to—count—a new yos'Galan."

"So? And did Er Thom also explain that what Korval acquires Korval does not relinquish? You have seen our shield."

"The dragon over the tree—yes." She hesitated, looked from his intent face to Er Thom's, equally intent. "Shan yos'-Galan is my son," she said to him, voice excruciatingly even. "Whether he is—of—Clan Korval or not."

"Yes," Er Thom said, meeting her gaze straightly, hand half-lifting toward her. "How could it be otherwise?"

"Scholar." Daav yos'Phelium's voice brought her eyes back to his face, which was no less serious than it had been. "Scholar, if you are at all unsure—stand away. There is no dishonor in taking time to be certain."

She stared down at him where he knelt in the grass, holding her son by the hand. Leaf-stained as he was, with his fox-face and bold eyes, lean and tough as a dock-worker—He was beyond her experience: Half-wild and unknown; utterly, bewilderingly different than Er Thom, who was her friend and who—she *knew*—wished her well—and wished to do well for their son.

"It's what we came to do," she said slowly, voice cracking slightly. She shook her head, as much from a need to break that compelling black gaze as from a desire to deny—anything.

"Shan was to be shown to Delm Korval and then Er Thom could be easy again, and the clan not be—embarrassed—by there being a—rogue yos'Galan loose in the galaxy—one the delm hadn't counted. It was—my error," she explained, looking back to his face. "I—custom on my homeworld is to name the child with the father's surname in—respect. In—*acknowledgement.* I hadn't understood that there would be—complications for Er Thom when I followed my—my world's custom. Having made the error, it is—fitting—that I do what I can to put the error into—context—and repair any harm I may have done."

"Hah." For two long heartbeats, the bold eyes held hers, then he inclined his head.

"So it is done." He extended the hand that bore the broad enameled band and cupped Shan's cheek.

"Korval Sees Shan yos'Galan, child of Er Thom yos'Galan and Anne Davis," he announced. The High Liaden words rang like so many bells across the garden, startling the birds into silence. He bent forward and kissed Shan on the lips before taking his hand away.

"Welcome, Shan yos'Galan. The clan rejoices."

And that, Anne thought, around a sudden and astonishing surge of joy, *is that. I hope Er Thom thinks it was worth all that worry.*

Shan laughed and reached forward on tiptoe to pluck the leaf from his uncle's hair and hold it up for inspection.

"Flower."

"Leaf, I believe," Daav corrected gently. "Quite a nice one." He rose in a single fluid motion, one hand still holding the child and the other sweeping up in a extravagantly wide gesture.

"Thus, matters requiring my attention! Let us go within and have wine—and luncheon, too! For I do not scruple to tell you, brother, that you behold a man who is famished."

"No new sight," Er Thom replied calmly, stepping across to offer an arm to Anne and smiling up into her eyes. "Will you take wine and food before we go on to Trealla Fantrol, friend?"

The sense of joy was dizzying, exhilarating beyond reason, so that it was all she could do not to bend and kiss him, with full measure passion, on the lips. Only the understanding that it would not do—not here—kept her emotion in check.

So instead of kissing him, she smiled at him and slid her arm through his.

"Wine and food sounds delightful," she said warmly and allowed him to lead her into the house.

CHAPTER EIGHTEEN

In an ally, considerations of house, clan, planet, race are insignificant beside two prime questions, which are:
1. *Can he shoot?*
2. *Will he aim at your enemy?*

—Excerpted from Cantra yos'Phelium's Log Book

A light luncheon had been called for, to be brought to the Small Parlor, to which they had repaired. Wine had been poured for each adult—Shan was given a small crystal cup half-filled with citrus punch—and tasted with all due ceremony.

Very shortly after, Er Thom excused himself to place a call to his parent, and left the room. Daav and Shan went to the window, where the man was apparently pointing out sections of shrubbery most likely to yield rabbits, if a boy were patient, and had sharp eyes.

Momentarily left to herself, Anne walked slowly around the room, sipping the slightly tart white wine and trying to absorb everything at once.

The rug—the rug was surely Kharsian wool, hand woven by a single family across several generations. She had seen a hologram of such a priceless treasure once and recognized the signature maroon and cobalt blue among the lesser colors, all skillfully blended to create a riotous garden of flowers, each bloom unique as a snowflake.

At one side of the room, the rug broke and flowed around a hearth of dark gray stone laid with white logs. The mantle that framed the fireplace was of a glossy reddish wood she could not identify, carved with a central medallion slightly larger than her fist. The design tantalized a moment before she named it—a Compass Rose, pure in the smooth red wood.

Turning from the fireplace, she nearly fell over the table and two comfortable-looking chairs. On top of the table was a board, margins painted with fanciful designs. The center of the board was marked into blue and brown squares, bounded by larger borders, like countries. There were twelve countries in all, Anne counted, each containing twelve small squares.

On the table outside the board were four twelve-sided ebony dice. Two shallow wooden bowls likewise sat to hand, each filled with oval pebbles. The pebbles in the right bowl were red; those in the left, yellow.

"Do you play, Professor Davis?" Daav yos'Phelium inquired suddenly from her side.

She glanced up with only a slight start and shook her head. "It's a counterchance board, isn't it?"

"Indeed it is. You must ask my brother to teach you—he's a fiend for the game, you know. And very good, besides." He flashed a smile up into her face, humor crinkling the corners of his eyes. "Although of course it wouldn't do for him to hear I've said so."

Anne laughed. "No, I can see that would be a—bad move."

"Precisely," he agreed, raising his glass. "I've left young Shan scouting for rabbits," he continued after a moment, gesturing toward the window and the child kneeling motionless before it, nose pressed to the glass.

"That should keep him busy until lunch," she said, grinning. "There's a shortage of rabbits on University."

"Ah. Well, there are more than enough here for him to enjoy, never fear it." He tipped his head slightly, black eyes quizzical.

Anne lifted her glass—and brought it down as a low move to the right caught her attention.

"What a beautiful cat!" she breathed.

Daav yos'Phelium turned his head. "Lady Dignity, how kind of you to join us! Come in, do, and give grace to the guest."

The cat paused in her progress across the carpet, considering him out of round blue eyes. After a moment, she sat down, brought up a paw and began to wash her face.

"Wanton," the man said calmly and Anne laughed.

"Lady Dignity?" she asked. "Is she very shy?"

"Merely shatterbrained, I fear, and a great deal set up in her own esteem. She does well in her role, however, so I don't like to complain."

"Her role?" She glanced expressively around her. "Tell me you have mice!"

He laughed—full and rich, a world apart from Er Thom's soft, infrequent laughter. "No, how could I? But she's useful, nonetheless."

Anne looked to where the cat had settled, chicken-fashion, onto the carpet, front paws tucked under creamy chest, blue eyes half-closed within the mask of darker fur.

"She frightens off unwanted guests," she suggested and Daav opened his black eyes wide.

"Isn't that why I keep a butler? No, I will tell you—" He sipped wine, glanced over at the cat, then back to Anne.

"My sister is very proper," he began earnestly, "and I am a great trial to her. She says I have no dignity and I fear she may be correct. Still, scolding will not create what the gods have not provided and I confess I grew tired of being reminded of my deficiency."

He used his chin to point at the drowsing cat. "So I have employed this lady, here, to act in my behalf. Now, whenever my sister demands to know where my dignity is, I can produce her upon the instant."

Anne stared at him, a smile growing slowly, curving her big mouth and lighting her eyes. The smile turned to a chuckle and she shook her head at him in mock severity.

"Your poor sister! I don't expect she was amused."

Daav sighed dolefully, eyes glinting. "Alas, the gods were behindhand in Kareen's sense of fun."

"Daav!" This from Shan, vigilant at the window. "Look, Daav! Cat!"

"Good gods, in *my* garden?" He was gone, moving across the carpet with a quick, silent stride to lean over the boy's shoulder.

Anne drifted over just in time to see an enormous orange-and-white cat slink into the bushes at the base of a small tree.

"Relchin," Daav said. "Doubtless gone birding." He glanced up at Anne. "He never catches any, you know, but the chase does amuse him."

"Exercise," she agreed, seriously.

"Indeed," he murmured and seemed about to say something else, when there was a step at the door.

"Ah, there you are, brother! We were only just wondering when you might return and free us all to dine!" He slid past Anne and crossed the room, blocking her view of Er Thom's face. "How do you find your mother my aunt?"

"A trifle—distressed—today." Er Thom's voice was soft and smooth as always, yet Anne felt apprehension shiver through her as she reached down to take Shan's hand.

"Er Thom, if your mother is not—able—to take on the burden of a guest—" she began, and that quickly he was before her, looking seriously up into her eyes.

"No such thing," he told her, softly, though she was cold with sudden dread. "She sends apology to the guest, that she will be unable to greet you instantly upon your arrival. She looks forward to the pleasure of your company at Prime meal this evening."

She stared down into his eyes, feeling—*knowing*—that there was something wrong—badly wrong. Er Thom was lying to her. The thought—the surety—shocked her into still wordlessness.

"Anne?" He extended a hand and she caught it tightly, as if it were a thrown rope and she floundering far out of her depth.

"What's wrong?" she demanded, voice raspy and dry. "Er Thom—"

His fingers were firm, giving back pressure for pressure; his eyes never wavered from hers.

"My mother is—inconvenienced," he said patiently. "She is not able to meet you at once, but shall surely do so at Prime." His grip increased, painfully, but she made no move to withdraw her fingers. "You are welcome in my House, Anne. Please."

She held his eyes, his hand, for another heartbeat, trying desperately to plumb the wrongness, identify the ill. At last, defeated, she bowed her head and slid her fingers free.

"All right," she said softly, and raised her head in time to see Daav yos'Phelium's bold black eyes move slowly from her face to Er Thom's.

Luncheon passed in a flurry of small-talk, of which Er Thom's brother apparently possessed an unending supply. It seemed absurd, Anne thought as she nibbled cheese, that she should have found him strange and formidable scarcely an hour ago. Now, he was merely an amusing young man with a flair for the dramatic and a penchant for telling the most ridiculous stories with an entirely straight face.

He's a bit like Jerzy, really, she thought around a stab of homesickness.

Er Thom's contributions to the conversation were slight: Set-ups for his cha'leket's absurd stories and tolerant corroborations of unlikely events. Mostly, he busied himself with feeding Shan bits of cheese and slices of fruit from the plate he had filled for himself.

Anne, watching surreptitiously, thought Shan accounted for nearly all of the plate's contents, and that Er Thom perhaps had a taste of cheese with his wine. *Worried,* she thought, and wondered how ill his mother was.

When at last Luncheon was over, Daav walked them down the long hall to the door and gave Er Thom another hug.

"Don't keep yourself far," he said and Er Thom smiled—wanly, Anne thought, and caught his brother's arm.

"Come to Prime, do."

Daav's eyes opened wide. "What, tonight?"

"Why not?"

"An excellent question. I shall come in all my finery. In the meanwhile, commend me to your mother."

Er Thom's smile this time was a little less tense. Daav bent to hug Shan and kiss his cheek.

"Nephew. Come and visit me often, eh? I think we shall deal famously."

Shan returned the embrace and the kiss with exuberance, then stood back to wave.

"'Bye, Daav."

The man bowed lightly—as between kin, Anne read. "Until soon, young Shan."

"Professor Davis." The bow he accorded her was of respect. "We shall speak again, I hope. I have read your work, you know, and would welcome a chance to discuss your ideas more fully, if you will grant it."

"That would be pleasant," she told him, returning his bow with one of respect to a delm not one's own. "I look forward to it."

"Good." His eyes were intent on hers and she felt again that he was utterly beyond her, more alien than she could fathom.

"In the meanwhile," he said, all gentle courtesy, "if there is any matter in which I may serve you, please know that I am entirely at your disposal."

"Thank you," she said, matching his inflection as precisely as possible. "You are gracious and—kind—to a stranger."

For one moment more, the black eyes seared into hers, then he was bowing them gracefully out the door.

"Until Prime," he called, lifting a hand as Er Thom started the landcar. "Keep well, all."

CHAPTER NINETEEN

The best advice for any Terran with a yen to visit the beautiful planet of Liad is: Stay home.

—From *A Terran's Guide to Liad*

"The name of the valley," Er Thom said, deliberately—Anne thought—to cut off any additional questions she might ask, "is Valcon Berant'a. Korval's Valley, they say in Solcintra. It was ceded by the passengers to Cantra yos'Phelium and Tor An yos'Galan, for the piloting fee. Jelaza Kazone was built first, of course, after the Tree was planted. Trealla Fantrol—the house of yos'Galan—that came later. It was built as a—sentinel post, you would say—to guard the in-road, to act as first deterrent—and to give warning to the delm."

Anne looked out the window at the lush landscape, turning this burst of information over in her mind. *Valcon Berant'a?* The Liaden name Er Thom had given did *not* mean "Korval's Valley." It meant, she decided after a moment of concentrated thought, "Dragon's Price," or perhaps "Dragon Hoard."

"A sentinel post," she asked as Er Thom slowed and made the turn into another drive. "Were there wars?"

"Ah, well, in the old times, you know, there were—disharmonies. Things did not always run smoothly and the Council of Clans did not always agree. Daav says civilized behavior is never to be depended upon." He laughed his soft laugh, so different from his cha'leket's. "Do not fear that I ask you to guest in a fortress, friend. Trealla Fantrol has—amenities. Very soon, now . . ."

It was, in fact, a matter of three more minutes and two more twists in the tree-lined drive. The car passed under an arch rich with yellow flowers and entered a sweeping curve.

Er Thom pulled up to the bottom of the stairway and turned the car off. Anne sat and tried not to stare, Shan completely still on her lap.

Trealla Fantrol was a mansion, with a marble stairway and towering granite facade. Windows glittered like diamonds among the gray stone and lawns like plush green velvet sloped away on both sides.

"This is the outpost?" she demanded in a voice that cracked. After the warm hominess of Daav's house . . .

"All of us would live at Jelaza Kazone," Er Thom said quietly, "if we could." He lay a light hand on her arm and immediately took it away.

"Come, allow me to show you and our son to your rooms. I will leave you for a time, so that you might refresh yourselves and rest. One has been engaged to care for our son—Mrs. Intassi, who had been our nurse when we were young. She will arrive before Prime. I shall instruct Mr. pak'Ora to conduct her to you immediately . . ."

Chattering, Anne thought, in no little wonder, as Er Thom came around to her side of car and lifted Shan to his feet. *Er Thom is actually* chattering.

Chattering, he brought them up the marble stairway, through the front door and across the echoing lobby, up the Grand Staircase—each riser hand-carved with a scene from the Great Migration—down an interminable hallway to her room.

"The house has your palmprint on file," he told her as the door slid open. "If you do not find all precisely as you would wish it, only tell me and the deficiency will be corrected." He looked up at her, chatter suddenly broken as his eyes took fire. He glanced away.

"I am sorry to leave you so abruptly, Anne. I—necessity. Later, if you like it, I shall show you the house—and the grounds." He lay a hand on her arm and this time did not remove it so quickly. "My private code is in your computer. If there is— any way—in which I may serve you, do not hesitate . . ."

"All right," she said soothingly and against all sense extended a hand to stroke his cheek, meaning only to ease his nervousness.

As soon as she touched him, she knew it was a mistake; she barely needed to hear the sharp intake of his breath, or see the blaze of his eyes, which echoed the re-awakened blaze of her desire.

Ensorcelled yet again, she looked helplessly into his eyes, her hand trembling against his cheek, unwilling—unable—to move.

It was Er Thom who moved.

A single step, backward, his eyes hot on hers. Her hand fell, lifeless, to her side and he bowed: Esteem and respect.

"I shall return," he said, very softly indeed. "Please. Be at ease in our House."

He turned on his heel and was gone, the door closing behind him with the barest whisper of sound.

He came as ordered to her private parlor, dressed in plain shirt and trousers, with the dust of the Port still on his boots, and made his bow, dutiful and low.

"Mother."

"My son."

Petrella surveyed him from her chair, meaning to make him writhe while she leisurely surveyed the wind-rumpled golden hair, the delicate wing of brow over eyes more purple than blue, the pleasing symmetry of face, and the firm, give-me-no-nonsense mouth. Er Thom, the son who was not her son. Chi's work, this one, returned at last to the mother who bore him on his twelfth name day, when he boarded *Dutiful Passage* as cabin boy.

He had Chi's look, Petrella allowed, which meant her own, since she and her twin had been as like as two seeds in a pod. She knew him to be mannerly and biddable, dutiful to a fault—far different than his volatile cha'leket, who looked more changeling than Korval.

"Are that woman and her child in this house?" she demanded abruptly, letting him hear the rasp of her displeasure.

He swayed a bow, discomfited not one whit. "The House is honored by the guesting of Professor Anne Davis," he said in his soft way, "mother of Shan yos'Galan, Seen by Korval."

"Oh, is it?" Petrella straightened to her full height in the chair, preparing to attack.

"Shan yos'Galan," Er Thom continued smoothly, "is the son of Er Thom yos'Galan, and grandson of Petrella yos'-Galan." He lifted his head, purple eyes bland. "It would be— gracious—of the thodelm to complete what the delm has begun."

"You *dare*," she breathed, anger filling her with vivid energy. "Is your thodelm a counterchance token, Er Thom yos'-Galan, to dance when you choose the tune? Your cha'leket the delm has Seen your bastard, has he? You provide an accomplished fact, and I—too weak to protest dishonor—make my bow meekly and am ruled by the whim of an upstarting boy. Think again—*Master Trader.* That child is none of mine."

The firm mouth had tightened somewhat, she noted with satisfaction; the bow he gave her was grave.

"Mrs. Intassi," he murmured, as if all she had said were mere pleasantry, "has been engaged to care for my son. She arrives this afternoon to take charge of the nursery."

For a heartbeat she could only gape at him, then she drew a careful breath, fingers tightening ominously on the arm rests.

"I see. And if your thodelm requires you to engage a house in town in which these delightful arrangements may continue as planned?"

Once again, courteous and grave, he bowed. "Then of course I will remove myself immediately."

And the so-proper contract marriage with Syntebra el'Kemin, Petrella understood from that, would never be consummated. She glared at him, considering her next move.

"Enlighten me," she ordered after a moment. "Precisely where did you meet this—person—who has the honor of being yos'Galan's guest?"

The winged brows twitched—smoothed.

"Professor Davis and I became acquainted on Proziski, at

the time when *Dutiful Passage* had been transport for the Liaden contingent of the Federated Trade Mission. Professor Davis had been engaged in field research under a grant from University Central, where she teaches." He paused.

"We met at the port master's rout," he finished gently, "and contracted an alliance of pleasure."

"With so many Liadens by your side, you take a *Terran* as pleasure-love?" She stared at him in disbelief.

The purple eyes sparked—and were shielded immediately by the sweep of long golden lashes. Er Thom said nothing.

"Speak, sirrah! I will know how a son of this House came to so far forget himself as to—"

"It was myself I considered!" he interrupted sharply, and there was no shielding the anger in his eyes now. "She cared nothing for bedding an a'thodelm, or for the daring of coming so near to Korval! She barely cared of *this*—" He flung out his hand, the master trader's ring flashing violet lightnings, "save it said I was competent, and she a lady who admires competence."

"Indeed! You fascinate me. And what did she care for, pray, if not for any of what you are?"

He drew a hard breath, his mouth a tight, straight line. "She cared for who I was," he said quietly, passion seeming spent as quickly as it had been struck. He moved a hand, softening the statement.

"It may have been at first, that I was Liaden, and exotic, and of a form that pleased her. What reasons do *Liaden* lovers need? For me, it was that she gave friendship with no eye to profit, and opened her door and her heart as if I were no less than kin."

"And got your child, to her honor!" Petrella commented caustically. "A strange accident, for one who admires competence."

Er Thom inclined his head. "So I also thought, at first," he said surprisingly. "Anne—Professor Davis—is not, as we have discussed, Liaden. In spite of this, she is a person of honor and meticulous melant'i. That her necessity required her to bear my child without proper negotiation is—regrettable. Having bowed to necessity, however, she strove to place honor properly, after the custom of her homeworld, and thus the child is yos'Galan. To the increase and joy of the clan."

Petrella glared. "I *will not be played,* sirrah! Strive to bear it in mind."

"As you say." He bowed obedience and went into stillness, hands loose at his sides, face bland and attentive.

Almost, Petrella laughed, for that was a trick from Chi's bag, designed to unnerve an opponent and force a response— and very often a blunder. She let the silence stretch, teasing his patience. When she spoke at last, her voice was almost mild.

"So, Shan yos'Galan has been Seen by the delm. Tell me, do, what the delm has Seen."

"A child of a little less than three Standard Years," Er Thom said gently, "with pale hair and silver blue eyes, bold and alert. He successfully completes puzzles and match-problems designed to challenge children half again his age. He sees *sparkles,* as he calls them, from which he may interpret another's emotional state."

Petrella stared. "A *Terran?*" she demanded.

Er Thom was seen to sigh. "A *yos'Galan,*" he said patiently, "which has given dozens to the Healers and the dramliz over the years since the Exodus. Why stare that another child of the Line shows these abilities?"

Petrella closed her eyes. A Terran—blast it all! At best, a half-blood yos'Galan. And already he showed sign of Healer talent? Rare to show so early, certainly. And coupled with the promise of pilot skills—Easy to see the attraction of this irregular child for Delm Korval. Very nearly understandable, that he would risk Thodelm yos'Galan's anger to gain such promise for the clan.

"Professor Davis," Er Thom murmured, "is a scholar of much acclaim in her field. You may wish to read of her work—"

Petrella opened her eyes.

"I have no interest in scholars," she said flatly. "Especially Terran scholars."

There was a moment of electric stillness before Er Thom bowed.

"In that wise," he said softly, "I shall after all engage a house in town. I will not have her shown any dishonor."

"You will not *what*?" Petrella demanded, disbelief in her voice.

"I spoke plainly," Er Thom replied, giving her all his eyes.

She met them, and saw determination—and thus the lines were drawn: Honor to the Terran scholar, or abandon all hope of a more legitimate heir to yos'Galan.

"It's my belief you've run mad," Petrella announced, trading him stare for stare.

He bowed, accepting her judgment with graceful irony.

"So." She moved her shoulders, feeling the edge of exhaustion.

"Very well," she told him crisply. "The Terran scholar is yos'Galan's guest. For a twelve-day. If her business on Liad holds her beyond that, she may guest elsewhere. In the meanwhile, all honor to her."

For a moment, she thought he would not be satisfied with the compromise. Then he bowed acceptance.

"It is heard."

"Good," Petrella snapped. "Let it also be remembered. Go now and leave me in peace. I shall see you and the guest of the House at Prime."

"Yes, mother," he said, and added, "Daav will be with us, as well."

"Of course he will," she said tiredly. "Go away."

He did, though without alacrity. After all, Petrella thought, he was far too accomplished a player to give her the advantage of seeing him either relieved or dismayed by the outcome of their interview.

Petrella closed her eyes and allowed herself to go limp in the chair, concentrating on her breathing. Her mind wandered a bit, as it tended to do nowadays, rather than face the dreariness of continued pain, and she found herself remembering a long-ago interview with her twin.

"Daav is a forest creature, all eyes and teeth," Chi had murmured, sipping her wine. "He knows the forms, the protocols—but will he bide with them? There's the question." She smiled. "Ah, well. The Scouts will tame him, never fear it. As for your own . . ."

Petrella sipped her wine, waiting with accustomed ease while her twin tidied knowledge into words.

"Your own is—a marvel, considering his place in the Line Direct, son of the Delm's Own Twin—" They shared a glance of amusement for that, before Chi moved her hand and went on.

"He's a sweet-natured child, your Er Thom: mannerly, dutiful and calm. He knows the forms and applies them correctly, with neither rebellion nor irony. From time to time I see him hint Daav—the wonder is my wild thing takes such hinting with grace! But you mustn't fear he is dull—both of them are sharp enough to cut! It is only this attitude of dutiful sweetness that disturbs me, sister—so unlike Korval's more usual attributes . . ."

Petrella remembered that she had laughed, waving away her twin's misgivings.

"What cause to repine, that at last Korval has—through whatever accident!—got itself a biddable child?"

"Biddable—" Chi sipped wine, eyes gazing miles, perhaps worlds, away. She focussed abruptly and gave her wide, ironic smile. "I suspect he may surprise us one day, sister. And I know enough of history to worry how he might go about it. Though I allow when it comes it will doubtless be amusing."

Petrella had laughed again, and refilled her twin's cup with wine, and the talk had moved to other matters.

And now, Petrella thought, eyes opening onto the pain-racked present, *Er Thom has at last surprised.*

She wondered if Chi would have been amused, after all.

CHAPTER TWENTY

If honor be your clothing, the suit will last a lifetime.

—William Arnot

It was quite the nicest dress she had ever owned.

Indeed, Anne thought, as she opened the closet, it was the only *formal dress* she possessed, and, hopefully, formal enough for a Liaden dinner party comprised not only of the delm and the delm's heir, but of her lover's thodelm, grandmother of her son.

Until Er Thom yos'Galan, Anne would have laughed at the notion of owning a piece of clothing as extravagant as the luscious green confection she had purchased on Proziski. But— *An ambassadorial affair, with dancing,* Er Thom had said in his soft, sweet way. Would it amuse her to accompany him?

It would have amused her to accompany him to Hell, she recalled ruefully as she took the dress down. She had accepted his invitation with more joy than sense—then spent an entire day—and far too much of her meager personal funds—in pursuit of the green gown.

The delicious fabric swirled round her shoulders, fell and settled, water-smooth, against her skin as she slipped on the matching slippers and turned to face the mirror.

"Oh—my."

The gown still had magic to work, she thought, staring

dazedly at the vision in the mirror. The regal lady caught there stared haughtily back, brown skin rich against the pure greenness, chestnut hair glowing, eyes all velvet seduction.

From slim waist to full bosom, the gown was laced with golden chains so delicate they might have been worked at a elf-lord's forge. She had a matching length, provided by the dressmaker, to wear around her throat.

On the occasion of the ambassadorial affair, she had also worn a gold ribbon, threaded through painstakingly-arranged hair. The ribbon was long-lost—and the hair soon woefully disarranged. For the dance had proved insipid and they had left early, smuggling out a napkin filled with delicacies pilfered from an hors d'oeuvre tray and a split of wine offered by a sympathetic waiter.

Dazzling in his own finery, Er Thom had driven them to the Mercantile Building, and pulled the sample bolt from the flitter's boot.

"You mustn't spoil your dress," he had murmured, shaking a prince's ransom worth of lace back from his beautiful hands and spreading the scarlet silk like a blanket . . .

Anne shook herself. "That will do," she informed her reflection sternly, and deliberately turned away.

The vanity had been arranged by the same invisible hands that had unpacked her clothing and carefully put it away.

To the right were her comb, brush and mirror, the black oak veneer battered, the silver-wrapped handles tarnished. To the left sat the chipped lacquer chest that contained her few pieces of jewelry.

Careful of stressed plastic hinges, she lifted the lid and propped it open. Along the back of the box, glowing like a candle in the shiny dark interior, was the carved ivory box that held the necklace Er Thom had given her—"to say good-bye." For a moment, she was tempted to wear that piece tonight, for it was inarguably the most beautiful of her paltry jewels.

He asked you not to wear it, she reminded herself as her fingers touched the exquisitely-carved ivory. With a sigh, she shook her head and fastened the dressmaker's golden chain around her throat instead.

She hung a simple pair of gold hoops in her ears and used plain gold combs to hold her hair back from her face.

The entire effect was a little more austere than she had hoped for, despite the green gown's magic.

Well, she thought wistfully, *and maybe Er Thom's ma will pity you, Annie-gel, since it's plain you've no sort of melant'i to boast on.*

Or, Er Thom's mother might just as easily take the plainness of her guest's adornment as a personal affront. Anne swallowed against a sudden uprising of butterflies inside her stomach.

"Maybe I'll have a cup of soup and some toast in my room," she said aloud, and with no conviction at all, for that *would* be an insult, and Er Thom's mother well within her rights to avenge it.

Just when she was beginning to think that would be no bad thing, the entrance-chime sounded.

Green dress swirling around her, she left the bedroom, went through the spacious kitchenette and luxurious common room. She paused a moment before laying her hand against the admittance plate, composing her face and trying to calm her racing heartbeat. It would never do for Mr. pak'Ora, come to do butler's duty and guide the guest to the dining room, to see her panting with fright.

Hoping that her face betrayed only serene expectation, she opened the door.

Er Thom bowed, low and eloquent, looked up and smiled into her eyes. "Good evening."

"Good evening," she managed, though her tongue suddenly seemed cleft to the roof of her mouth. She stepped back, motioning him inside with a sweep of her ringless hand. "Please come in."

"Thank you," he said gravely, as if the door weren't coded to his palm as well as hers. He stepped within and the portal in question slid shut behind him.

Er Thom wore the form-fitting dark trousers deemed appropriate formal wear for Liaden males. She knew from experience that the fabric was wonderfully soft to the touch. His wide-sleeved white shirt was silk, or something more precious; the lace frothing at his throat contained by an emerald stickpin. Emeralds glittered in his ears and on his slender hands, half-hidden by more lace.

"Anne?" His gaze warmed her face. "Is there something wrong?"

She shook herself, aware that she had been staring.

"I was just thinking how beautiful you are," she said and felt her face heat, for the man was here to take her to meet his *mother*—

Er Thom laughed his soft laugh and bowed, slightly and with humor.

"And I," he murmured, "was trying most earnestly *not* to think the same of you."

Dear gods, a compliment. She very nearly blinked; rescued the moment with a bow of her own, accepting his admiration.

His eyes gleamed, but he turned a little aside, gesturing around the room.

"Everything is as you wish it? Is there anything else the House may provide for you?"

"Everything is perfectly delightful," she told him soberly. "I'll miss all this elegance, after we go back home." She *did* blink then, seeing him among the wide, comfortable chairs and high-set desk.

"Do you guest Terrans often?"

"Eh?" Winged brows drew together in puzzlement. "I believe you are the first."

"Oh." She bit her lip, then plunged ahead, waving her hand at the room.

"It's just that everything's—*convenient*—for someone who is—of Terran height. I assumed—"

"Ah." Enlightenment dawned in a smile. "My mother has redecorated," he murmured, running his eyes in rapid inventory around the parlor. He looked back to Anne, feeling his blood heat with desire for her even as he forced himself to make civil reply.

"She would have wished to have everything as it should be for the guest," he explained. "Why should you not be comfortable in our house?"

She looked at him doubtfully, then took a breath, the golden laces stretching tight across her delightful bosom.

"Your mother redecorated—*rebuilt*—this whole apartment just so I'd be comfortable for few weeks?"

"Of course," he said reasonably. "Why not?" He moved a hand, drawing her attention away from the subject.

"Mrs. Intassi came to speak with you?" he asked, though he had just come from an interview with that lady. "You have seen the nursery and find it acceptable?"

Anne laughed, head tipped gracefully back. "Your notions of—*acceptable*—" she said, and he heard her unease through the laughter even as she shook her head and made her face more serious.

"The nursery looks lovely. Mrs. Intassi seems—very competent." She hesitated. "It's going to be a little strange—for Shannie and for me, too—to have him sleeping so far away . . ."

"Not so far away," he said softly. "You may visit him whenever you like. The door has your code." Almost, he reached to take her hand; gamesmanship strangled the impulse before it went beyond a finger-twitch.

"Shan is your son," he said, repeating his comfort of the afternoon, and saw the tiny lines of tension around her eyes ease.

Smiling then, he bowed and offered his arm.

"May I escort you to the First Parlor, friend? My mother is eager to make your acquaintance." He slanted a mischievous look into her face, feeling irrationally gay. "Never fear," he told her lightly, "there will be wine close to hand."

She laughed at that and took his arm, resting her hand lightly over his, intertwining their fingers in the way he had taught her.

Just at the door, she checked and looked down into his eyes, her own shaded with trouble, so that he felt his gaiety fade.

"Don't let me make a mistake," she said, fingers tightening around his.

Astonishment held him for half a heartbeat, to be replaced by flaring joy. For here at last was the sign of her intention he had hoped for since she had turned her face from contract-marriage.

Don't let me make a mistake. She placed her melant'i in his hands for safekeeping, as if they were kin. Or lifemates.

"Er Thom?" Her eyes were still troubled, doubt beginning to show.

As if she could think that what she asked was any else than his own ardent wish—He stopped himself, recalling that she was Terran and unsure of custom.

Gently, and with extreme caution, he lifted his hand, barely brushing her lips with his fingertips.

"No," he said, solemn despite the burgeoning joy, "I will not let you make a mistake, Anne." A laugh burst free despite his best efforts.

"But if we are late for the Gathering Hour with my mother," he predicted, "nothing may succor either of us!"

Her son and the guest were late—oh, a few minutes, merely, Petrella allowed, as she settled more comfortably into her chair—but late, nonetheless.

Almost, she had time in their tardiness to imagine herself the victor. To suppose that seeing his Terran tart *here,* in his very homeplace, surrounded by all that was elegant, proper and *Liaden* had awakened Er Thom's swooning senses to sanity.

Almost, she began to weigh the wisdom of accepting this child—this *Shan*—to yos'Galan. Not, most naturally, as Er Thom's heir—young Syntebra would doubtless serve them well enough *there.* But it could not be denied that the clan could ill afford to turn away one who was potentially pilot and Healer merely because tainted blood ran his veins.

Her hand moved, almost touching the button that would fetch Mr. pak'Ora—and paused.

There were voices in the hall.

Er Thom's murmur came first to her ears. She missed the words, but the cadence was of neither High Liaden nor Low.

The voice that answered him was all too clear; carrying without being shrill, with the hint of such control found in the speech of those trained as prena'ma.

"I've sent a message to Drusil tel'Bana," the carrying voice announced in perfectly intelligible Terran, "telling her I'm on-planet and hoping for an early meeting. I'll have to go to her, of course, which means renting a car, if you would give me the name of a—"

"The House," Er Thom's words were now clear, as well, "will provide you a car, friend. And a driver, should you wish."

Oh, and will it? Petrella thought, stiffening against the cushions—but that was only ill-temper, for surely Er Thom owned vehicles enough in his own right that the Terran scholar need never walk.

Honor to the guest, she reminded herself, composing her face into that look of courteous blandness with which one dealt with those not of one's clan.

Asked, she could not have precisely said what portrait imagination had painted of Anne Davis beforehand. Sufficient to its accuracy to say that the woman who crossed the threshold on Er Thom's arm surprised. Entirely.

To be sure, she was a giantess, looming above her tall and shapely escort, but she did not move ill. Indeed, there was that in her stride which seemed peculiarly pilot-like, and her shoulders sat level and easy, as with any person of pride.

Though she was large in all things, Petrella acknowledged her not out of proportion with her height, and of her form there was a pleasing—yet not overcommanding—symmetry.

Her gown suited her figure, and was not—to an old trader's eye—overexpensive. Her plain necklet and earrings, the lack of ostentation in the matter of rings—all this proclaimed her a person who knew her own worth and was neither ashamed of her station nor eager to show herself as more than she was.

The face, to which Petrella now raised her eyes, was large-featured: The nose was too prominent for beauty, the mouth too full, the eyes set a fraction too close, the willful jaw square, the forehead high and smooth. Not a beautiful face, but, rather, an *interesting* face—intelligent and humorous, enlivened by a pair of speaking brown eyes, with a sweetness about the mouth that did much toward balancing the stubborn jaw.

Had Anne Davis been Liaden, Petrella might at this juncture very well admitted to some small portion of interest in her.

But Anne Davis was unremittingly Terran; Er Thom, by guiding her here, was seen to be still in the throes of his madness; and their child, by all that meant winning, must remain a half-bred bastard, unacknowledged by yos'Galan.

With a determination that was surprisingly difficult to rally, Petrella turned a stone-like face toward her son.

"Good evening," she said, chilly and in all of the High Tongue, barely inclining her head.

"Good evening, mother," he returned gently, bowing re-

spect. He brought the Terran woman forward as if she were
some outworld regina and bowed once more.

"I bring you Anne Davis, Professor of Linguistics, mother
of my child, guest of the House." He put the woman's hand
lingeringly aside, and turned to make his bow to her.

"Anne, here is Petrella, Thodelm yos'Galan, whose child I
have the honor to be."

Pretty words, Petrella thought grumpily, *from one who has
not also the honor of being obedient.* It surprised her that he
gave the introductions in High Liaden, for surely a Terran, no
matter how scholarly—

The woman before her bowed with an ease astonishing in
one so large, in the mode of Adult to Person of Rank, a choice
that charmed by its very lack of innuendo.

"Petrella yos'Galan," she said in her clear, storyteller's voice,
"I am glad to meet you. Allow me to thank you at once for the
generosity which has admitted me as a guest in your house."

Petrella very nearly blinked. That this graceful acknowledgement was made in High Liaden must amaze, though the de-
livery was necessarily marred by a rather heavy accent. Still, it
was understood that not everyone spoke with the accent of Solcintra, and balancing this was the fact that the sentences had
been spoken in proper cadence and with a thoughtfulness indicating the speaker understood her own words, rather than
merely repeating what had been learned by rote.

It was necessary to answer grace with grace—her own
melant'i demanded it, even had there not been this other matter between herself and her son. Petrella inclined her head
with full ceremony.

"Anne Davis, I am glad to meet you, as well. Forgive me
that I do not rise to greet you more properly."

"Please do not concern yourself," the guest replied. "Indeed, it is your kindness in having myself and my son here
when you are so ill that has particularly touched my heart. I
wish that we will not be a burden to you."

Petrella was still trying to gauge whether this astonishing
speech carried any deliberate offense—given leave to be ill,
forsooth!—when Mr. pak'Ora entered to announce the arrival
of the delm.

CHAPTER TWENTY-ONE

Liaden clans are primarily social organizations, amended by centuries of ever more exacting usage. Some Terran investigators compare them without amendment to military organizations, perhaps not realizing that the line of command is to some extent fluid, with variation due to considerations of melant'i. Though the delm is "supreme commander" and the thodelm his "second," an adroit junior with an agenda may at times be as much of an impediment to those commanders as any external enemy.

—From *The Lectures of a Visiting Professor, Vol. 2*
Wilhemenia Neville-Smythe, Unity House, Terra

"Daav yos'Phelium, Delm Korval," Mr. pak'Ora informed the room, and stepped aside so the gentleman might pass.

Unhurried and silent, he came across the rug, dressed in much the same way as Er Thom, his dark hair tied neatly at the nape with a length of silver ribbon. Deep and respectful, he made his bow before Petrella yos'Galan's chair.

"Aunt Petrella. Good evening to you."

"Good evening to you, nephew," the old lady replied, with an inclination of her head, her tone nearly cordial. She lifted a thin, shaking hand, directing the man's attention aside. "I believe you have had the honor of making your bow to yos'Galan's guest."

He made another, nonetheless. "Professor Davis. How
good it is to see you again!"

The words were High Liaden, the mode as between equal
adults, which was about as friendly as the High Tongue got,
Anne thought, returning his greeting with pleasure.

"You are kind," she said, meaning it. "I am glad to see you
again, also, sir."

She thought she saw a smile glimmer at the back of his
eyes, but before she could be certain, Petrella commanded his
attention once more.

"I will also make you known to Er Thom, a'thodelm of
yos'Galan, master trader and heir to the delm. I am persuaded
you can never have seen his like before."

Her nephew considered her out of bright black eyes, head
tipped a little to one side.

"You wrong me, Aunt Petrella," he said after a moment,
and with utmost gentleness. "Though it is entirely true that I
have never seen his like anywhere else." He turned his head,
smiling at Er Thom with throat-tightening affection.

"Hello, darling."

Er Thom's smile was no less warm. "Daav. It's good of
you to come."

"Yes, let us by all means extol my virtues," his cha'leket
said with a grin. "Certainly the party has a moment or two at
leisure!"

Anne laughed and Daav turned to her, one hand flung out,
face comically earnest.

"What! You doubt me virtuous to even that extent?"

"On the contrary," she assured him, with matching earnest-
ness. "I think it very good of you to round out the dinner
party—especially when you clean up to such good advantage!"

In her chair, the old lady stiffened. Anne caught the movement from the corner of an eye and half-turned in that direction, worry overcoming fun, and found Daav someway before
her.

"Well, you know," he said, still in that tone of bogus gravity, "my aunt has been saying the same of me any time these
ten years—have you not, Aunt Petrella?"

"Indeed," the old lady agreed, with, Anne thought, a touch

of acid, though her parched face remained as bland as formerly. "It only remains to discover how to influence you to behave in concert with your finery." She shifted abruptly, signaling Er Thom with a wavering fingertip.

"Doubtless, the guest would welcome a glass of wine. Daav, I want you, if you please."

"Certainly," he murmured as Er Thom and the guest walked downroom toward the wine table, "it must always please me to obey you, Aunt Petrella. In the face of such pleasure it does seem churlish to observe that I would welcome a glass of wine, as well."

She merely stared at him, face composed, until she judged the others sufficiently well-embarked on their own conversation to care little of what was being said behind them.

"So," she said at last, meeting his eyes fully. "It comes to my attention that the delm now decides for yos'Galan."

Daav lifted an eyebrow. "I am desolate to be the first before you with the news—the delm decides for Korval."

"And you see nothing that might offend, that the delm should decide—for Korval!—before ever the Line has made decision. I see."

Petrella drew a hard breath, eyes wandering, then stopping where Er Thom stood with his—with yos'Galan's guest—sipping wine and gazing up into her face with such a look of admiration as must give pause—if not actual pain. She brought her attention forcibly back to Daav.

"It is understood," she said, though without any effort to soften her tone, "that the clan must not at this point in its history turn away any who are—never care how irregularly!—of the Line. That the one now offered is likely pilot and perhaps Healer must make him doubly advantageous to the clan. That he is the child of beloved kin must make him more than acceptable to yourself. All this is crystalline." She paused, considering his face, which was merely attentive, black eyes shadowed by long dark lashes.

"However," Petrella continued after a moment, "yos'-Galan at present is engaged in a disciplinary matter of no small moment. Respect for authority must be taught in such a way as to leave an indelible impression upon the a'thodelm. It is no less than my duty to the delm, who must at all times be

certain his directives *will be* obeyed. I do not know how it is
come about that the a'thodelm has become so careless of obedience, but as head of his Line, the fault is mine to correct."

Daav bowed, slightly and gravely. "And young Shan?"

She sighed, fingers tightening on the arms of her chair.

"You will say I am cruel, to use a child as the whip which
will humble his parent. But I very much fear, my Delm, that
you have Seen a child for Korval who has no other home
than—Korval."

"Hah. And this is your last word upon the matter?"

She moved her shoulders, fretfully. "If he learns his lesson
well," she said, meaning Er Thom, "perhaps the child may be
admitted—eventually. Certainly, the thodelm will do as he
pleases, when I am dead. In the meanwhile, however, I will
trouble the delm to arrange a fostering for this—Shan. yos'-
Galan will not have him here."

"Removal of the child at this time will likely distress the
guest," Daav commented. "Unless that is also your intention?"

"The guest remains for a twelve-day," Petrella answered
calmly. "It is understood that a proper fostering may take even
as long as that to arrange. Scholar Davis need experience no
grief from an untimely parting."

"You are kind," he observed, in such a tone of bitterness
that she raised her eyes in surprise to his face.

His countenance was hidden from her, however, by reason
of his bow, which was low and full of respect as always.

"By your leave, Aunt Petrella, I am now in desperate need
of wine."

"Go, then," she snapped, pleased to have an excuse to be
annoyed with him. "And send my son to me, do."

"Turnabout, darling!" Daav cried as he approached the couple tête-à-tête at the wine table. "You to your mother and I at
long last to drink and fashion pretty compliments for the
delectation of the guest!"

Er Thom turned, showing a tolerably composed face in
which the violet eyes were heated far beyond the prettiest
compliment. Anne Davis, her own eyes bright, ventured another of her delightful laughs.

"We've already dealt with the dress and the hair and the hands," she told him gaily. "You shall have to be inventive, sir!"

He smiled at her in appreciation. "But you see, I may admire your abilities in the High Tongue, which are as new to me as our acquaintance, and if Er Thom has not already been delighted with your manner before my aunt, I can only call him a dullard."

"I have never found Anne's manner other than a delight," Er Thom said calmly, while his eyes betrayed him and his brother wondered more and more.

"Best answer the summons quickly, you know," Daav said when a moment had passed and Er Thom made no move to go to his parent. "Try to comport yourself well. Scream, should the pain go beyond you, and I swear to mount a rescue."

Er Thom laughed his soft laugh and bowed gently to his companion. "My mother desires my presence, friend. Allow Daav to bear you company, do. I engage for him that he will not be entirely shatterbrained."

"Bold promises!" Daav countered and Anne laughed. Er Thom smiled faintly and went at last to wait upon his mother.

"Wine is what I believe I shall have," Daav announced, moving toward the table. "May I refresh your glass?"

"Thank you." She came alongside him and held out a goblet half-full of his aunt's best canary.

He shook the lace back from his hand, refilled her glass and took a new one for himself, into which he poured misravot. He had just replaced the decanter when the woman beside him spoke, in a very quiet tone.

"Delm Korval?"

He spun, startled by such an address *here,* when more proper solving would call for privacy and time and—

Her face showed confusion at his alacrity; indeed, she dropped back a step, fine eyes going wide as her free hand lifted in a gesture meant, perhaps, to ward him.

"Hah." Understanding came, as it often did to him, on a level more intuitive than thoughtful: She meant courtesy, that was all, and called him by the only title she knew for him. He inclined his head, face relaxing into a smile.

"Please," he said, going into Terran for the proper feel of friendly informality. "Let me be Daav, if you will. Delm

Korval is for—formalities." He allowed his smile to widen, showing candor. "Truth told, Delm Korval is a tiresome fellow, always about some bit of business or another. I would be just as glad to be shut of him for an evening."

She smiled, distress evaporating. "Daav, then," she allowed, following him into Terran with just a shade of relief in her voice. "And I will be Anne, and not stodgy Professor Davis."

"Agreed," he said, bowing gallantly. "Though I must hold that I have not yet found Professor Davis stodgy. Indeed, a number of her theories are exciting in the extreme."

She tipped her head. "You're a linguist?"

"Ah, no, merely a captain specialist of the Scouts—retired, alas." He sipped his wine and did not yield to the strong temptation to look aside and see how Er Thom got on.

"My area of speciality was cultural genetics," he told Anne Davis, "but Scouts are all of us generalists, you know—and linguists on the most primitive level. We are taught to learn quickly and to the broad rule of a thumb—" She laughed, softly. "And, truly, there are several languages which I speak well enough to make myself plain to a native of the tongue, yet still could not make available to yourself." He sighed. "My skill as a lexicographer falls short, I fear."

"As does mine," she said. "I've been working forever on a translation guide between High Liaden and Standard Terran." She shook her head, though not, Daav thought, in order to deny anything, unless it was a point made in her own mind. "I'm beginning to think I'm barking up the wrong tree."

Daav took note of the idiom for future exploration. "Perhaps your time on Liad will enlighten you," he suggested.

"Maybe," she allowed, though without observable conviction. "It's just *frustrating*. With the back-language so—" She started, flashing him a conscious look.

"You don't want to hear me rant for hours about my work," she said, smiling and taking a nervous sip of wine. "Professors can bore the ears off of the most sympathetic listener— as my brother often tells me! It would be much safer, if we were to talk about you."

But he was saved from that bit of fancy dancing by the advent of Mr. pak'Ora, come to say that Prime meal awaited them in the dining room.

CHAPTER TWENTY-TWO

Wicked men obey from fear; good men, from love.

—Aristotle

Prime went off without too much event, though Daav fancied he saw Er Thom once or twice hint Anne to the proper eating utensil. Still, there was no harm done, and the attention no more than a dutiful host might without offense offer to a guest of different manner.

Anne had apparently settled upon the more-or-less neutral mode of Adult-to-Adult for her conversation, a point of Code which Petrella was at first inclined to dispute. However, as neither of the remaining party found it beyond them to answer as they were addressed, Adult-to-Adult became the mode of the evening.

There were to have been cards afterward, but as the guest had never used a Liaden deck, the play was a trifle ragged, and Petrella soon excused herself, pleading, so Daav thought, a not-entirely fictitious exhaustion.

As if this were her cue, Anne also announced an intention of retiring, turning aside Er Thom's offered escort by saying she wished to stop in the nursery for a few moments. Both ladies then quit the drawing room in the wake of Mr. pak'Ora.

And so the brothers were abruptly alone, trading bemused glances across the card table.

"Well," commented Daav, "and to think we shall live to tell the tale!"

Er Thom laughed. "Now I suppose you will make your excuses, as well."

"Nonsense, what would you do with yourself all the long evening if I were to be so craven?"

"There are several hundred invoices awaiting my attention," Er Thom replied with abrupt seriousness, "and a dozen memoranda from my first mate. The evening looks fair to overfull, never fear it."

"Hah. And I wishing to share a glass and a bit of chat . . ."

Er Thom smiled his slow, sweet smile. "As to that—a glass of wine and some talk would be very welcome, brother. The invoices quite terrify me."

"A confession, in fact! Very well—you see to the door, I shall see to the wine. I suppose you're drinking red?"

"Of your goodness." Er Thom was already across the room, pulling the door closed with a soft thud.

"None of my goodness at all, I assure you! The wine is from yos'Galan's cellars." He brought the two glasses back to the table and settled on the arm of a chair, watching as Er Thom gathered in the cards they had spread out for Anne's instruction.

Delm, Nadelm, Thodelm, A'thodelm, Master Trader, Ship, then the twelve common cards, until the three suits—red, blue and black—were all joined again. Absently, Er Thom tamped the deck and shuffled, fingers expert and quick among the gilded rectangles.

Daav sipped misravot. "Your mother my aunt appeared somewhat—fractious—this evening," he murmured, eyes on the lightning dance of the deck. "How did you find her earlier?"

The shuffle did not waver. "Less inclined to be courteous even than this evening," Er Thom said composedly. "She refused to acknowledge the child, which was not entirely unexpected, though—regrettable. I feel certain that, after she has had opportunity to meet Shan, she will—"

"Thodelm yos'Galan," Daav interrupted neutrally, "has requested that the delm arrange fostering for Shan yos'Galan, child of Korval alone."

The shuffle ended in a snap of golden fingers, imprisoning the deck entire. Daav looked up into his brother's face.

"He will come to me, of course," he said, and with utmost gentleness, for there was that in Er Thom's eyes which boded not much to the good.

"I am—grateful," Er Thom said, drawing a deep breath and putting the cards by. "I point out, however, that such an arrangement will most naturally—distress—Professor Davis."

"Yes, so I mentioned as well." Daav tipped his head slightly, eyes on his brother's set countenance. "Thodelm yos'Galan informs me that the guest remains for only a twelve-day."

"Thodelm yos'Galan is—alas—in error. There are—matters yet to be resolved—but I feel confident that Anne—Professor Davis—will be making a much longer stay."

"Oh, do you?" Daav blinked. "How much longer a stay, I wonder? And what is it to do with Anne—forgive me if I speak too plainly!—should Korval make what arrangements are deemed most suitable for one of its own?"

Er Thom glanced down, found his glass and picked it up. "It is not necessary," he told the sparkling red depths, "that my—our—child be—deprived—of association with his mother. They have been in the habit of spending many hours a day in each other's company. Even so small a separation as Shan's removal to the nursery has caused Anne—anxiety, though certainly he is old enough—" He seemed to catch himself, to shake himself, and brought his gaze up to meet Daav's fascinated eyes.

"My thodelm had suggested I might take a house in Solcintra," he said, with a calm that deceived his cha'leket not at all. "I believe that this course is, at present, wisest. Anne will be more at ease in—a smaller establishment—and may be free to pursue her business at the university. Mrs. Intassi shall continue to care for Shan—"

"And yourself?" Daav murmured.

"I? I should naturally live with my son and—and his mother. Anne is not—she is not up to line, you know, and depends upon me to advise her."

"Yes, certainly. What of young Syntebra? Shall she be added to your household?"

For a heartbeat Er Thom simply stared at him, eyes blank. Then recollection glimmered.

"Ah. Nexon's daughter." He glanced aside, perhaps to sip his wine. "That would be—entirely ineligible."

"So it would," Daav agreed. "Nearly as ineligible as setting up household with a lady with whom you share no legitimate relationship, save that she has borne you a child outside of contract!"

Er Thom gave him a solemn look. "You had never used to care for scandal."

"And if it were myself," Daav cried, mastering a unique urge to throttle his cha'leket, "I should not care now! But this is yourself, darling, on whom I have always depended to lend me credence among the High Houses and untangle me from all my ghastly scrapes! How shall we go on, if both are beyond the Code?"

Er Thom seemed to go suddenly limp; he sagged down onto the arm of the chair, eyes wide and very serious.

"I asked Anne," he said slowly, "to become my contract-wife."

"Did you?" Daav blinked, remembered to breathe. "And she said?"

"She refused me."

And all praise, Daav thought gratefully, *to the Terran scholar!*

"Surely then there is nothing more to be said. If she will not have you, she will not. To talk of sharing houses only ignores the lady's word and belittles her melant'i. Certainly, you owe her better—"

"It is my earnest belief," Er Thom interrupted gently, "that she wishes a lifemating. As do I."

It was Daav's turn to stare, and he did, full measure. When he at last spoke again, his voice was absolutely neutral, a mere recitation of the information he had just received.

"You wish a lifemating with Anne Davis."

Er Thom inclined his head. "With all my heart."

"Why?"

The violet eyes were steady as ever, holding his own.

"I love her."

"Hah." Well, and that was not impossible, Daav considered, though Er Thom's passions had not in the past run so very warm. He recalled his brother's eyes, hot on the scholar's face; the care he took to shield her from error during the meal and then after, going so far as to lay out the entire deck and painstakingly delineate each card. Love, perhaps, of a kind. And yet . . .

"It had been three Standard Years since you had seen her," he said evenly. "In all that time—"

"In all that time," Er Thom murmured, "I saw no face that compelled me, felt no desire stir me. In all that time, I was a dead man, lost to joy. Then I saw her again and it was as if— as if it were merely the evening after our last, and I expected, welcomed. Wished-for. Desired."

Oh, gods. It was all he could do to remain perched on his chair-arm, glass held loose while he met his brother's eyes. Within, jealousy had woke, snarling, for Er Thom was *his,* Er Thom's love *his* perquisite, not to be shared with any—

He drew a deep, careful breath, enforcing calm on his emotions. Er Thom was his brother, the being he loved best in all the worlds, his perfect opposite, his balancing point. To wound his brother was to wound himself, and what joy gained, should both be mortally struck?

"This is," he said, and heard how his voice grated. He cleared his throat. "This is the matter you would have brought before the delm?"

Er Thom inclined his head. "It is." His eyes showed some wariness as he looked up.

"I would have—spoken—some time—with my brother before arousing the delm."

"As who would not!" Daav extended a hand across the table, Korval's Ring flaring in the room's light, and felt an absurd sense of relief as Er Thom caught his fingers in a firm, warm grip.

"The delm does not yet take notice," he said earnestly, damning his melant'i and the defect of genes that made Kareen unable to take up the Ring. But Kareen would never have Seen young Shan at all and would likely have sent the Terran scholar briskly about her business, richer by neither cantra nor solving, while Er Thom became the victim of whatever punishment spite was capable of framing. He sighed sharply, fingers tight around his brother's hand.

"You must tell me," he said. "Brother—this bringing home of your child—and most especially his mother!—how does this make you ready to contract-wed in accordance with your thodelm's command?"

Er Thom's mouth tightened, though he did not relinquish Daav's hand. "You will think I am mad," he murmured, violet eyes showing a sparkle of tears.

"Darling, we are all of us mad," Daav returned, with no attempt, this once, to make light of the truth. "Ask anyone—they will say the same."

A small smile was seen—no more, really, than a softening of the corners of Er Thom's mouth, a glimmer that dried the sparkling tears.

"Yes," he said softly; "but, you see, I am not entirely in the way of seeming so to myself." He squeezed Daav's hand; relinquished it.

"When I left you, these few weeks ago, it was to accomplish one plan, which I felt *must* be accomplished, after which I—hoped—to be able to show the Healers a calm face and come away from them obedient."

Daav shifted on his chair-arm. "The Healers—that was not necessity, except as you had not accomplished your plan."

"Yes." Er Thom sighed. "And yet necessity did exist. It had been three years, as I said, since I had looked upon a face that pleased me. Three years of—mourning—for she to whom I had given nubiath'a. What right had I to bring such business to the contract-room? Nexon's daughter is young, this her first marriage. In all honor, her husband must be attentive, capable of—kindness. I had ought to have had the Healers time a-gone, myself, except I *would not* forget . . ." He drew a hard breath and took up his glass, though he did not drink.

"I went to Anne," he said softly, "to say only that I loved her. It was knowledge I knew she would treasure. Knowledge that I could not allow to be lost entirely to the Healers' arts. It was to have been—a small thing, simply done."

"And the child?" Daav murmured.

Er Thom lifted a hand to rake fingers through his bright

hair, a habit denoting extreme distraction of thought, very little seen since he had put boyhood behind him.

"There was no child," he said, and his voice was distracted, as well. "There was no child nor mention of a child, three years ago."

"Hah." Daav glanced down, caught sight of the deck and took it up, then sat holding it in his hand, staring hard at nothing.

"You hunger yet for this lady?" he asked and heard Er Thom laugh, short and sharp.

"Hunger for her? I starve without her! I astonish myself with desire! There is no sound, save her voice; no sensation, save her touch."

Daav raised his head, staring in awe at his brother's face. After a moment, he touched his tongue to his lips.

"Yet she refuses a contract-marriage," he persisted, pitching his voice deliberately in the tone of calm reason. "Perhaps the—depth of your passion—may be—no dishonor to her!—inadequately returned."

"It is returned," Er Thom told him, with the absolute conviction of obsession, "in every particular."

Daav bit his lip. "Very well," he allowed, still calm and reasonable. "And yet unalloyed passion is not the foundation upon which we are taught to build a lifemating. You speak in such terms as make me believe you have indeed erred, by giving nubiath'a too soon, before your passions were slaked. In such case, a wiser solving is to go with the lady to the ocean house, indulge yourselves to the full extent of joy, to return home, when you have had your fill—"

"Fill!" Er Thom came to his feet in a flickering surge; instinct brought Daav up, as well, and he met his brother's eyes with something akin to dread.

Er Thom leaned forward, hands flat on the card-table, eyes vividly violet.

"There is no fill," he said, absolutely, utterly flat.

Scouts are taught many tricks in order to ensure the best chance of survival among potentially hostile peoples. Daav employed one such trick now, deliberately relaxing the muscles of his body, letting his mouth soften into a slight smile, his fingers curl half-open. After a moment or two, he had the satisfaction of seeing Er Thom relax, as well, shoulders loosening and eyes cooling even as he sighed and straightened, looking somewhat sheepish.

"Forgive me, denubia," he said softly. "I had never meant to contend against you."

"Certainly not," Daav said gently. "Though I will say it seems a sticky enough coil you plan to lay before the delm." He tipped his head. "Perhaps it would be—illuminating— were I to speak with Anne apart—" He raised a deliberately languid hand, stilling the other's start of protest. "Only to hear what she herself considers of the matter." He tipped his head, offering a smile.

"I shall have to hear it, soon or late, you know."

The smile was answered, faintly. "So you shall."

"Indeed—and tomorrow soon enough, for it is come time—alas!—to make my excuses and leave you to that dreadful pile of invoices." He tipped his head.

"In the meanwhile, promise you will engage no houses in the city—for at least tomorrow, eh?"

"Promised." Er Thom inclined his head and then came around the table to offer his arm.

Arm in arm, they went down the various hallways and across the moon-bathed East Patio. At the car, Er Thom embraced him, and Daav cursed his treacherous muscles, which stiffened, only slightly.

It was enough. Er Thom drew back, staring into his moonlit face.

"You are angry with me." He made some effort to keep his voice neutral, but Daav heard the pain beneath and flung himself into the embrace.

"Denubia, forgive me! My wretched moods. I am *not* angry—only tired, and such a muddle as you bring the delm must make my head spin!"

"Hah." Er Thom's arms tightened and when Daav asked for his kiss a moment later, he bestowed it with the alacrity of relief.

She had wandered through the beautiful, strange, suite for a time, but her pacing failed to tire her. Finally, she plucked a bound book at random from a shelf and, robe swirling around her, settled into a corner of the wheat-colored sofa, resolving to read until sleep overtook her.

An hour later she was still there, sleepless as ever, pursuing the Liaden words from page to page, resolutely not thinking of how lonely she was, or of how much she missed him, or of—

The door-chime sounded, once.

She was up in a flurry of blue skirts, across the room and hand on the admittance plate before she thought to tighten the sash at her waist—which was not really necessary, after all. The one who stood there had seen all she had to show, many times.

Er Thom bowed and straightened, looking up at her from eyes of molten violet.

"I had come," he said softly, "to make my good-night."

Throat tight, she reached out and took his hand, drawing him inside. The door closed, silent, behind him.

CHAPTER TWENTY-THREE

The guest is sacrosanct. The welfare and comfort of the guest will be first among the priorities of the House, for so long as the guest shall bide.

— **Excerpted from the Liaden Code of Proper Conduct**

Daav yos'Phelium, fourth of his Line to bear the name; master pilot; Scout captain, retired; expert of cultural genetics; Delm Korval, lay beneath the Hebert 81 DuoCycle, one shoulder braced against the cool stone floor as he worked to loosen a particularly troublesome gasket-seal. Oil dripped from the gasket and he was careful to keep his face stain-free, though neither the thick old shirt he wore nor the scarred leather leggings were so fortunate.

For a time he had worked with only the flutter of bird song from outside the garage for company, and the now-and-again rustle that was rabbits foraging through the dew-sheathed grass. Now, however, he became aware of something different—a deliberate, plodsome rhythm that vibrated through his braced shoulder and into his head.

Attention on the gasket, he wondered briefly if there was an elephant loose on the lawns. He was mildly disappointed, but not really surprised, when a few minutes later the plodding became the harsh click of boot heels striking stone flooring and a sound was vented in the sudden silence that his Scout sensibilities cataloged as a human sigh.

"What," demanded the voice of his sister, speaking in the mode of Elder Sibling to Child, "are you doing under there?"

The gasket-seal at last heeded his promptings and fell free, releasing a minor downpour of oil. He flinched back from the splatter that liberally redecorated his shirt-front and peered around the Hebert's front wheel.

Creamy leather boots met his gaze, striped here and there with light blue grass-stains. The stiff silk trousers that belled over them, falling precisely to the instep, were of an identical cream color. Daav turned his attention back to the gasket.

"Good morning, Kareen," he called, mindful of his manners, and phrasing the reply in Adult Siblings.

The Right Noble Kareen yos'Phelium allowed herself a second sigh. "What are you doing under there?" she asked again, still in that tone of exasperated scolding.

"Replacing the winder-gasket and repairing the sync-motor," Daav said, carefully using a solvent-soaked towel to clean the gasket seat.

There was a short silence before his sister asked, with lamentable predictability, "And that is a task of such urgency you must attend it before you receive your own kin?"

"Well," Daav allowed judiciously, working the new gasket around to the proper orientation. "There is some urgency attached to it, yes. The final part required for the repair only arrived from Terra last evening and as soon as I have the sync-motor geared, the cycle will be in fine state for racing. I confess I have been wanting to race it anytime this last Standard, but it would not do, you know, to enlist an unsafe machine."

"Race!" Kareen's voice carried a wealth of loathing much more suited to the elder sibling mode she yet insisted upon than the mode he had offered. "One hopes you have more care for your duty than to endanger the person of Korval Himself in a race. Most especially as you have not yet seen fit to provide the clan with your heir."

"Oh, no!" Daav said, as the gasket clicked satisfyingly into place. "Please do not tease yourself on that account one moment longer! Of course I have designated an heir. Only this morning I re-initialed the document pertaining to the matter."

"Only this morning," Kareen repeated, voice suddenly silken with malice. "How very busy you are, younger brother. No doubt this reinitialing has much to do with yos'Galan's latest impropriety."

"yos'Galan's impropriety?" Daav demanded, letting go the gasket and staring wide-eyed at the boots. "Never tell me Aunt Petrella's been brawling in taverns again!"

"Yes, very good. The clan hovering on the brink of ruin and you in one of your distempers!" She stopped herself so sharply Daav fancied he had heard her mouth snap shut.

"On the brink of ruin?" he repeated, in accents of wonder. "Are we impoverished, then? Small wonder you disturb yourself to come to me here! I honor your sense of duty, that you brought the news yourself."

One of the boots lifted. Daav watched it with interest, wondering if he had so easily driven Kareen to the point of stamping her foot at him.

The boot hesitated, then sank, with only the faintest of heel-clicks, to the floor.

"Will it please you to come out?" she asked with astonishing mildness. "It would be best, could we discuss a certain matter face to face."

Beneath the cycle, Daav frowned. Kareen's conversation rarely descended into civility. She must want something from him very badly, indeed.

"Well," he said, by way of seeking a range, "I had hoped to effect the necessary repairs this morning . . ."

"I see." That, at least, was as acerbic as a brother might wish, but the sentence that followed was nothing short of alarming. "If you will name a time when it will be convenient to speak with me regarding a matter of utmost seriousness, I shall endeavor to wait upon you then."

Oh, dear, Daav thought. *If this goes on we'll actually have her calling me by name.*

He toyed with the notion of sending her away until the afternoon, but reluctantly gave it up. The interview with Anne Davis might well prove lengthy and he had no wish to crowd himself on a matter of such importance.

Sighing lightly, he turned onto his back and called out, "A moment! I shall attend you forthwith!"

He then scrambled out from beneath the Hebert, an operation not abundant of grace, and came 'round to lean a hip against the fender, stripping off his oily gloves as he considered his sister's face.

"All right, Kareen. What is it?"

She flinched at the state of his clothes, which was expectable in one who regarded dirt as a personal affront, but forbore from comment.

Instead, she bowed, if not respectfully then at least with that intent, and straightened to look him in the eye.

"It has come to one's attention," she said, mildly, "that the delm has Seen a child called yos'Galan, which yos'Galan has not likewise Seen. Such an irregular circumstance must, alas, awaken the liveliest speculations among those who move in the world. That the child exists outside of any recorded contract thickens the sauce, while the fact of mixed parentage adds piquancy for those whose favorite dish is scandal broth."

Herself chiefest among them, Daav thought uncharitably. He raised his eyebrows.

"I must say, it seems a very bad case, put thus."

"And yet not entirely hopeless," Kareen assured him. "Given one who is known in the world, who possesses the necessary skills, working with the clan's interest at heart—the broth may never gain the dining board." She inclined her head.

"It is thus that I may serve Korval."

"You offer to undertake damage control, do you?" He grit his teeth against a surge of anger at the effrontery of it. Kareen, to wash Er Thom's face for him? More likely the scheme of letting a house in Solcintra would find the delm's favor than—

"How much?" he snapped, barely resisting the temptation to address her in the mercantile mode.

Kareen stared. "I beg your pardon?"

"Oh, come, come!" He moved a hand in a sweeping, deliberately meaningless gesture. "Surely we know each other too well to pretend of coyness! You offer to perform a service.

I desire to know your price. I will then decide if the price is fair or dear." He met her eyes, his own hard as black diamond.

"Tell me what you want, Kareen."

She touched her tongue to her lips, though she matched him, stare for stare.

"I want my heir returned me."

Of course. Daav reached up and fingered the silver twist hanging in his ear, souvenir of his Scouting days.

"Your heir," he mused, letting his gaze wander from hers and fix upon a point slightly above her head. He continued to play with the earring. "Enlighten me. Has your heir a name?"

"His name is Pat Rin, as you well know!"

Well, at least they had done with that unnatural civility. Daav very nearly smiled as he let the earring go.

"And have you seen Pat Rin of late?"

"I saw him not twelve-day gone," she answered, somewhat snappishly.

"So nearly as that. Then you will be able to tell me of his latest interest."

"His interest?" Kareen glanced aside. "Why, his studies interest him, naturally, though I must say that Luken bel'Tarda does not insist upon the level of achievement I consider—" She broke off, respiration slightly up, and fingered the brooch at her throat before continuing.

"He is forever rambling about outdoors, so I expect, as all boys, he is fond of falling in streams and—and climbing trees and fetching down bird's nests . . ."

"Guns," Daav said gently. Kareen's head jerked toward him as if he had pulled a wire.

"Guns?" she repeated blankly.

"He bids fair to become an expert on guns," Daav told her. "Everything about them interests him. How they work. Why one sort is superior to another sort. How they are put together. How they are taken apart. Relative benefits of velocities versus projectile size. The theory of marksmanship." He bowed slightly. "When I last visited, I took him a beginner's pistol and we had a bit of target practice. I would say, should his interest continue, that he holds potential as a marksman of some note."

"A *marksman*." Kareen did not even try to mask the loathing in her voice.

Daav raised an eyebrow. "Our mother belonged to Tey Dor's, did she not? And successfully defended her place as club champion for five years together. Why should Pat Rin not be as good—or better? Or at very least have the chance to explore his interest to its fullest?

"But you are not interested in such matters," he continued after a moment. "You are most naturally interested in knowing whether the service you offer will be accepted." He moved a hand in negation. "Your price is found too high."

"So." It was nearly a hiss. "Er Thom yos'Galan is to be allowed a bastard mongrel and not required to make so much as a bow to society! But I, who have done duty and desire only to serve the clan, must have my son fostered away without my consent, for no reason other than *you* had decided—"

"I will remind you that the delm decided," Daav cut in. "I shall also give you two pieces of advice: The first is to compose yourself. The second is that you drop the words 'bastard' and 'mongrel' from your vocabulary. The child's name is Shan yos'Galan. He is the son of Er Thom yos'Galan and Anne Davis, both of whom acknowledge him as their own, so you see that 'bastard' is inexact."

" 'Mongrel' however is no more than plain truth!" Kareen cried, apparently choosing to ignore his first piece of advice.

"I find the word offensive," Daav said evenly, and sighed sharply. "Come, Kareen, have sense! Your concern is that those with nothing better to do than scrounge for trouble will scan back through *The Gazette* and find that there has been no contract between Er Thom yos'Galan and Anne Davis, with the child to come to Korval. Eh?"

"Yes, certainly—"

"And yet you choose to ignore the fact that persons of such mind will without difficulty find listed in that same *Gazette* the information that Pat Rin yos'Phelium has been taken from his fostering and returned to his mother. And that they will think to themselves, *bribe*."

"And you consider yourself equal to the task of cleaning Korval's melant'i among the High Houses—"

"I remind you again that I am delm," Daav interrupted

with exquisite gentleness. "Should Korval's melant'i require repair, it is no less than my duty to see such repair done. However, there is nothing to be mended. The clan accepts who it will, and no explanations due any outside of the clan." He took a careful breath.

"I advise you to leave me, Kareen. Now."

Her lips parted but no words came and in a moment she had made her bow.

"Good-day," she stated, in a tone so absolutely neutral it might be said to be mode-less. She left him then, quickly, heavy steps rattling the paving stones.

Daav stood where he was until he heard a motor start up, far down the hill. Then and only then did he allow his shoulders to lose their level rigidness and, pulling the gloves back over his hands, went to put his tools away.

They woke early, shared a glass of morning wine and a leisurely, sensual shower. Then, like children sneaking a holiday, they had gone to explore the house.

Anne was soon thoroughly lost, her head a muddle of Parlors, Public Rooms and Receiving Chambers, and at last stopped in the middle of an opulent hall, laughing.

"Don't leave me, love, for if you did I'd never find my rooms again!" She shook her head. "I can see I'll have to carry a sack of bread crumbs with me and remember to scatter them well!"

"Yes, but you know, the servants are very efficient," Er Thom murmured, swaying close and smiling up into her face. "Likely they would have the crumbs swept up far ahead of the time you wished to return."

"Then I'm lost! Unless you'll draw me a map, of course."

"If you wish," he replied and she looked down at him, exotic and achingly beautiful in the embroidered house-robe. He shook the full sleeves back and caught her hands in his.

"Shall I show you one more thing?" he murmured, eyes bright with the remains of his smile. "Then I swear I will allow you to eat breakfast."

"One more thing," she agreed, giving herself a sharp mental rebuke: *Don't gawk at the man, Annie Davis!*

"This way," Er Thom said, holding tight to one hand and keeping so close to her side that his robe bid fair to tangle in her legs.

They walked the hallway without mishap, however, and went midway down one slightly shorter.

"Here," he said, squeezing her hand lightly before he let it go.

Stepping forward, he twisted an edge-gilt china knob and stepped back with a fluid bow. "Enter, please."

Anne hesitated fractionally. The bow had been of honored esteem, but Er Thom's eyes showed an expectation that was nearly hunger. Smiling slightly, she went into the room.

The walls were covered in nubby bronze silk, the floor with a resilient grass-weave the color of Jelaza Kazone's leaves. A buffet along the back wall supported two small lamps and there were bronze sconces set at precise intervals around the walls. Three rows of twelve chairs each were arranged in a precise half-circle before a—

"It's beautiful," she breathed, going across the woven mat as if the omnichora had reached out a hand and pulled her forward. She stroked the satiny wood, pushed back the cover and ran her fingers reverently over the pristine ivory keys.

"It pleases you?" Er Thom asked from her side.

"Pleases me? It overwhelms me—an instrument like this . . ."

"Try it," he said softly and she shot him a quick look, shaking her head as she lifted her hand from the silent keys.

"Don't tempt me," she said, and he heard the longing in her voice. "Or we'll be here all day."

He caught her hand, lay it back on the keyboard, fingertips lazing over her knuckles.

"Turn it on," he murmured. "Play for me, Anne. Please."

It took no more encouragement than that, so hungry was she to hear the 'chora's voice, to test its spirit against her own.

She played him her favorite, *Toccata and Fugue in D Minor*, an ancient piece meant for the omnichora's predecessor, the organ. It was an ambitious choice, without the notation before her, but her fingers remembered everything and threw it into the perfect keyboard.

The music filled the room like an ocean, crashing back at her, bearing her up on a wave of sound and emotion until she thought she would die there, with the music so close there was no saying where it stopped and Anne Davis began.

Eventually, she found an end, let the notes die back, let herself come out of the glory, and looked at Er Thom through a haze of tears. She scraped her sweat-soaked hair back from her face and smiled at him.

"What a glorious instrument."

"You play it well," he said, his soft voice husky. He moved a step closer from his station at her side. It was then that she saw he was shivering.

"Er Thom—" Concern drove all else before it. She spun around on the bench, reaching out for him.

"Hush." He caught her questing hands, allowed himself to be pulled forward. "Anne." He lay his cheek against her hair, gently loosed a hand to stroke her shoulder.

"It is well," he murmured, feeling the way her muscles shivered with strain, in echo of his own. He stepped back and smiled for her, tugging lightly on her hand. "Let us go and eat breakfast. All right?"

"All right," she said after a moment, and turned to power-off the 'chora, and to cover the glistening keys.

They were in the dining room, rapt in each other, various dishes scattered near them on the table. Er Thom was wearing a house-robe, the Terran scholar a plain shirt and trousers.

Petrella glared at them for several minutes, her fingers gripping Mr. pak'Ora's arm. When she was convinced that neither her son nor the guest would soon turn a head and decently see her, she hit the floor a sturdy thump with her cane.

Both heads turned then, but it was Er Thom's eye she wanted.

"You, sir!" she snapped, "a word, of your goodness." She stumped off with no more than an inclination of the head as good-morning to the guest.

Er Thom sighed lightly and put his napkin aside.

"Excuse me, friend," he said softly, and went off in the wake of his mother.

CHAPTER TWENTY-FOUR

A Dragon will in all things follow its own necessities, and either will or will not make its bow to Society. Nor shall the prudent dispute a Dragon's chosen path or seek to turn it from its course.

—From *The Liaden Book of Dragons*

"You will have the goodness to explain," Petrella announced as the patio door closed behind the butler, "why *three* messages to your personal screen have gone unanswered from the time of sending to this moment?"

Er Thom bowed. "Doubtless because I have not gone by my rooms since an hour before last evening's Prime meal, nor have I collected messages from the house base."

Petrella took a deep breath, fingers tightening ominously around the head of her cane. A breeze played momentary tag with the flowers at the edge of the patio, gave up the sport to tease the sleeves of Er Thom's robe, then veered again, showering Petrella with flower-scent as it chased off.

"Mother, allow me to seat you," he murmured, slipping a solicitous hand beneath her elbow. "You will overtire yourself."

It was just such gentle courtesy as he was wont to offer. Tears filled Petrella's eyes as she accepted it, though she could not have said whether they were tears of rage or of love.

Love or rage, her voice shook when next she spoke.

"If you think that I will close my eyes to any impropriety you and that—*person*—chose to perform in this house—"

"Forgive me." He did not raise his voice, but some slight edge, immediately recognizable to those who were of Korval—and those who dealt with them—warned her to silence.

"Professor Davis is a guest of the House," he continued after a moment, voice unremittingly gentle. "The Code teaches us that the well-being of the guest is sacred. Professor Davis is—accustomed—to depending upon me for certain comforts; she felt herself adrift among strangers, alone on a world far different than her own. Shall I doom her to sleeplessness and worry from a concern for *propriety*? Or shall I offer accustomed and much-needed comfort, that she might rest easy in our House?"

"All from concern for the guest," Petrella said acidly. "I am enlightened! Who would have considered you possessed the genius to twist Code in such a wise, all with an eye to gain your own way! *I* had thought you a person of melant'i, but I see now that judgment—and the judgment of your foster mother—was in error. I see that what I have is a clever halfling, strutting his own consequence and flaunting his faulty understanding for all the world to see! Never fear that I am too ill to lesson a disobedient boy. Give me that ring!"

Er Thom froze, eyes wide in a face gone somewhat pale.

"Well, sir? Will you have me ask it twice?"

Slowly, then, he raised his hands; slowly, drew the master trader's amethyst from his finger. He stepped forward and bowed, and lay the ring gently in her palm.

"So. We have at least a base of obedience upon which to build. You relieve me." She clenched her fingers, feeling the edges of the gem cut into her palm. "With this ring you give me your pledge, Er Thom yos'Galan. You pledge you will withhold such—comforts—as you have been accustomed to provide the Terran scholar, beginning immediately. Carry through your pledge and in eleven day's time, when her guesting is done, you may ask me for your ring." She gripped the gem tighter as she spoke, grateful for the slight, simple pain.

"Fail of your pledge and I shall return this ring to the Trade Commission, and ask that your license be withdrawn."

There was little chance that the Trade Commission would revoke the license of Master Trader Er Thom yos'Galan. But a request for revocation would mean a review. And a review would suspend Er Thom's ability to trade for a minimum of two Standard Years.

Er Thom drew a deep breath. Perhaps he meant to speak. If so, he was rescued from that indiscretion by the cheery voice and sudden advent of his cha'leket.

"Good-morning, all! What a lovely day, to be sure!" Daav paused beside his foster-brother and made his bow, all grace and easy smiles.

"Aunt Petrella, how delightful to see you looking so rested! I am come to speak with the guest. Is she within?"

"In the dining hall," Petrella told him, with scant courtesy, "when last seen."

"I to the dining hall, then." He turned and caught Er Thom's hand. "Good-morning, darling! Have you been naughty?"

Er Thom laughed.

Daav smiled and raised the hand he held, bending his head to kiss the finger which the master trader's ring had lately adorned.

"Courage, beloved," he said gently. Then he loosed his brother's hand and vanished into the house.

"Another mannerless child!" Petrella snapped peevishly, flicking her hand in dismissal. "Leave me," she commanded her son. "Take care you recall your pledge."

Anne lowered her coffee cup, glancing up eagerly as a shadow flickered across the dining room door.

Alas, the shadow was not Er Thom, returning from his interview with his mother, but Er Thom's foster-brother. She rose quickly and bowed good-morning, but some of her disappointment must have shown in her face.

"Ah, it is only Daav!" that gentleman cried, striking a pose eloquent of despair in the instant before he swept his own bow of greeting. "Good-day, Scholar."

It was a bit of incidental theater worthy of one of Jerzy's more manic days and she gave it the laughter it deserved.

"But I thought we'd agreed that I was to be Anne, not 'Scholar'," she protested.

"My dreadful manners," he said mournfully and Anne grinned.

"If you're looking for Er Thom, his mother needed to speak with him for a—"

"Yes, I've seen them," Daav interrupted, leaving Adult-to-Adult and entering Terran. "But it's you I've come to speak with. Have you half-an-hour?" He tipped his head. "There's a room down the hall where we may be private."

"The whole house is full of rooms where people can be private," she told him, coming slowly around the table.

"Have you seen all of Trealla Fantrol? You must be entirely exhausted." He bowed her through the door ahead of him.

"Only a corner of it, I'm afraid." She sighed. "My head's in a muddle. I'm not even sure I can find the 'chora room again."

"So you have seen that," he murmured. "How did you find the omnichora?"

"It's magnificent," she said frankly. "The Academy of Music on Terra has none finer."

He sent her a glance from beneath his lashes, a trick he shared with Er Thom, else she would never have caught it.

"Have you been to the Academy of Music on Terra, I wonder?"

"I was there on scholarship for two years," she said evenly. "Funding slipped in the third year and there was no way my family could—" She shrugged, cutting herself off.

"I went home and finished out college, snared a fellowship and went on to advanced work."

In record time, she added silently. Driven by the grief of losing her first love, determined to make a success of her second, studying to the exclusion of everything, even—especially—friendship . . .

"I see," Daav said, guiding her into a small room and pulling the door closed. He waved toward a pair of overstuffed, almost shabby chairs.

"Please, sit. May I give you wine?"

"Thank you—white, please."

The chair she chose was delightfully comfortable, the seat wide enough for her hips, the tall back sweeping 'round her shoulders, and sufficiently high-set that she barely needed to fold her legs at all.

Daav sat opposite her, placing two glasses on the low table between them.

"So, now." He settled back into his chair. "I have questions which must be answered. Believe that I do not wish to distress you in any way." He smiled. "Er Thom would hand me my ears if I did, you know."

She laughed. "Yes, very likely!"

"Ah, you don't think so? But surely it's no more than duty to protect the peace of a proposed spouse?"

"A proposed—oh." She shook her head. "Er Thom told you that he asked me to sign a marriage contract. I turned him down, and if he didn't tell you that he should have."

"He did," Daav said gently.

"Then what—" She frowned, searching his thin, foxy face. "I don't understand."

"Hah." He tasted his wine, considering her over the edge of the glass.

"May I know," he said eventually, "your intentions toward my brother?"

She barely knew, herself. It was plain she would have to give the man up—soon. Unfortunately, it was equally plain that giving him up was like to rip the living heart out of her.

Anne reached for her glass, buying time with a sip of wine. When she had put the glass aside, she was no closer to an answer.

"Should we," she asked, flicking a glance at Daav's face, "be having this conversation in—the High Tongue?"

"Certainly, if you would feel more comfortable," he said agreeably. "But I find Terran so free, don't you? No need to sift through a dozen modes in search of one particular nuance . . ."

She grinned. "It's only that I thought, since I seem to be speaking with the delm—"

"Ah, my regrettable manners! The delm, stuffy fellow that he is, remains aloof for the moment. You are speaking to Daav yos'Phelium, on behalf of his brother, who asked that I talk with you."

"Regarding my intentions?" Drat the man, why couldn't he ask her himself, then?

"Or your feelings," Daav murmured. He tipped his head. "It's an impertinence, I know. Alas, I've always been a impertinent fellow—and my brother is very dear to me."

She glanced up, charmed by his candor.

"Well," she said wryly, "he's very dear to me, too. How I'm going to give him a tolerable good-bye at the end of semester break is more than I can see." She shook her head.

"I should never have come to Liad—I see that now. It was only that he—he came to find me. *Me*. He was in trouble—" she smiled, recalling Er Thom's way of it—"in *difficulty*. And I thought, foolishly enough, that I could help . . ." She glanced aside.

"Nothing foolish at all," Daav said gently, "in wishing to aid a friend."

"Yes, but I should have thought it through," she said, biting her lip. "Naturally, you, or his mother or—other friends—would be more able to help him than—than a Terran." She raised her eyes to meet Daav's black gaze.

"I'm a handicap to him here, whatever his trouble is. But he wanted the delm to count Shan—it was so important—and then I had word from Scholar yo'Kera's associate and—oh, it all seemed to fall into some sort of pattern! Shan would be counted—that was small enough—my friend's associate would get her assistance, and—" She faltered, swallowing against sudden tears.

"And you would help Er Thom extricate himself from his difficulty," Daav finished for her. There was a slight pause. "You didn't think of parting?"

She laughed ruefully. "At the beginning, I was braced—waiting for him to leave. Of course he would have to leave, I knew that. But he stayed and he kept insisting that we go to Liad and I kept insisting that Shan and I would stay on University—" She shook her head.

"Quite a donnybrook—and all wasted effort. Er Thom got his way, of course—*that* should teach me not to argue with a master trader! The more we were together, the less I thought of parting. He was with me and I loved him—more now—much more now—than—before." She glanced down, saw her fingers twisted around each other on her lap, sighed and looked up. "Is that what you wanted to know?"

Daav's eyes met hers with a curious intensity.

"You never thought of a lifemating?" he asked.

Anne frowned. "I'm Terran."

"And a Terran wife must necessarily be a burden," he commented dryly. "Yet, if he offered a lifemating—"

"No." She shook her head decisively. "No, I couldn't let him do that. It's not—necessary—that he make such a—I'll be able to—to show him a dry face, when it's time to leave."

"Will you?" His voice was very soft, one eyebrow well up.

Anne looked at him, feeling the tightness in her chest. "Yes, I will," she said with a certainty she was a long way from feeling. "I've done it before, after all."

"I might indeed give him his ring back," Petrella informed her nephew tersely. "He knows what he must do to earn it."

"Yes, but only consider the unnecessary speculation awakened in the minds of the idle," Daav urged, "does he but go into Solcintra thus."

"There is no reason for Er Thom to go into the city."

Daav stared. "Why, there is *every* reason for him to do so!" he cried. "The normal demands of his duty take him to Solcintra and the Port many times over a twelve-day." He checked his pacing. "Unless you've relieved him of those, as well?"

"Certainly not," she said, righteously. "Only the Trade Commission may relieve a master trader of his duties."

Daav clamped his jaw against a sharp return to that and mentally reviewed a Scout's relaxation exercise, deliberately bringing his anger under control.

"Aunt Petrella," he said after a moment, with credible, if fragile, calm. "If you believe Er Thom will keep from duty simply because you choose that he not wear mark of rank, you have a very odd view of his character."

"Thank you!" she snapped. "I choose to teach him obedience, sir, as I told you last evening. You will not interfere in this."

"You wish to shame the clan's master trader before the Port entire and claim it's none of mine? Aunt—"

She struck the floor with her cane. "I will not have him interpreting Code for his own benefit!"

Daav froze, staring at her out of wide eyes.

"Isn't that what it's for?"

Petrella glared, thin chest heaving with rage, hands gripped like talons about the head of her cane.

"I may die before your eyes this moment," she said grimly, "and leave you a wrongheaded, disobedient boy as thodelm. It's no less than you deserve."

"I don't *want* a dog broken to heel!" Daav shouted, control and gentle-speaking alike be damned. "I want intelligence, clear sight, strength of duty—as my mother did before me! And I tell you now, Chi's sister, if you break Er Thom yos'-Galan, you break Korval!"

She straightened in her chair as if he had struck her, sucked in breath for she barely knew what reply—

Too late. Daav was gone.

CHAPTER TWENTY-FIVE

The dramliz want young Tor An's genes. Farseers predict twins from the match and offer the girl-child to us—to Clan Korval—as settlement.

Jela would say that a wizard on board tips the scale to survival—which remains sound reasoning, though we're planet-bound now and in honorable estate, or so the boy will tell me . . .

As it transpires, Tor An met his proposed wife several days ago, through Dramliza Rool Tiazan's good graces, I make no doubt! The boy's smitten, of course, so the marriage is made.

Perhaps the girl-child will fail of being dramliz . . .

—**Excerpted from Cantra yos'Phelium's Log Book**

"**Master Merchant bel'Tarda,**" Mr. pak'Ora announced from the doorway. "Master Pat Rin yos'Phelium."

Petrella glanced up from her desk with ill-concealed irritation as Luken, looking every inch the rug merchant he was, crossed into the room, holding a dark-haired boy of about six Standard Years by the hand.

The man bowed greeting between kin, a certain trepidation marking the gesture. The boy's bow, of Child to Clan Elder, was performed with solemn exactitude. He straightened, shifting the brightly-ribboned box he carried from the left hand to the right, and showed Petrella a sharp-featured face dominated by a pair of wary brown eyes.

"Good-day, Luken," Petrella said, inclining her head. For the boy, she added a smile. "Good-day, Pat Rin."

"Good-day, grand-aunt," Pat Rin responded politely, nothing so like a smile in either lips or eyes.

Stifling a sigh, she looked to the man, who gave the impression of fidgeting nervously, though he stood almost painfully still.

"Well, Luken? What circumstance do I praise for this opportunity to behold your face?"

The face in question—blunt, honest, and mostwise good-humored—darkened in embarrassment.

"Boy's come to bring a gift to his new cousin," he said, dropping a light hand to Pat Rin's thin shoulder and flinging Petrella a look of respectful terror. "Just as his mother would wish him to do, all by the Code and kindness to kin."

It was perhaps the piquancy of a point of view that could suppose Kareen yos'Phelium capable of wishing her heir to associate in any way with an irregularly-allied child of lamentable lineage that saved Luken the tongue-flaying he so obviously anticipated. Petrella contented herself with a sigh and the observation that news traveled quickly.

Luken moved his shoulders. "No trick to reading *The Gazette*," he commented. "Do so every morning, with my tea."

Petrella, who had failed of her own custom of *The Gazette* with breakfast only this morning, openly stared.

"You wish me to understand that there is an announcement of Shan yos'Galan's birth in this morning's *Gazette*?" she demanded.

Luken looked alarmed, but stuck to his guns.

"Right on the first page, under 'Accepted.'" He closed his eyes and recited in a slightly sing-song voice: "'Accepted of Korval, Shan yos'Galan, son of Er Thom yos'Galan, Clan Korval, and Anne Davis, University Central.'"

He opened his eyes. "That's all. Simple, I remember thinking."

"Indeed, a masterwork of simplicity," Petrella said through

gritted teeth and was prevented of saying more by the unan-
nounced arrival of her son, dressed at last in day-clothes.

"Luken. Well-met, cousin." Er Thom's voice carried real
warmth, as had his bow. He smiled and held out a ringless
hand. "Hello, Pat Rin. I'm glad to see you."

The tense face relaxed minutely and Pat Rin left his foster-
father's side to take the offered hand. "Hello, Cousin Er
Thom." He held up the festive box. "We have a gift for Cousin
Shan."

"That's very kind," Er Thom said, matching the child's seriousness. "Shall I take you to him, so that you may give it?"

Pat Rin hesitated, glancing over his shoulder at his foster-
father.

"Of course you would welcome the opportunity to meet
your new cousin," Luken coached gently and Pat Rin turned
his serious eyes back to Er Thom.

"Thank you. I would like to meet my new cousin."

"Good. I will take you to him immediately. With my
mother's permission . . ." He bowed respect in her direction,
gathered Luken with a flicker of fingers and moved toward
the hallway.

Petrella gripped her chair.

"Er Thom!"

He turned his head, violet eyes merely polite in a face still
somewhat pale. "Mother?"

"An announcement of your child's acceptance," she said,
with forced calm, "appears in this morning's *Gazette*."

"Ah," he said softly, and, seeing that she awaited more,
added: "That would be the delm's hand."

"I see," Petrella said, and spun back to her desk, releasing
him.

He had just reviewed the last of the day's pressing business
and was considering a climb up the Tree. Seated on the plat-
form he and his brother had built as children, the world below
reduced to proper insignificance, surrounded by the benign
presence of the Tree—there he might profitably begin to consider Er Thom's tangle.

Indeed, he had pushed away from the desk and was halfway across the room when he heard his butler's familiar step in the hallway beyond and paused, head tipped to one side, wondering—

In another moment, wonder was rewarded by delight.

Mr. pel'Kana bowed in the doorway, "Scout Lieutenant sel'Iprith," he announced, standing aside to let her pass.

"Olwen."

Smiling, Daav went to meet her. Mr. pel'Kana discreetly withdrew, pulling the door shut behind him.

She was in leathers, as if new-come from space, and carried a small potted plant carefully in both hands. Looking up, she returned his smile, though somewhat less brightly than usual, and went past to put the pot on the desk.

Daav watched her, abruptly cold.

"Olwen?"

She spun away from the desk and flung against him, arms hard around his waist, cheek pressed to his chest.

She was sweet and familiar, warm where he was so suddenly chill. Daav hugged her close, rubbing his face in her hair.

They stood thus some time, neither speaking, then she stirred a little, muscles tensing as if she would move away.

He loosened his embrace, though he did not entirely free her. Olwen sighed and seemed to melt against him.

"Wonderful news, old friend," she said, so softly he could barely make out the words. "I'm recalled to active duty."

"Ah." He closed his eyes, acutely aware of the softness of her hair. He drew a careful breath.

"When do you leave?"

"This afternoon." Her arms tightened bruisingly; she released him and stepped back, one hand rising to brush his cheek. "Be well, Daav."

He caught her hand and kissed the cool fingertips. "Good lift, Olwen. Take care."

"As ever," she returned, which was the old joke between them.

He walked with her to the door, and watched as she went down the path and slipped into her car.

When the sound of the engine had gone beyond his hearing, he returned to his office, taking care that the door was well-closed behind him.

Nubiath'a sat upon the corner of the desk, where she had placed it. He shivered and bent his head, gasping, hands coming up to hide his face, though no one was there to see him cry.

"It's none of my business," Luken muttered for Er Thom's ear alone as they strolled along the hall, Pat Rin well ahead, "and you needn't bother snatching my hair off if I'm expected to turn a blind eye. But I wonder what's happened to your ring."

Er Thom lifted an eyebrow. "My thodelm keeps it for me," he said mildly, and smiled. "More than that loses you hair, Cousin."

"Fairly warned," the older man said with the good humor that won him friends in both the Port and the City.

"Announcement in *The Gazette* took me unaware—" he confided—"felicitations, by the way! But the last I knew of matters, yos'Galan was looking to Nexon to provide your heir—" He threw Er Thom a sudden look. "Not that it concerns me, of course!"

Er Thom laughed. "Poor Luken. Do we abuse you?"

"Well," the other replied candidly, "you and Daav cut up a trifle rash as cubs—and it's a certified wonder you weren't drowned as halflings. Though," he said hastily, as if recollecting himself, "I believe that to be the case with most halflings."

"And as adults we daily snatch you hairless," Er Thom murmured, "and do you no better good than setting Kareen at your throat."

"No," Luken said as they climbed the stairs. "No, I wouldn't have it that way. Daav visits often, you know—he and the boy are quite fond. I find him much easier now he's come back from the Scouts and taken up the Ring. You—you were always the sensible one, Cousin, and if you have from time to time been sharp, why, it's doubtless no more than I deserved. I'm not a clever fellow, after all, and it must be a trial to you quick ones to always be bearing with us slow. Kareen, now—" Luken sighed, eyes on the child who went so solemn and unchildlike ahead of them.

"The boy makes gains," he said eventually. "No more nightmares—well, none to speak of." His mouth tightened.

"My back's broad. Kareen yos'Phelium may do her worst to me, if it buys the child his peace."

Er Thom lay a hand on the other's arm, squeezing lightly. "Thank you, Cousin."

"Eh?" Luken gave a startled smile. "No need for that, though you're very welcome, I'm sure." He moved his shoulders. "That's always been the difference between you lot and Kareen. Good-hearted, the both of you, and not dealing hurt for the joy of hurting." He raised his voice.

"Ho, there, boy-dear, you've gone past the door!"

Up ahead, Pat Rin turned and came slowly back, holding the gift between his two hands.

Er Thom lay his palm against the nursery door and bowed his cousins within.

"Catch!" Anne tossed the bright pink sponge-ball in a lazy arc.

Shrieking with laughter, Shan grabbed, the ball skittered off his fingertips and he flung down the long room after it, giggling.

Anne shook her hair back from her face, clapping as he caught up with the ball and snatched it high.

"Now throw it back!" she called, holding her hands over her head.

"Catch, Ma!" her son cried and threw.

It wasn't too bad an effort, though it was going to fall short. Anne lunged forward on her knees, hand outstretched for the grasp—and turned her head, distracted from the game by the door-chime.

"Mirada!" Shan ran and threw himself with abandon into his father's arms, ignoring the other two visitors entirely. Anne came off her knees and went forward, ball forgotten.

Er Thom caught Shan and swung him up into an exuberant hug. "So, then, bold-heart!"

Beside them, the older of the two visitors—a sandy-haired man of perhaps forty-five, with a bluff, good-humored face—pursed his lips and lay a lightly-ringed hand on the thin shoulder of his companion. Anne smiled at the fox-faced little boy and received a solemn stare out of wide brown eyes.

"Play ball, Mirada!" Shan commanded as Er Thom set him down.

"Indeed not," he murmured. "You must make your bow to your cousins." He turned his head and caught Anne's eye, giving her a smile that jelled her knee-joints.

"Anne, here are my cousins Luken bel'Tarda and Pat Rin yos'Phelium. Cousins, I make you known to Scholar Anne Davis, mother of my child and guest of the House."

"Scholar." Luken bel'Tarda's bow puzzled for an instant, then she had it: Honor to One Providing a Clan-Child. "I'm glad to meet you."

"I'm glad to meet you also, Luken bel'Tarda." Honor-to-one-providing had no neat corollary, so Anne chose Adult-to-Adult, which was cordial without leaping to any unwarranted conclusions regarding Luken bel'Tarda's melant'i.

"Well, that's kind of you to say so," he said, with apparent pleasure. He squeezed the little boy's shoulder lightly. "Make your bow to the guest, child-dear."

Bow to the Guest it was, delivered with adult precision, and a quick, "Be happy in your guesting, Scholar Davis," delivered in a husking little voice, while the brown eyes continued, warily, to weigh her.

Anne bowed Honor to a Child of the House, adding a smile as she straightened. "You must be Daav's little boy," she said gently. Pat Rin ducked his head.

"Begging the lady's pardon," he said quickly, "I am the heir of Kareen yos'Phelium."

"But he has his uncle's look, certain enough," Luken added, rumpling the boy's dark hair with casual affection and sending Anne a glance from guileless gray eyes. "His mother's dark, as well. I don't doubt you'll be meeting her soon. Never one to allow a duty to languish, Lady Kareen."

"I look forward to the pleasure of meeting her," Anne told him, with was only proper, and wondered why he blinked.

"And here," Er Thom said gently, "is Shan yos'Galan. Shan-son, these are your cousins Luken and Pat Rin. Make your bow, please."

Shan hesitated, frowning after the Liaden words.

"Shannie," Anne prompted in Terran. "Bow to your cousins and tell them hello."

There was another momentary hesitation, followed by a bow of no particular mode. On straightening, he grinned and offered a cheery "Hi!"

Luken bel'Tarda sent a startled glance to Er Thom. "I'm afraid—oversight, of course!—I've never learnt—aah—Ter-ran—"

"Hi!" Shan repeated, advancing on his cousins. Pat Rin tipped his head, brown eyes wide.

"Hel-lo?" he said uncertainly.

Shan nodded energetically. "Hello, yes. Hi!" He thrust out a hand. "Shake!"

Pat Rin flinched and stared. Then, lower lip caught between his teeth, he reached out and brushed Shan's fingers with his.

"Hel-lo," he repeated and snatched his hand back. "I am glad to meet you, Cousin Shan," he said in rapid Liaden and held out the package he carried. "We've brought you a gift."

Shan took the package without a blink. "Thanks. Play ball?"

"My son thanks you for your thoughtfulness," Er Thom said for Luken bel'Tarda's benefit. "He asks if his cousin might play."

"That's very kind." Luken looked gratified. "It happens the boy and I are promised in the City today, but I'd be delighted to bring him to visit again soon. He might spend the day, if you've no objection, Cousin."

"Of course Pat Rin is always welcome," Er Thom said and Anne saw the tense little face relax, just a bit.

"That's fixed then," Luken said comfortably. He turned and bowed, giving Anne the full honor-to-one-providing treatment.

"Scholar Davis. A delight to meet you, ma'am."

"Luken bel'Tarda. I hope to meet you again."

Unprompted, Pat Rin made his bow, and then the two of them were ushered out by Er Thom, who turned his head to smile at her as he was departing.

"Well!" Anne sighed gustily and grinned at her son. "Do you want to open your present, Shannie?"

CHAPTER TWENTY-SIX

There is nobody who is not dangerous for someone.

—Marquise de Sevigne

The chime recalled him, blinking, from the world of invoices, profit and cargo-measures. He rose, half-befogged, and keyed the door to open.

"Anne." The fog burned away in the next instant, and he put out a hand to catch hers and urge her within.

"Come in, please," he murmured, seeing his delight reflected in her face. "You must forgive me, you know, for thrusting Luken upon you, all unexpected. I had not known you would be with our son—"

"Nothing to forgive," she said, smiling. "I thought he was delightful." The smile dimmed a fraction. "Though Pat Rin is very—shy . . ."

Trust Anne to see through to the child's hurts, Er Thom thought, leading her past his cluttered worktable, to the double-chair near the fireplace.

"Pat Rin progresses," he murmured, which was only what Luken had told him. "I thought him quite bold in dealing with our rogue."

She laughed a little and allowed him to seat her. He stood before her, availing himself of both her hands, smiling into her face like a mooncalf.

Her fingers exerted pressure on his, and a frown shadowed her bright face. She bent her head; raised it quickly.

"You've taken off your ring." The tone was mild, but the eyes showed concern—perhaps even alarm.

"Well, and so I have," he said, as if it were the merest nothing. He raised the hand that should have borne the ornament, and silked her hair back from her ear, the short strands sliding through his fingers.

"How may I serve you, Anne?"

She moistened her lips, eyes lit with a certain self-mockery. "Keep that up, laddie, and neither of us will get to our work." She turned her head to brush a quick, pulse-stirring kiss along his wrist.

"And that?" he murmured.

She laughed and shook her head so that he reluctantly dropped his hand.

"It happens I'm going to need that car you offered," she said, in a shocking return to practicality; "and probably a driver, too. Drusil tel'Bana can see me this afternoon."

"Ah. Shall I drive you?"

"I'd like that," she said, with a regretful smile. "But I'm liable to be some time. If Doctor yo'Kera's notes are in as bad a way as she's led me to think—" She shook her head. "No use you kicking your heels for hours while a couple of scholars babble nonsense at each other. It's a shame to even force a driver . . ."

"Nonetheless," Er Thom said firmly, laying a daring finger across her lips. "You *will* have a driver. Agreed?"

"Bully." She laughed at him. "I'd like to see what would happen if I *didn't* agree—but as it happens, I do. I'm not at all certain of my directions, and if the work should keep me until after dark . . ."

"It is arranged," he said. "When shall you leave?"

"Is an hour too soon?"

"Not at all," he returned, around a stab of regret. He stepped back, reluctantly releasing her hand.

Anne stood. "Thank you, Er Thom."

"It is no trouble," he murmured and she sighed.

"Yes, you always say that." She touched his cheek lightly

and smiled. "But thank you anyway. For everything." She lay a finger against his lips as he had to hers.

"I'll see you later, love," she whispered, then whirled and left him, as if it were too chancy a thing to stay.

"**Scholar** Davis, how delightful to meet you at last!" Drusil tel'Bana's greeting was warmth itself, couched in the mode of Comrades.

Anne bowed and smiled. "I regret I was not able to come sooner."

"That you came at all is sufficient to the task," the other scholar assured her. "I had barely dared hope—But, there! When I wrote I had not known you were allied so nearly with Korval. I do not always read *The Gazette*, alas, and with Jin Del's death—" She gestured, sweeping the rest of that sentence away. "At least I did read today's issue! Allow me to offer felicitations."

"Thank you." Anne bowed again. "I will share your felicitations with my son and his father."

Drusil tel'Bana's eyes widened, but she merely murmured, "Yes, certainly," and abruptly turned aside, raising a hand to point.

"Let me show you Jin Del's office. His notes—what are remaining—have been kept just as they were found when—The state of disorder, I confide to you, Scholar, is not at all in his usual way. I thought, at first, you know, that—but it is foolishness, of course! What sense to steal the notes for a work that will perhaps excite the thought of two dozen scholars throughout the galaxy? No. No, it must only have been that he was ill—much more ill, I fear, than any of us had known."

Anne glanced down at the woman beside her, seeing the care-grooved cheeks, the drooping line of her thin shoulders, the jerky walk.

"Doctor yo'Kera's death has affected you deeply," she offered, cautiously feeling her way along the border of what the other would consider proper sympathy and what would be heard as insult. "I understand. When I received your letter, I could barely credit that he was gone—he had seemed so vital, so brilliant. And I had only known him through letters. What one such as yourself, who had the felicity of working with him daily, must feel I may only surmise."

Drusil tel'Bana threw her a look from tear-bright eyes and glanced quickly aside.

"You are kind," she said in a stifled voice. "He was—a jewel. I do not quite see how one shall—but that is for later. For now, there is Jin Del's work to be put into order, his book to be finished. Here—here is his office."

She turned aside, fumbled a moment at the lockplate and stepped back with a bow when the door at last swung open and the interior lights came on.

"Please."

Anne stepped into the room beyond—and smiled.

Overcrowded shelves held tapes, bound books, disks and unbound printouts. Two severe chairs were crowded together at the front of the computer-desk, a battered, rotating work chair sat behind it. A filing cabinet was jammed into one corner, a double row of books at its summit. Next to it was a plain table, bookless, for a wonder, though that lack was more than made up by the profusion of 'scriber sheets, file folders and note cards littering its surface.

The floor sported a dark red rug that had once very possibly been good. The walls were plain, except for a framed certificate which declared Jin Del yo'Kera, Clan Yedon, a Scholar Specialist in the field of Galactic Linguistics, and a flat-pic, also framed, of three tall Terran persons—two women and a man— standing before an island of trees in a sea of grasslands.

"He had gone—outworld—to study, as a young man," Drusil tel'Bana said from the doorway. "Those are Mildred Higgins and Sally Brunner with their husband, Jackson Roy. Terrans of the sort known as 'Aus.' Jin Del had stayed at their—station—one season. They taught him to—to shear sheep." Anne glanced over her shoulder in time to see the other woman give a wavering, unfocused smile.

"He had another picture, of a sheep. He said that they were—not clever."

Anne grinned. "My grandfather kept sheep," she said, "back on New Dublin. He contended that they were smarter than a radish—on a good day."

Drusil tel'Bana smiled and in that instant Anne saw the

woman as she had been: Humorous, vivid, intelligent. Then
the cloud of grief enfolded her again and she gestured toward
the laden table.

"These are his notes. Please, Scholar, of your kindness . . ."

"It's what I came for," Anne said. She spun the desk chair
around to the table, reached out a long arm and snagged one
of the straight-backed 'student's' chairs.

"Do you have time to sit with me?" she asked Drusil
tel'Bana. "In case I should have questions as I go through?"

"My time is yours," the other woman said, sitting primly
on the edge of the straight chair.

Anne, perforce, sat in the battered, too-small desk chair,
and pulled the first stack of folders toward her.

Hours later, she sat back and scraped the hair from her face,
staring blankly at the blank wall before her. Her shoulder and
back muscles were cramped and she didn't doubt her legs
would stiffen up when she finally tried to stand—but none of
that mattered.

Disordered as his notes undoubtedly were, it was plain to
one who had corresponded with him and who tended in certain directions of thought herself, that Jin Del yo'Kera had
found it. He had found what she herself had been looking
for—the proof, the empirical, undeniable evidence of a common mother tongue, which had then given birth to its dis-
parate, triplet children: Liaden, Terran, Yxtrang.

Jin Del had found it—his notations, his careful reasoning,
his checks and double checks—all here, needing only to be
re-ordered, culled and made ready for presentation.

All here, all ready.

All, except the central, conclusive fact.

Anne looked aside, to where Drusil tel'Bana still sat patiently in her hard chair, face grooved with grief, but otherwise composed, calm.

"Is there," Anne asked slowly. "Forgive me! I do not wish
to ask—improperly, but I must know."

Drusil tel'Bana inclined her head. "There is no shame in an
honest inquiry, Scholar. You know that is true."

Anne sighed. "Then I ask if there are—people—who

would feel their—melant'i at—risk, should a fact be found that linked Terra to Liad?"

"There are many such," the other woman said, with matter-of-fact dreariness. "Even among your own folk, is there not the Terran Party, which would wish to deny Liad the trade routes?"

The Terran Party was a gaggle of cross-burning crackpots, but it *did* exist. And if the Terran Party existed, Anne thought wildly, why shouldn't there be a Liaden Party?

"You feel," Drusil tel'Bana said hesitantly, "that there is something—missing—from Jin Del's work?"

"Yes," Anne told her. "Something very important—the centerpiece of his proof, in fact. Without it, we merely have speculation. And all his notes lead me to believe that what he had was proof!"

Beside her, the other woman sagged, tears overflowing all at once.

"Scholar!" Anne reached out—was restrained by a lifted hand as Drusil tel'Bana shielded her face.

"Please," she gasped. "I ask that you do not regard—I am not generally thus. I shall—seek the Healers, by and by. Only tell me if you are able, Scholar."

Anne blinked. "Able?"

"Able to take on Jin Del's work, to find his proof and finish his lifepiece. I cannot. I lack the spark. But you—you are like him for brilliance. It was your thought that started him on this path. It is only fitting that you are the one to complete what you caused to begin."

And there was, Anne admitted wryly, a certain justice to it. Jin Del yo'Kera had unstintingly given of his time and his knowledge to the young Terran scholar he had graciously addressed as 'colleague'. Together, the two of them had constructed the quest represented by the notes now spread, helter-skelter, before her. That one of the two was untimely called aside did not mean that the quest was done.

She sighed, trying not to think of the years it might take to recapture that one vital fact.

"I will need to take this away with me," she told Drusil tel'Bana, waving a hand at the littered table. "I will require permission to go through his files—the computer. The books."

"Such permissions are on file from the Scholar Chairman

of the University. If you find it necessary to take anything else, only ask me, Scholar, and I shall arrange all." The Liaden scholar rose and went to the desk, pulled open a drawer and extracted a carry-case.

"What you have upon the table should fit in here, I think."

CHAPTER TWENTY-SEVEN

Love: the delusion that one woman differs from another.

—H. L. Mencken

"Sacrifice?"

Er Thom sagged to the edge of the desk, staring at Daav out of stunned purple eyes.

"Anne said it would be a *sacrifice* for me to become her lifemate?"

"She stopped short of the actual word," Daav acknowledged, "but I believe the sentence was walking in that direction, yes."

"I—" He glanced aside, moved a slender, ringless hand and rubbed Relchin's ears.

"There—must be an error," he said as the big cat began to purr. "She cannot have understood." He looked back to Daav.

"Anne is not always as—certain—of the High Tongue as—"

"We were speaking Terran," Daav interrupted and Er Thom blinked.

"I—do not understand."

"She said that, also." Daav sighed, relenting somewhat in the face of his brother's bewilderment. "She admits to being in love with you, darling—very frank, your Anne! However, she is sensible that a Terran lover makes you vulnerable, as she would have it, and that a Terran wife must make you doubly so." He smiled, wryly. "An astonishingly accurate summation, given that she does not play."

Er Thom chewed his lip.

"She asked me," he said, all his confusion plain for the other to read. "She asked me to guard her melant'i."

"She did?" Daav blinked. "In—traditional—manner?"

"We were speaking Terran," Er Thom said slowly. "Last evening, when I had gone to escort her to Prime. We were about to leave her apartment and she suddenly paused and looked at me with—with all of her heart in her face. And she said, *Don't let me make a mistake . . .*"

"And you accepted this burden on her behalf?"

"With joy. It was the avowal I had longed for, which she had not given, though there was certainly sufficient else between us—" He broke off, eyes wide. "It was plain," he said stubbornly. "There could have been no error."

"And yet," Daav said, "the lady spoke—plainly, I assure you!—of her intention to show you a dry face, when time had come for her to end her guesting and return to University."

"No." Er Thom's voice broke on the denial. He cleared his throat. "No. She cannot—"

Daav frowned. "Would you deny an adult person the right to her own necessities?"

"Certainly not! It is only that there must be some error, some nuance I am too stupid to see. Anne is honorable. To ask for the care of a lifemate and in the next breath speak of giving nubiath'a—it is not her way. Something has gone awry. Something—"

"And how," Daav cut in gently, hating what he must put forth. "if the lady asked not for lifemate's care, but for that of kin?"

"Kin?" Er Thom's face showed blank astonishment. "I am no kin of Anne."

"Yet her son is accepted of Korval," Daav murmured, "which might encourage her to believe herself in a manner—kin—to you."

A vivid image of Anne's body moving under him, a recollection of her kiss, her face transcendent with desire—Er

Thom glanced up. "I am not persuaded she believes any such thing."

"Hah." Daav's lips twitched, straightened.

"Another way, then. Understand that I honor her abilities in the High Tongue. However, you, yourself, say her proficiency sometime wavers. How if her understanding of custom is likewise uncertain? How if she should consider that a guest of the House might ask this thing of a son of the House?" He moved his shoulders.

"She has already made one error of custom, has she not?" He asked his brother's stubborn eyes. "In the matter of naming the child?"

"Yes," Er Thom admitted after a moment. "But there is no—" He broke off, sighing sharply.

"I shall endeavor to arrive at plain speaking," he said slowly, "and show Anne—" He stopped, wariness showing in his face.

"Is it—possible—that the delm will allow a lifemating between myself and Anne Davis?"

"The delm . . ." Daav moved from his chair, took two steps toward the desk and his brother—and halted, hands flung, palm out, showing all.

"The delm is most likely to ask you to consider what this affair has thus far bought you," he said levelly. "He is likely to ask you to think on the anger of your thodelm, who refuses to See your child, and who is prepared to ring such a peal over you as the world has never witnessed! The delm may ask you to look on the disruption your actions have introduced into the clan entire." He took a gentle breath, meeting his brother's eyes.

"The delm is likely to ask you if another coin might spend to better profit, brother, and the Terran lady released to her necessities."

Er Thom was silent, eyes wide and waiting.

"The delm may well ask," Daav concluded, with utmost gentleness, "that you give this lady up."

"Ah." Er Thom closed his eyes and merely sat, hip on the desk, one foot braced against the carpet, hand quiet along Relchin's back.

"With all respect to the delm," he murmured eventually,

and in the Low Tongue, so Daav understood that as yet the delm was safely outside the matter. "Might it be—permitted—to mention that one has striven for several years to put this lady from one's mind?" He opened his eyes, tear-bright as they were.

"Whatever the success of that enterprise, certainly she remained in one's heart." He moved his shoulders, almost a shudder. "The delm needs no reminder of one's—adherence to duty—saving this single thing. To give her up—that is to go now, tonight, to Solcintra, and give myself to the Healers."

And have Anne Davis ripped not only from his memory but from his daily mind, Daav thought, overriding his own shudder. *Which commission the Healers certainly would refuse.*

However, were Anne Davis to depart according to her stated intention, the Healers would very easily agree to assuage what measure of grief Er Thom might experience from the parting.

Daav stared at his brother's face, seeing the pain there, *feeling* his longing, and his need.

It's ill-done, he warned himself, though he already knew he would fail to heed his own warning. *You set him up to fail; you bait the trap that will spring forgetfulness with that which he most desires to recall . . .*

"Daav?"

He started, went forward and enclosed his brother in embrace. Laying his cheek against the warm, bright hair, he closed his eyes, and allowed himself a fantasy: They were boys again, the lie went, and nothing loomed to mar their love. They were one mind with two bodies, neither ascendant over the other. There was no dark power that one held which with a word would change the other, irrevocably and forever . . .

"A wager," Daav whispered, never caring that his voice trembled. It did not matter. Er Thom would take the bait. He must.

Daav stepped back and met his brother's eyes. "A wager, darling," he repeated softly.

"Tell me."

"Why, only this: Woo the lady while she is here. Win her—plainly, mind—and with full understanding between you! Win her aye, and win all. The delm shall overrule yos'Galan, the lady shall stand at your side, the child shall be your acknowledged heir. All." His mouth twisted wryly.

"Does your wooing fail to sway the lady from her necessities, then the day she leaves Liad is the day you make your bow to Master Healer Kestra."

"Hah." Er Thom's lips bent in a pale smile, eyes intent on Daav's face.

"Shall I lose, brother?" he asked softly.

"I will tell you," Daav said with the utter truth one owed to kin, "that I think you shall."

"So little faith!" Er Thom moved his shoulders. "It is only a continue of the throw made three years past. The game continues." He smiled more widely and gave a little half-bow from his perch against the desk. "We play on."

Daav returned the bow, speechless and grief-shot, in a fair way to hating delm and clan and homeworld and the necessities the weaving of all created—

"Never mind." Er Thom came off the desk and moved forward, raising a hand to cup Daav's cheek, to trace the line of a bold black brow.

"Never mind, beloved," he whispered, and touched the barbaric silver earring, sending it to trembling. "I shall not lose."

Some hours later, Daav leaned far back in his work chair and stretched mightily, fisted hands high over his head.

"Well," he said, righting himself and glancing over to where Er Thom sat beside him, silently perusing the screen. "Does that cover everything, do you think?"

"I believe it is a solid beginning," Er Thom replied, picking up his glass and sipping. "A contract of formal alliance between Clan Korval and Anne Davis. Free passage on any Korval ship. Right of visit to our son . . ."

"And half your personal fortune," Daav finished, tasting his own wine. "Your mother will dislike that excessively, darling."

Er Thom shrugged, much as he had earlier when this point had been raised.

"Money is easy to come by," he murmured now, dismissing his parent's displeasure as the merest annoyance. "Why should Anne not have comfort in her life?"

"Why, indeed?" Daav sighed. "I do wonder—"

Er Thom flashed him a quick purple glance. "What is it you wonder?"

"Only if the lady's understanding of custom was equal to the knowledge that her child belongs to Korval. I had the distinct impression that she meant to take him away with her when she returned to University." He sipped wine. "Though I could be mistaken."

"I am certain that she understands that Shan is of Korval," Er Thom said. "We had discussed it—several times."

"Quite a *donnybrook*, as the lady described it," Daav agreed. "Still, I wonder if she does know."

"Since I am already embarked upon a mission of clarity, I shall undertake to be certain that she does." Er Thom frowned. "What is a *donnybrook*?"

"An argument," Daav murmured, "named in honor, or so I am told, of a possibly mythic town on Terra where fisticuffs is the pastime of choice." He grinned. "A language to love, admit it!"

"I fear my proficiency falters daily," Er Thom said mournfully. Far down the hall, a clock could be heard striking the hour.

"Gods, only hear the time! And I expected early at Port tomorrow—"

Daav eyed him doubtfully. "Are you?"

"Yes, certainly. I must tend some matters on the *Passage* first, then there are orders to place, people to see . . ."

"Naturally enough, since you have been away for some time. However," Daav hesitated.

"Your thodelm expects there is no reason for you to go into Port. Or so she said."

Er Thom glanced down at his naked hands; back to Daav's face.

"My thodelm," he said levelly, "is—alas—mistaken."

"Yes," Daav agreed, "I thought that she might be." He waved a hand at the screen. "Get you home, then. I shall send this lot on to Mr. dea'Gauss. He should have the framed contracts to you within a two-day. You and I can then discuss any modifications that may be necessary before the final papers are presented to Anne."

"All right." Er Thom rose and smiled. "Thank you, Daav."

"Thank me, is it? Go home, darling, you're in your cups."

He let himself in through the door off the East Patio and went, surefooted and quiet, through halls illuminated by night-dims.

In the upper hallway, he lay his hand against a door-plate, and stepped gently into the darkened room beyond.

Anne lay in the long, wide bed, fast asleep in the wash of star shine from the open skylight. She looked vulnerable, thus, and incalculably precious: a jewel for which a man must gamble—and never think of losing.

He sighed as he stood over her, for he understood Daav's wager well enough, knew the dangers that dodged his steps and his brother's distress—who could have no less failed to offer the wager than Er Thom declined to take it. To be delm was an awesome and perilous duty. Daav had never wanted the Ring, which was Er Thom's certain knowledge. He had, indeed, begged his delm to pass him by, to place the Ring in abler hands—

In Er Thom's hands.

She had refused, which was wisdom, and Daav was thus Korval, gods pity him. Daav possessed full measure that trait which allowed him to offer such a thing as this twisty wager to his cha'leket, expecting him to fail—for the good of the clan.

It is a terrible thing, Er Thom thought, leaning above his sleeping love, *for a delm to have a brother.*

Beneath the star-glown blanket, Anne stirred and lifted a hand.

"Er Thom?" Sleep-drugged and beautiful, her voice. He caught her questing hand and bent to gently kiss the palm.

"Hush, sweeting," he murmured, soothing in the Low Tongue. "I had not meant to wake you. Sleep, now . . ."

"You, too," she insisted in Terran. "It's late."

"Indeed, and I am to go early to Port . . ."

"Tell the computer to wake you up," she mumbled, her

hand going slack in his as she slid back toward sleep. "Come to bed . . ."

With exquisite care, he lay her hand back atop the coverlet, then stood still in the starlight, watching her and recalling what his thodelm had ordered.

Thinking on Daav's damned, labyrinthine wager.

Woo the lady. Win her aye and win all . . .

Anne feared that a lifemate's burden of shared melant'i put him at risk in the world. Such fear did her only honor, so he considered it, and proved—if it happened he required proof—the depth of her love.

To win her, he must cross custom one final time, show her his heart and his innermost mind—as if they were already lifemated many years.

There was nothing dishonorable in such a path, as he conceived it. Anne was the one his heart had chosen; his lifemate, in truth, whatever a new dawn might bring.

Decided, he crossed the room to the house console and tapped in instructions to wake him at dawn.

Back at the bed, he removed his clothing and slid under the covers, curled against Anne's warmth—and plummeted into sleep.

CHAPTER TWENTY-EIGHT

A person of melant'i deceives by neither word nor deed and shall have no cause to hide his face from the world.

—Excerpted from the Liaden Code of Proper Conduct

He entered his office aboard *Dutiful Passage*, jacket collar still turned up against the rain in the Port below. One moment he paused as the door shut behind him, eyes closed, breathing in the elusive taste of ship's air, listening to the myriad, usual sounds that meant the *Passage* was alive all around him.

Sighing with something like relief, he opened his eyes and crossed the room to his desk, spinning the screen around to face him.

Twenty minutes later, he was still standing there, quick fingers plying the keypad. He barely registered the whisper of the door opening at his back and very nearly started at his first mate's voice.

"Ah, you are here!" Kayzin Ne'Zame exclaimed in Comrade, the mode in which they usually conversed. "I might have known you'd come up ahead of the early shuttle. Felicitations, old friend, on Korval's acceptance of your child! When shall I be pleased to make his acquain—"

Er Thom took a careful breath and deliberately turned to face her, hands in plain sight.

She chopped off in mid-word, her eyes leaping to his.

"Old friend?" Very careful, that tone, even from Kayzin, who had known him from his twelfth name day. Almost, Er Thom sighed.

Instead, he gave her courtesy, and the gentleness due a friend.

"My rating is intact," he murmured, gesturing toward the computer. "You may call the Guild Hall to be certain, if you wish."

"Yes, naturally." She moved her shoulders. "Ken Rik is concerned of Number Eighteen Pod and requests the captain's earliest attention. The radio-tech sent by the Guild was—unable to meet our standards. I took the liberty of dispatching her Port-side. Shipment from Trellen's World will meet us at Arsdred, something about the trans-ship company's credit record. I will look into that, of course . . ."

Er Thom leaned a hip against the desk and Kayzin drifted over to perch on the edge of a chair, both caught in the business they knew best, no blame nor shadow of doubt between them.

The afternoon among the warehouses was slightly less felicitous than the morning on his ship. There were none who actually refused to take his requisitions, though there were enough glances askance to leave one's belly full down the length of a long lifetime.

One fellow did demand a cantra to "hold" the order, to the very visible horror of his second. Er Thom gave him a long stare, then flicked the coin from his pocket to land, spinning, on the counter.

"A receipt," he said, entirely bland. The merchantman swallowed.

"Of course, Master Trader," he stammered, fingers jamming at the keys.

Still bland, Er Thom took the offered paper and gave it leisurely perusal before folding it into his pocket and going his way, setting his boot heels deliberately against the worn stone floor.

Some while later, he was in the public room of the Trade

Bar, having just concluded a trifle of business with Zar Kin pel'Odma. Wily old trader that he was, Zar Kin had not allowed himself even a glance at Master Trader yos'Galan's hands. Which, Er Thom thought, sipping a glass of cold, sweet wine, told as much about Trader pel'Odma's melant'i as it did about the speed at which news traveled, Port-side.

He touched the port-comm's power-off, sipped again at his wine and closed his eyes, wondering if it were worth walking to the Avenue of Jewels on the chance that Master Jeweler Moonel would be disposed to see him.

"Captain yos'Galan, how fortunate to find you here, sir!"

The voice was not immediately familiar, the accent unabashedly Chonselta.

Er Thom opened his eyes and looked up, encountering a pair of hard gray eyes in a determinedly merry face. Her hair was also gray and clipped close to her skull in the manner favored by Terran pilots. It was a style that showed her ears to advantage, and all the dozen earrings piercing each. On her hands she wore, not the expected hodgepodge jewelry of a Port-rat, but a single large amethyst, carved with the symbol of the Trader's Guild.

"Master Trader Jyl ven'Apon." So she introduced herself, clanless, bowing as between equals. She straightened and gave him a knowing look. "Captain."

Er Thom acknowledged her introduction with a bare nod of his head and fixed her with a gaze that would have given anyone of melant'i serious doubts regarding the wisdom of imposing further.

Jyl ven'Apon was far from entertaining any such doubts. Uninvited, she pulled out the chair Zar Kin pel'Odma had lately vacated and sat, arms folded on the table before her.

"One hears," she said, leaning forward with a show of candor, "that Er Thom yos'Galan has been seen about the Port this day, devoid of his master trader's ring. Of course, this can but pain those of us who wish him well, of whom there are—most naturally!—dozens. It is indeed fortunate that one such well-wisher as myself should have the means to offer—easement in loss."

"Oh, indeed?" Er Thom raised his eyebrows. "You fascinate me. But you merely mean to sell me another ring, of course."

The gray eyes narrowed and the face lost a little of its merriness, though she did bend her lips slightly in the parody of a smile.

"The—captain—will have his joke," she allowed. "But the matter in which I can provide easement is in the area of trade." She sent a sharp glance into his face. "You perhaps did not receive my correspondence regarding a certain extremely lucrative business venture. Several traders have already seen the advantages of this—venture—not merely in terms of the cantra to be earned, but in the sense of winning greater rank. Indeed, I do not think any who assist in bringing the project to fruition can escape the notice of the Trade Commission. In the case of some, the prospect of gaining—or regaining—the rank of master trader must carry all other considerations before it."

So that was the bait that had snared yo'Laney and Ivrex. Er Thom stared at her coldly.

"I recall the correspondence," he said flatly. "I will tell you that I hold severe doubts regarding the viability of your enterprise and am distressed to find you still enjoy hopes of luring others into a scheme that must fail. I suggest—most strongly—that you re-evaluate your plan of business in this instance, else a review before the Guild must be inevitable."

"Oh, must it?" She laughed, and deliberately poured herself a cup of wine from the pitcher.

"Will you call me up for review, *Captain*? I wish you might try!" She drank deeply of her cup and grinned. "But of course if you no longer care for amethyst, there's nothing more to be said."

Er Thom put his wine cup aside, turned the port-comm's screen around and pushed the keyboard across the table.

"You might," he suggested gently. "Call up today's Guild list of master traders in Port." He leaned back in his chair, hands folded before him on the table, face and eyes composed.

Her startlement showed clearly for an instant, then she spared him another hard-edged grin, hit the power-on and typed in the request.

Still grinning, she finished the dregs of her wine, poured more and turned her eyes back to the screen.

The grin faded.

Er Thom inclined his head.

"I had been taught that a master trader was made by skill, and that the ring bestowed upon attaining that level of skill was an acknowledgement, not a license." He lifted an eyebrow. "Doubtless, other clans teach other wisdom."

Jyl ven'Apon touched her tongue to her lips. "As you say."

"Ah. Allow me to offer advice, from one who is master of trade to one who wears the ring. Let the lithium deal go. Return the buy-ins you have collected. This would be equitable and not likely of failure, nor notice to the Guild for review."

"You threaten me, in fact."

"I am of Korval," Er Thom said softly. "I merely tell you what is."

She managed another laugh at that, though not so convincingly as formerly, and threw the rest of the wine down her throat. She then rose to bow a seemly enough farewell—and went away down the room, swaggering like a Low Port bravo.

Moonel had been in and willing, for a wonder, to talk, by which circumstance he did not arrive home until well after Prime, to find his mother at tea with Lady Kareen.

He made his bows from the doorway and, obedient to his mother's gesture, came forward to sit and take refreshment.

"I ask pardon," he murmured with all propriety, "that I show myself in all my dust. I am only this moment come from the Port."

His mother shot him a sharp glance. Kareen's was more leisurely—and, naturally, thorough.

"Why, Cousin Er Thom," said she, in tones of false concern, "I believe you may have misplaced your ring."

Bland-faced, he met her eyes. "You are mistaken, cousin. I am well-aware of the location of my ring."

"But to go thus to the Port," Kareen insisted, eyes gleaming with spite, "where the lack of rank-ring must be noted and commented upon, is—surely—foolish?"

"Is adherence to duty foolish?" Er Thom wondered, sipping his tea. "I cannot agree with that."

Kareen's eyes narrowed, but before she could launch another attack, his mother introduced a change of topic and the rest of the visit passed almost agreeably.

He stood and bowed as Kareen took her leave and was on the point of departure himself, when his mother snapped, "Stay."

Eyebrows up, he resumed his seat, folded his naked hands upon his lap and assumed an attitude of dutiful attentiveness.

"To the Port, is it?" Petrella snarled after a moment. "I bow to your sense of duty, sir. And where, one wonders, did duty dictate you sleep yestereve?"

Er Thom merely looked at her, eyes wide and guileless.

"I see," his mother said after a long minute. She closed her eyes. "In the time of the first Daav," she said eventually, "a certain Eba yos'Phelium was publicly flogged by her thodelm. The instrument employed was a weighted leather lash, from which Eba received six blows, laid crosswise, along her naked flesh. History tells us she carried the scars for the rest of her life." She opened her eyes and regarded her son's bland face.

"I bore you," she surmised. "Or perhaps you believe me too weak to wield the lash. Never mind—we shall speak of pleasanter things! Delm Nexon's delightful visit of this afternoon, for an instance."

Only silence from Er Thom, who kept his eyes and face turned toward her.

"Delm Nexon," Petrella said, "wonders—most naturally!—what Korval means by the announcement that appeared in yesterday's *Gazette*. She wonders if Korval has been toying with Nexon, by raising hopes of a match advantageous to both sides—*she* says!—and then withdrawing all hope in this churlish manner. Delm Nexon wonders, my son, if she has been insulted, though she does hope—very sincerely—that this will be found not to be the case."

When he still remained silent, she fixed him with a stern eye. "Well, sir? Have you anything to say, or will you sit there like a stump until dawn?"

Er Thom sighed. "Delm Nexon," he said softly, "is entirely aware that no insult has been given. No contract exists. Preliminary negotiations of contract-marriage flounder and fall awry every day. As to what Korval might mean by publishing notice of Shan's acceptance to the clan—that is entirely by the Code, and nothing to do with Nexon at all."

"Bold words," Petrella commented. "Bold words, indeed, A'thodelm. Especially as there is yet the matter of an heir to the Line—which is nothing to do with this *Shan.* I will have a proper heir out of you, sir, and I find in Nexon's daughter your suitable match." She held up a hand, stilling his move of protest.

"You will say that you do not know the lady—that we are no longer in the time of the first Daav. True enough. Nor do I wish to thrust you into the contract-room with a lady whose face you have not seen. You shall meet her beforehand."

"I will not—" Er Thom began and Petrella cut him off with a slash of her hand through the air.

"We have had quite enough of what you will and will not! What you *will* is what you are commanded by your thodelm. And you are commanded to attend the gathering that will be held in this house two evenings hence. At that time you will meet Syntebra el'Kemin, who I suggest you begin to think of as your contracted wife."

Er Thom's eyes were hot, though his voice remained cool. "Scholar Davis will yet be a guest in this house."

Petrella moved her shoulders. "The scholar is welcome to join the party, if she is so inclined. It may prove—instructive—for her."

"No!" He snapped to his feet, towering over her, slim and taut as a cutting cord. "Mother, I tell you now, I shall not—"

"Silence!" she shouted, pounding her cane on the floor. She lifted it, agonizingly slow, until the point was on a level with his nose.

"You do not raise your voice to me," she told him, Thodelm to Linemember. "Beg my pardon."

For a long moment he stood there, quivering with the fury that filled his eyes. Then, slowly, he bowed apology.

"I beg your pardon."

Eyes holding his, she lowered the cane-tip to the floor.

"Leave me," she said then. "If you are wise, you will go to your room and meditate upon the path of duty."

He hesitated a fraction of a heartbeat before he bowed respect to the thodelm—and obediently quit the room.

CHAPTER TWENTY-NINE

On average contract-marriages last eighteen Standard Months, and are negotiated between clan officials who decide, after painstaking perusal of gene maps, personality charts and intelligence grids, which of several possible nuptial arrangements are most advantageous to both clans.

In contrast, lifemating is a far more serious matter, encompassing the length of the partners' lives, even if one should die. One of the pair must leave his or her clan of origin and join the clan of the lifemate. At that time the adoptive clan pays a "life-price" based on the individual's profession, age and internal value to the former clan.

Tradition has it that lifemates share a "bond of heart and mind." In view of Liaden cultural acceptance of "wizards," some scholars have interpreted this to mean that lifemates are "psychically" connected. Or, alternatively, that the only true lifematings occur between wizards.

There is little to support this theory. True, lifematings among Liadens are rare. But so are life-long marriages among Terrans.

—From *Marriage Customs of Liad*

Anne sighed and pushed back from the computer. Standing, she stretched high on her toes, ceiling tiles an inch beyond her fingertips.

It takes going to Liad and living among folk half your own size to find a ceiling that's tall enough. She grinned and finished her stretch, glancing to Doctor yo'Kera's work table, where Shan sat, silky white head bent over his *Edu-Board.*

The *Edu-Board* was a self-paced, self-programmed wonder, sure enough, and it held Shan's attention like nothing before. Anne tipped her head, watching her son work, feeling a buzz of determined concentration somewhere in the behind of her mind.

Just like his ma, she thought, and felt her mouth twist into a smile. *And his da, too, truth be told.*

The smile grew a bit wistful. She had woken in the gray of dawn, to feel warm lips on her cheek and a light hand caressing her hair.

"Sleep again, darling," Er Thom whispered in the intimate, only-for-kin Low Tongue. "I shall see you this evening."

Drowsily obedient, she had nestled back into the quilt, waking again several hours later to full sunlight and the wonder of having *two* endearments from Er Thom within the space of a single night.

Gods love the man, she thought in exasperation. *How am I ever to leave, if he turns up sweet now?*

"Ma?" Shan looked up from his device. "Says play and rest."

"Module full?" She moved, bending over him to peer at the miniature screen.

EXERCISE TIME! The top line was in Terran, scribed in cheery blue letters. Below, in green letters, was the Liaden approximation: PLAY WITH THE BODY, REST THE MIND.

Anne blinked and looked down at the top of her son's bright head.

"What does this say?" she asked, pointing at the Terran letters.

"Time to exercise," Shan said, patient, if inaccurate.

Anne pointed at the Liaden line. "What does this say, Shannie?"

"I'ganin brath'a, vyan se'untor." He craned his head backward to look at her out of wide silver eyes. "Play in body, rest in mind. Mirada says. Mirada says, pilots run *and* think."

"Well, Mirada's certainly right there," Anne said wryly, recalling Er Thom's hair-raising dash between the lumbering big-rig and his son.

Planned that trajectory to a hair, laddie, she thought. *And then called it nevermind.* She sighed and reached down to touch her son's face.

"You like Mirada a lot, Shannie?"

"Love Mirada." He blinked solemnly. "Play now, Ma?"

She laughed and rumpled his hair. "Regular con artist." She shook her head ruefully.

"I expect I could use a rest, too. How's this meet your fancy, boy-o? We'll have us a race down to the snack shop at the end of the hall, nibble a bit, then come back for an hour more so I can finish my search line. OK?"

"OK!" he said energetically and popped out of his seat. "Last winner's a rotten egg!"

It was Jerzy who had taught Shan first winner and last winner, a philosophical concept that was about as alien to Liaden thought as you could get. Anne hesitated, turning to stare around Doctor yo'Kera's tiny, comforting office.

Liad.

Liadens.

An entire culture that counted coup, that held melant'i and the keeping of melant'i to be vital work. A culture cutthroat and competitive in every imaginable area, where people were divided into two camps—kin and opponents.

On Liad, there were never first winners and last winners.

On Liad, you won. Or you lost.

Anne shivered, remembering Drusil tel'Bana's grief-filled half-ravings. Had there been some esoteric balancing of social accounts which Doctor yo'Kera had lost, thus forfeiting the central proof of his life-work?

Forfeiting, as well, his life?

"Ma?" Shan tugged at her hand, bringing her out of her morbid dreamings. She smiled down at him.

"Ma's being a rare, foolish gel. Never mind." She opened the door, turned and made certain it was locked before she looked back to her son and dropped his hand with a flourish.

"Last winner's a rotten egg!" she cried and they were off.

•   •   •

It had taken more than an hour—or even two—to finish her systematic search of Doctor yo'Kera's private terminal. Somewhere in the midst of it, she roused herself to call Tre-alla Fantrol and leave two messages: One for the host, regretting that she would be unable to attend Prime meal.

And one for Er Thom—rather warmer—regretting the same and hoping to see him later in the evening.

You're shameless, she told herself. *Why not practice leaving go of the man now?*

But, after all, there would be plenty of time to practice life without Er Thom—later. Anne sighed and glanced over at Shan, who was curled up atop the work table, fast asleep in the nest of her jacket, white head resting on Mouse.

He woke on his own just as the data-core copy was completed. A disk sighed out of the side slot. She pulled it free and shut down the main system, shaking her head.

Fruitless.

She'd known it would be, of course, but hope had been there. The next task, she supposed, tucking the disk safely away into her case, was a search of the books—a daunting task, and one likely to take more time than remained of semester break.

She wondered if Er Thom might give her a special rate on shipping the things to University.

Books as ballast, she thought with a tired giggle. *Why not?*

"All right, now, laddie, it's home for us!"

Shan yawned and wriggled free of her jacket. She caught him under the arms and swung him to the floor.

"Gather your things and let's be off."

"OK."

In very short order, the *Edu-Board* was stowed in her carry-all, Shan was in his jacket and Mouse was in his arms. Anne shrugged into her own jacket, glanced once more around the tiny office, got a grip on her case and nodded to her son.

"Stay by me, now."

She made sure of the door, checking the lock twice, turned—and nearly fell over a man hovering at her elbow.

"For goodness'—" She retreated a step, which put her

back against the door, her hand rising toward her throat in a gesture of surprise.

The man—perhaps thirty, with a peculiarly blank face and curiously flat brown eyes, neat, forgettable clothing, neat, nondescript hair—also fell back a step, bowing profoundly.

"I beg your pardon," he said in expressionless Trade. "It seemed you were experiencing difficulty with the door and I had thought to offer aid."

Anne looked down at him—rather a way, as he was significantly shorter than Er Thom—and returned his bow of Stranger to Outworlder precisely.

"Thank you," she said, choosing the High Tongue mode of Nonkin, which was cool. Very cool. "I am experiencing no difficulty. I had merely wished to be certain the mechanism was engaged."

The man's eyes flickered. He bowed again—Respect to Scholarship, this time—and when he answered, it was in the High Tongue, Student to Teacher.

"You must forgive me if my use of Trade offended. I did not at first apprehend that of course you must be the Honored Scholar who shall complete Doctor yo'Kera's work." He lay his hand over his heart in a formal gesture. "I am Fil Tor Kinrae, Linguistic Technician, Student of Advanced Studies."

Anne inclined her head. "I am Anne Davis of University, Linguistics Scholar."

"Of course. But I keep you standing in the hallway! Please, allow me to carry your bag and walk with you to your—"

"Ma!" Shan's voice was sharp. She looked at him in surprise, saw him staring in—fright?—at the man before her.

"Go home, Ma! Go home *now*!"

"Oh, dear." She swooped down and gathered him up, felt him shivering against her, and threw a distracted, apologetic smile at the bland-faced grad student.

"I regret, sir. My child requires attention. Another time and we shall talk."

"Another time." Fil Tor Kinrae bowed precisely. "An honor to meet you, Scholar Davis."

"An honor to meet you, as well." Anne barely knew what she replied. Shan was never—*never*—afraid of strangers. Her

stomach cramped in fear as she turned and walked rapidly
down the hall, toward the carport.

The patient driver settled them in the back of the car and
wasted no time in putting the campus behind them. Gradually,
Shan's shivering stilled. He sighed and snuggled into her
arms.

"OK now, Shannie?"

"Uh-huh."

Anne rubbed her cheek against his hair, feeling decidedly
better herself. *Really,* she thought. *Of all the foolish starts,
Annie Davis . . .*

"What happened?" she asked her son softly.

He pushed his face against her neck.

"No sparkles," he whispered—and shuddered.

She was leaving the nursery, her thoughts on finding Er
Thom, when she was intercepted by no less a personage than
the yos'Galan butler.

"Scholar Davis." Stately and austere, he inclined his head.
"Thodelm yos'Galan requests the pleasure of your company
in the Small Parlor."

Which request, she thought wryly, had the force of command. She stifled a sigh and inclined her head.

"I shall be delighted to bear Thodelm yos'Galan company," she said, glad that the Mode of Acceptance leached any
flavor of untruth from her words.

"Follow me, please," the butler replied, and turned briskly
on his heel.

"Wine for Scholar Davis," Petrella yos'Galan directed and
wine there was.

Mr. pak'Ora also refreshed the cup on the table at the old
woman's side, then left, the door snicking shut behind him.

Petrella took up her wine and sipped, her movements firm
and formal. Anne followed suit—a solitary taste of wine, and
the glass put gently aside.

"You are comfortable in our house, Scholar?" Petrella's choice of mode this evening was Host to Guest.

Anne inclined her head and responded in like mode. "I am extremely comfortable. Thank you for your care, ma'am."

"Hah." Petrella glanced down, made a minute adjustment to the enameled ring she wore on the second finger of her left hand. Abruptly, she looked up, faded blue eyes intense.

"Your command of the High Tongue is praiseworthy, if I may extend a compliment," she said with formal coolness. "It is perhaps not to be expected that your grasp of custom be so exact." She smiled, slightly, coolly. "Indeed, I know well how slippery custom becomes, world-to-world. One would require Scout's eyes, to never err. Few of us, alas, are able to achieve so wide an understanding."

Anne eyed her dubiously, wondering if the old lady were going to give her a tongue-lashing for missing dinner. She inclined her head carefully.

"One hears that Captain yos'Galan's cha'leket had been a Scout."

"So he had. The children of yos'Phelium are often sent to the Scouts; it's found the training tames them." She paused. "The Scouts teach that all custom is equally compelling, which may well be true in the wide galaxy. On Liad, matters are quite otherwise."

Anne kept silent, hands folded tightly in her lap, waiting for her host to come to the point.

A smile ghosted Petrella's pale lips and she inclined her head as if the younger woman had spoken.

"A word in your ear, Scholar Davis?"

"Certainly."

"You have," Petrella said after a moment, "borne my son a child. Understand that we are grateful. At such a time in the clan's history, when the Line Direct is become so few, every child, no matter how irregularly gotten, is a jewel. You must never doubt that the clan's gratitude shall show itself fitly, nor that the child shall receive all care, nuturance and tutelage."

She paused, eyes sharp, and Anne hoped fervently that her face was properly bland, giving away nothing of her bewilderment.

"Necessity, however, exists," Petrella continued slowly. "It

existed before the advent of yourself and the child you give to
Korval. It exists now, unchanged. As much as your son shall
be a treasure to the clan, it cannot be denied that he is but half
of the Book of Clans. Such a one cannot be accepted as the
heir of he who will soon be Thodelm yos'Galan. The a'thodelm is aware of this. He is also aware that a contract-wife has
been chosen for him and that he is required now to wed. Indeed, a gathering in honor of the to-be-signed contract shall
be held in this house two evenings hence. You are welcome to
attend the gather, should you care to wish the a'thodelm and
his bride happy."

Care to wish him happy? Anne thought, around a jag of
icy, incredulous grief. *Could ye not have waited until I was
gone?* She wanted to scream the question at the woman across
from her. Instead, she swallowed and remained silent, hands
fisted on her lap, face determinedly smooth.

Once more, Petrella's faded eyes scrutinized. Once more,
she inclined her head as if Anne had made some fitting reply.

"My son speaks highly of you, Scholar. I believe that such
delight as you shared must long remain in fond memory.
However, it is now time for the a'thodelm to do his duty. He
will expect you to stand aside." She glanced down, rubbing
her ring with an absent forefinger.

"Surely," she murmured, eyes coming back to Anne's face,
"even among Terrans a pleasure-love must yield to a wife."

Sleep again, darling, Er Thom murmured tenderly in memory.

Confusion washed through her, threatening to tear away
her fragile mask of calm; she thought she must be trembling.
Fatal to call Thodelm yos'Galan's word into question. Even to
ask for a clarification of Shan's status in Clan Korval would
expose weakness, make her vulnerable . . .

Carefully, she inclined her head.

"I am grateful for the care of the House," she said, concentrating on keeping precisely to the mode of Guest to Host.
"Naturally, one would not wish to be untoward . . ." It was all
she could think of, but it seemed it was sufficient.

Petrella smiled her cool, ravaged smile and raised a hand
on which the thodelm's enameled band spun loosely.

"Pray do not say more. It is the honor of the House to guide the guest."

"Yes, of course." Anne stood, desperately willing her trembling legs to support her, and made her bow to the host. "I am certain you will forgive me for leaving you so soon," she said, though she was certain of no such thing. "My day was long and somewhat arduous. I feel the need of rest."

"Certainly," Petrella said, moving her hand with a remnant of grace. "Good health to the guest."

"And to the host," Anne responded properly, and forced herself to walk, slow and steady, from the room.

CHAPTER THIRTY

A Healer should be contracted to attend every birth for the purpose of keeping the mother's soul attached to her body and for easing the way through childbirth.

Such attention is doubly necessary in the case of one who has the honor to bear a child for an allied clan. In this instance, the child's clan must instruct the Healer in addition to blur memory and assuage any painful emotions the mother may otherwise experience.

A Healer should also be summoned before the one who gave the child-seed rejoins his own kin.

—From The Liaden Code of Proper Conduct

The child shall receive all care, nuturance and *tutelage . . .*

Sleep again, darling . . .

Even among Terrans, a pleasure-love must yield to a wife . . .

I am not a thief, to steal our son . . .

No sparkles!

The clan shall show its gratitude—

"Anne?"

Gasping, she spun, hands outflung, half-curled and protective.

Er Thom caught both, his fingers shockingly warm, reas-

suringly strong. Her friend, her love, her ally against Liad and
the terrors of Liaden custom—

Who had lied, after all, and stolen her son; who came to
bed with endearments in his mouth even as he planned to wed
someone other—

"Anne!" His grip tightened; worried violet eyes looked up
at her out of a face that showed clear consternation.

She made a supreme, racking effort. Fatal to antagonize Er
Thom. Fatal to assume, to assume—

"You're hurting me." Her voice sounded flat, cold as iron.
Cold iron, to bane an elf-prince . . .

His fingers eased, but he did not let her go. Face turned to
hers, concern showing plain as if it were real, he bespoke her
in the Low Tongue.

"What has happened, beloved? You tremble . . ."

"I've just come from your mother—" She blurted the truth
in Terran before she considered what lie would best cover her
agitation.

But it seemed the truth served her purpose very well.
Anger darkened Er Thom's eyes, his mouth tightened ominously.

"I see. We must speak." He glanced around the hallway.
"Here." He tugged on her hands. "Please, Anne. Come and sit
with me."

She let him lead her down the unfamiliar hall, into a room
shrouded in covers, illuminated by the dusty light from a cen-
ter-hung chandelier.

Her mind was working now, smoothly and with preternat-
ural efficiency, laying out plans in some place that was beyond pain and bewilderment, that was concerned only with
necessity.

"Here," Er Thom said again, his Terran somewhat
blurred—a certain sign of his own agitation. He left her to
swirl a dust-sheet from the sofa before the dead hearth, rolled
the cloth into a hasty bundle and cast it aside.

"Please, Anne. Sit."

She did, curling into the high-swept corner. Er Thom sat
next to her, turned sideways, one knee crooked on the faded
brocade seat, one elbow propped along the back cushion. He

looked elegant, all grace and beauty in his wide-sleeved shirt and soft-napped trousers. Anne looked away.

"My mother has distressed you," Er Thom said gently. "I regret that. Will you tell me what she has said?"

She considered that, deliberately cold. First and foremost, she must have verification of her worst suspicions. Yet she must gain such verification without alerting Er Thom to her plan.

"Your mother—confused me—on a couple things. I thought I understood—" She hesitated, then forced herself to meet his eyes.

"Shan is accepted of Clan Korval, isn't he?"

Something flickered in Er Thom's eyes, gone too quickly for her to read.

"Yes, certainly."

"But your mother said that he wasn't—wasn't good enough to be your heir," Anne pursued, watching him closely.

Anger showed again, though she sensed it was for his mother and not for herself. He extended a slim, ringless hand. "Anne—"

"It's just—" She glanced at the dead hearth, feeling how rapidly her heart beat. *Gods, gods, I'm no good at this . . .*

"It's that—" she told the cold bricks, "if Shannie's going to be a burden on your clan, maybe it would be best if I just took him back to University—"

"Ah." His hand gripped her knee very briefly; her flesh tingled through the cloth of her trousers. "Of course Shan shall not be a burden upon the clan. The clan welcomes children—and doubly welcomes such a child as our son! To snatch him away from kin and homeplace, when the clan has just now embraced him as its own . . ." He smiled at her, tentatively.

"Try to understand, denubia. My mother is—old world. She has held always by the Book of Clans, by the Code—by Liad. To change now, when she is ill and has lost so much in service of the clan—" He moved his shoulders. "I do not think that she can. Nor, in respect, must we who hold her closest demand such change of her." He seemed for an instant to hesitate. One hand rose toward her cheek—and fell again to his knee.

"I regret—very much—that she found it necessary to

speak to you in such terms of our son. If you will accept it, I ask that you take my apology as hers."

A rock seemed lodged in her throat, blocking words, nearly blocking breath. That he could plead so sweetly for a parent who showed him not an ounce of affection, who ordered him to her side as if he were her slave rather than her son . . . Anne managed at last to get a breath past the blockage in her throat.

Verification, announced the strange new part of her mind that was busily molding its plans. *We proceed.*

"I—of course I forgive her," she told the hearth-stones. "Change is difficult, even for those of us who aren't—old— and—and ill . . ." She cleared her throat sharply and closed her eyes, hearing her heartbeat pounding, crazy, in her ears.

"I find I'm to wish you happy," she whispered, and there was no iron in her voice now at all. "Your mother tells me you're going to be married—"

"No."

His hands were on her shoulders, his breath shivering the tiny hairs at her temple. Anne shrank back into the corner of the sofa, a sob catching her throat.

"Anne—no, denubia, hear me . . ." His hands left her shoulders and tenderly cupped her face, turning her, gently, inexorably, toward him. "Please, Anne, you must trust me."

Trust him? When he had just confessed to lying, to kidnapping, to using the trust she had borne him to—no.

On Liad, you won. Or you lost.

It was absolutely imperative that she win.

She allowed him to turn her face. She opened her eyes, looked into his and saw, incredibly, tenderness and care and longing in the purple depths.

Er Thom smiled, very gently, ran his thumbs in double caress along her cheekbones before taking his hands away.

"I love you, Anne. Never forget."

"I love you, too," she heard herself say, and it was true, true, gods pity her, and the man had stolen her son.

Never mind, the cold planner in the back of her mind told her. *Disarm him with the truth, so much the better. Put any suspicions he may have fast asleep. Then the plan will work.*

He sat back, reluctantly, to her eye, and folded his hands

carefully on his knee. The face he showed her was earnest, the eyes tender and anxious.

"This marriage which my mother desires," he said softly. "It is old world, and as a dutiful son I should accept the match and give the clan my heir, which is duty long past fruition." He tipped his head, anxiety overriding tenderness for the moment. "You understand, this is the—manner in which things are done—and no slight to you is intended."

"I understand," she said, hearing the iron back in her voice.

Er Thom inclined his head. "So. But it happens that there is you and there is our son and we two—love. There is that bond between us which—after even such a time—remains unabated. Unfilled. That is true, Anne, is it not?"

"True." *True . . .*

"I had thought so," he said, very softly, and she saw the shine of tears in his eyes.

"Since we wish not to part—since we wish, indeed, to become lifemates—this marriage that my mother hopes for is—a nothing. I have taken counsel on the matter. A lifemating between us shall be allowed, does the delm hear from your lips that it is your desire as well as my own. Alas, that my mother has sought to—to force the play—striving to divide us and burst asunder the bond we share." He reached out and took her hand; her traitor fingers curled tight around his.

"If we stand together, if we hold now as the lifemates we shall soon become, she cannot win," Er Thom said earnestly. "It will be difficult, perhaps, but we shall carry the day. We need only give her what she desires—in certain measure. She desires to have the lady here to meet me. So we acquiesce, you see? The lady is a child. She does not want me. She wants the consequence of bedding an a'thodelm, of having borne a child to Korval.

"The—infelicity—of the proposed match can easily be shown her, gently and with all respect, in the course of such an affair as my mother plans." His fingers gripped hers painfully, though Anne made no demur.

"We need only stand together," he repeated earnestly. "You must not allow yourself to be frightened into leaving our house. To do so ensures my mother's victory. You must only attend the gather and show a calm face. Why should you not?

When the gather is done, we shall go hand-in-hand before the delm and ask that he acknowledge what already in fact exists."

Lifemates? For a moment it seemed she spun, alone in void, the familiar markers of her life wiped clean away. For a moment, it seemed that here was a better plan, that kept her son at her side, and her lover, too, with no duplicity, no lies, no anguish. For a moment, she hovered on the edge of flinging herself into his arms and sobbing out the whole of her pain and confusion, to put everything into his hands for solving—

The moment passed. Cold reason returned. Er Thom had lied. From the very beginning, he had intended to steal Shan from her, though he swore he would do no such thing. There was no reason to believe this plea for lifemates was any truer than his other lies.

"Anne?"

She stared down at her lap, at her fingers, twisted like snakes each about the other, white-knuckled and cold.

"Your mother," she said, and barely recognized her own voice, "will be just as well served if I shame you."

"It is not possible," Er Thom said quietly, "that you will shame me, Anne."

She had thought herself beyond any greater agony, foolish gel. She stared fixedly down at her hands, jaw clenched until she heard bone crack.

"We may go tomorrow into Solcintra," Er Thom continued after a moment, "and arrange for proper dress."

"I—" *What?* she asked herself wildly. *What will you say to the man, Annie Davis?*

But she had no more to say, after all, than that bare syllable. Er Thom touched her knee lightly.

"Lifemates may offer such things," he murmured, "without insult. Without debt."

Oh, gods . . . From somewhere, she gleaned the courage to raise her head and meet his eyes levelly.

"Thank you, Er Thom. I—expect I will need a dress for—for the gather."

Joy lit his face, and pride. He smiled, widely, lovingly. "We play on," he said, and laughed lightly. His fingers grazed her cheek. "Courageous Anne."

She swallowed and tried for a smile. It was apparently not an entirely successful effort, for Er Thom rose and offered his arm, all solicitude.

"You are exhausted. Come, let me walk you to your rooms."

In the moment of rising, she froze and stared up into his eyes.

"Anne, what is wrong?"

"I—" Gods, she could *not* sleep with him. She wouldn't last through one kiss, much less through a night—she would tell him everything, lose everything . . .

"I was thinking," she heard her voice say, "that maybe we should—sleep apart—until the gather is over. Your mother—"

"Ah." He inclined his head gravely. "I understand. My mother shall see that all goes her way, eh? That the guest has heeded her word and behaves with honor regarding the House's wayward child." He smiled and it was all she could do not to cry aloud.

Instead, she rose and took his arm and allowed him to guide her through unfamiliar hallways to the door of her room.

Once there, she hesitated, and some demon prompted her to ask one last question.

"Your mother had said that the clan would be—grateful— for Shan's adoption. I didn't quite—"

"That would be the proposal of alliance," Er Thom said gently, "as well as other considerations. Daav and I had drafted the papers yesterday, and a trust fund has been created in your name." He smiled up at her, sweetly. "But these matters are moot, when we are lifemates."

Speechless, she stared down at him, wondering what— *considerations*—what possible sum of money—Clan Korval had thought sufficient to buy a child.

"You are tired," Er Thom murmured. "I say good-night. Sleep well, beloved." He raised one of her hands, kissed the palm lightly and released her.

Tear-blinded, Anne spun and fumbled her hand against the lock-plate, escaping at last into grief-shot solitude.

• • •

"**Why** now?" Daav demanded.

Petrella regarded him calmly from the comm screen. "Why not now? He has been coddled long enough. Nexon calls Korval's melant'i into question. What better way to give such question rest than by proceeding as planned?"

"As *you* planned!" Daav snapped and sighed, reaching up to finger his earring.

"Aunt Petrella, be gracious. The guest will still be with you two nights hence. She holds Er Thom precious, whether you will see it or no. What can possibly be gained by wounding her in this manner? Such action does more harm to Korval's melant'i than all Nexon's petulance can accomplish!"

Petrella raised her hand. "I hope we are not rag-mannered, nor behind in our duty to the guest," she said austerely. "Certainly, there was instruction given. The guest cannot hope to know our custom. A word in her ear was sufficient, as it happens. I find Scholar Davis a very sensible woman."

"Oh, do you?" Daav closed his eyes briefly, running a Scout's calming exercise, trying not to think of Er Thom's desperate gamble and what must be made of his wooing now.

"Indeed I do," Petrella replied. "Shall I have the honor of seeing you at the gather, my Delm?"

"Why certainly," he said, hearing the snap in his voice despite the exercise. "I can always be depended upon to dance for you, Aunt Petrella. Good-night." He swept the board clear with a violent palm and surged to his feet as if he would run immediately out into the night.

Instead, he walked very slowly over to the windowsill and reached down to stroke the leaves and white flowers of the plant Olwen had left with him. Nubiath'a.

"Ah, gods, brother," he whispered to the little plant, "what a coil we have knotted between us . . ."

CHAPTER THIRTY-ONE

Accepted of Clan Korval: Identical twins, daughters of Kin Dal yos'Phelium and Larin yos'Galan.
Accepted of Line yos'Galan: Petrella, daughter of Larin.
Accepted of Line yos'Phelium: Chi, daughter of Kin Dal.

**—From The Gazette for Banim Fourthday
in the Third Relumma of the Year Named Yergin**

Two days ago she had dreamed of such a visit to the City of Jewels. Then, Solcintra had gone past the car window in a dazzle of possibility, and she had imagined walking the wide streets safe on Er Thom's arm, enclosed by his melant'i, guided by his care.

Today, she stared, sand-eyed, at a city gone gray, and listened to the cold, back-brain planner make its cold and necessary plans.

Tomorrow and today were her last on Liad. On the morning after Er Thom's betrothal party, she and her son would be gone. That was the plan.

The plan called for precise timing. It called for the ingenuity to forestall Er Thom immediately petitioning the delm to acknowledge lifemates. It called for pulling a few strands of wool across the eyes of an unsuspecting yos'Galan driver. It required the fortitude to leave everything—*every*thing—behind, save her son and what could be carried in her briefcase.

Necessity existed. These things could be done.

It required sufficient funds to book passage for herself and her child on the first available ship.

Cash was the sticking point: She had a little, in Terran bits, which enjoyed an—unequal—exchange rate on Liad.

Of course, she would sell her jewelry, paltry stuff that it was. Er Thom's good-bye gift would fetch the most of the lot, but she was not fool enough to suppose it would cover even a tenth of the passage price to New Dublin.

For it was to New Dublin she had determined to go, where laws were sane and where she would have her brother's staunch and stubborn support.

From Liad to New Dublin the price will be dear, she told herself wearily, as she had told herself all last night, pacing, exhausted and shivering, through the luxurious, alien apartment.

She wondered if she dared ask Er Thom how to access the trust fund he had set up for her.

While she was weighing that question, the car pulled into a parking slot and stopped.

"We arrive," Er Thom said softly, and turned to look at her. "Are you well, Anne?"

He had asked her that once already, this morning at breakfast. Anne had a moment of despair, that a whole day in her company would reveal to him that she was sick with fright, bloated with deception. She would lose—

I will not lose, she thought firmly. *Clan Korval does not own Shan. My son is not for sale.*

Resolutely, she summoned the best smile stiff face muscles could provide.

"I'm fine," she lied. "Just—tired. I didn't sleep very well."

"Ah." He touched the back of her hand with light fingertips. "When we are lifemated, perhaps . . . The clan keeps a house by the southern sea. We might go there, if you like it, to rest and—grow closer."

Pain twisted, a mere flicker of agony in the larger pain of his betrayal. Anne smiled again.

"That sounds wonderful," she said, and it was true. "I'd like that very much, Er Thom."

If it all was different. If you hadn't lied. If you hadn't schemed and connived. If I could dare even pretend that this might be true . . .

"Then it is done." He smiled. "Come and let us put you into Eyla's hands."

Eyla dea'Lorn stood back, gray head cocked to a side, lined face impish.

"So, Your Lordship brings me a challenge," she said to Er Thom, and rubbed her clever hands together. "Good."

To Anne, she bowed slightly, eyes gleaming.

"Ah, but you will provide such opportunity, Lady—I give you thanks! Nothing usual for you, eh? Nothing the same as so-and-so had it at Lord Whomever's rout. Hah! No, for you, everything must be new, original!" She shot a gleaming glance aside to Er Thom.

"An original. There is no possible comparison between this lady and any other lady in the world. In this, the world has failed us, but the lady shall be accepted on the terms of her own possibility. I accurately reflect Your Lordship's thought?"

"As always," Er Thom told her, lips twitching, "you are a perfect mirror, Eyla."

"Flattery! Recall who made your first cloak, sir, and speak with respect!" She beckoned Anne. "Come with me if you please, Lady. I must have measurements—ah, she walks as a pilot! Good, good. Put yourself entirely in my hands. We shall send you off in a fashion the world has rarely seen! Such proportions! So tall! The bosom, so proud! The neck—Ah, you are a gift from the gods, Lady, and I about to expire of boredom, or strangle the next same-as who walked through my door!"

The little woman's eagerness pierced even the iron-gray dreariness that enclosed Anne. She smiled.

"I fear I may prove a little too far out of the common way for such a debut as that," she murmured as she was led back to the measuring room.

"Never think it!" Eyla told her energetically. "The world is a great coward. Merely keep a level gaze and a courteous face and the world will bow to you. Some will scoff, certainly, but you needn't mind those. An original is a Code unto herself. And you have the advantage of sponsorship by Korval, which has elevated originality to an art form." She rubbed her hands together, looking Anne up and down with eager appraisal.

"And now," she said, going over to a discreet console. "If I may ask you to disrobe . . ."

The gown would be brought to Trealla Fantrol no later than mid-morning, tomorrow. The color was to be antique gold, to "show that delightful brown skin." Eyla gave Er Thom a patch of fabric, which he solemnly placed in his pocket.

"We shall be going along to Master Moonel presently," he murmured. "When the design is fixed, perhaps you might call and allow him to name a suitable jeweler."

"He'll want the work himself," Eyla predicted with a smile. "Only show her to him. The deadline will mean nothing to Moonel, with such a showcase for his craft." She clasped her hands together and bowed them out with energy.

"And to think that only last evening I was considering retirement!"

"You and Eyla are good friends?" Anne asked, because it was necessary to say something. It was imperative that Er Thom think everything was just the same between them, and to put down any oddness in her behavior to the effects of a restless night.

"dea'Lorn and Korval are old allies," he murmured, guiding her along the flower-scented street with a gentle hand on her elbow. "Eyla will want to make your entire wardrobe."

"Would that be wrong?"

"Not—wrong. Indeed, it might well be prudent. Eyla has the gift of seeing exactly what is before her, rather than what she believes is there." He smiled up at her. "It has in the past been considered—expedient—to engage the services of several tailors, so Korval's patronage may not be used to undue advantage."

"But if your Houses are allied—"

"Not allied. Not—precisely—that. Doubtless my Terran

falls short. It is—in the time of my fourth-great-grandfather—
the youngest of dea'Lorn, who had just finished his appren-
ticeship, came with a proposal for trade. The dea'Lorn would
undertake to make whatever clothes Korval required at cost,
in return for materials at cost."

Anne frowned. "That sounds rather audacious."

"Indeed it was. But audacity amused my grandfather. He
inspected those items the dea'Lorn offered as samples of his
work, and made a counter-offer. He would provide shop space
in one of Korval's Upper Port warehouses and a very favor-
able discount on materials, as well as options on certain—exotic—fabrics. These things would constitute his buy-in and
make him one-half partner in the dea'Lorn's business, which
would indeed make Korval's clothes. Free of charge."

"But in return he got free advertising," Anne said, "and the
opportunity for his clothes to be seen at society functions . . ."

"And so he prospered," Er Thom concluded. "The
dea'Lorn's daughter was able to move the shop to its present
location and to retire Korval's partnership. The trade agree-
ments remain in place—and dea'Lorn from time to time
makes Korval's clothes. At cost." He sent her a glance from
beneath his lashes.

"Anne?"

She drew a careful breath, willing her face to be neutral.
"Yes?"

"I wish," Er Thom said, very softly, "that you will tell me
what troubles you."

Oh, gods . . . She swallowed, glanced aside, groping for a
lie—

"I—it's foolish, I know," she heard herself saying distractedly, "but I can't seem to get it out of my mind."

Annie Davis, she demanded in internal bewilderment,
what are ye nattering about?

"Ah." The pressure of Er Thom's fingers on her elbow
changed, guiding her to the edge of the sidewalk and a bench
beneath a flowering tree.

"Tell me," he murmured.

The bench was not particularly roomy. Er Thom's thigh
against hers woke a storm of emotion, of which lust and an-

guish were foremost. Anne bit her lip and almost cried out when he took her hand in his.

"Anne? Perhaps I may aid you, if I can but understand the difficulty."

Well, and what will you tell him? she asked herself with interest.

But the back-brain planner had been busy.

"It's probably nothing," she heard her voice say uncertainly. "But—I took Shannie with me yesterday to Doctor yo'Kera's office. I was doing an inventory of his research computer, and it took longer than I had expected—I sent you a note."

"Yes, so you did," Er Thom murmured, apparently not at all put out by this rather rattle-brained narrative.

"Yes. Well, it was late when we finally did leave—the night lamps had come on in the hallway. I made sure the office door was locked, and when I turned around there was—a man. He startled me rather badly, though of course—" She shook her head, half in wonderment at herself, half in remembered consternation.

"A Liaden man?" Er Thom wondered softly.

"Oh. Yes. Very ordinary-looking. He spoke to me in Trade at first—I'm afraid I was pretty sharp in setting him straight. He was polite after that—offered to carry my case—and of course he had a perfect right to be there, since he's a grad student . . ."

"Do you recall his name?"

"Fil Tor Kinrae," she recited out of memory, "Linguistic Technician and Student of Advanced Studies."

"Ah. And his clan?"

Anne frowned. "He didn't say."

"Did he not?" Er Thom's glance was sharp.

"No," she said defensively, "he didn't. Why should he? It was more important for me to know that he was a linguistics student with a perfectly legitimate right to be where he was."

"Yes, certainly." Er Thom squeezed her hand gently. "What disturbed you, then?"

"It was Shan," she said and shivered, recalling her son's fright. "He's never—you know he's never afraid of anyone!

But he was afraid of Fil Tor Kinrae. Demanded to go home *now*." She looked down into Er Thom's eyes.

"In the car, I asked him what had happened. And he said— *no sparkles*—and hid his face . . ."

Er Thom's eyes darkened. "*No* sparkles?" He glanced aside, chewing his lip.

"There is—a thought," he said after a moment. "My grandmother had been a Healer, you know. I recall she once said that no one holds the key to all rooms. That those who are locked and dark to one Healer may be open and full of light to another." He looked up into her face.

"Shan is young. If this is the first person he has met who does not—broadcast on the same frequency, Daav would say—he may well have been frightened." His gaze sharpened, a little.

"It might be wise, were we to ask the delm to call a Healer to our child. He is very young to be experiencing these things. There is perhaps something that may be done to alleviate such distress as was occasioned last evening."

And only another Healer would know what to do, she thought, suddenly cold. *Whatever are ye about, Annie Davis, to be taking the laddie away from such aid? How will he learn what to do with his sparkles, when there's no one who's Terran can teach him?*

She snatched at his hand. "Er Thom!"

"Yes, denubia." His voice was soothing, his fingers firm. "What else troubles you?"

Almost, she told him. It hovered on the tip of her tongue, the rollygig of loss and love, hope, denial and confusion. She was a heartbeat away from burying her face in his shoulder and sobbing out the whole.

Down the walkway beyond the tree came a couple, very fine in their day-clothes and jewels. The woman turned her head and met Anne's eyes. Disgust washed over her perfect Liaden features; she clutched her companion's arm, leaning close to whisper.

He turned his head, face and eyes cold.

They walked on.

Anne cleared her throat.

"It's nothing," she said, and could not meet Er Thom's eyes. "I—Thank you, Er Thom—for listening."

There was a long silence, and still she could not bring herself to raise her face to his. Finally, she felt him move, coming smoothly to his feet, his hand still firmly holding hers.

"I shall listen whenever you wish," he said gently. "Will you come with me now to Port?"

"Yes," she said numbly and stood, and let him lead her back to the car.

Master Jeweler Moonel was as taciturn as Eyla dea'Lorn was voluble. He took the bit of fabric from Er Thom's hand and glared at it as if he suspected it held a flaw.

"Tomorrow?" he snapped and moved his eyes to Anne. "This the lady for whom the items are destined?"

"Scholar Anne Davis," Er Thom murmured, "guest of Korval. Please feel free to give Eyla another name, Master, if the deadline is too near."

"Yes, very likely." Moonel spun on his stool, showing them his back as he reached for his tools. "I'll send them 'round by mid-day. Good morning."

"Good morning, Master Moonel," Er Thom said, bowing to the older man's back. He smiled at Anne and held out his hand.

Hand-in-hand they came out into the narrow Avenue of Jewels.

"Would you care for luncheon?" Er Thom asked as they turned down a slightly wider side street.

"Good-day to you, Captain yos'Galan!" The passerby who gave the greeting had close-cropped gray hair and a multitude of earrings. She raised a hand from across the way and the sunlight gleamed on her master trader's ring.

"I've yet to hear from the Guild, sir!" the little woman added gaily. Her sharp eyes swept once over Anne's face and then she was gone, swallowed in the crowd.

Er Thom's face was stiff with anger, his mouth a tight line. Anne blinked in amazement.

"Who was that?"

He took a deep breath and sighed it out forcefully, then looked up into her face, violet eyes bland.

"No one," he said flatly. "Let us go to Ongit's for luncheon."

CHAPTER THIRTY-TWO

The last of those who had hand in Eba yos'Phelium's capture and shaming seven years ago is dead. Balance achieved.

—Daav yos'Phelium, Sixth Delm of Korval
Entry in the Delm's Diary for Trianna Seconday in the
Fourth Relumma of the Year named Sandir

"Morning wine or red?"

"Red, if you please," Er Thom answered absently, eyes on the counterchance board sitting ready before the hearth.

Daav filled the glass and put it into his brother's hand, added a splash of morning wine to his own cup and shot a shrewd glance at the other's abstracted face.

"What's amiss?"

"Hmm?" Er Thom had wandered over to the board. He picked up a pair of dice, idly shook and released them: Eighteen.

"Is it true," he murmured, perhaps to the dice, "that Eba yos'Phelium was publicly whipped by her thodelm?"

Daav's eyebrows rose. "Yes," he said matter-of-factly, "but you must understand that it was the means by which her life was preserved."

Violet eyes flashed to his face. "Ah, was it?"

"Certainly. Times were—unsettled. To make a complex tale simple, Eba fell into the hands of those who wished Korval ill. They then showed her, still bleeding from the abduction, knife along her throat, to her thodelm, who was also her cha'leket.

"The enemies of Korval were adamant that Eba be punished for some insult they had concocted. The one with the knife claimed the right to her life and professed herself willing to do the thing at once. However, there were cooler heads present, who saw that their ends would be met as well by a public shaming." Daav sipped his wine.

"The young thodelm judged Eba's odds of survival, not to say recovery, significantly better did he wield the lash himself, so he contended for, and won, the right."

Er Thom picked up the dice and made another cast: Six. "And?"

Daav moved his shoulders. "And he laid the stripes, then ran, weeping, to cut her down, his back guarded by all of the clan who could hold a weapon. Balance commenced immediately she was safe at Jelaza Kazone and her wounds had been treated. Seven years were required for fruition, as there were several Houses involved." He lifted an eyebrow.

"Shall I show you the entries in the Diaries?"

"Thank you," Er Thom murmured, raising his glass and meeting Daav's eyes across the rim, "that will not be necessary."

"Ah." Daav lifted his own glass, but did not drink. "Has your thodelm threatened to flog you, darling?"

Er Thom grinned. "One is amazingly disobedient, after all."

"So I've heard. Does it occur to you to wonder whither Aunt Petrella has purchased these sudden notions of propriety?"

"Perhaps her illness . . ." her son offered, and sighed. "I miss our mother," he said, very softly.

"As I do." Daav drifted over to the table, picked up the dice and threw. Eleven.

"Our mother would have liked your Anne, I think," he murmured. "The devil's in it that I believe Aunt Petrella would like her well enough, were we only able to show her Line and House!"

Across from him, Er Thom shifted. Daav looked up, eyebrows high.

"You wonder that the delm would ask you to give her up, eh? But the lady's summation was unfortunately correct: Accepting a Terran makes the clan vulnerable. It can be managed, if it must be managed. But how very much easier, to go on as always we have. As for Daav—" he moved his shoulders and threw again: Seven.

"Daav likes her very well indeed and thinks it a great pity that Liad must be so overfull with Liadens."

Er Thom laughed. "Spoken like a Scout! But there. When have we ever gone on as proper Liadens? The Diaries tell us that is not our contract. Here are our mothers born aside the Delm's Own Word, simply because Kin Dal and Larin could not keep from each other!"

"And they send us to be Scouts and traders," Daav agreed. "Which makes us even odder." He tipped his head. "How does Anne take news of your betrothal?"

"Unhappily," Er Thom said, frowning. "For one who states she will not be played, my mother throws the dice with energy."

"Will Anne show her face at the gather, I wonder?"

"Certainly. We have settled it between us." He smiled. "I believe I may soon bring you proof of a win, brother, and ask the delm to See my lifemate."

"So? I will wish you joy gladly, darling. Is there reason the win must wait upon the gather?"

"Kindness for Nexon's daughter," Er Thom said softly. "At the gather I shall have opportunity to show her that we would not suit. Also, a matter of balance, in part. It is ill-done to hold such an event at this moment. Add to that the manner in which my mother chose to speak to Anne regarding our son—I will tell you, brother, it has disturbed Anne greatly! She is distracted—anxious . . . It is a shame to the House, that a guest be treated so, never mind what punishment thodelm finds proper for a'thodelm!" He raised his glass and drank, showed a rueful smile.

"Still, she has agreed to attend the gather, bold heart that she has—and show a calm face to Nexon and her daughter, not to speak of Thodelm yos'Galan."

"Honor to the lady," Daav said, with sincerity. "She may yet learn to be a player to fear." He sipped.

"Should you bring a lifemate before the delm," he said after a moment, "certain things shall be required, for the good of the clan. You will be required to provide the clan several more children. Your lifemate shall be required to take pilot's training."

Er Thom inclined his head. "I shall discuss these things with Anne."

Daav eyed him with a touch of wonder. "Oh, and will you?"

"Of course," Er Thom said. "How else?"

"How else, indeed?" his brother replied politely.

"There is a matter which might be brought to the delm's attention, however," Er Thom continued, oblivious to—or ignoring—irony.

"Our son has recently met with one who frightened him—an unusual occurrence. The reason he gave his mother for this fright was that the person in question possessed 'no sparkles.' In view of his extreme youth and the apparent precocity of his talent, it may be wise to call a Healer, before he experiences another—perhaps needless—fright."

"Yes, I see." Daav frowned down at the counterchance board. "He is very young for this, is he not? Mostwise, talent shows when one comes halfling . . ." He shook himself and looked up.

"Certainly, a Healer must be summoned. The delm shall see it done."

Again, Er Thom inclined his head. "I shall inform Anne of the delm's care." He lifted his glass and drained it.

"I shall have to leave you now. Is there a commission I may discharge for you in Port?"

"Thank you, no. My steps are for the City this morning. The delm and Mr. dea'Gauss are called to renegotiate with Vintyr."

"Pah." Er Thom made a face. "Vintyr is never satisfied, brother."

"So I begin to notice. I believe I may mention it to Mr. dea'Gauss, in fact. It seems a change of course is indicated."

"Good lift to the delm, then," Er Thom said, with a light-hearted bow. "I shall see you at the gather, shan't I?"

"Indeed, how could I stay away, when Aunt Petrella was so gracious as to order my appearance?"

Er Thom lifted troubled eyes.

"Her illness weighs more heavily upon her, I think."

"I think so, as well," Daav said, and resolutely shook off his sudden chill. "I shall be there to support you this evening, never fear it. Until soon, darling."

"Until soon, Daav."

Well, Annie Davis! And you preened in the green gown and thought yourself so fine.

The new gown, like the old, was cut low over her bosom, close in to her waist. There, all similarity was done.

A wide collar swept up to frame her throat, belling, flower-like, to cup her face. Long sleeves fell in graceful pleats, calling attention to her hands, and the floor-length skirt, deceptively slim, was slashed to permit all of her accustomed stride.

Eyla dea'Lorn twitched the skirt into more perfect order and smiled.

"Yes," she said, standing back and clasping her hands before her. "I believe His Lordship will be pleased."

Before Anne could make answer to that, the little tailor held up a finger.

"Attend me, now, Lady. The dress is all very well, and Moonel's jewels will shame no one. However, if you are wise, you will take my advice in a few certain matters. First—hair. Sweep yours up—yes, I know it is not long! Up and back, nonetheless. The collar's work is to frame the face—a little daring, I admit, but not wanton. Of a sophistication, perhaps, that a master trader might encounter—and admire—far out-side of Liad's orbit." She rubbed her hands together.

"You walk well, with a fine smooth stride. The dress is made to accommodate you. Your hands—so beautiful, your hands! Show them, thus—" She extended an arm and flicked her wrist. "Try."

Anne copied the other woman's gesture; the sleeve flipped

smoothly back from her hand, revealing strong, slender fingers.

"Good," Eyla approved. "An original is a Code unto herself. There is not your like on all of Liad. The rules that bind you are not found within the world, but within yourself. Recall it and carry your head—so! Eh? There are those who must crane to admire you—that is their concern, not yours. There are those who will turn their face away and cry out that you are not as they." She lifted a hand to cover a bogus yawn.

"Boors, alas, are found in even the highest Houses."

Anne smiled, palely, and inclined her head. "You are kind to advise me."

"Bah!" Eyla swept thanks away with an energetic hand. "I will not have my work shamed, that is all." She smiled and bent to gather up her work-kit. "His Lordship means to fire you off with flair, which is profit to me, does this gown please." She straightened.

"It will be amusing to see what the world makes of you, Lady. And what you will make of the world."

Shan was fractious and weepy. He jittered from one end of the nursery to the other; even the *Edu-Board* failed to hold his attention for more than a few seconds. All Anne's attempts to ease him into a less frenzied state were met with utter failure.

At last, feeling her own frazzled nerves about to go, she gathered him into her lap, thinking that a cuddle might do them both good.

"No!" He jerked back, body stiff, silver eyes wide.

"Shannie!"

"No!" he shouted again and smacked her hand aside, so un-Shan-like that she let him go in astonishment.

"Mirada!" He stamped his foot, glaring up at her. "I want Mirada! Go away! Go away, bad Ma!"

And with that he was gone, running pell-mell down the long playroom—and into the arms of Mrs. Intassi, who had just stepped through the door that led to the nursery's kitchen.

"Bad Ma!" Shan cried, hurling himself against the nurse's legs and hiding his face in her tunic. "I want Mirada!"

"That's all very well," Mrs. Intassi said in firm and unsympathetic Terran. "However, you are not very kind to your mother. You should beg her pardon."

"No," Shan said stubbornly, refusing to raise his head.

Sick to her stomach, shivering and weary, Anne rose, shaking her head at the tiny ex-Scout.

"Never mind," she said, hearing how her voice shook. "If he doesn't want me here, then I'll go." She turned toward the door, missing the concerned glance Mrs. Intassi flung her.

"Good-bye, Shannie," Anne called. "Maybe I'll see you tomorrow."

The nursery door slid closed behind her with a sound like doom.

She was lying on her bed some while later, staring blankly through the overhead window. The Liaden sky was brilliant, blue-green and cloudless.

The brilliance pierced her, searing the tumbling thoughts from her mind, scalding emotions to ash.

Seared, scalded and gone to ash, she closed her eyes against the brilliance.

When she opened her eyes again, the brilliance had faded. She turned her head against the pillow. The clock on the bedside table told her there were two hours left to prepare for the gather.

Sighing, feeling not so much exhausted as drained—of thought, of emotion, of any purpose save the plan—she rolled out of the wide bed, glanced at the mirror across the room—and frowned.

On the vanity beneath the mirror, among her familiar belongings, were two unfamiliar boxes.

The large box was covered in lush scarlet velvet. Anne lifted the lid.

A rope braided of three gold strands: Pink, yellow and white, weeping drops of yellow diamond exactly matching her gown. Tiny yellow diamond drops to hug her earlobes, glittering allure. Woven gold combs and pins, dusted with yellow chips, to hold her hair, up and back.

Anne looked down at the velvet box's treasure, at jewels

that cost more than she would likely earn in a lifetime, created to grace one dress, created in turn for one gathering . . .

His Lordship means to fire you off with flair.

Anne sighed, feeling, perhaps, a distant relief.

Now she would have enough money to buy passage. Home.

The smaller box was wood, carved with vines and flowers, a center medallion inlaid with bits of ivory. She opened it, found a folded square of ivory-colored paper. Her name, written in uncertain Terran characters, adorned the outer fold.

Inside, the words were in Liaden, the letters true and bold.

For my love. To say hello, and never to say good-bye. Er Thom

Nestled in a satin pillow was a band of rosy gold. The gem set flush to the metal, simply cut and pure as pain, was precisely the color of his eyes.

For a long moment she simply stood there, wondering if her heart would take up its next beat, if her lungs would accept another breath.

When it seemed that she would, after all, live, she closed the little box and set it gently aside. The scrap of creamy paper she placed in her briefcase, sealed in the pocket with the disk from Jin Del yo'Kera's computer.

The velvet box she let stand open, giving its expensive glitter to the room while she began at last to ready herself for the gather.

CHAPTER THIRTY-THREE

Here we stand: An old woman, a halfling boy, two babes; a contract, a ship and a Tree.
   Clan Korval.
   How Jela would laugh.

—**Excerpted from Cantra yos'Phelium's Log Book**

A'thodelm yos'Galan, Syntebra reminded herself forcefully, *is a person of melant'i, son of an old and respected House. It is a signal honor to be chosen as his wife.*

To be sure, she thought, cold fingers twisted together beneath her cloak, to marry an a'thodelm of Korval would be a very great thing, indeed.

Except her heart—that traitor which had lifted so quickly upon hearing Korval had Seen a child of A'thodelm yos'-Galan—her heart, now an ice-drenched stone pitted in her chest, did not seem to find it a great thing at all. She had said as much, tentatively, to her father.

"Not marry the yos'Galan?" Her father stared, as well he might, Syntebra allowed fairly. "Are you mad?"

Syntebra felt the easy tears rise to her eyes, and her father's face softened.

"Doubtless you're thinking now a child is Seen there's no cause for him to marry. Nothing could be farther from the case, I assure you. Korval is in sorry state of late—wretched luck for them, certainly, but golden fortune for us, do we throw the dice canny!" He leaned forward with the air of one offering a treat.

"Why, if the yos'Galan does not want you, there's Korval Himself still in need of an heir!"

But that was even worse, for Korval was a Scout, all the world knew that! And Syntebra was afraid of Scouts.

Tearfully, she had attempted to explain this to her parent. She met Scouts from time to time at the Port, where she went—dutifully—to put in her hours of flying. Scouts possessed the oddest manners imaginable, and a bold, unnerving way of looking directly into one's eyes.

Scouts forever seemed to be enjoying some obscure joke, or secretly laughing at *some*thing. Syntebra rather thought that they were laughing at her.

"Oh, posh!" her father cried, all out of patience. "You'll do as you're told, and none of your vapors! Hearing you, one would think the yos'Galan scar-faced and Korval dissolute! You are very fortunate, my girl. I recommend you seek solitude and consider that aspect of the case."

Which is how Syntebra came to be at her delm's side in Trealla Fantrol's great formal entry hall, handing off her cloak to a servant and dutifully striving to recall that it would be a very great thing indeed, to wed A'thodelm yos'Galan.

"**Rakina** Lirgael, Delm Nexon," Mr. pak'Ora announced. "Syntebra el'Kemin."

They came slowly down the long room, the elder lady leaning lightly upon the younger's arm. Neither was dressed in the first style of elegance, though the younger lady's gown was slightly more elaborate, designed to show a winsome shape to perfection.

Stationed beside his mother's chair, Er Thom watched their progress. Young Syntebra's plentiful hair had been pinned high, then allowed to tumble with calculated artlessness to kiss her bare shoulders. Here and there a diamond winked among the rioting dark ringlets. Diamonds glittered in each tiny ear and a solitaire suspended from a chain fragile as thought trembled at the base of her throat.

"Delm Nexon," Petrella said from her chair. "Be welcome in our House."

Nexon bowed, the glitter of her dress-jewels all but obscuring sight of the clan Ring.

"Your welcome is gracious," she stated. Straightening, she indicated the younger lady. "Allow me to make you known to Syntebra el'Kemin, a daughter of Nexon's secondary Line. Syntebra, here is Thodelm yos'Galan."

Syntebra's bow was charmingly done, though to Er Thom's eye a trifle ragged at the start.

Petrella inclined her head and raised a hand that trembled visibly. Er Thom felt a stab of concern. His mother was pushing her limit tonight. Gods willing, she would not push it too far.

"My son," his mother was telling the guests, "Er Thom, A'thodelm yos'Galan."

He made his bow to Nexon, receiving in return an inclined head and a civil, "Sir."

To Syntebra then he bowed, which was rather a trickier undertaking, for he must neither appear cool to the careful eye of his parent, nor so warm to the eye of the lady that impossible hopes were nourished.

Thereby: "Syntebra el'Kemin," he murmured, all propriety and very little else. "I am pleased at last to meet you, ma'am."

Wide, opal-blue eyes looked up at him from a tight little face, the luscious red mouth pinched pale.

Gods abound, the child's terrified! Er Thom thought, and felt a spate of anger at their respective parents, for insisting upon this farce.

Syntebra made her bow—not quite as pretty as her first.

"Sir," she returned in a breathless, husky voice. "A'thodelm yos'Galan. I am—very—pleased to make your acquaintance."

Well, Er Thom thought wryly, as he obeyed his mother's hand-sign and went 'round to pour wine for the guests, *it should be no very great thing to show her that we shall not suit . . .*

●   ●   ●

It was all Syntebra could do to keep the tears at bay. Certainly, she could not bring herself to look up at the tall gentleman beside her, nor could she think of one gay or witty or even *sensible* thing to say.

He would think she was a fool. He would—her delm would—

"Drink your wine, child."

The voice was very soft, the mode Adult-to-Adult. Syntebra looked up in startlement.

Violet eyes met her gaze straightly from beneath winged golden brows.

"You'll feel the better for it," he murmured, raising his own glass for a sip. When he lowered it, she saw he was smiling, just a little. "I won't eat you, you know."

Almost, the ever-ready tears escaped. She had not expected kindness. Indeed, she had expected nothing but scorn from so grand a gentleman. Of course, he was quite old, and it was perhaps not entirely flattering to be addressed as "child," when she had all of twenty Standards . . .

"One is informed," A'thodelm yos'Galan said in his soft voice, "that you have but recently attained your second-class license. Do you plan to pursue first class?"

First class? She wished she had never attained second! The sorriest day of her life thus far had been the day she tested well in the preliminaries. She hated piloting. She hated ships. She hated the Port, with all its noise and rabble and bewildering to-and-fros—

But, of course, one could scarcely voice such sentiments to a man who was both master pilot and master trader. Syntebra took a hasty swallow of wine—and was saved from answering by the dismaying call of the butler:

"Daav yos'Phelium, Delm Korval!"

Delm Korval was more terrifying than she had anticipated.

He spent some time speaking with Nexon and Thodelm yos'Galan, as was only proper. However, after the introduction, in quick succession, of Mr. Luken bel'Tarda and Lady Kareen yos'Phelium, he had turned his silent Scout steps toward her tête-à-tête with A'thodelm yos'Galan.

Now, Syntebra had long been wishing for something like this to happen. It was only ill-chance that her rescuer should be more dreaded than he from whom she was rescued.

"Ma'am." He gave her the grace of a small bow, and such a look from his bold black eyes that she wished she might sink into the floor.

Happily, the bold eyes moved in the next instant as Korval addressed his kinsman.

"Good evening, darling. Shall the guest be with us, after all?"

"I believe so," A'thodelm yos'Galan said in his soft way. He turned to Syntebra. "Scholar Anne Davis, guest of the House, is to be present this evening, as well."

Syntebra very nearly blinked. Scholar Anne Davis? But surely—She became aware that she was the object of study of two very vivid pairs of eyes, and raised a hand to her throat.

"I—ah—the Terran lady?" she managed, trying to seem as if she were quite in the way of meeting Terrans.

A'thodelm's yos'Galan's golden brows rose slightly. "Indeed," he murmured politely, "the Terran lady."

"You needn't be nervous of her, you know," Korval added in his deep, coarse voice. "She's quite gentle."

She looked up at him, but his face was composed, without a hint of the laughter she suspected he harbored in his heart.

"It is merely that one does not speak Terran," she said, striving to recover her dignity. "And to converse in Trade would seem out of the way."

"Ah, no, acquit her as the cause of such inconvenience, I beg." Korval said. "Her grasp of the High Tongue is entirely adequate."

"Scholar Davis," A'thodelm yos'Galan murmured, "specializes in the study of linguistics."

At that moment Lord and Lady yo'Lana were announced, then Delm Guayar. Syntebra, looking aside from the progress of these luminaries, saw A'thodelm yos'Galan exchange a quick glance with his kinsman.

"Scholar Anne Davis," the butler announced, and Syntebra saw A'thodelm yos'Galan smile.

"Hah." He bowed gracefully to Syntebra, gave his delm a nod. "Pray excuse me."

In the next moment he was gone, crossing the room to meet the lady who had just entered.

Syntebra fairly gaped. She had considered A'thodelm yos'-Galan and Delm Korval out-of-reason tall, but Scholar Davis revised that thought.

A'thodelm yos'Galan greeted her with the bow between equals and, looking warmly up into her face, offered his arm. The lady took it and they went down the room, pausing here and there to make proper introductions.

"There," Delm Korval said. "She doesn't look at all savage, does she?"

Undeniably, he was laughing at her. Of course the lady didn't look savage, though how such an immoderately tall, deep-bosomed creature could contrive to seem so regal went beyond Syntebra's understanding. She went 'round the room on A'thodelm yos'Galan's arm as if she were precisely High House, making her bows with grace, her clear voice carrying effortlessly to all corners of the suddenly quiet room.

"She bears an accent," Syntebra said to Delm Korval. The gentleman lifted one eyebrow.

"Well, and so do I," he said equably. "My Terran is quite marred by it, I fear."

She was spared any answer to this by the advent of the guest and A'thodelm yos'Galan.

"Daav." The Terran smiled, making free of Korval's personal name, as if, Syntebra thought, they were kin. She shrank into herself, anticipating the withering set-down to be delivered the lady for her audacity.

On the contrary.

"Anne," Korval returned with a smile that transformed his face into something approaching beauty. He bowed gently. "You look magnificent. Dance with me later, do."

The Terran actually chuckled, mischief lighting her eyes. "Do you only dance with magnificence, sir?"

"Ah, do not tease!" Korval returned in desperate tones. "If you won't have me there's nothing for it save I dance with my sister."

"A fate to be most ardently avoided." She smiled and inclined her head. "Count me your rescue, then." She turned her attention to Syntebra.

"Syntebra el'Kemin, Clan Nexon," A'thodelm yos'Galan said softly, "Scholar Anne Davis, guest of Korval."

Really, Syntebra thought, making her bow, *that dress is entirely wanton.*

However, there was no wantonness in the Terran lady's bow, or in her very correct, "Syntebra el'Kemin, I am pleased to meet you."

"Anne Davis, I am pleased to meet you," Syntebra replied, since she must.

She had to crane her neck to see the Terran's face. It was in no way a beautiful face, further marred by lines around the eyes and mouth. There was the suggestion of a smile in the grave brown eyes, and it was the outside of enough, Syntebra thought pettishly, to be laughed at by a *Terran*.

"Allow me to give you wine," A'thodelm yos'Galan said.

The Terran lady agreed to the suggestion and they went off, leaving Syntebra alone with Delm Korval.

"Will you tell me," Er Thom said in soft Terran, "if the ring displeases?"

It was wrong to ask it; twice wrong to ask it here, now. But the sight of her naked hands had hurt—appallingly. It was as if he had leaned to kiss her and she turned her face aside.

"The ring is—lovely," Anne said, keeping her eyes steadfastly from his. "I—I chose not to wear it."

His breath was out of pace and he felt uncannily close to tears. Exercising stern control, he poured her wine and held the glass. She took it, looking down.

"Anne . . ." Gods, he was going to break and shame them both by weeping before all these gathered. He swayed a daring half-step closer, not caring who marked it.

"Anne, I beg you will tell me what is wrong!" The whispered plea came out with the force of a shout, and at last she raised her head.

Her eyes were desolate—determined. He saw the lie form in their depths, felt the price she paid for speaking it as if it were wrung from his own soul.

"There is nothing wrong," she said, and took a breath. "Shouldn't you be attending to that pretty child?"

"That pretty child," he said, hearing the edge on his voice, "is terrified of me. The best I might do for her is to arrange matters so we need never meet again."

Anne glanced around in time to see Luken bel'Tarda approach Syntebra and Daav.

"Then you won't mind if you lose her to Luken," she said, raising her glass to sip.

"If Luken can abide her, he's welcome." He turned away and poured himself a glass of the red.

"At least tell me," he said, looking back to her, "if you yet intend to allow me the honor of becoming your lifemate."

Agony. Boiling lye poured across the open wound of his heart. He gasped, clutching his glass as the room spun dizzily out of control—and steadied. Before him, Anne's face was stark, desolate eyes sparkling tears.

She will lie, he thought around the singing in his ears. *Gods, I cannot bear it, if she lies to me again.*

Anne turned her head sharply, breaking his gaze.

"I must ask Daav to make me known to his sister," she said abruptly, and with no more ceremony than that she left him, walking so smoothly the gown barely rustled.

Er Thom took a sip to calm himself—and another—and moved out into the room, meticulously taking up his duties as host.

CHAPTER THIRTY-FOUR

The Lower Docks of Solcintra Port are the sphere of thieves, murderers, rogues and criminals of every description. Clanless and desperate, they have nothing to lose, and are completely willing to relieve the unwary of their purses and, often enough, their lives.

—From *A Terran's Guide to Liad*

The final guest at long last bowed out, Er Thom leaned dizzily against the wall and raked his hands through his hair.

He'd lost track of Daav during in the evening; he supposed his cha'leket to have simply slipped away when the crush became too wearisome. He remembered that Anne had retired about mid-way through the dancing. Daav, her self-appointed cavalier, would have likely made his escape soon after.

The two dearest to him in someway accounted for, Er Thom closed his eyes, trying to ignore the roaring in his ears and consided what he could recall of the evening.

He had a vague notion that he had performed his hostly duties with competence, if not flair. Daav had attached himself to Anne, for which kindness his brother loved him all the more.

Luken had taken young Syntebra in to dinner, and danced with her several times. Duty had compelled Er Thom to claim the lady's hand for at least one dance, which he had done, and come away wondering how Luken could bear the chit hanging on his sleeve all evening.

But there, he thought, leaning his head back against the wall, Luken was a patient, good-hearted fellow. The child's apparent distress would be sufficient to assure her of his good offices.

Of the rest of the evening, he could recall nothing, save a feeling of bone-deep coldness, nausea, and the desire to break into tears at the most inopportune moments.

Ill, he thought, clawing his hair back from his face. *I must be ill.*

He'd been ill, once or twice, so long ago he could scarcely remember the occasions, much less the symptoms. He tried to recall when he had first felt poorly this evening—and gasped, coming up straight in the hallway.

Anne.

He'd been speaking with Anne. Anne who had not been her accustomed self for several days. Anne who had lied to him and who, reasonless, declined to wear his ring. Anne—

Gods, if Anne is ill—

He was on his way down the hall, half-running, shivering now with fear, lest she be lying in need and he unaware—

The door to the Smaller Salon opened. His mother came one step into the hallway and held up her hand.

"A word with you, sirrah. Now."

"Your pardon," he stammered, barely knowing what he said. "I must go to Anne immediately."

His mother's hand moved, flashing out with all her old speed, fingers locking around his wrist, crushing his lace, biting into his flesh.

"I think not," she said ominously.

For all her sudden strength, he could have easily broken the hold. But she was kin; she had borne him and given him aside, that he might be raised with Daav yos'Phelium, his beloved other self—and for that she was owed.

"Mother," he said gently, standing where she held him. "I have reason to believe the guest is ill."

"I see," she said, remotely polite. "A very grave affair, I

agree. Mr. pak'Ora shall be dispatched to inquire into the guest's health. You will come with me."

For a heartbeat he thought he would not; thought he would break with clan entirely, rip away his arm and run abovestairs to his heart's own love.

But he felt the deep tremors in the hand that held him, saw the exhaustion in her face and the half-mad glitter in her eyes that said she kept her feet by will alone.

"Certainly," he murmured and they went together into the Smaller Salon, she leaning heavily on the arm of her supposed captive.

Er Thom seated her in a chair by the busy fire, then stood back, solemnly studying the table at her side.

Petrella's glittering eyes raked his face.

"Think I'm beyond keeping my word, do you?" she snapped and pulled the intercom to her.

The order to inquire into the state of the guest's health was given, brusquely, and the intercom shoved aside.

"Satisfied, A'thodelm?"

Er Thom bowed. "My thanks, mother."

She made no answer to this, but simply sat for a time, staring into his face, fingers gripping the arms of the chair.

"The Terran scholar looked uncommonly fine this evening," she said at last, and in milder tone than he had anticipated. "Eyla dea'Lorn's work, I think?"

Er Thom said nothing. In spite of the fire he was *cold*— cold. He felt certain his mother could see him shiver.

"And the jewels," she pursued, after a moment. "Who but Moonel would think a yellow diamond rope? Allow me to offer my compliments, A'thodelm: You do handsomely by your light-loves." She paused, eyes burning into his.

"You will now have the goodness to name the day in this relumma on which you shall wed Syntebra el'Kemin."

Er Thom inclined his head. "I shall not marry Syntebra el'Kemin," he said steadily. "Not in this relumma or in any other."

"Ah, so?" His mother lifted her eyebrows in polite interest, her voice dangerously mild. "Pray, why not?"

"For the first part, because the child is frightened of me."

"A condition," Petrella pointed out, still in that tone of

menacing mildness, "you did very little to alleviate this evening. But I interrupt! If there is a first part, then a second must be at hand! Enlighten me, I beg."

His hands were ice; he felt sweat gathering along his hairline; his stomach was cramped and there was a roaring in his ears that overrode the crackling of the fire. Er Thom grit his teeth and bowed.

"Scholar Davis and I are agreed to become lifemates," he said, around a strangling tightness in his throat. "We go to seek the delm tomorrow."

Silence. Petrella was seen to close her eyes—and open them.

"I forbid it."

"You cannot," he answered.

"Ah, can I not?" She leaned forward, fingers clawed into the carven arms of the chair. "I remind you that I am Thodelm yos'Galan. It is I who decides issues of Line and I have decided that it is not necessary to take a Terran into yos'Galan. Why should we do so? We are Liaden!"

"We are Korval!" Er Thom's shout startled him as much as his mother. "There is strength in diversity, weakness in samehood! You have read Cantra's logs—" He flung his hands out, showing her his empty palms.

"Mother, you have not even seen the child we made," he said, voice somewhat calmer. "Bright, bold-hearted and quick—as quick as any in the clan at his age—quicker than many! How is this ill-done? Why, the clan can use a dozen such!"

"And may have them yet, should I decide to breed you thus often!" Petrella pushed to her feet, face nearly white in the fire glow.

"Mother—"

"Silence!" The Command Mode: Thodelm to Line Member. She pinned him with glare.

"You are forbidden," she stated, all in High Command. "You are forbidden from this moment forward to see, touch, speak to or think upon Anne Davis. She is not for you. You are commanded to name a day when you shall wed Syntebra el'Kemin. Now."

"Never!" he cried. "As for denying Anne, I shall not! We

are lifemates, in all but word! Tomorrow morning, we shall be lifemates entirely! You cannot stop us from seeking the delm, you cannot—"

"I forbid this lifemating!" Petrella snarled. "Pursue it at your peril, A'thodelm, unless you wish make a way for yourself and your *lifemate* on the Lower Docks!"

Er Thom froze, jaw tight. He met his mother's eyes straightly.

"There is no need for a master trader to seek the Low Port," he said, and the inflection of his voice was nearer Terran than any proper mode. "And if you will have my license called in question, then I remind you there is yet no reason for a master pilot to go further than the Guild House in the Upper Port." He bowed.

"If you will have it so, ma'am, then you will. I wish—with all my heart—that it were otherwise. As it is not, I shall take myself and mine—"

"Enough!" The Command Mode: Delm to Clanmember. Er Thom bit off his sentence as Daav came, quick and silent, across the room.

"You!" He flung a hand out to Petrella, black eyes bright in a face that might have been carved of gold. "We bar none from the clan tonight! You!" The hand flashed to Er Thom, Korval's Ring snagging the firelight. "We drag none unwilling into the clan. Ever!"

Er Thom started, was stilled by a flare of black eyes. "The lady has told me—tonight!—that she would have none of you. She swore it, and I believe her. The game is done."

"No!" Er Thom shook off his delm's gaze. "I will see her, speak with her! There is something gone ill and she—"

"Silence!" Korval commanded and Er Thom gasped, staring into black, black eyes. In the fireplace, a stick broke noisily, releasing a rain of sparkles.

"You will go to your rooms," Korval commanded then, "and await the Healer. Anne Davis is none of yours. I trust you will not trouble her further."

She had denied him. His mind logged the thought into a loop, that began at once to repeat, over and over: Anne had denied him. Anne had denied him. Anne . . . Anne.

His body moved, graceless and wooden—a bow to the

delm's honor, followed by another, to the thodelm. His—legs—moved, carrying him past delm and thodelm, out of the room, into the hall, down corridors pitch black and bitter cold, until at last he came to an end of walking.

He stared around the place where he found himself: Stared at the laden worktable, the mantelpiece cluttered with bric-a-brac from an hundred worlds, the pleasant grouping of chair and doublechair before the laid and unlit hearth.

He walked toward the hearth, eyes caught by a flutter of red and gold among the mantel's clutter. Reaching, he had it down, and stood gazing at the thing.

A scrap of red silk no longer than his hand, that was all. That, and a length of tarnished, gold-colored ribbon, elaborately knotted into a fraying flower, through which the red silk had been lovingly threaded.

"Anne!" Her name was a keen, jagged with agony. He crashed to his knees, clutching the bit of silk as if it were a lifeline, bent his head and wept.

"Well." Petrella sank into her chair, quivering in every muscle. She looked up into her nephew's set face. "Better late than never arrive, I suppose. It comforts me that at last you perceive the good of the clan."

"The good of the clan," Daav repeated tonelessly. He stared down at her, eyes black and remote. "Is Korval so wealthy, aunt, that we might cast aside a master pilot, and shrug away the cost? Or has your intention always been to end yos'Galan with yourself? Speak plainly, I beg you."

"End yos'Galan—Ah." Petrella closed her eyes and let her head fall against the chair's padding. "You heard me threaten him with the Lower Docks, did you? Then you also heard that he was raving. I spoke to frighten, and to shock him into sanity."

"And failed in both intents," Daav snapped. "He was on the edge of accepting your terms, ma'am, when the delm ordered him to cease!"

There was a small silence. Petrella opened her eyes.

"I believe you had mistaken the matter, nephew."

"Oh, had I?" Daav returned bitterly. " 'I shall take myself

and mine—' was what he said! Am I the only one of us who can clearly hear the end of that sentence?" He bowed, deeply and with irony. "My compliments, aunt—In one throw you make your son clanless and a thief."

In the depths of her chair, Petrella shivered, assailed by a pain far different than that which wracked her body.

"He—is ill," she achieved after a moment. "To turn his face from the clan and follow a Terran? It is—"

"Master Healer Kestra will be with him tomorrow. Would that she had been able to come tonight." Daav turned away to stare into the fire. Suddenly, he whirled.

"Damn you for a meddlesome old woman!" he cried. "Why could you not have let it be? The lady had said she would not have him! She loved him too well, for your interest, aunt—too well to allow him the *sacrifice* of aligning himself with a Terran. If only his mother loved him half so well! But you—you must needs demand and shame and assert your dominion, sowing pain with every throw!" He came forward, one step, and stopped himself, staring down at her as if she were prey.

"The lady would have gone!" he shouted. "Of her own will, she would have left us and sought what healing she might. My brother would have likewise sought the Healers, to ease the grief of her going. There would have been honor for both in this, and a minimum of pain." He paused and Petrella found she could breathe again, though she dared not take her eyes from his.

"All thanks to your wisdom," he finished with brutal calm, "we have now two bleeding from wounds which may never heal clean, and a child abovestairs, crying aloud for both."

He swept a low, mocking bow, his lace rustling in the utter silence of the room.

"Sleep well, Aunt Petrella. I shall return tomorrow."

She made him no answer; barely knew that he was gone. She watched the fire—and, later, the embers—letting her mind ride the waves of pain, until she was back in a time when her twin was alive and all of life stretched before them.

CHAPTER THIRTY-FIVE

Er Thom fell from the Tree this morning.

I hasten to add that all is well, though of course he took damage. A matter of broken ribs and dislocated shoulder—that's the worst of it. Nothing beyond the auto-doc's capabilities.

I cannot for certain say how far he fell, for all Daav can tell me is that the pair of them had "never been so high." Er Thom was craning for a better sight of the Port when an end-branch broke under his weight.

He was caught, twig-lashed and unconscious, by the big by-branch about seven meters up—you know the one, sister. The luck is in the business twice: The child doesn't remember falling.

Daav saw the whole, and kept a cool head—far cooler than I should have kept at eight Standards, and so I swear! 'Twas he climbed down, fetched me out of a meeting with dea'Gauss, and showed me where Er Thom lay.

Nor would he be parted from his cha'leket, but kept vigil at 'doc-side and bed. I at last persuaded him to lie down whilst I kept watch, and he fell instantly asleep—to wake a quarter-hour later shrieking for Er Thom to come back, "Come back! The branch is breaking!"

I await the Healer as I write this . . .

—Excerpted from a private letter to
Petrella yos'Galan from Chi yos'Phelium

Shan took her hand listlessly and went without any of his usual chatter down the long hallway toward Doctor yo'Kera's office, Mouse clutched tight against his chest.

Anne eyed him worriedly. According to Mrs. Intassi, he had passed a restless night, his sleep broken by bad dreams and bouts of crying. It sounded remarkably like Anne's own night and she wondered, half-dazedly, if she had caused her son's unrest or he had caused hers.

She shook her head. *Sure and there's plenty of pain for everyone to have their own share.* Er Thom's night would have surely been no better; she recalled the look in his eyes, as he begged her to tell him what was wrong.

Annie Davis, I hope you know what you're doing.

But after all, she told herself, working the lock on Doctor yo'Kera's door, there was nothing else to do. By now, Daav would have told Er Thom that Anne had lied when she had agreed to be his lifemate. Er Thom could not possibly forgive such a lie, such a strike at his melant'i. Of course, he would come after her—but he would do so in any case, once he found Shan was gone. It was her intention to be firmly within Terran jurisdiction by the time Er Thom finally caught up with her.

"Ma?" Shan looked up at her from heavy-lidded silver eyes. "Where's Mirada?"

Oh, gods. She dropped her bulging briefcase and went to her knees, gathering her son's small body close.

"Mirada can't come, Shannie," she whispered, cheek tight against his hair. "His clan needs him."

He slipped his arms around her neck, she felt him sigh, then: "We stay here? With Mirada?"

"No, baby," she whispered and closed her eyes to hold back the tears. "We're going home—to visit Uncle Dickie. A nice, long visit."

She thought briefly of her post on University: Good-bye tenure track. Well, she could get a job on New Dublin, surely. She could be a translator at the Port, or a teacher of Standard Terran in the private school.

Or she could raise sheep. Her arms tightened around her son.

"I love you, Shannie."

"Love you, Ma." He pushed back against her arms and lifted a hand to her face. His fingertips came away wet. "Sad."

"Sad," she repeated, voice cracking. She tried a smile; it felt wrong on her face. "We'll be happy again. I promise."

She stood and lifted him onto the table; plucked Mouse from the floor and laid it across Shan's knees.

"I'm going to call a cab," she told him. "Then we can go to the Port."

It took a few minutes and some ingenuity to thread the university's comm system, but she finally got an outside line and placed her call. The cab was promised in fifteen minutes, at the secondary door, as directed. Anne nodded to herself and cut the connection, glancing around Doctor yo'Kera's cluttered, comfortable office for the last time.

In an ocean of hurt, the pain of leaving his work undone, of walking away from the mystery of missing corroboration, was imbued with special flavor. Jin Del yo'Kera had been her friend, steadfast down a dozen years. In a way, she had loved him. Gods knew, she owed him more than she could ever repay. To leave him this way, with his research in shambles, his brilliance dimmed in the memories of his colleagues . . .

She shook her head, denying the tears that made a glittering riot of the book-crammed shelves. Turning from the shelves, she found herself contemplating the flat-pic of three Aus at their sheep station: Mildred Higgins, Sally Brunner, Jackson Roy. Strong, straightforward people they seemed, smiling out of the battered frame. People who would see nothing odd in teaching a Liaden scholar to shear sheep.

The flat-pic was slightly wrinkled, as if someone had lately had it out of its frame and reseated it imperfectly. Or, Anne thought, perhaps the picture was so old the paper was beginning to dissolve. She had a moment's urge to take the thing off the wall and smooth the pic tidy. Shaking her head at the impulse, she turned back to Shan.

"Time to go, laddie," she said, swinging him to the floor. "Hold tight to Mouse, now."

She picked up her briefcase, took her son's hand and stepped out into the hall.

Shan uttered a sharp squeak and fell silent, his hand gone cold in hers.

Fil Tor Kinrae finished his bow and smiled, coldly, up into her eyes.

"Scholar. How fortunate that I meet you. We have much to speak about."

Anne inclined her head and allowed a note of irritation to be heard. "Alas, sir, I am unable to accommodate you today. I am bound for the Port."

"Then I am twice fortunate," he said in his curiously flat voice. "I go to the Port, as well. Allow me to drive you."

"Thank you, no. I have transport." She made to go past him down the hall, but he was abruptly before her.

The gun in his hand was quite steady. He was pointing it at Shan.

"You do not seem to grasp the situation, Scholar," he said, and the mode was Superior to Inferior. "You will allow me to drive you to the Port. You will continue to do precisely as I command. Fail, and I shall certainly harm—that." The gun moved minutely, indicating Shan.

"He's only a child," Anne said slowly. Fil Tor Kinrae inclined his head.

"So he is. Walk this way, if you please, and pray do not do anything foolish."

He came to himself in the gray of foredawn, face crushed into the hearth rug, one outflung hand clutching a tattered piece of red silk and a tawdry, fraying love knot.

His body ached amazingly, but that was no matter. His mind was clear.

He had dreamed.

Baffling, grief-laden dreams, they were, that robed the veriest commonplace in twisty, alien menace until his stomach churned with the strangeness of it and his head felt likely to burst asunder.

There were tolls demanded, now and again—he gave what was asked: His ring, his fortune, his peace. In return he was promised safe passage through the surrounding menace. He was promised love, melant'i and a return of peace.

The toll-man demanded his son.

"He's my son, Er Thom!" he cried out and felt as if his

heart were broken anew. "He's a Terran citizen! Your clan doesn't know and your clan doesn't care!" He covered his face and wept aloud.

"I came home," he whispered distractedly, "and you were gone . . ."

Full awake, lucid and calm, he rolled to his back, careless alike of complaining muscles and ruined finery. He stared up at the gray-washed ceiling and considered his own folly.

Of course Anne did not care of Shan's place in Line—that would be to think as a Liaden. To think as a Terran—to think like *Anne*—one would weigh the answers to such questions and find in them proof that the man she had asked to guard her melant'i—the man she loved too well to allow his *sacrifice*—had willfully cheated her, stolen her child and placed him beyond her reach—forever.

Comes the same man pursuing his suit and Anne is flung headlong and frightened into a game so complex it might well give a seasoned player pause.

The man cries lifemates—does he lie? He had lied once, had he not? Assume he lies—necessity demands it. Lie to him in return, a little; better, allow him to deceive himself. Play for time, play for the single, slender moment of escape.

She had played well—brilliantly well, for one unused to the game. Yet she had been unable, even for necessity, to lie entirely. Honor would not allow her to wear the ring he had given.

He wondered, lying there, if she had known her confidence to Daav would end thus, with Er Thom safely out of the way, and her path clear from nursery to space port. It seemed likely.

He sighed and moved his head from side to side against the floor.

Anne's window of opportunity was today—this morning. She would take it—she must, or all play was for naught. He rather thought she would try to barter Moonel's jewelry for passage away, an enterprise she might find more difficult than she had supposed.

His course was clear. He spared a thought for his brother— but it seemed he was beyond feeling any new pain. The Healer would soon arrive; she must find an empty room when she did.

He came to his feet, wincing a little at the protest of his muscles, and went along to the shower, stripping off his formal clothes as he walked.

Muscles eased by a hot shower, Er Thom dressed in plain, serviceable trousers, plain shirt, comfortable boots. Each of the boots carried a cantra in the heel.

The belt he ran around his waist carried two dozen cantra between the layers of leather; the cunningly-made silver buckle could be traded either for melt-price or as an artwork.

From the lock-box he took other sorts of money: Terran bits, loops of pierced shell and malachite, rough-cut gems. These he disposed in several secret pockets about his person, and closed the safe on a dozen times the amount he had taken.

He shrugged into his leather pilot's jacket, feeling it settle heavily across his shoulders. Coins were sewn between the outer lining and the inner; more coins weighted the waist.

For a moment he fingered his jewel-box, frowning—and decided against. He pulled a second, smaller box toward him, lifted the lid and brought the gun out.

Quickly, he cracked it, checked it, reassembled it and slipped it into a jacket pocket. Extra pellets went into still other pockets. He closed the box and put it meticulously back in its place.

So. He looked around his room, reviewing his plan.

Anne's first object must be to leave Liad. Thus, he would find her at the Port. Necessity might dictate that she bear her son away, but she loved Er Thom yos'Galan. He knew that. She would allow him to come close enough to speak to her— close enough to touch her.

The gun weighed like a stone in his pocket. For a moment he hated it with an intensity that should have been shocking— then he shook the emotion away. He must make haste. Daav would be here with the Healer very soon.

Pilot quick, he went back to the parlor and opened the window wide. The door was unlocked; he didn't bother locking it or scrambling the access code. Such tactics would scarcely slow Daav. The best plan was to be gone, and quickly.

He spared a glance for Jelaza Kazone, stretching tall and

true across the valley, visible sign of Cantra yos'Phelium's love for Jela, her partner, and the father of her child. Tears pricked his eyes; he dashed them away, swung over the sill and began the downward climb.

Daav ran across to the open window, heart in his mouth. *Gods, no, he would not—*

But his brother's broken body did not lie on the path so far below. Indeed, a cooler perusal of the vine that grew along the window and below discovered disturbed leaves, torn runners, crushed flowers—damage one would expect a climber to inflict.

Daav swore, though with more relief than anger, for it was an appalling climb down a sheer rock wall and the vine very little aid, in case one should fall.

"However, he did not fall," Master Healer Kestra commented from behind him. "So you may lay that fear aside, if you please."

He turned back to her and bowed fully. "My apologies, Master Healer. It appears my brother had—business elsewhere."

"Urgent business," she agreed in her dry way. She paced to the hearth rug, bent to pick up a scrap of red fabric and a bit of gold ribbon.

"The room," she murmured, her face losing its accustomed sharpness as she reached for nuance beyond the mere physical.

"The room tells me of great distress, of two people—wounded, yet fighting for understanding—of—resolution . . ."

"Two?" Daav demanded, for surely Er Thom would not have been so disobedient as—A breeze from the window mocked the thought.

From the hearth-rug, Master Kestra frowned. "Two? Of course—No. No, I believe you are quite correct. *Three* people. But surely one is—a child? A rather exceptional child. I would be interested in making the child's acquaintance, I think."

"It had been intended," Daav said as his mind raced, placing piece against piece until he had the shape of how it must have been.

The lady would not leave without the child, he thought, with icy calm. *Er Thom would not stay without the lady. The luck send I'm in time to catch them at the Port!*

"Master Healer, I am wanted urgently elsewhere."

She turned from her study of the mantelpiece and gave him a look of sleepy amusement, running the red-and-gold ornament absently through her slender fingers.

"Go along, then. I shall await your return."

Without even a bow he was gone, running at the top of his considerable speed.

A few moments later the sound of a landcar's engine came through the open window and faded rapidly into the distance.

The Healer sat cross-legged upon the hearth rug, dreamy-eyed and languorous. She smoothed the tattered little love token flat on her palm, closed her eyes, and prepared herself to listen.

CHAPTER THIRTY-SIX

To be outside of the clan is to be dead to the clan.

—Excerpted from the Liaden Code of Proper Conduct

She spoke once on the ride to Solcintra Port, to offer their captor the jewels in her briefcase, in trade for their freedom.

"I am not a patient man, Scholar," Fil Tor Kinrae replied without sparing a glance at her face.

Anne sat back in the short, cramped seat, shoulder bumping the opaqued window, put her arms around her son and tried to think.

Marksmanship had been part of her required course of study at the Academy of Music. She had never been comfortable carrying a gun, though, and given the habit up on her return to New Dublin.

Of course, she attended the mandatory self-defense practice course for faculty every other semester. But the prospect of taking a gun away from an undoubted professional while ensuring he did not shoot her child iced her blood.

Perhaps a chance would present itself when they left the car. If she could keep between Shan and the gun—in her lap, Shan twisted to push his face against her breast.

He hadn't uttered a sound since his squeak of terror in the hallway, miles and minutes ago. Anne lay her cheek against

his hair and stroked him silently, hearing the echo of his
fright, feeling her own muscles tense in response.

Don't, she warned herself sharply. *For the gods' sake, gel,
don't set up a loop. The laddie's frightened enough—and you
need your wits about you.*

She closed her eyes and deliberately thought of Er Thom
as he had been back on University, after it was settled that
Shan would come to Liad—after they could be easy with each
other again. She thought of his understated humor, his care
and his thoughtfulness. She thought of him cross-legged on
the floor, assisting in the design of a block tower; she thought
of him holding Shan in his lap, telling a story in his soft, sweet
voice . . .

In her lap, Shan relaxed, the hand that clutched her sleeve
loosened. Anne resolutely thought of the good times, and it
seemed that she could see him before her, his hair brighter
than gold, his eyes purple and compelling beneath winged
brows. The mind-image grew sharper until it seemed she need
only extend a hand to feel the silked surface of his old leather
jacket, to finger the new scar along the shoulder, to touch his
cheek—once more . . .

The car stopped.

She sat up, Shan tensing against her. Now, perhaps . . .

The door popped open. Fil Tor Kinrae reached in, grabbed
Shan by one arm and dragged him from Anne's lap.

"Ma!" he shouted, then gasped into silence. Anne flung out
of the door——and froze, staring at the gun.

"Good," the man said without inflection. "Have the goodness to bring the case, Scholar. If the child makes another
sound he will regret it. Impress that upon him, won't you?"

Anne licked her lips and looked down into her son's wide
silver eyes. "Shannie," she said, keeping her voice firm and
even, "you have to be very quiet, OK?"

He swallowed and nodded, keeping his face turned away
from the man who held him. Anne reached into the car and
pulled out her briefcase.

"Good," Fil Tor Kinrae said again and moved the gun.
"This way, Scholar."

They were in an alley, thin, dirty and deserted. Anne
walked past two empty shop fronts and turned into a third,

obeying the movement of the gun. The man pushed ahead and shouldered the door open, dragging Shan into a dank vestibule. He pointed the gun at a set of twisty, ill-set steps.

"Up."

Obediently, she went up, minding the shallow stairs and hearing, in the hidden pocket of her mind, the sound of her son's silent sobbing.

At the top of the flight was another door, this one slightly ajar.

"In."

Anne pushed the door wide and walked in. Behind her the door closed, tumblers falling loudly.

The woman at the console spun in her chair, snapping to her feet in such haste her many earrings jangled.

"Cold space, it's the yos'Galan's Terran!" The hard gray eyes went past Anne. "And the mongrel. Have you gone mad?"

Fil Tor Kinrae sent Shan reeling against Anne's legs with negligent brutality and walked within, moving his shoulders.

"What business of mine, if the yos'Galan keeps cows?"

"And is so very careless as to lose them," the woman agreed, running a hand on which a master trader's amethyst gleamed over her close-cropped head. "Well enough. But that child is Korval, my friend, and if you believe the Dragon will not tear the Port to ground to find him, you *have* run mad!"

"But they're not at the Port, Master ven'Apon," Kinrae explained in his flat voice. "They're at the university."

"Oh, are they?" The hard eyes flickered over Anne's face. "That might serve," she allowed. "I trust no one saw you take them." Her face shifted. "And I trust you'll allow them to be found far away from here, as well. I need no trouble with Korval, thank you. The yos'Galan has already done me the favor of calling my name before the Guild, scar his face!"

Kinrae stared at her. "If I chose to leave them here, I hope to hear no word from you, Master."

"Leave your dirty linen to me, will you?" the little woman demanded hotly, putting her palms flat on the desktop. "Damn you, wash your own laundry."

The gunman looked at her blandly. "I believe you've had handsome payment."

"And worked handsome hard!" the woman retorted. "I've told you I'm called before the Guild! How if I scrub clean and show the gentles the way of buying a master trader's license?"

"Would you sing that song?" he wondered flatly. "But birds have such short lives, Master ven'Apon." He moved his gun, negligently.

"I shall be using the back room and I expect I shall not be disturbed." The gun was on Anne, who was holding Shan against her and stroking his hair.

"Touching. This way, Scholar." He reached out and pulled Shan away, fingers twisted in the back of the child's collar. "Bring the case."

She had not attempted to sell the jewels back to Moonel, nor had she been seen in the Gem Exchange. He considered it unlikely that she knew of the less-savory establishments on the border of Mid-Port. Besides, they would not give her near the sum she must have.

It could perhaps be judged an error of play, that she had not asked him for money. How simple a matter, after all, to point out that her purse was slimmer than she liked. He would have emptied his pockets at her word. It was thus, between lifemates.

But Anne, Er Thom thought, standing at the curb on Exchange Street—Anne would see such asking to be dishonorable, the coins themselves tainted, devalued by deceit.

Wondering where next to seek her, he stuck his hands into his pockets, shuddering when his fingers touched the gun.

Ah, gods, beloved, must it be this path?

But there: Anne had chosen their course; to unchoose it was not possible. Bound to her as he was, with spider-silk lines of love and lies, it was his part, now, to follow.

He stepped off the curb and crossed the busy street, walking back to his car, puzzling over where she might have gone. Frowning and abstracted, he lay his hand against the door, and spun around, certain he had heard someone call his name.

The street behind him was very nearly empty. No one stood near, hand raised in greeting.

He heard the call again—slightly louder. His name, cer-

tainly, the voice seeming to come from—the east. Toward
Mid-Port.

Holding his breath, he slipped into the car, started the engine—and sat waiting, stretching his ears, though of course
that was foolish. When the call came again, he put the car into
gear and followed the fading echoes through the noisy chatter
of the outside world.

"**You** will have the goodness to produce the piece of bogus
evidence linking Liaden language to Terran."

Anne eyed Fil Tor Kinrae carefully. The gun was steady,
but at least he had let Shan sit next to her on the hard wooden
bench. The crying in the back of her mind had stopped, replaced by a kind of exhausted half-trance.

"If the evidence is bogus, why bother with it?" she asked
the gunman.

He returned her scrutiny blandly. "I collect lies, Scholar; it
is an avocation. Produce the material or pay the price. Please
understand that I am able to extract whatever payment I will.
Behold the destruction of the Languages Department on University and believe me." He moved the gun. "The proof,
Scholar. Now."

"I don't have it," she said, meeting his disturbingly expressionless eyes and willing him to believe the truth.

"Jin Del yo'Kera had it," he returned.

"So I believe. However, the central argument is missing
from his notes. I thought it might be in his research computer,
but I was not able to find it." She nodded toward the briefcase
leaning against the wall. "I copied the core. The disk is in my
case. You're welcomed to take it."

"Am I? But how kind. However, I am not interested in
negative results, Scholar. I give you one more opportunity to
cooperate: Produce this central argument of Jin Del's, this
masterpiece of error that attempts to link Liad and Terra to a
common mother tongue."

Her son's body was a torch, scorching her side, his presence in her mind an alert somnolence. She met the gunman's
eyes fully, and saw Jin Del yo'Kera's death in their depths.

"I have no such information."

"I see. It is my belief, Scholar, that you are not fully awake to the vulnerability of your position. Perhaps a demonstration is in order."

The voice no longer called his name.

Indeed, Er Thom thought, threading the narrowing streets toward Mid-Port with rapid skill, that which guided him was no longer voice, but—compulsion. He followed it and in good time pulled over to the side of an alley, just behind another, nondescript and slightly battered, landcar.

He got out of the car and walked a short distance. It took less than a minute to persuade the street door to admit him, after which he lost no time in going up the rag-tag stairway.

Jyl ven'Apon spun round as he burst through the door, her hand flashing toward the weapon set ready on the desk—too late.

Er Thom's gun was already out and aimed, with regrettable accuracy, at a point in the precise center of her forehead.

Anne tried to block the man with her body and earned a fist against her shoulder for her efforts. He grabbed for Shan.

The child flung himself back against the wall, soft-booted feet flailing at the man's face.

"Mirada!" he screamed in piercing hysteria. "Mirada! Mirada!"

Fil Tor Kinrae swore and snatched again, clawed hand grabbing for fragile throat. Anne twisted, flung the man half backward and used her elbow in the way she had been taught.

One blow to crush a man's windpipe. Kinrae dropped like a stone. Before he hit the floor, Anne had the gun out of his hand and caught Shan to her.

"Hush, baby. Hush, OK?"

Face against the side of her neck, he nodded. Anne held him, mind working feverishly. The woman in the other room: She would have to be prepared to kill her, as well. Anne swallowed, feeling the gun in her hand, the plastic still warm from Kinrae's grip.

"Shannie, listen to me. You listening?"

"Yes."

"OK. I'm going out for a minute. You need to stay here *(with a dead man on the floor, Annie Davis?)*. I'll be back in a minute and then we'll leave. *(Gods willing.)* Promise me you'll stay here until I come for you."

"Promise, Ma."

"Good." She hugged him tight. "I love you, Shannie."

The warning was little enough—a light step in the hall beyond. Anne came to her feet, thrusting her son behind her, gun held ready.

The door burst open.

"Mirada!"

Er Thom's eyes flashed over her face, took in Shan and what was left of Fil Tor Kinrae on the floor. He slipped his gun away and held out a hand.

"Come away now. Quickly."

Er Thom had the briefcase, Anne was carrying Shan, uncertain if the shaking she felt was his or her own.

They went through the console-room. A glance revealed no body bleeding its life out on floor or desk. Anne swallowed around a mingled sense of nausea and relief, recalling what was left behind on the back room floor.

"How did you get here?" she asked Er Thom, voice sounding thin in her own ears.

He spared her a quick violet glance. "I heard you calling."

"Oh." She gulped, hugging Shan tight. "We're leaving Liad, Er Thom."

"Yes," he said, leading the way down the tricky stairs. "I know." At the bottom of the flight he turned to her.

"You and our child must be attended by a Healer as soon as possible. We should thus book passage on *Chelda,* which leaves this afternoon and has a Healer on-staff. After we are safe away, we may modify direction."

She stopped, blinking into his beautiful, beloved face. "We?"

He met her eyes, his own unguarded, his face fully open to her.

"If you will have me."

Have him? Anne drew a careful breath, aware of Shan, trembling in her arms. "We have to talk," she said.

Er Thom bowed slightly. "We do, indeed. Let us board *Chelda*. The Healers shall tend to you and to our son. We shall talk. Fully, I swear it. If you choose then that we must go separate paths, I shall trouble you no further." He held out a tentative hand.

"Can you trust me in these things, Anne?"

She touched his fingertips lightly with her own. "Yes."

"Good," he said gravely. "Let us go away from here."

CHAPTER THIRTY-SEVEN

In the case of a clan's loss of an individual member through the actions of a person unrelated to the clan, balance-payment is hereby set forth. Such payment weighs equally the occupation, age, and clan-standing of the individual who has been lost. The attached chart shall henceforth be the standard by which all clans shall compute such balance-payment.

—From the Charter of the Council of Clans,
Fifth Amended Edition

"Yes, I see." The Healer folded neat hands into his lap. "For the child, forgetfulness. And for yourself as well, if you wish it, Lady."

Anne found herself looking into a pair of bright brown eyes.

She frowned, fighting to think with a mind that seemed frozen and unwieldy. Er Thom had handled the arrangements at the reservation office, slicing through what Anne dimly perceived as a daunting mountain of red tape. He had bespoken them a suite aboard *Chelda,* she remembered that he had said so. But what else he might have told her, she could not presently call to mind.

On consideration, they might very well be on *Chelda* now, in the very suite Er Thom had rented, though the shuttle trip seemed likewise lost to recollection. The only thing she clearly remembered was the scene in the Mid-Port back room, where she had killed a man and left him lying on the floor . . .

The Healer was looking at her, head tipped to one side, face alert and friendly.

"Forgetfulness," she managed. Her voice was shaking badly, she noted with detachment. "You can make Shan forget what happened?"

The Healer inclined his head. "Very easily, Lady. Shall I?"

"It would be best," she heard Er Thom murmur beside her.

She hugged Shan tight against her chest. "Yes," she said awkwardly, the dead man looming before her mind's eye. "If you please."

"Very well." He stood, a diminutive man with a quantity of curly gray-shot hair, and held out a hand. "We shall have to be alone, Shan and I. It will not take long."

On her lap, Shan stirred, looking up at the tiny man out of dull silver eyes. Abruptly, he wriggled upright and leaned forward in Anne's hold.

"Beautiful sparkles," he announced, and raised a hand toward the Healer. "Show me."

The Healer smiled. "Certainly."

Shan wriggled again, and Anne took her arms away. Her son slid from her lap and clasped the Healer's hand. Together they disappeared into an anteroom.

"Anne?" Er Thom's voice was worried. She turned to look at him. "Shall you take forgetfulness, as well?"

Forget . . . She wanted, desperately, to forget. Especially, she wanted to forget that last moment, when her body had taken over from her mind and—she had killed a man. She had *intended* to kill him. He had threatened her child, herself. He had murdered Jin Del yo'Kera, by his own word, he had destroyed the Language Arts building and only pure luck that no one had died of it—

"Anne!" Er Thom's hands were on her shoulders.

She realized she was trembling, looked wildly into his face.

"What happened—happened to the—master trader?"

His fingers were kneading her shoulders, setting up a rhythm in counter to her trembling. "She need not concern you."

"You killed her."

"No." He lifted a hand and tenderly cupped her cheek. "There was no need. She ran away." Gently, he bent and lay his lips against hers, whisper-light and warm.

Tears spilled over. She lurched forward, face buried in his shoulder, arms tight around his waist. The trembling turned to violent shaking, the tears to half-cries, gritted out past locked teeth.

Er Thom held her, one hand stroking her hair, the vulnerable back of her neck. He spoke in the Low Tongue, honoring her, loving her. Indeed, he barely knew what he said, except it came full from the heart. It seemed the sound of his voice soothed her.

The storm passed, quickly for all its passion. She lay shivering in his arms, her cheek pillowed against his shoulder.

"Remember something for me," she said huskily, her breath warm against the side of his neck.

He stroked her hair. "What shall I recall?"

"That—Fil Tor Kinrae. He wanted the central argument—the material that was missing from Doctor yo'Kera's proof. I know—I think I know where it is." She drew a shuddering breath. "It's behind the flat pic of—of the Aus sheep farmers. In his office. Remember that, Er Thom." Her arms tightened around him. "It's important."

"I will remember," he promised.

"Thank you." She sighed and nestled her cheek against him, seeming more peaceful, though she trembled still.

The door to the anteroom opened and the Healer spoke with the ease of one for whom there are few surprises in life.

"The child is asleep. If the lady will come with me, I shall see what might be wrought."

She stirred and moved her arms from his waist. Er Thom stepped back, took her hand and helped her to rise. Slipping her arm through his, he guided her to the doorway and gave her over to the Healer.

"I will be with you," he said, smiling up into her beloved and careworn face, "when you wake."

She gave him an uncertain smile in return. "All right," she mumbled, and allowed the Healer to lead her away.

•   •   •

The Healer's exhaustion showed clearly in his face. He accepted a glass of wine with unfeigned gratitude and slumped into the offered chair with a sigh.

Er Thom sat in the chair opposite, sipped his wine and put it aside.

"It is fortunate," the Healer said after a sip or two of his own, "that they were able to be seen so quickly after the event. I anticipate no complications for the child: The dream will be hazy when he wakes from trance and will continue to fade over the next two or three days.

"The lady I believe capable of recapturing the entire experience, did necessity exist. She has a disciplined mind and a very strong will. If she should find it difficult to concentrate, if her sleep is disturbed, if she is troubled in any way—only call. I shall be honored to assist her."

Er Thom inclined his head. "I thank you."

"It is joy to serve," the Healer replied formally. He had recourse once more to his glass.

"The child," he said then and met Er Thom's gaze. "Your Lordship is perhaps not aware that the child is something out of the common way. It would be wisdom, were he to be shown—soon—to a master Healer, or brought to a Hall."

Again, Er Thom inclined his head. "I shall discuss the matter with my lady."

"Certainly." The Healer finished his wine and rose to make his bow.

Er Thom rose, returned the man's salute with gravity, straightened and held out a hand in which a six-cantra gleamed.

"Please accept tangible evidence of my gratitude for the service you render my lady and our son."

"Your Lordship is gracious." The coin disappeared. The Healer inclined his head.

"Good day, sir. Fair fortune to you and yours."

"And to you, Healer."

Er Thom walked the smaller man to the door and let him out into the wide, cruise-ship hallway. He closed the door and locked it—and went back through the parlor to the bedroom, there to keep watch at Anne's bedside until such time as she should wake.

• • •

Coming out of sleep was like coming out of heavy cloud, into lighter cloud, to dense fog, to mist—to bright, unencumbered sun.

Anne stretched luxuriously. She felt wonderfully well, without care or grief; lucid and joyful for the first time in days.

She stretched again, knowing that they were booked on the cruise ship *Chelda,* bound for Lytaxin and points outward, scheduled to leave Liad orbit this very afternoon. Her son was safe and happy—deeply asleep at the moment, she knew. Er Thom was traveling with them—she forgot precisely how that had come about, for surely—

The thought slid away, vanishing into a warm glow of happiness.

"Hello, Anne." His voice, in gentle Terran. "Are you well?"

"Well?" She opened her eyes and smiled up into his, extended a languid hand and brushed his cheek with her fingertips, relishing the slow stir of passion. "I'm wonderful. I guess I needed a nap."

"I—guess," Er Thom agreed softly. He traced her eyebrows with a light fingertip. "You are beautiful."

She laughed. "No, laddie, there you're out. I am *not* beautiful."

"You really must allow me to disagree with you," he murmured, fingertips like moon-moths against her lips. He smiled, eyes smoky, fingers running the line of her jaw. "Beautiful Anne. Dar-ling Anne. Sweetheart."

She gasped, as much from surprise as from the tingle of pleasure his caresses evoked.

"You don't—You never say—things . . ." His fingers were tracing a line of fire along the curve of her throat.

"My dreadful manners," he murmured, bending his bright head as his clever fingers worked lose the fastening of her shirt. "Forgive me."

His mouth was hot over the pulse at the base of her throat. His fingers were teasing a nipple to erection.

"Teach me," he whispered, raising his head and kissing her cheek, her eyelids, her chin. "What else should I say, Anne?"

She laughed breathlessly, cupping his face in her two hands and holding him still.

"I don't think you need to say anything more at the moment," she murmured, and kissed him, very thoroughly, indeed.

She woke again, sated and a-tingle in every nerve, opened her eyes and saw him leaning above her, face suffused with tenderness. She shivered and reached for him.

"Er Thom, what's wrong?"

"Ah." He stroked her hair softly back from her forehead. "I shall—miss—my clan."

Coldness leached into her, riding confusion. Why was he here? The plan—hadn't the plan been to take Shan and herself away to New Dublin? Er Thom was to have stayed with his clan, wasn't that the plan? How—She groped after the precise memory. It eluded her, leaving her blinking up into his eyes, feeling half-ill with loneliness, vulnerable as she had never been vulnerable.

"You could—" Gods, she could scarcely breathe. She pushed her voice past the tight spot in her throat. "The ship's still in orbit, isn't it? You could—go home . . ."

"No, how could I?" He smiled gently and lay his finger along her lips. "You and our son are leaving Liad. How can I stay?" He kissed her cheek. "I shall learn, sweetheart. I depend upon you to teach me."

She stared at him, speechless—then blinked, attention diverted.

"Shan's waking up."

"I shall go to him," Er Thom said, slipping out of the wide bed and bending to retrieve his clothes. He smiled at her. "If you like, we three may go up to the observation deck and watch the ship break orbit."

He was going to stay with them, loneliness and vulnerability be damned. She felt his determination echo at the core of her. He was turning his back on his clan, on wealth and position; throwing his lot in with Linguistics Professor Anne Davis, untenured.

"Er Thom—"

"Hush." He bent quickly over her, stopping her protests with his lips. "I love you, Anne Davis, with all of my heart. If you will not have Liad, then you must lead me to another place, and teach me new customs. Only do not put me aside . . ." His voice broke, eyes bright. "Anne?"

"You lied," she said uncertainly, for that had suddenly come crystal clear. "You said you weren't a thief—"

"Nor am I." He sat on the edge of the bed and caught her hands in his. "Anne, listen. If there were a child who was Davis, and I caused him to brought into Korval, that is thievery. But a child named yos'Galan, brought into Korval—how may yos'Galan steal a yos'Galan?" His fingers were tight on hers; she felt the truth in him, like a flame, melting away old fears.

"I erred. That, yes. I mistook local custom and thought I had explained enough. I thought, having done honor in name, you now passed the full joy of another yos'Galan to the clan, as was right and proper. Liaden. I plead stupidity. I plead pride. But you must acquit me of lying to you, Anne. That, I never undertook."

"You'll come with us?" she said, wonderingly. "To New Dublin?"

"Is that where you are bound?" Er Thom moved his shoulders. "I shall stand at your side. It is what I wish." He tipped his head. "We may need to tarry upon Lytaxin. Our son should be seen in the Healer's Hall—unless there is such on New Dublin?"

She shook her head. "We'll need to talk," she said, and heard a vague, fog-shrouded echo. She let it fade away, uncurious.

Er Thom inclined his head. "So we shall. I will go to our son now."

"I'll sort out my clothes," Anne said, with wry humor, "and meet the two of you in the parlor very soon."

Shan pronounced himself both hungry and thirsty. He submitted with a certain ill-grace to having his hair combed and a wet cloth passed over his face, but took Er Thom's hand willingly enough and went with him into the parlor.

One step into the room, Er Thom froze, staring at the man in the black leather jacket who lounged at his ease on the low-slung sofa, long legs thrust out before him and crossed neatly at the ankle. He lifted a glass of blood-red wine in salute and sipped, room lights running liquid off the enamel-work of his single ring.

"Daav!" Shan cried joyously.

"Hello, Nephew," the man replied gently. His black eyes went to Er Thom. "Brother. I perceive I am in time."

CHAPTER THIRTY-EIGHT

Take the course opposite to custom and you will almost always do well.

—Jean Jacques Rousseau

Shan was settled at a low table in the corner, a crystal glass of juice and some tidbits of cheese to hand. Er Thom came back to the center of the room and stood staring down at the man on the sofa.

"My family and I," he said eventually, and in Terran, "are bound for New Dublin."

Daav raised his glass, lips pursed in consideration.

"A pastoral location," he allowed in the same language. "Do you plan a long stay?"

"I believe Anne means us to settle there."

"Really?" Daav lifted an eyebrow. "I don't see you as a farmer, denubia."

"That has very little to say to the matter," Er Thom informed him flatly.

"Ah. Well, that is lowering, to be sure." He flourished the glass, switching to Low Liaden. "Drink with me, brother."

"I regret to inform you," Er Thom said, keeping stubbornly to Terran, "that your brother is dead."

"Oh, dear. But you are misinformed, you know," Daav said kindly, pursuing his end of the conversation now in Low Li-

aden. "My brother was seen not very many hours ago, book-
ing passage for three upon *Chelda*. Unless the line's service
has gone entirely awry, I believe we may assume he is enjoying his customary robust health."

"Mirada!" Shan called from across the room. "More juice.
Please!"

"You will have to teach him to call you otherwise," Daav
murmured, and lifted an eyebrow at Er Thom's start.

"Father," he suggested in soft Terran, meeting the determined violet eyes. "Papa. Da. Something of that nature."

"Mirada?" Shan called.

Er Thom went to him, refilled the glass and ruffled his
frost-colored hair. Then he came back to stand and stare. Daav
sipped wine, unperturbed.

"I repudiate the clan," Er Thom said, the High Tongue cold
as hyperspace.

"Yes, but you see," Daav returned earnestly in the Low
Tongue, "the clan doesn't repudiate you. If things were otherwise, I might very well wave you away. An off-shoot of the
clan on New Dublin might be amusing. But things are not otherwise, darling. The clan needs you—you, yourself, not simply your genes. I cannot allow you to leave us. Necessity." He
used his chin to point at Shan, engrossed in his snack.

"And if you think I shall allow that child beyond range of
a Healer Hall any time before he has completed formal training, I beg that you think again." He cocked a whimsical eyebrow. "Come home, darling, do."

Er Thom's mouth tightened, his eyes wounded.

"My family and I," he repeated steadfastly, though his Terran had gone rather blurry, "are bound for New Dublin. The
ship leaves within the hour."

Daav sighed. "No," he corrected gently. "It does not."

Er Thom drew a careful breath. "The schedule—"

"I see I have failed of making myself plain." He swirled
what was left of his wine and glanced up, black eyes glinting.

"This ship goes nowhere until I leave it. And I shall not
leave it without yourself and your son in my company." He
raised his glass and finished the last of the wine.

"There is an important package due from Korval," he said,
somewhat more gently. "The ship is being held for its arrival.

It will make rather a hash out of traffic, of course, but that's the port master's problem, not mine." He put the glass aside.

"When I leave the ship, the package will be delivered and *Chelda* may be on its way." He moved his hand as if he cast dice. "It is now your throw, brother. How long shall we hang in orbit?"

There was a long silence.

"Anne and I are—tied together," Er Thom said eventually, and in, his brother heard with relief, the Low Tongue. "Understand me. I heard her call—from across the Port. I followed her thought to a place—" He moved his shoulders. "There is a dead man named Fil Tor Kinrae in the back room of a warehouse in Mid-Port."

"How delightful. Your work?"

"Anne's. In rescue of our son." He lifted a hand and ran it through his hair. "The Healer has been to both."

"Very good. I hesitate to mention that Master Healer Kestra awaits you at Trealla Fantrol."

Er Thom stiffened. "Anne and I are tied. I had just told you."

"My dreadful memory," Daav murmured. "I do however seem to recall that the lady swore she would have none of you. This leads me to the unfortunate conclusion that any— bonding—that exists is on your side alone."

Er Thom bowed with exquisite irony. "As you will. One-sided or not, it exists. I go with Anne, since choice is necessary. I cannot do otherwise."

"Ah, can you not?" Daav frowned; turned his head.

The door to the bedroom slid open and Anne came into the room. She advanced to Er Thom's side and looked down, her face tranquil, as the faces of those newly Healed tended to be. Daav inclined his head.

"Good-day, Anne."

"Daav," she returned gravely. "Have you come to take Shan away?"

"Worse than that," he said, watching her face with all a Scout's care. "I've come to take your son and your lover away."

Something moved in her eyes; he read it as anger.

"Er Thom makes his own choices," she said flatly. "My son comes with me."

"To New Dublin?" Daav asked, keeping his voice gentle, his posture unthreatening. "Anne, your child bodes to be a Healer of some note, if he does not come to halfling as one of dramliz. How shall New Dublin train him to use these abilities? Will you wait until he harms someone through ignorance—or until he begins to go mad—before you send him back to Liad to be taught?" He showed her his empty palms.

"How do I serve my cha'leket by denying his son the training he must have to survive? How does flinging talent into exile serve Korval?" He lowered his hands and gave her a rueful smile.

"For good or ill, Shan is of Korval. We are in Liaden space, subject to the law and customs of Liad. Shan's delm commands him to bide at home. The law will find no different."

She licked her lips. "Terran law—"

Daav inclined his head. "You are free to chart that course. However, for the years such litigation will doubtless encompass, the child bides with Clan Korval, his family of record." He shifted; came to his feet in one fluid move, hand out in a gesture of supplication.

"Anne, hear me. The luck was in it, that you brought your child to Liad. There is nowhere else in the galaxy where his talents are understood so well. I am not your enemy in this, but your friend. Only think and you will see that it is so!"

Her mouth was tight, fine eyes flashing. "You seem to have me over a barrel," she commented. "What do you propose I do, hang on as Clan Korval's guest until my son is come of age?"

Daav tipped his head, watching Er Thom's face out of the side of an eye.

"Why, as to that," he said calmly, "here is my brother says he can do nothing other than stand at your side, whatever ground you choose. He makes a rather compelling case for himself, casting aside his delm's word and escaping from his rooms down a vine. If things were otherwise, I might well give such devotion its just reward. But the devil's in it, you see—I need him. Korval needs him. He comes with me, if I must have him off this ship in chains."

"So the great House of Korval holds hostages, does it?" Anne flashed. "Is this honor?"

"We had been—wishing—to talk," Er Thom said, very softly, from her side. "Perhaps—we might find the proper compromise—on Liad."

Anne spun to look at him, eyes wide.

Er Thom met her gaze. "Is the intent of the trade to keep we three together?" he asked. "Or is it to keep us forever at—at—"

"Loggerheads," she supplied, almost absently. "You would burden yourself with a Terran on Liad?" There was a note of wistfulness beneath the disbelief. Daav relaxed, carefully. Er Thom took her hand and smiled up into her eyes.

"You would have burdened yourself with a Liaden," he murmured, "on New Dublin."

Daav felt a small hand slip into his and looked down into Shan's bright silver eyes.

"Hi, Daav," that young gentleman said comfortably. He smiled impartially at all three adults. "We go home now?"

"May I offer you more fruit, Master Healer?" Petrella yos'-Galan asked from the head of the table, "Cheese?"

"Thank you, my needs have been well provided for." Master Healer Kestra inclined her head.

Thodelm yos'Galan's displeasure with her son was entirely audible to the Healer's inner ears. It was, of course, bad form to broach the subject of emotional turmoil with one who had not specifically requested aid, and Kestra had scrupulously kept to good form. Thus far. She could not help but admit, however, that her sympathies lay on the side of the abruptly absent a'thodelm and the lady his heart would not relinquish.

The shabby little love-knot had been compelling, as had the struggle she had perceived in the room's echoes. Two people who loved each other, each striving for right conduct. More the pity that the two were persons of melant'i and that right conduct shifted like moon shadow, world to world.

"I must offer apology," Petrella yos'Galan said ill-temperedly, "for my son's lack of manner. Of late he has come unruly, to the clan's distress."

"No need of apology," Kestra returned mildly. "Those of Korval are understood to be unruly." She smiled.

"I recall when the delm—Scout Cadet yos'Phelium he was at the time—applied for Healing, after his ship was disabled. Four Healers were required for the task of smoothing the memory—myself and another of Master rank, with two high adepts—and he wished to forget!" She sipped tepid tea and set the cup down with a tiny click.

"For all of that, we did not entirely accomplish our goal. We succeeded in blurring the experience, but he recalls it. I am certain that he does. I believe it to be a distant recollection, devoid of emotion, as if he had read of the incident in a book. But I am entirely certain he could tap the memory in all its horror, did he become convinced of necessity."

Her host said nothing to this and after a moment the Healer continued, in not so *very* good form:

"It has perhaps—forgive me!—escaped notice that your son's love for this lady and their child goes very deep."

"So?" Petrella said harshly. "We have all lost that which we loved, Healer. It is the nature of the game."

"True," Kestra allowed. "But it is not the purpose of the game."

"Enlighten me," the thodelm requested, with acid courtesy, "is it myself you have been requested to Heal?"

Kestra inclined her head. "Ma'am, it is not. You must forgive me and lay fault with my years. I find that old women are often impertinent."

"Not to say incorrigible," Petrella remarked, and Kestra smiled, feeling the tingle of the other's amusement.

"I had told Korval I should await his return," Kestra said. "If it does not inconvenience the House—"

But she got no further. There was a subdued clatter in the hallway, the door to the dining room swung open and Delm Korval entered with his long, silent stride, accompanied by a very tall lady and a fair-haired man carrying a child. The Healer came to her feet, inner eyes a-dazzle.

Fumbling like a novice, she Sorted the images. Thodelm

yos'Galan she could now ignore; likewise Korval's vivid emotive pattern. The others . . .

The strongest was a dazzle of tumbling color and untamed light—rather as if one had fallen head-first into a kaleidoscope. With difficulty, the Healer traced the tumbling images to their source, bringing the pattern to overlay what was perceived by the outer eyes—gasped and automatically damped her own output.

"I am—honored—to meet Shan yos'Galan," she said, perhaps to the room at large. "I would welcome—indeed, require!—opportunity to spend more time with him. But if my primary concern is to be A'thodelm yos'Galan, I must ask that the child be removed. He is—enormously bright."

Korval was already at the wall-mounted intercom. A'thodelm yos'Galan also moved, leaving the tall lady standing alone near the door.

"Mother," he said, going gracefully to one knee by Petrella yos'Galan's chair. "I bring your grandson, Shan, to meet you."

The old lady's pattern, seen dimly through the rioting light show that was the child, registered yearning, even affection. However, the face she showed the one who knelt before her was bitterly hard. She did not so much as lift her eyes to the child.

"Sad sparkles," the child said suddenly and wriggled in the a'thodelm's grasp. Set upon his feet, he reached out and took one of Petrella's withered hands in his.

"Hi," he said in Terran, and then, in Low Liaden, "Tra'sia volecta, thawlana."

"Grandmother, is it?" Petrella glared into the small face, then sighed, suddenly and sharply. "Good-day to you as well, child. Go with your nurse now, before you blind the Healer."

"Come along, Shan-son," the a'thodelm said softly. He took the child's hand and led him to the nurse hovering at the door.

"Mrs. Intassi," Shan cried, flinging himself against her, "we went to the Port!"

"Well, what an adventure, to be sure!" Mrs. Intassi returned and led him out, carefully closing the door behind her.

Master Healer Kestra let out a sigh of heartfelt relief, ran an exercise to calm her jangled nerves, and trained her inner sight on the a'thodelm.

It was a pleasing pattern: Sharp-edged and cunning; subtly humorous, with a deep, well-guarded core of passion. The Master Healer nearly sighed again: Here was one who loved deeply—or not at all. There were signs of stress on the overlay, which was expectable, and a tenuous, almost airy construct that—

The Healer frowned, focusing on that anomaly. There, yes, feeding straight to that core place where he kept himself so aloof. And it fed from—where?

Laboriously, she traced the airy little bridge—and encountered another pattern entirely.

This one was also orderly, well-shaped and passionate, overlain with the fragile skin of a recent Healing. The humor was broader, the heart-web less guarded, more expansive. The Healer lost the bridge in a twisting interjoin of passion and affection.

"Oh." Master Healer Kestra opened her outer eyes, seeking Korval's sparkling black gaze. "They're lifemates."

CHAPTER THIRTY-NINE

There are those Scouts—and other misinformed persons— who urge that the Book of Clans be expanded to include certain non-Liaden persons.

I say to the Council now, the day the Book of Clans includes a Terran among its pages is the day Liad begins to fall!

—Excerpted from remarks made before the Council of Clans by the chairperson of the Coalition to Abolish the Liaden Scouts

"I beg your pardon," Petrella said acidly, "they are certainly not lifemates."

The Master Healer turned to her. "Indeed they are," she said, striving for gentleness. "It is very nearly a textbook case—a shade tenuous, perhaps, but beyond mistake."

Petrella turned her head and glared at the tall a'thodelm and his taller lady, standing side-by-side at the door.

"I forbid it," she said, the Command mode crackling minor lightnings.

Kestra saw the flicker in the a'thodelm's pattern and acted to prevent a response which could only pain all.

"Forgive me," she said firmly to Petrella. "It is plain you have failed of grasping the fullness of the situation. I am not speaking of pleasant signatures on a contract and a formal announcement in *The Gazette*. I speak of a verifiable, physical *fact* which is not in any way subject to your commands."

"Lifemates?" Petrella flung back with pain-wracked scorn. "Which of them is a wizard, pray?"

"Well, now, the gaffer, he was a water-witch," the tall lady said in a peculiar, lilting voice, a glimmer of half-wild humor lighting her pattern.

The Healer frowned after the sense of the words, feeling a similarity to Terran, but unable to quite—

"A water-witch," Korval murmured in Adult-to-Adult, "is one who has the ability to locate water below ground without use of instrumentation." He flicked a glance at the Terran lady. "Correct?"

She moved her head up and down—Terran affirmative. "He found other things, too," she said in accented, though clear, Liaden. "Lost sheep. Jewelry, once or twice. A missing child. But mostly he stuck to water." She shrugged. "If you listen to the talk on New Dublin, all the ancestors were—*fey*, we say. It adds color to the family tree."

"You are yourself a wizard, then?" Petrella's voice was sharp.

The Terran lady shook her head. "No, a language professor."

"You know when the child wakes," the a'thodelm murmured from her side. "You know when I am troubled. I heard you calling me, from many miles away, and followed your voice."

"And yet neither are of the dramliz," the Master Healer said, firmly. "I recall when the a'thodelm was tested at Healer Hall as a child. We tested twice, for, after all, he *is* of Korval." She moved her shoulders and caught Korval's attentive eye.

"Plain meat and no sauce, the a'thodelm. Yourself—you have *some*thing, my Lord. If we are ever able to quantify it, I shall tell you."

He inclined his dark head. "You are gracious."

"*You* are dangerous—but, there. It is what one expects of Korval." She turned her attention once more to Petrella.

"Neither pretends to wizardhood, Thodelm. I suspect the only talent either ever held was the ability to recognize and meld with the other. That work has proceeded as it must—hindered, alas, by the demands of custom, melant'i—and kin. It may not be stopped, nor may it be undone." She showed her empty hands, palm up.

"You speak of wrapping the a'thodelm in forgetfulness, of sending the lady far away. To speak of these things is to be ill-informed. If they are separated by the length and breadth of the galaxy, still they will find each other. They are lifemates, Thodelm. If your pride cannot be thwarted, you must have the lady killed—and the child, as well. Then, the a'thodelm will be free of her."

"Yet history tells us that Master Wizard Rool Tiazan's lady lived in him after the death of her body," Korval commented from across the room.

Kestra hid her smile with a bow. "Indeed. You understand that the tie between these two may not be so potent—or it may well be potent enough. Certainly they are both strong-willed. Certainly they both love. It may be that the areas where the match is not entirely perfect are those which are not so—very—important. Who can say?"

There was a silence in the room. Korval shifted slightly, drawing all eyes to himself.

"Cry grace, Aunt Petrella," he said gently. "The game has gone to chance."

"Chance," the Terran lady murmured, a flutter of panic through her steady, beautiful pattern. "Chance without choice."

"Choice was made," A'thodelm yos'Galan said, "several times over." He took her hand, looking earnestly up into her face. "I love you, Anne Davis."

It thrilled along all the matrices of her pattern, resonating within his. She smiled. "I love you, Er Thom yos'Galan." The smiled faded, and she spoke again with a certain sternness. "But we still have to talk."

"Certainly," he returned, smiling as if they were quite alone in the room. "Shall I show you the maze? We may be private there."

"All right . . ."

He turned back to the room, making his bows, pattern a dazzling, sensuous clatter.

"Master Healer," he murmured, with a propriety that be-

lied the joy ringing through him. "Mother." He turned to face
Korval and checked, the clamoring joy within him stuttering.

Carefully, silently, he bowed respect for the delm.

Straightening, he stepped back, opened the door and allowed his lady to proceed him into the hall.

"Master Merchant bel'Tarda," Mr. pel'Kana announced
from the doorway.

Daav looked wearily up from his work screen.

Luken had got a new jacket—an astonishing affair in
bright blue with belled sleeves and citron buttons. The buttons
flashed irritatingly when he made his bow.

"Wine for Master bel'Tarda," Daav instructed Mr.
pel'Kana and waved a hand. "Sit, Cousin, do, and tell me
what brings you so far from the City."

"Well, it's not as far as that," Luken said seriously, disposing
himself with unusual care in the leather chair across the desk.
"Matter of an hour's travel, if you're unlucky in the route." He
received his glass from Mr. pel'Kana and took the required sip,
watching Daav trepidatiously over the rim.

Daav smiled, picked up his near-empty cup and also drank,
setting the thing aside as Mr. pel'Kana closed the door.

"Well, Luken, you might as well make a clean breast, you
know. I can hardly be expected to go before the Council of
Clans on your behalf unless I know the awful whole."

"Council of Clans! Here now, it's nothing—" Luken sput-
tered, caught himself and sighed.

"It's no wonder the world finds us odd," he said severely,
"when you go on giving rein to that sense of humor of yours."

"Horrid, isn't it?" Daav agreed. "Now you've vented your
feelings, shall you tell me what is wrong? Pat Rin?"

"Eh? Oh, no—no. Ease your heart there—the boy's fine,
though we had his mother yesterday. Why that woman insists
on—Well." He glanced down and brushed an imaginary fleck
of dust from one of his improbable sleeves.

"It's about young Syntebra," he said, and raised a hurried
hand. "Now, I know she's intended for Er Thom, but the thing
is—well, damn it, it just won't do!"

Daav lifted an eyebrow, momentarily diverted. "No, won't it?"

"Terrified of him," Luken said warmly. "Of you, too, if it comes to that. Nothing against her. But she's only a child, you see—and mid-House, beside. Hardly knows how to go on in that world, much less rubbing High House shoulders. I'm not saying she can't make a success of things—but she needs more work than Er Thom's likely to have time to give. He's a busy one, and he stands too close to the delm."

Daav looked sharply away, picked up his glass and drained it. "Does he?"

"Well, he's your heir, isn't he? And the pair of you as cutting quick and twisty bright as any would wish—I'll tell you what, it's *tiring* trying to keep abreast! The girl would be miserable, lost and uncertain of herself." He eyed Daav consideringly.

"You alarm me, Cousin. I certainly would not wish one of Korval to be the agent of such distress. However, I feel sure you are about to offer me a solution to young Syntebra's troubles."

Luken grinned, rather shamefacedly. "See through me like glass, can you? Well, it's no matter—I know I'm not a clever fellow. Here it is: I'll engage to marry Syntebra. Another child is no hardship on me—the eldest is away at school more often than she's home now-days, and Pat Rin's no trouble at all. Nexon will be put to rest and a more equitable wife can be found for Er Thom."

"Undoubtedly, a more equitable wife can be found for Er Thom," Daav murmured, possibly to himself. He looked at Luken with a grin.

"I take it the lady does not find yourself—aah—*terrifying*, Cousin?"

"Not a bit of it," Luken said comfortably and smiled. "I get on with most, after all."

"So you do." Daav closed his eyes and resisted rubbing his aching forehead. He opened his eyes.

"I shall speak with Thodelm yos'Galan tomorrow," he told Luken. "However, I feel certain that your solution will be adopted. Now there is an active nursery at Trealla Fantrol, Pat

Rin may be relocated for the duration of your marriage." He cocked an eyebrow. "Unless you think that unwise?"

Luken pursed his lips. "I'll speak with the boy," he said eventually, "and let you know his wishes." He sent a sharp look at Daav. "Not that he isn't fond of his cousin Er Thom, nor that young Shan doesn't look a likely child. But I would dislike going against the boy's strong inclination, if he has one."

"Certainly." Daav inclined his head. "You do well by us, Cousin," he said in sudden and sincere gratitude. "I find you honor and ornament the clan."

Luken blushed, dark gold spreading across his cheeks. He glanced aside and picked up his glass.

"Kind of you," he muttered, and drank.

It took two rather hefty swallows to recover his address. He glanced at Daav.

"I'll hear from you, then?" he said hopefully.

Daav inclined his head. "I expect you may hear from me as soon as tomorrow."

"Good," said Luken. "Good." He rose. "You're a busy man, so I'll be taking my leave. Thank you."

"No trouble," Daav said, rising also and coming 'round the desk. He forestalled Luken's bow by the simple maneuver of taking him by the arm and turning him toward the door.

"Allow me to see you to your car, Cousin . . ."

It was rather late.

Daav had no clear notion of precisely how late. He had put the lights out some time back, preferring the room in firelight while he drank a glass or two in solitude.

Firelight had become emberlight and the glass or two had become a bottle. Daav leaned his head against the back of his chair and thought of his brother's cold face and unwarm bow.

Gods, what have I done?

He closed his eyes against the emberlight and strove not to think at all.

"You're going to have a dreadful headache tomorrow," the sweet, beloved voice commented.

With exquisite care, Daav opened his eyes and lifted his

head. Er Thom was perched on the arm of the chair across the counterchance board. Someone had thrown a fresh log on the fire. His hair gleamed in the renewed brightness like a heart's ransom.

"I have," Daav said with a certain finicking precision, "a dreadful headache *now.*"

"Ah." Er Thom smiled. "I rather thought you might."

"Have you come to cut my gizzard out?" Daav asked, dropping his head back against the chair. "I believe there's an appropriately dull knife in the wine table."

"I don't know that I'm particularly skilled at gizzard-cutting," Er Thom said after a moment. "Shall you like some tea?"

"Gods, at this hour? Whichever it is—" He moved a hand in negation. "No, don't disturb the servants."

"All right," Er Thom said softly. He rose and vanished into the fringes of the firelight. A minor clatter was heard from the direction of the wine table. Daav wondered somewhat blearily if the other had decided upon the knife after all.

"Drink with me, brother."

Daav opened his eyes. Er Thom was before him, limned in the firelight, holding two cups.

"Thank you," Daav said around a sudden start of tears. He accepted a cup and drank—a full mouthful—swallowed—and laughed. "Water?"

"If you drink any more wine you're likely to fall into a snore," Er Thom commented, lifting his own glass. There was a gleam of purple on his hand.

"Reinstated, darling?"

"My mother attempts to accept the outcome equitably." He smiled. "She speaks of—perhaps—accepting the child."

"Gracious of her." Daav sighed. "Will your Anne be happy with us, do you think?"

The smile grew slightly wider. "I believe it may be contrived."

"Hah. So long as my work as delm is not entirely confined to scrambling planetary traffic and threatening my kin with chains—" He shuddered and looked up into bright violet eyes.

"The window was—distressing."

Er Thom inclined his head. "I apologize for the window,"

he murmured. "But there is no way to close it, you see, once you are climbed through."

Daav grinned. "I suppose that's true."

Er Thom tipped his head. "May I know what balance the delm may require of me?"

"Balance." Daav closed his eyes; opened them. "How shall the delm require balance, when it was he did not listen to what you would tell him?"

Er Thom frowned. "I do not believe that to be the case," he said in his soft, serious way. "How should any of us have expected such an extraordinary occurrence? Recall that I gave nubiath'a! Indeed, it may be that such—adversity—as we met with enlivened and strengthened our bond." He bowed, slightly and with whimsy.

"Delm's Wisdom."

"Amuse yourself, do." Daav tried for a look of severity, but his mouth would keep twitching in a most undignified manner. He gave it up and grinned openly.

"*All's well that ends well*," he quoted in Terran, "as your lady might agree. Tell her: *Be fruitful and multiply*."

Er Thom laughed. "Tell her yourself. We shall want the delm to See us tomorrow, after all."

"Whatever for? I distinctly recall Master Healer Kestra informing us that your arrangement is beyond the ken of command or Code."

"Ah, but, you see," Er Thom said earnestly. "There is local custom to be satisfied. I would not wish to be backward in any attention the world might deem necessary."

"Certainly not. Korval has its standards, after all."

Er Thom laughed.

CHAPTER FORTY

The first attack was a hammer-blow at the Ringstars. A dozen worlds were lost at once, including that which was home to the dramliz and the place the Soldiers call Headquarters. There was rumor of a seed-ship—as high as a hundred seed-ships—sent out from Antori in the moment before it died. Much good it may do them.

Jela says The Enemy means to smash communications, then gobble up each isolated world in its own good time.

Jela says anyone with a ship is a smuggler, now. And every smuggler is a soldier.

I've never seen anything like this . . .

—**Excerpted from Cantra yos'Phelium's Log Book**

It was early, the halls yet empty of scholars, save the one who walked at Er Thom's side. When they came to a certain door, he stood away, and watched her bend over the lock, quick brown fingers making short work of the coding.

Straightening from her task, she flung him a smile and caught his hand, pulling him with her into a tiny, cluttered office smelling of book-dust and disuse.

Just within, he paused, holding her to his side while he scanned the shabby and book-crammed interior. Satisfied that they were alone, he allowed them another step into the room, then turned to lock the door.

Anne laughed.

"As if we were in any danger among a crowd of fusty professors!"

Er Thom bit his lip. Of course, she did not recall. He had not doubted the wisdom of immediately summoning a Healer to ease Anne's distress. To be abducted at gunpoint, to have one's child and one's own life threatened, to make one's bow to necessity and take a life—these things were certainly best quickly smoothed from memory and peace restored to a mind unsettled by violence.

Yet now it seemed that in doing her the best service he might, he had placed her in the way of future peril. One madman with a gun did not necessarily argue another, but it was only wise to be wary.

And difficult to be wary when the memory of past danger was washed clean away.

"Er Thom?" She was frowning down at him, concern showing in her eyes. "What is it?"

He caught her other hand in his and looked seriously into her face.

"Anne, I wish you will recall—I am in very earnest, denubia! I wish you will recall that Liad is not a—safe place. There are those who love Terrans not at all. There are those who actively hate—who may seek to do you harm for merely being Terran, or for the direction your work takes you . . . Liadens—there is pride, you understand. It pleases many to think Liad the center of the universe and all others—lower. With some, this pleasure becomes obsession. Korval's wing is broad, but it is far better to be vigilant, and avoid rousing the delm to balance."

"Better to be safe than sorry," Anne murmured and inclined her head. "I understand, Er Thom. Thank you." She hesitated; met his eyes once more.

"I knew how to use a pistol, once. I'm willing to brush up and carry a gun."

He smiled in relief. "That would be wise. I shall teach you, if you like it."

"I like it." She grinned, squeezed his hands and let them go, crossing the room in three of her long strides and taking a framed flat-pic down from the wall between two reverent palms.

"Er Thom," she said, as she lay the frame face down and began to ease the back away. "Aren't *you* Liaden?"

He drifted over to the desk, watching her face, downturned and intent upon her task.

"We are Korval," he said, softly. "You understand, we are not originally from the Old World—Solcintra, it was called. Cantra came from the Rim, so it states in the logs, and her co-pilot in the endeavor which raised Liad—young Tor An had been from one of the Ringstars, sent to Solcintra for schooling. Poor child, by the time his schooling was done, the Ringstars were no fit place for return."

Anne had raised her head and was watching him intently. "Every other clan on Liad can trace its origins to—Solcintra?"

"Yes, certainly. But Solcintra was only one world in what had been a vast empire." He smiled into her eyes. "And not a particularly—forward—world, at that."

"You know this," she said, very carefully, "*historically*?"

He bowed. "It is of course necessary for one who will be Korval Himself—and for one who may be delm—to have studied the log books of Cantra yos'Phelium, as well as the diaries of the delms who had come before."

She bit her lip. He had a sense of—hunger?—and a real-ization that, for one who studied as Anne did, such information as he had just shared might be pearls of very great price.

"One empire," she murmured. "One—language?"

"An official tongue, and world-dialects. Or so the logs lead one to surmise." He showed her his empty palms. "The logs themselves are written in a language somewhat akin to Yxtrang—so you see they are not for everyone. Korval is counted odd enough, without the world deciding that we are spawn of the enemy."

"May I see them?" Anne's voice was restrained, intense. "The logs."

Er Thom smiled. "It is entirely likely that you will be *required* to see them, beloved."

Her face eased with humor. "Home study for the new Dragon," she quipped, and turned her attention once more to the task of easing the back from the rickety old frame.

This went slowly, for Anne seemed as intent on keeping the frame in one piece as the frame itself seemed determined to fail. Her patience won in the end, however, and the frayed backing was set aside.

Atop the pic-back lay one thin square of gray paper.

Anne picked it up, frowning at the single row of letters.

"What is it?" Er Thom wondered, softly, so not to shatter her concentration.

"A notation," she murmured. "I don't quite—" She handed him the paper, shaking her head in perplexity.

A notation, indeed, and one as familiar to him as his brother's face.

"Lower half of the second quadrant, tending toward eighty degrees." He read off the piloting symbols with ease and raised his eyes to Anne. "Alas, I lack board and screens."

She stared at him. He saw the idea bloom in her eyes in the instant before she caught his arm and turned him with her toward the overfull bookshelves.

"Lower half," she murmured, moving toward the shelves, her eyes on the books as if they might up and bolt if she shifted her gaze for a moment. ". . . of the second quadrant . . ." She knelt and lay her hand along a section of spines, eyes daring to flash a question to him.

He inclined his head. "Just so."

"Tending," Anne ran her fingers lightly, caressingly, down the spines. "Tending. Toward eighty de—Dear gods."

It was a small, slim volume her forefinger teased from between two of its hulking kinsmen, bound in scuffed and grit-dyed leather, looking for all the worlds like someone's personal debt-book that had been left out in the rain.

Anne opened it reverently, long fingers exquisitely gentle among the densely-noted leaves, her face rapt as she bent over this page and that.

Er Thom moved to kneel beside her. "Is this the thing you were seeking?"

"I think . . ." She closed it softly and held it cupped in her hand as if it were a live thing and likely to escape. "I'll have to study it—get an accurate dating. It looks—it looks . . ." Her voice died away and she bent her head sharply over the little book with a gasp.

"Anne?"

She shook her head, by which he understood he was to be still and allow her time for thought.

"Er Thom?" Very unsteady, her voice, and she did not raise her face to his.

"Yes."

"There was a man—a man with a gun. I—the grad student. He killed Doctor yo'Kera. For this. To suppress this." At last she raised her head, showing him a face drawn with sorrow and eyes that sparkled tears.

"He wanted the information from me—threatened Shan." She swallowed. "I killed him. Fil Tor Kinrae."

"Yes." He reached out and stroked her cheek, lay his fingers lightly along her brow. "I know."

She bit her lip and looked deep into his eyes, her own showing desperation. "They're going to come and demand balance," she said. "His clan."

Er Thom lifted an eyebrow. "More likely they will come and most abjectly beg Korval's pardon for the error of owning a child who would abduct and threaten yourself and our son." He moved his shoulders. "In any wise, it is a case for the delm."

"Is it?"

"Indeed it is," he returned firmly. "Shall I fetch you a Healer now, Anne?"

"You did that before." She bent her head and reached out to take his hand, weaving their fingers together with concentration, the ring he had given her scintillant against her skin.

"I think," she said softly. "I think I'll try it without—forgetting. It's not—it seems very—misty. As if it happened a long time ago . . ." She looked up with a smile. "If things start to slip, I'll let you know. OK?"

"A bargain. And in the meanwhile you shall practice with your pistol, eh?"

"I'll practice with my pistol," she promised, and glanced down at the little book she held so protectively. She looked back to Er Thom's face. "Will—the delm—want to suppress—assuming it's real!—this information?"

"The last I had heard, the delm was advised by his grandmother in matters such as these," Er Thom said carefully.

"That being, you understand, Grandmother Cantra. Her philosophy, as seen through the logs, leads me to believe that the delm will not wish to suppress anything of the sort, though he may very well have certain necessities with regard to the *manner* in which it is made available to the world." He inclined his head. "For the good of the clan."

"I—see." One more glance at the book, a brilliant look into his eyes and a warm squeeze of her hand. "Well, it's too valuable to stay here, so I guess I'll just drop it in the delm's lap before we go on our honey-trip." She grinned. "Which reminds me, if we don't move soon, we're going to be late for our own wedding."

"Now that," Er Thom said, "would be very improper. I suggest we leave immediately."

"I suggest," Anne murmured, swaying lightly toward him, "that we leave in just a minute."

"Much more appropriate," he agreed, and raised his face for her kiss.

Liaden/Terran Dictionary

A'nadelm: Heir to the nadelm

A'thodelm: Head-of-Line-to-Be

A'trezla: Lifemates

Al'bresh venat'i: Formal phrase of sorrow for another Clan's loss, as when someone dies.

Al'kin Chernard'i: The Day Without Delight

Balent'i Kalandon: Our local galaxy

Balent'i tru'vad: The starweb of all creation

Cha'leket: Heartkin (heartbrother, heartsister)

Cha'trez: Heartsong

Chernubia: Confected delicacy

Chiat'a bei kruzon: Dream sweetly.

Ckrakec: (derived from the Yxtrang) Approximately 'Master Hunter'

coab minshak'a: 'Necessity exits'

Conselem: An absurdity

Delm: Head of Clan (Delm Korval, Korval Himself/Herself)

Delmae: Lifemate to the Delm

Denubia: Darling

Dramliza: A wizard. PLURAL: dramliz (The dramliz...)

Dri'at: Left

Eklykt'i: Unreturned

Eldema: First Speaker (most times, the Delm)

Eldema-pernard'i: First-Speaker-In-Trust

Entranzia volecta: Good greetings (High Liaden)

Fa'vya: an aphrodisiac-laced wine sold at Festival

Flaran Cha'menthi: I(/We) Dare'

Galandaria: Confederate? Countryperson?

Ge'shada: Mazel tov; congratulations

Glavda Empri: yo'Lanna's house

I'ganin brath'a, vyan se'untor: Play with the body, rest the mind

I'lanta: Right

Ilania frrogudon palon dox: (approx) Young ladies should speak more gently

Illanga kilachi: (no translation available)

Indra: Uncle

Jelaza Kazone: The Tree, also Korval's Own House. Approx. "Jela's Fulfillment"

Lazenia spandok: Son of a bitch (REAL approximate)

Lisamia keshoc: Thank you (Low Liaden)

Megelaar: The Dragon on Korval's shield

Melant'i: Who one is in relation to current circumstances. ALSO who one is in sum, encompassing all possible persons one might be.

Menfri'at: Liaden karate

Mirada: Father

Misravot: Altanian wine; blue in color.

Nadelm: Delm-to-Be

Nubiath'a: Gift given to end an affair of pleasure

Palesci modassa: Thank you (High Liaden)

Prena'ma: Storyteller

Prethliu: Rumorbroker

Qe'andra: Man of business

Qua'lechi: Exclamation of horror

Relumma: Division of a Liaden year, equalling 96 Standard days. Four relumma equal one year.

Thawla: Mother (Low Liaden; approximately Mommy)

Thawlana: Grandmother

Thodelm: Head-of-Line

Tra'sia volecta: Good morning (Low Liaden)

Trealla Fantrol: The yos'Galan house.

Valcon Berant'a: Dragon's Price or Dragon Hoard, the name of Korval's valley

Valcon Melad'a: Dragon's Way, the Delm's Own ship

van'chela: beloved friend

va'netra: charity case, lame puppy

zerkam'ka: kinslayer

About the Authors

Sharon Lee and Steve Miller live in the rolling hills of Central Maine. Born and raised in Baltimore, Maryland, in the early '50s, they met several times before taking the hint and formalizing the team, in 1979. They removed to Maine with cats, books, and music following the completion of Carpe Diem, their third novel.

Their short fiction, written both jointly and singly, has appeared or will appear in *Absolute Magnitude, Catfantastic, Such a Pretty Face, Dreams of Decadence, Fantasy Book,* and several former incarnations of *Amazing.* Meisha Merlin Publishing has or will be publishing four books set in the Liaden Universe: *Plan B, Partners in Necessity, Pilots Choice,* and *I Dare.*

Both Sharon and Steve have seen their non-fiction work and reviews published in a variety of newspapers and magazines. Steve is the founding curator of the University of Maryland's Kuhn Library Science Fiction Research Collection.

Sharon's interests include music, pine cone collecting, and seashores. Steve also enjoys music, plays chess and collects cat whiskers. Both spend way too much time playing on the internet, and even have a webpage at:

www.korval.com/liad.htm